Simon Scarrow lives in Norfolk. He has in the past run a Roman History programme taking parties of students to a number of ruins and museums across Britain. Having enjoyed the novels of Forester, Cornwell and O'Brian, and fired by the knowledge gleaned from his exploration of Roman sites, he decided to write what he wanted to read – military page-turners set during the Roman invasion of Britain in AD 43. His five other action-packed novels featuring Macro and Cato, *Under the Eagle*, *When the Eagle Hunts*, *The Eagle and the Wolves*, *The Eagle's Prey* and *The Eagle's Prophecy*, are also available from Headline.

For more information on Simon Scarrow and his novels, visit his website at: www.scarrow.fsnet.co.uk

D1313191

The Eagle's Conquest

Simon Scarrow

First published in 2001
by HEADLINE BOOK PUBLISHING

First published in paperback in 2002
by HEADLINE BOOK PUBLISHING

This paperback edition published in 2005
by HEADLINE BOOK PUBLISHING

13

ISBN 0 7472 6630 1

Typeset in Times by Avon DataSet Ltd,
Bidford-on-Avon, Warwickshire

Printed and bound in Great Britain by
Clays Ltd, St Ives plc

HEADLINE BOOK PUBLISHING
A division of Hodder Headline
338 Euston Road
London NW1 3BH

www.headline.co.uk
www.hodderheadline.com

For Carolyn, who makes it all possible,
with all my love.

THE ROMAN ARMY CHAIN OF COMMAND IN 43AD

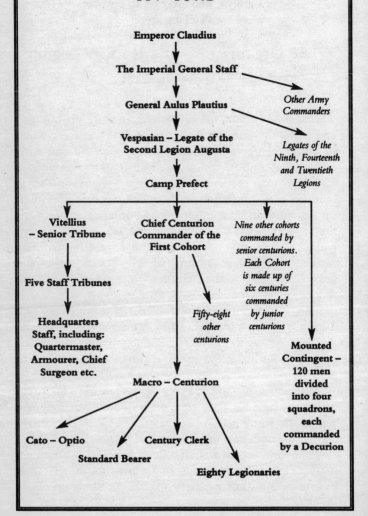

Emperor Claudius

The Imperial General Staff

General Aulus Plautius → Other Army Commanders

Vespasian – Legate of the Second Legion Augusta → Legates of the Ninth, Fourteenth and Twentieth Legions

Camp Prefect

Vitellius – Senior Tribune

Chief Centurion Commander of the First Cohort

Nine other cohorts commanded by senior centurions. Each Cohort is made up of six centuries commanded by junior centurions

Five Staff Tribunes

Headquarters Staff, including: Quartermaster, Armourer, Chief Surgeon etc.

Fifty-eight other centurions

Mounted Contingent – 120 men divided into four squadrons, each commanded by a Decurion

Macro – Centurion

Cato – Optio

Standard Bearer

Century Clerk

Eighty Legionaries

The Organisation of a Roman Legion

The Second Legion, like all legions, comprised some five and a half thousand men. The basic unit was the century of eighty men commanded by a centurion with an optio acting as second in command. The century was divided into eight-man sections which shared a room together in barracks and a tent when on campaign. Six centuries made up a cohort, and ten cohorts made up a legion, with the first cohort being double-size. Each legion was accompanied by a cavalry unit of one hundred and twenty men, divided into four squadrons, who served as scouts and messengers. In descending order the main ranks were as follows:

The *legate* was a man from an aristocratic background. Typically in his mid-thirties, the legate would command the legion for up to five years and hope to make something of a name for himself in order to enhance his subsequent political career.

The *camp prefect* would be a grizzled veteran who would previously have been the chief centurion of the legion and was at the summit of a professional soldier's career. He was armed with vast experience and integrity.

Six *tribunes* served as staff officers. These would be men in their early twenties serving in the army for the first time to gain administrative experience before taking up junior posts in civil administration. The senior tribune was different. He was destined for high political office and eventual command of a legion.

Sixty *centurions* provided the disciplinary and training backbone of the legion. They were hand-picked for their command qualities and a willingness to fight to the death. Accordingly their casualty rate far exceeded other ranks. The most senior centurion commanded the First Century of the First Cohort and was a highly decorated and respected individual.

The four *decurions* of the legion commanded the cavalry squadrons and hoped for promotion to the command of auxiliary cavalry units.

Each *centurion* was assisted by an *optio* who would act as an orderly, with minor command duties. Optios would be waiting for a vacancy in the centurionate.

Below the optios were the *legionaries*, men who had signed on for twenty-five years. In theory, a man had to be a Roman citizen to qualify for enlistment, but recruits were increasingly drawn from local populations and given Roman citizenship on joining the legions.

Lower in status than the legionaries were the men of the *auxiliary cohorts*. These were recruited from the provinces and provided the Roman Empire with its cavalry, light infantry and other specialist skills. Roman citizenship was awarded on completion of twenty-five years of service.

THE ROMAN INVASION OF BRITAIN IN 43AD SHOWING THE MAIN LINE OF THE ROMAN ADVANCE AND MAIN BATTLE SITES

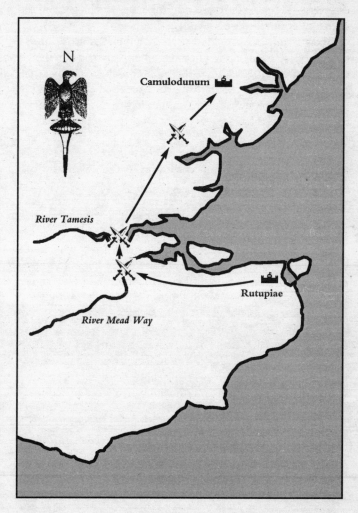

N

Camulodunum

River Tamesis

River Mead Way

Rutupiae

Chapter One

'I don't think I fancy the odds on the tall one,' muttered Centurion Macro.

'Why's that, sir?'

'Look at him, Cato! The man's all skin and bones. Won't last long against the opposition.' Macro nodded to the other side of the makeshift arena where a stocky prisoner was being armed with a buckler and short sword. The man took the unfamiliar weapons reluctantly and eyed up his opponent. Cato looked over to the tall, thin Briton, naked except for a small leather loin guard. One of the legionaries assigned to arena duties thrust a long trident into his hands. The Briton hefted the trident experimentally and adjusted his grip for the best balance. He seemed to be a man who knew his weapons and moved with a certain amount of poise.

'I'll bet on the tall one,' Cato decided.

Macro swung round. 'You mad? Look at him.'

'I have looked, sir. And I'll back my judgement with money.'

'Your judgement?' The centurion's eyebrows rose. Cato had only joined the legion the winter before, a fresh-faced youth from the imperial household in Rome. A legionary for less than a year and already throwing his judgements about like a veteran.

'Have it your own way then.' Macro shook his head and settled down to wait for the fight to begin. It was the last bout of the day's games laid on by the legate, Vespasian, in a small dell in the middle of the Second Legion's marching camp. Tomorrow the four legions and their support troops would be on the march again, driven on by General Plautius in his determination to seize Camulodunum before autumn closed in. If the enemy capital fell, the coalition of British tribes, led by Caratacus of the Catuvellauni, would be shattered. The forty thousand men under Plautius were all that Emperor Claudius could spare for the audacious invasion of the misty isles off the coast of Gaul. Every man in the army was aware that they were greatly outnumbered by the Britons. But as yet the enemy was dispersed. If the Romans could only strike quickly at the heart of British resistance before the imbalance in numbers weighed against the legions, victory would be within their grasp. The desire to push forward was in all their hearts, although the tired legionaries were grateful for this day's rest and the entertainment provided by the fights.

Twenty Britons had been paired against each other, armed with a variety of weapons. To make things more interesting the pairs had been picked by lot out of a legionary helmet and a handful of the bouts had been entertainingly unbalanced. Like this last one appeared to be.

The legion's eagle-bearer was acting as master of ceremonies and strode out to the centre of the arena, arms waving for silence. The eagle-bearer's assistants rushed to take final bets and Cato sat back down beside his centurion, having got odds of five to one. Not good, but he had staked a month's pay and if the man won, Cato would make a tidy sum. Macro had bet on the muscle-bound opponent with sword and buckler. Much less money, at much tighter odds, reflecting the assessment of the fighters.

'Quiet! Quiet there!' the eagle-bearer bellowed. Despite the holiday atmosphere, the automatic grip of discipline exerted itself over the gathered legionaries. Within moments over two thousand shouting, gesticulating soldiers stilled their tongues, and sat waiting for the bout to begin.

'Last fight, then! On my right I give you a swordsman, well-built, and a skilled warrior, or so he claims.'

The crowd howled with derision. If the Briton was so bloody good, why the hell was he here fighting for his life as *their* prisoner? The swordsman sneered at the audience, and suddenly raised his arms, screaming out a defiant war cry. The legionaries jeered back. The eagle-bearer allowed the shouting to continue a moment, before calling for silence again. 'On my left we have a trident. Says he's a squire to some chief or other. A weapon-carrier by trade, not a user. So this should be nice and quick. Now then, you lazy bastards, remember that normal duties begin right after the noon signal.'

The crowd groaned rather too much to be convincing and the eagle-bearer smiled good-naturedly. 'Right then, fighters – to your marks!'

The eagle-bearer backed away from the centre of the arena, a grassy sward, smeared with glistening patches of crimson where previous fighters had fallen. The contestants were led up behind two divots scored in the turf and made to face each other. The swordsman raised his short sword and buckler, and lowered himself into a tense crouch. By contrast the trident held his weapon vertically and almost seemed to be leaning on it, thin face completely expressionless. A legionary gave him a kick and indicated that he should prepare himself. The trident merely rubbed his shin instead, wincing painfully.

'Hope you didn't bet much on that one,' Macro commented.

Cato didn't reply. What the hell was the trident up to? Where was the poise of a moment ago? The man looked unconcerned, almost as if the whole morning had been a boring drill instead of a series of fights to the death. He had better be acting.

'Begin!' the eagle-bearer shouted.

At the word the swordsman howled, and hurtled forward at his opponent fifteen paces away. The trident lowered the shaft of his weapon and jabbed the wicked points towards the throat of the shorter man. The war cry died away as the latter ducked, knocking the trident to one side and thrusting for a quick kill. But the response was neatly worked. Rather than trying to recover the point of the trident, the tall Briton merely allowed the butt to swing round and smash into the side of the swordsman's head. His opponent dropped to the ground, momentarily stunned. The trident quickly reversed the weapon and moved in for the kill.

Cato smiled.

'Get up, you dozy bastard!' Macro shouted, hands cupped.

The trident lanced down at the figure on the ground, but a frantic sword swipe knocked the points aside from his neck. The trident still drew blood, but only from a shallow slash on the shoulder. Those in the audience who had taken the long odds groaned in dismay as the swordsman rolled to one side and got back onto his feet. He was panting, eyes wide, all arrogance gone now that he had been so neatly tricked. His tall opponent ripped the trident free of the soil and went into a crouch, a fierce expression twisting his face. There would be no more pretending from now on, just a trial of strength and skill.

4

'Get on with it!' Macro shouted. 'Stick the bastard in the guts!'

Cato sat silently, too self-conscious to join in with the shouting, but urgently willing his man on, fists clenched by his sides – despite his usual aversion to such fights.

The swordsman quickly side-stepped, testing the other man's reactions to see if the earlier move had been a fluke. But an instant later the tips of the trident were back in line with his throat. The crowd cheered appreciatively. This had the makings of a good fight after all.

The trident suddenly feinted, matched by his opponent's well-balanced backward hop, and the crowd cheered again.

'Good move!' Macro thumped one fist into the palm of the other. 'If we'd faced more like this it'd be us fighting out there. These two are good, very good.'

'Yes, sir,' Cato replied tensely, eyes fixed on the pair now circling each other over bloodstained grass. The sun blazed down on the spectacle. The birds singing in the oak trees surrounding the dell seemed quite out of place. For a moment Cato felt disturbed by the comparison between the fight-crazed soldiers hoarsely cheering men on to their deaths, and the placid harmony of wider nature. He had always disapproved of gladiatorial spectacles when he had lived in Rome, but that distaste was impossible to voice in the company of soldiers who lived by a code of blood, battle and discipline.

There was a metallic ring, and a frenzied exchange of clattering blows. With no advantage gained, the two resumed their circling motion. A swelling mood of frustration became evident in the cries of the watching legionaries and the eagle-bearer signalled the heated iron holders to move in behind the fighters, black rods tipped with red, glowing ends that wavered through the air. Over the shoulder of the swordsman, the trident caught sight of the approaching danger and threw himself into a furious attack, slashing at the shorter man's sword, trying to knock the blade from his grasp. The swordsman parried for his life, using both sword and buckler as he was forced back towards the side of the arena, straight into the path of the heated irons.

'Come on!' shouted Cato, waving his fist, caught up in the excitement. 'You've got him!'

A piercing shriek split the air as the heated iron came into contact with the swordsman's back and he instinctively recoiled, straight onto the barbed tips of the trident. He howled as one prong entered his thigh, high up near the hip, and tore free with a thick gout of blood which flowed down his leg and dripped onto the grass. The swordsman swiftly side-stepped away from the heated iron and tried to get some distance between himself and the wicked tips of the trident. Those who had bet on him shouted their support, willing him to close the distance and stick it to the trident while he still could.

Cato saw that the trident was grinning, aware that time was on his side. He just had to keep his opponent at a distance long enough for the loss of blood to weaken him. Then close in for the kill. But the crowd was in no mood for a waiting game and jeered angrily as the trident backed away from his bleeding foe. Up came the heated irons again. This time the swordsman sought the advantage, knowing that his time for effective action was short. He rushed at the trident, raining blows on the tip of his weapon, forcing the tall Briton back. But the trident was not going to fall for the same trick. He slid his grip down the shaft and suddenly swung it at the legs of the swordsman, then ran round to the side, away from the irons. The shorter man jumped awkwardly and landed off balance.

A series of thrusts and parries clattered out and then Cato noticed that the swordsman was swaying, his steps becoming more and more uncertain as his lifeblood ebbed from his body. Another attack from the trident was beaten off, but only just. Then the swordsman's strength appeared to give out and he slowly sank down onto his knees, sword wavering in his hand.

Macro jumped to his feet. 'Get up! Get up before he guts you!'

The rest of the crowd rose, sensing that the end of the fight was near, most of them desperately urging the swordsman to stand up.

The trident thrust forward, catching the sword between the prongs. A quick twist and the blade spun from the swordsman's grip and landed several feet away. Knowing all was lost the swordsman slumped onto his back, waiting for a quick end. The trident shouted his victory cry, and shifted his grip forward as he advanced to stand over his opponent and deal the final blow. Legs astride the heavily bleeding swordsman, he raised his trident high. The swordsman's buckler suddenly swung up with savage desperation and slammed into the taller man's groin. With a deep groan the trident doubled up. The crowd cheered. A second blow from the buckler smashed into the man's face and he went down on the grass, weapon slipping from his grip as he clutched at his nose and eyes. Two more blows to the head from the buckler and the trident was finished.

'Marvellous stuff!' Macro jumped up and down. 'Bloody marvellous!'

Cato shook his head bitterly, and cursed the trident's cockiness. It never paid to assume your foe was beaten simply because he appeared that way. Hadn't the trident tried that very trick earlier in the fight?

The swordsman rose to his feet, far more easily than a critically wounded man could, and quickly retrieved his sword. The end was merciful, the trident was sent to his gods with a sharp thrust under the ribcage into his heart.

Then, as Cato, Macro and the crowd watched, a very strange thing happened. Before the eagle-bearer and his assistant could disarm the swordsman, the Briton raised his arms and shouted out a challenge. In crudely accented Latin he screamed out, 'Romans! Romans! See!'

The sword swept down, the grip was quickly reversed and with both hands the Briton thrust it into his chest. He swayed a moment, head lolling back, and then collapsed onto the grass beside the body of the trident. The crowd was hushed.

'What the fuck did he do that for?' Macro muttered.

'Maybe he knew his wounds were fatal.'

'He might have survived,' Macro replied grudgingly. 'You never know.'

'Survived, only to become a slave. Perhaps he didn't want that, sir.'

'Then he was a fool.'

The eagle-bearer, concerned about the uncertain change in the audience's mood, hurried forward, arms raised. 'Right then, lads, that's your lot. Fight's over. I declare the swordsman the winner. Pay up the winning bets, and then back to your duties.'

'Wait!' a voice cried out. 'It's a draw! They're both dead.'

'The swordsman won,' the eagle-bearer shouted back.

'He was finished. The trident would have bled him to death.'

'Would have,' agreed the eagle-bearer, 'if he hadn't screwed it up at the end. My decision's final. The swordsman won, and everyone's to pay their debts. Or they'll have me to deal with. Now, back to your duties!'

The audience broke up, quietly streaming through the oak trees towards the tent lines while the eagle-bearer's assistants heaved the bodies onto the back of a wagon, to join the losers of the earlier bouts. While Cato waited, his centurion hurried off to collect his winnings from his cohort's standard-bearer, surrounded by a small mob of legionaries clutching their numbered chits. Macro returned a short while later, happily weighing up the coins in his purse.

'Not the most lucrative bet I've ever made but nice to win all the same.'

'I suppose so, sir.'

'Why the long face? Oh, of course. Your money went on that cocky twat with the trident. How much did you lose?'

Cato told him, and Macro whistled.

'Well, young Cato, you've still got a lot to learn about fighting men, it seems.'

'Yes, sir.'

'Never mind, lad. It'll come in time.' Macro clapped him on the shoulder. 'Let's see if anyone's got any decent wine to sell. After that we've got work to do.'

As he watched his men leave the dell from the dappled shadows of a large oak tree, the commander of the Second Legion silently cursed the swordsman. The men badly needed something to take their minds off the coming campaign, and the spectacle of British prisoners taking it out on each other should have been entertaining. Indeed, it had been entertaining, until the end of the last fight. The men had been in high spirits. Then that damn Briton had picked his moment for that pointless gesture of defiance. Or not so pointless, reflected the legate grimly. Maybe the

Briton's sacrifice had been deliberately aimed at undermining the morale-boosting diversion.

Hands clenched behind his back, Vespasian slowly walked out of the shadows into the sunlight. Certainly these Britons did not lack spirit. Like most warrior cultures, they clung to an honour code which ensured that they embraced warfare with a reckless arrogance and a terrible ferocity. More worrying was the fact that the loose coalition of British tribes was being led by a man who knew how to use his forces well. Vespasian felt a grudging respect for the Britons' leader, Caratacus, chief of the Catuvellauni. That man had more tricks up his sleeve yet, and the Roman army of General Aulus Plautius had better treat the enemy with more respect than had been the case so far. The death of the swordsman illustrated all too well the merciless nature of this campaign.

Pushing thoughts of the future aside for the moment, Vespasian made his way over to the hospital tent. There was an unfortunate matter he could put off no longer. The chief centurion of the Second Legion had been mortally wounded in a recent ambush, and had wanted to speak to him before he died. Bestia had been a model soldier, earning men's praise, admiration and fear throughout his military career. He had fought in many wars across the empire, and had the scars on his body to prove it. And now he had fallen to a British sword in a minor skirmish that no historian would ever record. Such was army life, Vespasian reflected bitterly. How many more unsung heroes were out there waiting to be snuffed out while vain politicians and imperial lackeys grabbed the credit?

Vespasian thought of his brother, Sabinus, who had raced up from Rome to serve on General Plautius' staff while there was still some glory to be won. Sabinus, like most of

10

his political peers, saw the army only in terms of the next rung on their career ladder. The cynicism of high politics filled Vespasian with a cold fury. It was more than likely that Emperor Claudius was using the invasion to strengthen his hold on the throne. Should the legions succeed in subduing Britain, there would be plenty of spoils and sinecures to oil the wheels of state. Some men would make fortunes, while others would be granted high office, and money would flow into the thirsty imperial coffers. The glory of Rome would be reaffirmed and its citizens be given further proof that the gods blessed Rome's destiny, yet there were men to whom such great achievements meant little, for they viewed events only in terms of the opportunities they presented for personal advancement.

This savage island, with its restless, feuding warrior tribes, might one day be afforded all the benefits of order and prosperity conferred by Roman rule. Such an extension of civilisation was a cause worth fighting for, and it was in pursuit of this vision that Vespasian served Rome, and tolerated those Rome placed over him – for now at least. Before that, the present campaign must be won. Two major rivers must be crossed, in the teeth of fierce resistance by the natives. Beyond the rivers lay the capital of the Catuvellauni – the most powerful of the British tribes opposing Rome. Thanks to their ruthless expansion in recent years, the Catuvellauni had swallowed up the Trinovantes and their prosperous trading city of Camulodunum. Now many of the other tribes viewed Caratacus with almost as much dread as they viewed the Romans. So, Camulodunum must fall before autumn to demonstrate to those tribes still wavering that resistance to Rome was futile. Even then, there would be more campaigns, more years of conquest, before every corner of this large island was incorporated into the empire. Should the legions fail to take Camulodunum then Caratacus might well win the allegiance of the uncommitted tribes, and raise enough men to overwhelm the Roman army.

With a weary sigh Vespasian ducked under the hospital tent's flap and nodded a greeting to the legion's senior surgeon.

Chapter Two

'Bestia's dead.'

Cato looked up from his paperwork as Centurion Macro entered the tent. The summer shower thudding down on the goatskin had drowned out Macro's announcement.

'Sir?'

'I said Bestia's dead,' Macro shouted. 'Died this afternoon.'

Cato nodded. The news was expected. The old chief centurion's face had been laid open right down to the bone. The legion's surgeons had done all they could to make his final days as comfortable as possible, but loss of blood, the shattered jaw and a subsequent infection had made death inevitable. Cato's first instinct was to welcome the news. Bestia had made his life a grinding misery throughout the months he had spent in training. Indeed, the chief centurion had seemed to positively enjoy picking on him and a smouldering hatred had grown in Cato in response.

Macro undid the clasp of his wet cloak and threw it across the back of a camp stool which he pulled up in front of the brazier. The steam from a variety of garments drying on other stools rose in orange wisps, and added to the muggy atmosphere of the tent. If the rain outside was the best weather that the British summer could offer, Macro wondered if the island was worth fighting for. The British exiles accompanying the legions claimed that the island had vast resources of precious metals and rich agricultural lands. Macro shrugged. The exiles might be telling the truth but they had their own reasons for wanting Rome to triumph over their own people. Most had lost land and title at the hands of the Catuvellauni and hoped to regain both as a reward for aiding Rome.

'Wonder who'll get Bestia's job?' Macro mused. 'Be interesting to see who Vespasian will pick.'

'Any chance of you, sir?'

'Hardly, my lad!' Macro snorted. His young optio had not long been a member of the Second Legion and was not wise to the promotion procedures of the army. 'I'm out of the running for that job. Vespasian has to choose from the surviving centurions of the First Cohort. They're the best officers in the legion. You must have several years of excellent service behind you before you get considered for promotion to the First Cohort. I'll be in command of the Sixth Century of the Fourth Cohort for a while yet, I think. Bet there are some pretty anxious men in the First Cohort's mess tonight. You don't get a chance to make chief centurion every day.'

'Won't they be grieving, sir? I mean, Bestia was one of their own.'

'I guess so.' Macro shrugged. 'But that's the fortune of war. Any one of us could have been for the Styx crossing. Just happened to be Bestia's turn. Anyway, he had had his time in this world. Two years from now he'd only have been going quietly mad in some dull veterans' colony. Better him than someone with something to look forward to, like most of the other poor sods who've copped it so far. And now, as it happens, there are quite a few vacancies to be filled in the centurionate.' Macro smiled at the prospect. He had been a centurion for only a few weeks longer than Cato had been a legionary and had been the most junior centurion in the legion. But the Britons had killed two of the centurions in the Fourth Cohort, which meant that he was now officially fourth in seniority, with the happy prospect of having two newly appointed centurions to lord it over. He looked up and grinned at his optio.

'If this campaign goes on for a few more years, even you might make centurion!'

Cato smiled at the back-handed compliment. Chances were that the island would be conquered well before anyone credited him with enough experience and maturity to be promoted to the centurionate. At the tender age of seventeen that prospect was years away. He sighed and held out the wax tablet he had been working on.

'The effective strength report, sir.'

Macro ignored the tablet. Barely able to read and write, he was of the opinion that attempting either was best avoided if at all possible; he depended heavily on his optio to ensure that the Sixth Century's records were kept in order. 'Well?'

'We've got six in the field hospital – two of those aren't likely to survive. The senior surgeon told me that three of the others will have to be discharged from the army. They're to be conveyed to the coast this afternoon. Should be back in Rome by the end of the year.'

'And then what?' Macro shook his head sadly. 'A pro-rata retirement gratuity and the rest of their lives spent begging on the streets. Some life to look forward to.'

Cato nodded. As a boy he had seen the disabled veterans scrabbling for a pittance in the filthy alcoves of the forum. Having lost a limb or suffered a disabling wound, such a lifestyle was all that was open to most of them. Death might well have been a more merciful outcome for such men. A sudden image of himself mutilated, condemned to poverty, and an object of pity and ridicule caused Cato to shudder. He had no family to fall back on. The only person who cared for him outside the army was Lavinia. She was far from him now, on the road to Rome with the other slaves in the household of Lady Flavia, wife of the Second Legion's commander. Cato could not hope that, if the worst happened, Lavinia would be able to love a cripple. He knew he could not bear her pity, or her staying with him out of any misguided sense of duty.

Macro sensed a change in the young man's attitude. It was strange, he considered, how much he had become aware of the lad's moods. Every optio he had ever known had been just a legionary on the make, but Cato was different. Quite different. Intelligent, well-read, and a proven soldier, yet perversely critical of himself. If he lived long enough, Cato would surely make a name for himself someday. Macro could not understand why the optio did not seem aware of this, and tended to regard Cato with a mixture of guarded amusement and admiration.

'Don't worry, lad. You'll live through this lot. If you were going to cop it, you'd have done so by now. You've survived the worst army life can throw at you. You'll be around for a while yet, so cheer up.'

'Yes, sir,' Cato replied quietly. Macro's words were false comfort, as the death of even the finest soldiers – like Bestia – had shown.

'Now then, where were we?'

Cato looked down at the wax tablet. 'The last man in the hospital is making a good recovery. Sword slash to the thigh. Should be back on his feet in a few more days. Then there's four walking wounded. They'll be back on our fighting strength soon. Leaves us with fifty-eight effectives, sir.'

'Fifty-eight.' Macro frowned. The Sixth Century had suffered badly at the hands of the Britons. They had landed on the island with eighty men. Now, only days later, they had lost eighteen for good.

'Any news on the replacements, sir?'

'We won't be getting any until the staff can organise a shipment from the reserve pool back in Gaul. Take them a week or more at least before they can ship them over the Channel from Gesoriacum. Won't join us until after the next battle.'

'Next battle?' Cato sat up eagerly. 'What battle, sir?'

'Easy, lad.' Macro smiled. 'The legate told us at the briefing. Vespasian has had word from the general. It seems the army is facing a river. A nice big, wide river. And on the far side Caratacus is waiting for us with his army – chariots and all.'

'How far from here, sir?'

'Day's march. The Second should arrive at the river tomorrow. Aulus Plautius doesn't intend to hang around, apparently. He'll launch the attack the following morning, as soon as we're in position.'

'How do we get at them?' Cato asked. 'I mean, how do we get across the river? Is there a bridge?'

'You really think the Britons would leave one standing? Just for us to use?' Macro shook his head wearily. 'No, the general still has to figure that one out.'

'Do you think he will order us in first?'

'Doubt it. We've been pretty roughly handled by the Britons. The men are still feeling very shaken. You must have sensed it.'

Cato nodded. The low morale of the legion had been palpable in the last few days. Worse still, he had overheard men openly criticising the legate, holding Vespasian responsible for the heavy casualties they had suffered since landing on British soil. That Vespasian had fought the enemy in the front rank alongside his men was of little account to most legionaries who had not witnessed his valour in person. As things stood, there was considerable resentment and mistrust of the legion's senior officers, and that did not bode well for the next engagement with the Britons.

'We'd better win this one,' Macro said quietly.

'Yes, sir.'

Both men were silent a moment as they gazed at the flickering tongues of flames in the brazier. Then a loud rumble from the centurion's stomach abruptly shifted his thinking to more pressing issues.

'I'm bloody hungry. Anything to eat?'

'There on the desk, sir.' Cato gestured towards a dark loaf of bread and a hunk of salted pork in a mess tin. A small jug of watered wine stood beside a battered silver cup, a memento of one of Macro's earlier campaigns. The centurion frowned as he looked at the pork.

'Still no fresh meat?'

'No, sir. Caratacus is doing a thorough job of clearing the land ahead of our line of march. The scouts say that nearly every crop and farm has been fired as far as the banks of the Tamesis, and they've driven their livestock away with them. We're stuck with what comes up to us from the victualling depot at Rutupiae.'

'I'm sick of bloody salted pork. Can't you get anything else? Piso would have got us something better than this.'

'Yes, sir,' Cato replied with resentment. Piso, the century's clerk, was a veteran who had known every dodge and scam in the book, and the men of the century had done very well by him. Only days before, Piso, a mere year off his honourable discharge, had been cut down by the very first Briton he encountered. Cato had learned much from the clerk, but the more arcane secrets of working the military bureaucracy had died with him, and Cato was on his own now.

'I'll see what I can do about the rations, sir.'

'Good!' Macro nodded as he bit into the pork with a grimace and started the long process of chewing the tough meat into a consistency soft enough to swallow. As he chewed he continued to grumble. 'Much more of this stuff and I'll quit the legion and take up the Jewish faith. Anything's got to be better than putting up with this. I don't know what the fuck those bastards in the commissariat do to the pigs. You'd have thought it would be almost impossible to screw up something as simple as salted pork.'

Cato had heard it all before and got on with his paperwork. Most of the dead men had left wills bequeathing their camp property to their friends. But some of those named as beneficiaries had died as well, and Cato had to trace the order of bequests through the documents to ensure that the accumulated possessions reached the right recipients. The families of those who had died intestate would require notification in order to claim the man's savings from the legion's treasury. For Cato, the execution of wills was a new experience, and since the responsibility was his, he dared not risk any errors that might lead to a lawsuit being brought against him. So he carefully read through the documentation, and checked and rechecked each man's accounts in turn, before dipping his stylus in a small ceramic inkpot and writing up the final statement of possessions and their destinations.

The tent flap swished open and a headquarters clerk hurriedly stepped inside, his sodden army cloak dripping all over the place.

'Here, keep that off my work!' Cato shouted as he covered the scrolls piled on his desk.

'Sorry.' The headquarters clerk stood back against the flap.

'And what the fuck do you want?' Macro asked as he bit off a piece of brown bread.

'Message from the legate, sir. He wants to see you and the optio in his tent, at your earliest convenience.'

Cato smiled. A senior officer's use of that phrase meant at once, preferably sooner. Quickly ordering the documents into a pile, and ensuring that none of the leaks in the tent were dripping anywhere near his campaign desk, Cato stood up and retrieved his cloak from its position in front of the brazier. It was still heavy with moisture and felt clammy as he pulled it round his shoulders and fixed the clasp. But the warmth in the folds of greased wool was comforting.

Macro, still chewing, pulled on his cloak and then waved impatiently at the headquarters clerk. 'You can piss off now. We know the way, thank you.'

With a longing look at the brazier, the clerk pulled his hood up and backed out of the tent. Macro crammed in a last mouthful of pork, crooked his finger at Cato and mumbled, 'Come on!'

The rain hissed down on the glistening ranks of the legion's tents and formed disturbed puddles on the uneven ground. Macro looked up at the dark clouds in the evening sky. Away to the south occasional flashes of sheet lightning marked the passage of a summer storm. The rain streamed down his face and he flicked his head to clear a loose strand of drenched hair from his forehead. 'What crap weather this island has.'

Cato laughed. 'I doubt it'll get much better, sir. If Strabo is anything to go by.'

The literary allusion caused Macro to grimace at the boy. 'You couldn't just agree with me, could you? Had to bring some bloody academic into it.'

'Sorry, sir.'

'Never mind. Let's go and see what Vespasian wants.'

Chapter Three

'At ease,' ordered Vespasian.

Macro and Cato, standing a pace back from the desk, adopted the required informal posture. They were rather shocked to see clear signs of exhaustion in their commander as he leaned back from the scrolls on his desk and the light from the overhead oil lamps fell on his heavily lined face.

Vespasian considered them for a moment, unsure how to proceed.

A few days ago the centurion, the optio and a small party of Macro's hand-picked men had been sent on a secret mission. They had been tasked with retrieving a pay chest that Julius Caesar had been forced to abandon in a marsh close to the coast nearly a hundred years earlier. The Second Legion's senior tribune, a smooth patrician named Vitellius, had decided to seize the pay chest for himself and, with a gang of horse archers he had bribed, had fallen on Macro's men amid the mists of the marsh. Thanks to the fighting skills of the centurion, Vitellius had failed and fled the scene. But the fates seemed to favour the tribune; he had come across a column of Britons trying to outflank the Roman advance and had been able to warn the legions of the danger just in time. As a result of the subsequent victory, Vitellius was now something of a hero. Those who knew the truth about Vitellius' treachery felt disgust at the praise that was showered on the senior tribune.

'I'm afraid I can't press any charges against Tribune Vitellius. I've only your word to go on, and that isn't enough.'

Macro bristled with barely contained rage.

'Centurion, I know the type of man he is. You say he tried to have you and your men killed when I sent you after the pay chest. That mission was secret, quite secret. I suspect that only you, me and the lad there knew about the chest's contents. And Vitellius of course. Even now it is still sealed, and on its way back to Rome under heavy guard, and the fewer who know about the gold it contains the better. That's the way the Emperor wants to keep things. No one will thank us for exposing this in court if charges are bought against Vitellius. In addition, you might not be aware that his father is a close friend of the Emperor. Do I need to say more?'

Macro pursed his lips and shook his head.

Vespasian let his words sink in, well understanding the expression of resignation settling on the faces of the centurion and his optio. It was too bad that Vitellius should be the one to emerge from the situation smelling of roses, but that was typical of the tribune's luck. That man was destined for high office, and the fates would let nothing stand in his way. And there was far more behind his treachery than Vespasian could ever let these two men know. Besides his duties as a tribune, Vitellius was also an imperial spy in the service of Narcissus, the Emperor's chief secretary. If Narcissus ever came to know he had been fooled by Vitellius, the tribune's life would be forfeit. But Narcissus would never find out from the lips of Vespasian. Vitellius had seen to that. While gathering information on the loyalty of the officers and men of the Second Legion, Vitellius had uncovered the identity of a conspirator involved in a plot to overthrow the new Emperor.

Flavia Domitilla, the wife of Vespasian.

For the moment, then, a stand-off existed between Vitellius and Vespasian; both had information that could fatally wound the other if it ever came to the ears of Narcissus.

Aware that he must have been staring vacantly at his subordinates for some time, Vespasian quickly turned his mind to the other reason he had summoned Macro and Cato.

'Centurion, there is something that should cheer you up.' Vespasian reached to the side of the table and picked up a small bundle wrapped in silk. Carefully unfolding the silk, Vespasian revealed a gold torc which he gazed at momentarily before holding it up in the dim light of the oil lamps. 'Recognise it, Centurion?'

Macro looked a moment, then shook his head. 'Sorry, sir.'

'I'm not surprised. You probably had other things on your mind when you first saw this,' Vespasian said with a wry smile. 'It's the torc of a chief of the Britons. It used to be the property of one Togodumnus, fortunately no longer with us.'

Macro laughed, suddenly recalling the torc as it had been, worn round the neck of the huge warrior he had killed in single combat a few days earlier.

'Here!' Vespasian tossed the torc and Macro, caught by surprise, fielded it awkwardly. 'A small token of the legion's gratitude. It comes out of my share of the spoils. You deserve that, Centurion. You won it, so wear it with honour.'

'Yes, sir,' Macro replied as he examined the torc. Plaited bands of gold gleamed in the wavering light, and each end curled back on itself round a large ruby that sparkled like a blood-soaked star. Strange swirling designs had been worked into the gold surrounding the rubies. Macro felt the weight of the torc and made a rough calculation of its value. His eyes widened as he registered the significance of the legate's gesture.

'Sir, I don't know how to thank you for this.'

Vespasian waved a hand. 'Then don't. As I said, you deserve it. As for you, Optio, I have nothing to give except my thanks.'

Cato coloured, his lips thinning into a bitter expression. The legate couldn't help laughing at the young man.

'It's true I may not have anything of value to give you. But someone else has, or had, rather.'

'Sir?'

'You're aware that Chief Centurion Bestia has died of his wounds?'

'Yes, sir.'

'Last night, before he lost consciousness, he made a verbal will in front of witnesses. He asked that I be his executor.'

'A verbal will?' Cato frowned.

'As long as there are witnesses, any soldier can state verbally how his camp property is to be disposed of in the event of his death. It's a custom rather than a rule enshrined in law. It seems that Bestia wanted you to have certain items of his property.'

'Me!' Cato exclaimed. 'He wanted *me* to have something, sir?'

'Apparently.'

'But why on earth? He couldn't stand the sight of me.'

'Bestia said he'd seen you fight like a veteran, with no armour, just helmet and shield. Going at it just as he had taught you. He told me he had been wrong about you. He'd thought you a fool and a coward. He learned otherwise, and wanted you to know he was proud of the way you'd turned out.'

'He said that, sir?'

'Precisely that, son.'

Cato opened his mouth, but no words came. He could not believe this; it seemed impossible. To have misjudged someone so completely. To have assumed that they were irredeemably bad and incapable of positive sentiment.

'What did he want me to have, sir?'

'Find out for yourself, son,' replied Vespasian. 'Bestia's body is still in the hospital tent, with his personal effects. The surgeon's assistant knows what to give you. We'll burn Bestia's body at dawn. You're dismissed.'

Chapter Four

Outside, Cato whistled with astonishment at the prospect of Bestia's bequest. But the centurion was paying little attention to his optio; he fingered the torc, relishing its considerable weight. They walked towards the hospital tent in silence until Macro looked up at the tall figure of the optio.

'Well, well. Wonder what Bestia's left for you.'

Cato coughed, clearing the tightness in his throat. 'No idea, sir.'

'I had no inkling the old boy had it in him to make that kind of gesture. Never heard of him doing anything like this the entire time I've served with the eagles. Guess you must have made quite an impression after all.'

'I suppose so, sir. But I can hardly believe it.'

Macro thought about it a moment, and then shook his head. 'Neither can I. No offence meant or anything but, well, you just weren't his idea of a soldier. Must admit, it took me a while to work out there was more to you than a beanpole bookworm. You just don't have the look of a soldier about you.'

'No, sir,' came the sullen reply. 'I'll try and look the part from now on.'

'Don't worry about it, lad. I know you're a killer, through and through, even if you don't know it. Seen you in action, haven't I?'

27

Cato winced at the word 'killer'. That was the last thing he wanted to be known as. A soldier, yes, that word had some measure of civilised credibility. Obviously being a soldier entailed the possibility of killing but that, Cato told himself, was incidental to the essence of the profession. Killers, on the other hand, were just brutes with few, if any, values. Those barbarians who lived in the shadows of the great German forests were killers. They slaughtered for the sheer hell of it, as their endless, petty tribal conflicts illustrated all too well. Rome may have had civil wars in its past, Cato reminded himself, but under the order imposed by the emperors the threat of internal conflict had all but passed. The Roman army fought with a moral purpose: the extension of civilised values to the benighted savages who lived on the fringes of the empire.

What of these Britons? What kind of men were they? Killers, or soldiers after their fashion? The swordsman who had died in the legate's games haunted his mind. The man had been a true warrior and had attacked with the ferocity of a born killer. His self-destruction was an act of sheer fanaticism, a trait in some men that deeply disturbed Cato, filling him with a sense of moral terror, and a conviction that only Rome offered a better way. For all its corrupt and cynical politicians, Rome ultimately stood for order and progress; a beacon to all those terrified huddled masses hiding in the shadows of dark barbarian lands.

'Still regretting your bet?' Macro nudged him out of his self-absorption.

'No, sir. I was just thinking about that Briton.'

'Ah, forget him. Stupid thing to do, and that's all there is to it. I might have more respect for him if he'd used the sword on us and tried to make a break for it. But to kill himself? What a waste.'

'If you say so, sir.'

They had reached the hospital tent, and waved away the insects crowding the oil lamps by the tent flaps, before ducking inside. An orderly was sitting at a desk to the side. He led them to the rear of the tent where the injured officers were quartered. Each centurion had been allotted a small sectioned area with a camp bed, side table and chamber pot. The orderly drew open a curtain and waved them in. Macro and Cato squeezed in either side of the narrow bed on which a linen shroud covered the chief centurion's body.

They stood a moment in silence, before the orderly spoke to Cato. 'The items he wanted you to have are under the bed. I'll leave you two here a while.'

'Thanks,' Cato replied quietly.

The curtain fell back across the opening and the orderly returned to his desk. It was quiet, only a faint groaning came from somewhere else in the tent, and the more distant sounds of the camp beyond.

'Well, are you going to look, or shall I?' asked Macro in a hushed voice.

'Pardon?'

Macro indicated the chief centurion with his thumb. 'One last look on the face of the old man before he goes up in smoke. I owe him that.'

Cato swallowed nervously. 'Go ahead.'

Macro reached down and gently pulled back the linen shroud, uncovering Bestia as far as his naked chest which bristled with grey hair. Neither of them had ever seen Bestia out of uniform and the mass of tightly curled body hair came as a surprise. Some kind soul had already covered the chief centurion's eyes with coins to pay Charon his fare for the crossing of the River Styx into the underworld. The injury that had finally killed him had been cleaned, but even so the mangled teeth, bone and muscle sinew that was visible where the flesh had been hacked from the side of Bestia's face was not a pretty sight.

Macro whistled. 'It's a wonder he managed to say anything to the legate in this state.'

Cato nodded.

'Still, the old bugger made it to the top, which is more than most of us achieve. Let's see what he's left for you. Shall I look?'

'If you want to, sir.'

'Fair enough.' Macro knelt down and rummaged about under the bed. 'Ah! Here we go.'

Rising, he held up a sword in a scabbard and a small amphora. The sword he passed over to Cato. Then he pulled the stopper from the amphora and sniffed cautiously. A smile split his face.

'Caecuban!' Macro crooned. 'My lad, whatever it is you did to impress Bestia, it must have been pretty damn miraculous. Do you mind if . . . ?'

'Help yourself, sir,' replied Cato. He examined the sword. The scabbard was black and inlaid with a striking silver geometric pattern. Here and there, the scabbard had been dented and marked with heavy use. A soldier's weapon then, not some ornamental device reserved for ceremonies.

Centurion Macro licked his lips, raised the amphora and made his toast. 'To Chief Centurion Lucius Batiacus Bestia, a hard bastard, but a fair one. A good soldier who did honour to his comrades, his legion, his family, his tribe and Rome.' Macro took a healthy swig of vintage Caecuban wine, his Adam's apple working furiously, before he lowered the amphora and smacked his lips. 'Absolutely wonderful stuff. Try some.'

Cato took the amphora thrust towards him and raised it over the body of the dead chief centurion, feeling slightly self-conscious about the gesture. 'To Bestia.'

Macro was right. The wine was uncommonly tasty, a rich fruitiness with just a hint of musk, and a dry aftertaste. Delicious. And intoxicating.

'Let's have a look at your sword.'

'Yes, sir.' Cato handed the sword over. After a cursory glance at the scabbard, Macro grasped the ivory handle with its ornately turned pommel of gold, and drew out the blade. It was well-tempered and polished, and glinted like a mirror. Macro raised his eyebrows in honest appreciation as he softly ran a finger down the cutting edge. It had been honed to unusual sharpness for what was essentially a thrusting sword. He felt the weight, and murmured approval at the fine balance between pommel and blade. This was a sword a man could wield with ease, never stressing the wrist the way that standard-issue short swords did. No Roman made this. The blade was surely the work of one of the great Gaulish forges which had been making the finest swords for generations. How had Bestia come by it?

Then he noticed an inscription, a small phrase near the guard, written in an alphabet he had come to recognise as Greek.

'Here, what's this say?'

Cato took the sword and mentally translated: 'From Germanicus to L. Batiacus, his Patroclus.' A shiver of wonder went down Cato's spine. He looked down on the hideously disfigured face of the chief centurion. Had this man once been an attractive youth? Attractive enough to win the affection of the great General Germanicus? It was hard to believe. Cato had only known Bestia as a harsh, cruel disciplinarian. But who knows what secrets a man holds when he dies? Some he takes with him to the underworld, some are revealed.

'Well?' Macro said impatiently. 'What's it say?'

Knowing his centurion's intolerances, Cato thought quickly. 'It's a gift from Germanicus, for his services.'

'Germanicus? *The* Germanicus?'

'I suppose so, sir. There's no more detail than that.'

'I had no idea the old boy was so well-connected. That deserves another toast.'

Cato reluctantly handed him the amphora, and winced as Macro guzzled more of the vintage wine. The amphora felt disappointingly light when he got it back. Rather than lose the balance of his bequest to the belly of his centurion, Cato toasted Bestia again and gulped down as much as he could handle in one go.

Macro belched. 'W-well, Bestia must have performed a pretty heroic deed to win that little beauty. A sword from Germanicus! That's quite something, quite something.'

'Yes, sir,' Cato agreed quietly. 'It must have been.'

'Look after that blade, lad. It's priceless.'

'I will, sir.' Cato was beginning to feel the effects of the wine in the hot, close confines of the tent, and suddenly craved fresh air. 'I think we should leave him now, sir. Let him rest in peace.'

'He's dead, Cato. He's not asleep.'

'Figure of speech. Anyway, I need to get out of here, sir. I need to be outside.'

'Me too.' Macro flipped the linen shroud back over Bestia and followed the optio outside. The rain had stopped and, as the clouds were clearing away, the stars flickered dully in the humid atmosphere. Cato drew in deep lungfuls of air. He was feeling the wine more than ever and wondered if he would suffer the indignity of being sick.

'Let's get back to our tent and finish the amphora,' Macro said cheerily. 'We owe the old boy that at least.'

'Do we?' Cato replied bleakly.

'Of course we do. Old army tradition. That's how we mourn our dead.'

'A tradition?'

'Well, it is now.' Macro smiled woozily. 'Come on, let's go.'

Holding tightly to his new sword in its scabbard, Cato relinquished control of the amphora and the pair of them steered an uncertain course back through the neat lines of tents to those of their own century.

At dawn the next morning, when Bestia's pyre was ignited, the centurion and optio of the Sixth Century in the Fourth Cohort gazed on with bleary eyes. The entire Second Legion was formed up to witness the event, and faced the pyre on three sides while the legate, the camp prefect, tribunes and other senior officers stood at attention on the fourth side. Vespasian had chosen his position well, upwind from the pyre in the light airs drifting across the British landscape. Directly opposite, the first tendrils of thick oily smoke, laden with the odour of burning fat, wafted across the legionaries standing at attention. A chorus of coughing broke out around Macro and his optio, and a moment later Cato's rather too delicate stomach clenched like a fist, and he doubled over and vomited the disturbed contents of his guts all over the grass at his feet.

Macro sighed. Even from beyond the shadows of death Bestia had the capacity to make his men suffer.

Chapter Five

'The problem, gentlemen, is that hillock over there.' The general pointed across the river with his baton, and the eyes of his senior officers followed the direction indicated. In addition to the commanders of the four legions, amongst the cluster of scarlet cloaks were Plautius' staff officers. Vespasian was finding it hard not to be amused by the amount of dazzling gilt that was adorning the burnished breastplate of his brother Sabinus, who was enjoying the honorific rank of prefect of horse. Almost as garish was the amount of gold being worn by the British exile accompanying Plautius. Adminius had been forced to flee his kingdom by his brother, Caratacus, and had joined the Roman army to act as a guide and negotiator. If Rome triumphed, his title and lands would be restored to him, although he would rule as a client king of Rome, with all the obligations that entailed: a poor reward for betraying his people. Vespasian shifted his scornful gaze from the Briton back to the river.

The far bank sloped up to a low ridge than ran alongside the river. The crest had been crudely fortified, and even as they watched, the tiny figures of the Britons toiled furiously to improve their initial efforts. Already a substantial ditch had been dug around the crossing point, with the spoil being added to the rampart behind. A crude palisade was being erected on top of the ramp, with a redoubt at each end, beyond which the ground became marsh.

'You may have noticed that this stretch of the river is tidal,' Plautius continued. 'And if you look closely at the far bank you can see that Caratacus has been laying submerged obstacles on the river bed. Is the tide flooding or ebbing, Tribune Vitellius?'

The general's latest staff officer was caught on the hop and Vespasian couldn't help smiling with satisfaction as Vitellius' usual smug expression fell prey to doubt and then embarrassment. The tribune was on secondment from the Second Legion as a reward for his recent heroics. This experience on the general's staff was an opportunity to make a name for himself, and ease the way for any future military career. For a moment it looked as if the tribune would try and bluff it, but then honesty won the day although, in perfect keeping with his character, Vitellius could not resist an attempt at damage limitation through evasion.

'I'll find out, sir.'

'Is that "I'll find out, sir" as in "I don't know, sir"?' Plautius asked drily.

'Yes, sir.'

'Then see to it immediately,' ordered Plautius. 'And from now on remember that it's your job to know these things. There'll be no excuses in future. Understand?'

'Yes, sir!' Vitellius snapped as he saluted and fled the scene.

'You just can't get the staff these days,' Plautius muttered.

The other officers present exchanged knowing smiles. It was unfair to expect a staff officer to be aware of the tidal conditions of a river he had only just encountered. But unless staff officers could be made to worry about each and every possible factor influencing the execution of a campaign, they were useless. A staff posting might be worth seeking, but the individuals concerned had all manner of crosses to bear.

Straining his eyes, Vespasian could just make out a series of ominous black tips protruding from the water's surface. Sharpened wooden stakes, driven into the river bed, and quite capable of impaling an infantryman or disembowelling a horse. The attackers would be forced to negotiate the crossing cautiously under volleys of slingshot and arrows from the enemy even before they emerged from the river and encountered the ditch and rampart.

'We could cover the assault with artillery, sir,' Vespasian suggested. 'The bolt-throwers would force them to keep their heads down, while the catapults took down the palisade.'

Plautius nodded. 'I have considered that. The prefect of engineers reckons that the range is too great – we'd have to use the smallest calibre of missile, not enough to do the required damage. I think we have to discount the possibility of a direct assault on its own. By the time any heavy infantry could cross the river and form up we'd have too many casualties. Furthermore, the front itself is too narrow for sheer force to carry the day. Our men would be exposed to fire from three sides as they approached the ditch. No, I'm afraid we must be a little more sophisticated.'

'Do we have to cross here, sir?' asked Sabinus. 'Can't we just march upriver until we find an easier crossing?'

'No,' the general replied patiently. 'If we march upriver, Caratacus can shadow us every step of the way and oppose any crossing we attempt. It might be days, weeks even, before we get across. Then he simply falls back to the Tamesis and we repeat the whole process all over again. And time is on his side, not ours. Every day more men will be joining his army. Every day we give him makes our chances of taking Camulodunum before autumn less likely. And unless Camulodunum falls, we won't be able to secure the alliance of those tribes still neutral. We must fight Caratacus here, and now.'

'Yes, sir,' Sabinus muttered, striving to hide his embarrassment at being lectured to as if he was no more than a green tribune.

Plautius turned to address his assembled officers. 'So, gentlemen, I'm open to suggestions.'

The legate of the Ninth Legion looked thoughtfully across the river. Hosidius Geta was a patrician who had opted to continue his army service rather than pursue a political career, and he had considerable experience of waterborne operations with his legion on the Danube. He turned to his general.

'Sir, if I may?'

'Be my guest, Geta.'

'This calls for a flanking movement, two flanking movements in fact.' Geta turned back towards the river. 'While the main army demonstrates here, we could throw a force across the river further downstream, under covering fire from some warships – provided the water's deep enough at that point.'

'We could use the Batavian auxiliaries for that, sir,' Vespasian suggested, and drew an irritated glance from Geta for his pains.

'I was going to suggest that,' Geta replied coldly. 'They've trained for this sort of duty. They can swim across rivers fully armed. If we can get them across without any significant opposition, we can launch a flank attack on the British positions over there.'

'You mentioned a second flanking attack,' said Plautius.

'Yes, sir. While the Batavians are crossing, a second force can move upriver until they find a ford and then turn the enemy's other flank.'

Plautius nodded. 'And if we get the timing right, we should hit them from three directions in a staggered attack. Should be over fairly quickly.'

'That's my belief, sir,' Geta replied. 'The second force need not require too many men, their chief role is to be the final surprise Caratacus cannot deal with. Catch him off balance, and we'll win the day. He'll never be able to cope with all three attacks. You know what these native irregulars are like. Of course, if either of our flanking forces is caught in isolation, then losses will be severe.'

Vespasian felt a cold chill at the nape of his neck as he recognised the chance he had been looking for. The chance to redeem himself and his legion. If the Second could play the decisive role in the coming battle, it would go a long way towards restoring the unit's spirits. Although Togodumnus' recent ambush of the Second Legion had failed, the unit had suffered grievous losses in men and morale was low. A successful attack, pressed home ruthlessly, might yet save the reputation of the Second and its commander. But would the men be up for it?

Plautius was nodding as he went over Geta's proposal. 'There is a risk in a divided assault, as you say, but there's a risk any way we cut it. Right then, we'll go with that plan. All that remains is the allocation of forces. Clearly, the right flank attack across the river will require the Batavians,' he said, with a faint nod towards Vespasian. 'The frontal assault will be carried out by the Ninth.'

This was it, Vespasian realised. Time to reclaim the Second's honour. He took a step forward and cleared his throat.

'Yes, Vespasian?' Plautius looked towards him. 'You have something to add?'

'Sir, I request the privilege of leading the left flank attack.'

Plautius folded his arms and cocked his head to one side as he considered Vespasian's request. 'Do you really think the Second can handle it? You're under-strength, and I imagine your men wouldn't be too pleased to find themselves in the thick of battle quite so soon after their recent experience.'

Vespasian coloured. 'I beg to differ, sir. I believe I speak for my men as much as for myself.'

'Frankly, Vespasian, a moment ago I had no intention of even considering the Second for this duty. I was going to hold you in reserve, and let a fresh unit do the job. And I don't see any reason why I should change my mind. Do you?'

Unless Vespasian could quickly find reasons to justify the Second Legion's position on the left flank, he would be doomed to live the rest of his tenure as a legate under a shroud of suspicion about his suitability for command. And if the men sensed that they were being denied an equal part in the campaign, and hence an equal share in the spoils, the Second's morale and reputation would never recover. Their reputation had been bought over the years with the blood of thousands of comrades, under an eagle that had led them into battle for decades. If that was to end, then it would be over his dead body. Vespasian needed to be firm with his general.

'Yes I do, sir. You seem to have been misinformed about the fighting spirit of my legion.' And Vespasian guessed that Vitellius was the source of that misinformation. 'The men are ready for it, sir. They're more than ready, they're thirsty for it. We need to avenge the men we've lost.'

'Enough!' Plautius cut in. 'You think that rhetoric will win out over reason? This is the front line, not the forum in Rome. I asked you to give me a good reason why I should give way.'

'All right then, sir. I'll speak straight to the point.'

'Please do.'

'The Second is under-strength. But you don't need a full legion for the attack. If it falls through, then you've only lost a unit that's already been pretty badly cut up rather than a fresh legion.' Vespasian looked at his general shrewdly. 'I dare say that you want to keep as many fresh units to hand as possible, in case you have to fight Caratacus again. You can't afford to face him with under-strength and tired forces across your battle line. Better to risk a more expendable unit now.'

Plautius nodded as he listened approvingly to this altogether more cynical reasoning. It neatly reflected the hard realities of command and, in the same hard way, made the most sense.

'Very well, Vespasian. A reprieve for you and your men then.'

Vespasian inclined his head in thanks. His heart jumped with excitement at having won his commander round, and then in anxiety at the dangerous duty for which he had just volunteered his men. He had been less than honest in his request to the general. He had no doubt that many of the men would curse him for it, but then soldiers complained about everything. They needed to fight. They needed a clearcut victory to boast about. To let the men continue in their present state of doubt about themselves would ruin the legion, and blight his career. Now that he had committed them to the attack he felt confident that the majority would share his desire to fight.

'Your orders,' Plautius stated formally, 'are to proceed upriver at dawn. Locate the nearest ford and cross to the far bank. From there you will march downriver, avoiding contact with the Britons. You will wait in hiding until the headquarters trumpets blow your legion's recognition signal, at which point you will join the assault on that hill. Is that clear?'

'Yes, sir. Perfectly.'

'Hit them hard, Vespasian. As hard as you can.'

'Yes, sir.'

'Your written orders will be with you later today. You'd best be on your way. I want you moving before daybreak. Now go.'

Vespasian saluted the general, nodded a farewell to Sabinus, and was making his way through the throng of officers back towards the horseline when Vitellius came running up the slope, panting heavily.

'Sir! Sir!'

Plautius turned to him in alarm. 'What is it, Tribune?'

Vitellius stood to attention, gulped in some air and made his report. 'The tide is flooding, sir. I got that from our scouts down there by the river.'

General Aulus Plautius stared at him a moment. 'Well, thank you, Tribune. That's very interesting. Very interesting indeed.'

Then he turned away to view the enemy's defences again and to hide his amused expression from view.

Chapter Six

The shadows were lengthening as Cato leaned unmoving against the trunk of a tree, his drab brown cloak cushioning him from the rough bark. In his left hand rested the hunting bow he had drawn from stores, a heavy barbed arrow notched to the drawstring. He had discovered a meandering trail where it crossed a rough track and had followed it down to this clearing. The track snaked across the low ferns and into the trees on the far side of the clearing. Beyond, the river glistened through the leaves and branches, sparkling with the reflection of the sinking sun. City boy as he was he had had the sense to ask for some advice from Pyrax, a veteran long used to foraging, before setting off into the woods. The area had been cleared of the enemy, and was ringed by the marching camps of Plautius' army, so the young optio felt that it was safe enough to try his hand at hunting. With luck, the men of the Sixth Century would not be dining on salted pork tonight, and would go into battle with a good meal in their bellies.

When news of the impending attack had been announced to the Sixth Century, Macro had cursed his luck. Some dangerous flanking manoeuvre was the last thing they needed when their numbers were so depleted. Back in his tent, he and Cato had made preparations for the next morning's attack.

'Take a note,' Macro instructed his optio. 'Each man is to leave all non-essential kit here. If we have to swim for it, we don't want to be carrying more than we need to. And we'll need some rope. Get three hundred feet of light cable from stores. Should be enough to reach across the river if we find a ford.'

Cato looked up from his wax note tablet. 'What if there isn't a ford? What will the legate do then?'

'That's the best bit of it,' Macro grumbled. 'If we don't find a ford by noon, we've been ordered to swim across. We'll have to strip down to our tunics and float the equipment across on inflated bladders. Make a note to indent a bladder for each man.'

He paused when Cato did not respond. 'I'm sorry, lad. I forgot about your aversion to water. If it comes to swimming across, stick with me and I'll see you get over safely.'

'Thank you, sir.'

'Just make sure you get some proper bloody swimming lessons in at the first available opportunity.'

Cato nodded, head lowered in shame.

'So where were we?'

'Bladders, sir.'

'Ah, yes. Let's hope we don't need them. If we can't find a ford I don't fancy tackling the Britons with just a woollen tunic between them and my vitals.'

Cato had wholeheartedly agreed.

The sun was now low over the western horizon and Cato again looked towards the river, which seemed wider than ever. He shuddered at the thought of having to actually swim across it; his swimming technique barely did justice to the words.

The sun was shining directly through the trees, casting a tangle of shadows with orange-hued edges across the clearing. A sudden flash of movement caught Cato's eye. Keeping his body still, he turned his head to follow the movement. A hare had cautiously hopped out onto the track from a patch of stinging nettles not twenty feet from where he stood. It rose up on its hind legs, cautiously sniffing the air. With its upper body and head haloed by the glow of the distant sun, the hare looked like a tempting target, and Cato slowly made to lift the hunting bow. One hare was not going to feed the men of the Sixth Century, but it would do until something larger came down the track.

Cato steadied the bow and was about to release the drawstring when he became aware of another presence in the clearing. The hare turned and scurried back into the undergrowth.

A deer ambled out of the shadows, heading for the point at which the trail entered the trees on the far side of the clearing. A much bigger target, even at twenty paces, and without hesitation, Cato adjusted his aim, allowing for drop and a tendency to shoot up and to the right. The drawstring hummed, the deer froze, and a streak of darkness hurtled through the air and landed in the back of the deer's neck with a loud whack.

The animal crashed down, thrashing its long neck as blood flecked the undergrowth. Cato hurriedly notched another arrow to the bowstring, and sprinted across the clearing. Sensing the danger, and maddened by the barbed arrowhead buried deep in its neck, the deer struggled up and leaped along the track towards the river. Heedless of the tangled vegetation straddling the track, Cato pursued his quarry down the slope, falling behind, then catching up again each time the deer stumbled. The injured animal burst onto the river bank and plunged into the river. The smoothly flowing surface exploded into a multitude of sparking droplets as they caught the evening sun.

Cato was close behind, and drew up at the edge of the river. It seemed much wider and more dangerous than when viewed from the clearing above. The deer splashed on and Cato raised his bow, furious that the animal might yet escape or be dragged off by the current.

The deer floundered on, fully thirty paces away now. The second arrow caught it right in the middle of the back and its rear legs crashed down senseless. Dropping the bow on the river bank, Cato plunged in. The bed of the river was firmly pebbled and less than a foot deep. Water sprayed up around him as he made for the deer with drawn dagger. The second arrow had shattered the deer's spine and it writhed in terror, desperately trying to use its front legs to drag itself on, and staining the water with its blood.

Cato stopped short, fearful of the flailing hooves, and worked his way round to the front. As his shadow fell across its face, the deer froze in terror, and seizing the opportunity Cato thrust his dagger into the animal's throat and ripped it clear. The end was mercifully quick, and after a brief final struggle the deer lay still, eyes staring lifelessly. Cato was trembling, partly from the nervous energy released by the frantic pursuit and kill, and partly through a peculiar sense of distaste and shame at having killed the animal. It was different to killing a man. Quite different. Yet why should it feel any worse? Then Cato realised he had never killed an animal like this before. Sure, he had wrung the neck of the odd chicken, but this felt unsettling and the swirls of blood eddying about his feet made him feel queasy.

He looked down at his feet again. Then up at the river bank he had come running down. Then across to the far side.

'I wonder.'

Cato turned away from the deer and headed for the far bank where the trees were starkly black against a deep orange sky. Squinting, he tried to make out the depth of the water ahead of him. It was too dark, and he nervously felt his way through the water, testing each step as he went. The river's depth gradually increased, and the current quickened, but by the time he reached midstream it had risen only as far as his hips. Thereafter the depth diminished again and he was soon standing on the other side of the river gazing back at the bank held by the legions.

He crouched down in the shadows and waited until the sun had fully set and stars were pricking the early evening sky, but there was no sign of anyone. No men on watch, no patrols, just the sound of wood pigeons and soft cracks as woodland creatures moved in the darkness about him. Satisfied that he was quite alone, Cato returned to the river, waded to the body of the deer and dragged it to where he had left the hunting bow.

The optio smiled happily. The men of the Sixth Century were going to eat well tonight, and tomorrow the rest of the legion were going to have something else to thank him for.

Chapter Seven

'Are you sure this is the place, Optio?'

'Yes, sir.'

Vespasian looked out across the river towards the far bank. Dawn had not yet broken, and the outline of trees was barely distinguishable from the night sky. The far bank was invisible, and the only sound that carried across the water was the hooting of an owl. Behind the legate the trail was packed with a silent mass of legionaries, tense and alert for the first sign of danger. Night marches were the bugbear of army life: no idea of how far one had progressed, frequent halts as columns bottlenecked or simply ran into one another, and the ever-lurking fear of ambush. They were a nightmare to co-ordinate as well, which was why army commanders rarely moved troops between dusk and dawn. But the plan of attack developed by Plautius and his staff officers required that the Second Legion be across the river and in position as quickly as possible, and preferably under cover of darkness.

Vespasian had not quite believed his good fortune when news was brought to him of the discovery of a ford not two miles from the legion's marching camp. It was almost too convenient, suspiciously so, and he had questioned the optio closely. Cato, he knew from previous experience of the lad's abilities, was intelligent and cautious – two qualities the legate particularly admired – and could be relied upon to report accurately. Nevertheless, if the optio had discovered the crossing so easily then surely the Britons were aware of its existence as well. It might well be a trap. There would be little time to test this hypothesis he realised as he looked back over his shoulder to where the darkness was thinning out against the horizon. A small scouting force had to be pushed across at once. If the Britons were guarding the ford, the legion would be forced to march further upstream in search of another. But the more time it took to get across, the less chance the general had of co-ordinating all three attacks on the British fortifications.

'Centurion!'

'Yes, sir!' Macro snapped back from nearby.

'Take your men across the river and scout half a mile in each direction from the far edge of the ford. If you don't encounter the enemy and you're satisfied that we can cross unobserved, send a runner back to me. Best use Cato here.'

'Yes, sir.'

'If you have any doubts about the situation, fall back across the river. Understand?'

'Yes, sir.'

'And do it quickly. We haven't got much darkness left to hide in.'

As the Sixth Century filed down the track and into the river, Vespasian passed the word down the column for the men to sit down and rest. They would need all their strength for the day ahead. Turning back to the river, he watched the straggling black mass wading across, seeming to make an inhuman din as they splashed through the gentle current. The tension only eased once the sound faded as Macro and his men reached the far side.

When the men had assembled on the river bank, Macro quietly issued their orders. He split them into sections and each one was assigned an axis of advance. Then section by section the men carefully picked their way into the trees.

'Cato, you're with me,' Macro whispered. 'Let's go.'

With a last glance at the other river bank, silent and dark against the greying horizon, Cato turned and carefully made his way into the woods. The passage of the other sections was clearly audible at first – the cracking of twigs, the rustling of undergrowth and snagging of equipment. But the sounds gradually died away as the men grew used to the unaccustomed movement, and the sections drew away from each other. Cato did his best to keep up with his centurion without stumbling or making too much noise. He counted off each pace against the half mile Vespasian had ordered. The woods seemed to go on for ever, gently sloping upwards. Suddenly the treacherous undergrowth gave way to much more solid ground, and the trees opened out into a clearing. Macro paused and crouched down, his eyes straining to make out their surroundings.

By the faint light breaking through the tree tops Cato was able to see dim details of the ancient grove they were in. The grove was ringed by ancient gnarled oak trees, upon which had been nailed hundreds of skulls, empty eye sockets and death's-head grins surrounding him on all sides. At the centre of the clearing stood a crude altar made out of monumental slabs of stone, down the sides of which ran dark stains. A grim atmosphere wreathed the grove in its coils and both men shivered, not entirely due to the coolness of the air.

'Shit!' Macro whispered. 'What in Hell is this place?'

'I don't know . . .' Cato replied quietly. The grove seemed almost supernaturally silent, even the first notes of the dawn chorus seemed muted somehow. Despite his adherence to a rational view of the world, Cato could not help being frightened by the oppressive atmosphere of the grove. He felt a compulsion to get away from this dreadful scene as soon as possible. This was no place for Romans, or any civilised men. 'Must be something to do with one of their cults. Druids or something.'

'Druids!' Macro's tone betrayed his alarm. 'We'd better get out of here, fast.'

'Yes, sir.'

Keeping to the fringes of the clearing, Macro and Cato crept past the trees with their grisly trophies, and continued through the woods. A palpable wave of relief washed over them as they left the grove behind. Ever since the Romans had first encountered the Druids, dark tales of their dread magic and bloodthirsty rituals had been handed down the generations. Both Macro and Cato felt an icy tension bristle beneath the hairs on the back of their necks as they trod softly through the shadows. For a while they progressed through the undergrowth in silence until, at last, Cato was sure that he could see lighter shades in the trees ahead.

'Sir!' he whispered.

'Yes, I've seen it. We must be close to the far tree line.'

More cautious than ever, they picked their way forward until the trees thinned out and only stunted saplings remained. They were at the top of the ridge that ran behind the river, and had a clear view down the far side and along the ridge in the direction of the British fortifications guarding the ford. Smoke from the campfires of both armies smeared the sky. To the east the sky was washed with pink and a light mist was visible down towards the river. The land to the west was still shrouded in gloomy shadows.

There was no sign of any movement and Macro waved his optio back into the trees.

'Get back to the legate and tell him it's all clear, the legion can start crossing. I'll stay here a little while to make sure.'

'Yes, sir.'

'You'd better tell him what the lie of the land is like from up here. We won't be able to approach along the top of the ridge – they'd see us a mile off. We'll have to follow the river bank until we're close to the Britons and then make for the ridge. Got all that? Now go!'

Cato made his way back down the slope more quickly than they had climbed it now that the light was strengthening, revealing all the treacherous roots and brambles. Even though he kept well clear of the grove, Cato reached the river bank far more quickly than he had anticipated. For a moment he panicked as he failed to see any sign of the rest of the legion on the far bank. Then a slight movement upstream caught his eye and there was the legate waving an arm from just within the trees. Moments later Cato was making his report.

'March along the river bank?' Vespasian reflected doubtfully as he surveyed the far side. 'That's going to slow us down.'

'Can't be helped, sir. The ridge is too exposed and the woods are too dense.'

'Very well. Return to the centurion, and tell him he's to scout ahead of the main force. Avoid all contact and report back on anything you see.'

'Yes, sir.'

As the column began to file across the ford, the scouting parties of the Sixth Century regrouped on the far bank around Macro. Once Cato had delivered the legate's orders,

Macro formed his men up, and sent the optio ahead with the first section. Cato was well aware of the responsibility placed upon him. He was now the eyes and ears of the Second Legion. Upon him depended the success of the general's plan, and the safety of his comrades. If the enemy were warned of the Second's approach, they would have ample time to prepare to receive the attackers. Even worse, they might have time to organise a counterattack. With this on his mind, the young optio crept forward along the bank, straining his senses to their limits. The untroubled river glided past in the pale air as the sun rose above the trees and filled the summer morning with light and warmth. So it continued for the best part of an hour, as Cato picked his way forward – until he came to a place where the river bank had given way, and many years before a mighty oak tree had tumbled into the water. It now lay across the broken ground at the river's edge, dead tangled branches rippling the passing flow. A mass of roots torn up from the earth provided a frame for new growth to cling to.

A sudden splash in the water caused him to freeze, and the men of the scouting party exchanged anxious glances before Cato spotted the kingfisher perched on a branch that overhung an expanding ripple on the river's surface. He almost laughed at the sudden release of tension before he noticed, not more than fifty feet away, a horse standing at the river's edge. The graceful neck lowered and the beast began to drink. A set of reins tethered the horse to the stump of a tree. Of the rider there was no sign.

Chapter Eight

'Signal the warships to open fire.'

'Yes, sir.' Vitellius saluted and turned smartly away. This posting to the general's staff was proving to be onerous in the extreme. Plautius sought any excuse to find him lacking and there was not a moment when he did not feel the scrutinising glare of the general resting upon him. Well, let the bastard have his fun for now, thought Vitellius. Time was on his side. With his father nicely ensconced in the Emperor's inner circle, his career would advance smoothly enough. He would bide his time and suffer the slights of old fools like Plautius until the moment was ripe to make his play. Already Vitellius was harbouring an ambition so audacious that the mere thought of it caused him to catch his breath at times. If Claudius could become Emperor, then so might any man with the patience and strength of will to see it through. But, he steadied himself, he must not act until he was sure of success. Until that glorious day he could only chip away at the ruling dynasty of the Claudians, invisibly undermining the Emperor, and his heirs, in any way he could.

Trotting down the slope to the makeshift headquarters, Vitellius waved to the assembled trumpeters. They snatched up their instruments and hurried into line. The signals orders had all been thoroughly outlined the night before and as soon as the tribune passed the word, the first notes blared out, splitting the morning air above the heads of the clerks scribbling away on camp tables. First the unit identification, then the instruction for the prearranged action. Below, four triremes lay on the smooth surface of the river, anchored fore and aft to present their beams to the British fortifications. As Vitellius watched, the pennant briefly dipped on the nearest vessel, acknowledging the order. Tiny figures hurried into position around the catapults fixed to the decks. Smoke trailed into the air from the portable ovens requisitioned from the army the previous evening. At first the prefect of the fleet had refused point blank to allow any fire-making apparatus on to his ships; the risk was just too great. The general had insisted; the enemy fortifications must be burned down to help the later infantry assault. In any case, he had pointed out, the fleet was no longer at sea. If the worst happened the sailors would be in easy reach of their comrades on the shore.

'And the galley slaves?' the prefect of the fleet had asked. 'What about them?'

'They're chained to their benches,' explained the prefect patiently. 'If there's a fire, there won't be much chance to get them out.'

'I expect not,' General Plautius agreed. 'But look on the bright side. Once we defeat that lot over the way, I guarantee that you will have first pick of the prisoners to replace any losses. Happy?'

The prefect considered the proposition and eventually nodded. Some fresh recruits to the slaves' benches would be well received by his captains – those who would still have ships, that is.

'Now,' Plautius had concluded, 'see to it that we have some incendiary artillery ready for the morning.'

Recalling the scene, Vitellius smiled as he climbed the slope back to the general's command post.

As the sun rose behind them, the ships' catapults opened up, their throwing arms smacking against their restraining bars. Thin coils of greasy smoke trailed up and over towards the Britons' fortifications, and then the pots smashed down, dousing them in bright pools of blazing oil. Bolt-throwers hurled heavy iron arrows at the palisade to discourage any attempt by the Britons to put the fires out.

Vitellius had seen the effects of a bolt-thrower barrage before and knew just how effective those weapons could be. The Britons, however, had not, and as the tribune watched, a swarm of natives rushed up over the earthworks and ran towards a section of the palisade that had taken a direct hit and was burning nicely. Reaching the spot, the Britons frantically shovelled earth onto the fire while those with buckets formed a chain down to the river. But before the chain could even begin to work, the bolt-thrower crews had trained their weapons against it, and in moments the ground was littered with figures struck down by a hail of bolts. The survivors fled back towards the earthworks, swiftly followed by their comrades with shovels.

'Shouldn't see much more of them this morning, sir.' Vitellius was smiling as he rejoined General Plautius.

'No. Not if they have any brains.' Plautius shifted his gaze to the right where the river's silvery surface curved round in a great sweep and disappeared between rising ground on the other bank. At this moment, four miles downstream, the Batavian cohorts should be swimming across; four thousand men in mixed cohorts of horse and infantry. Recruited from the recently subdued tribes on the lower Rhine, the Batavians, like all auxiliary cohorts, were supposed to harass the enemy until the legions could close in for the kill. With any luck they would gain the far bank and form up before the enemy scouts had time to summon forces to meet the threat. Plautius had no doubt that Caratacus would have men positioned along the river bank for several miles in both directions. Plautius was counting on the Britons not being able to react fast enough to quell each attack.

As soon as he detected enemy movement downstream, the frontal assault would begin. Directly below him, at the foot of the slope down by the ford, the massed ranks of the Ninth Legion stood still and silent, waiting for the order to advance on the enemy fortifications. Plautius well knew the cold dread that would be biting at the pit of their stomachs as they prepared themselves for the attack. He had been in their boots a few times in his youth, and now thanked the gods for being a general. True, there were now other fears and anxieties, but no longer the physical terror of hand-to-hand battle.

Glancing to the left, upriver, he stared hard into the forested river banks that all but swallowed up the silvered surface of the water, only permitting a gleam here and a glitter there. Somewhere in that rolling wilderness lay the Second Legion, moving down towards the enemy flank. Plautius frowned as he failed to detect any sign of movement. Provided Vespasian kept a cool head and arrived within the time the general had allowed, then victory over Caratacus was assured. But if Vespasian was delayed for any reason, the main assault might well be beaten back and the Batavians, isolated on the wrong side of the river, would be cut to pieces.

It all depended on Vespasian.

Chapter Nine

Small ripples glimmered outwards from where the horse's muzzle dipped into the river. It was a small horse but sturdy and well cared for, as the sheen on its flanks indicated. A thick woven saddlecloth lay strapped across its back, and on its far side the rim of a shield was visible.

Cato turned back to his men and waved his hand down to keep them quite still. Then he slowly rose, hidden behind the huge bulk of the oak tree's trunk, and peered over towards the horse. Holding his breath, as if it might be audible, he scanned the surrounding scene for any further signs of life. But there was none, only the horse. Cato cursed silently; where was its rider? The horse was tethered. The rider had to be nearby. Cato tightened his grip on the shaft of his javelin.

From no more than a few feet away someone coughed, and before a startled Cato could react, a man stood up on the other side of the tree trunk, facing away from him and pulling up his coarse woollen breeches.

'Oh shit!' Cato went to raise his spear.

The man spun round, eyes glaring, teeth bared under a red moustache. His lime-washed hair bristled in matted spikes beneath a bronze helmet. For an instant both men were still, staring at each other in numbed surprise. The Briton reacted first. He grabbed Cato by the shoulder straps, and with one powerful heave dragged him bodily across the trunk and threw him down on the loose shingle of the river bank. The impact drove the air from Cato's lungs. A fist smashed into his mouth, and the world went blinding white. There were shouts, vision returned and he saw the Briton standing over him, sword half drawn, glaring back across the tree trunk. Then the man was gone, shingle scattering in his wake as friendly hands hauled Cato up.

'You all right?'

'Don't let him get away!' gasped Cato. 'Stop him!'

Pyrax abruptly dropped his optio and ran off in pursuit, followed by the rest of the section as they scrambled across the tree trunk.

By the time Cato had recovered enough to stand up, it was all over. The Briton lay face down at the river's edge ten feet from his horse, a pair of javelins protruding from his back. The horse had jerked its reins free of the tether, and backed off. Now it was eyeing the newcomers uncertainly as it waited in vain for the reassurance of its master's return.

'Someone get the horse,' ordered Cato. The last thing he needed now was for the animal to run off and be discovered by some other British scouts. One of the men unstrapped his shield and helmet and moved quietly towards the horse.

'Make a noise like a carrot,' Pyrax suggested unhelpfully before he took his optio's arm. 'All right, Cato?'

'I'll live.'

'Nearly dropped yourself right in it!' Pyrax nodded at the trunk.

'Not funny.' Cato felt his jaw, throbbing from the blow, and saw blood on his hand from a split lip. 'Bastard!'

'Be grateful it wasn't worse. He had you bang to rights there.'

'I couldn't see him.' Cato began to blush.

'No shame, Optio. I'm just glad you were leading from the front.'

'Thanks,' Cato grumbled. He sent one man on to the next bend in the river to keep watch while he considered the situation. The body and horse had to be disposed of. The body was simple enough, and the patrol quickly bundled it under the trunk and piled up loose shingle and branches to hide it from view. The horse would be more of a challenge. With the beast securely tied to a stump, Cato drew the ivory-handled sword Bestia had left to him and gingerly approached. He was not looking forward to the task and the job was made no easier by the bright gleaming eyes and twitching muzzle that were raised towards him.

'Come on, horsey,' he said softly. 'Let's make this nice and quick.'

Raising the blade, he stepped to the side of the horse and looked for a point to strike.

'Optio!'

Cato glanced round and saw Pyrax gesturing downriver. The man on point was crouched down and waving frantically to get their attention. Cato waved back and the man dropped to the ground.

'Wait here. Keep the horse quiet.'

Cato hurried forward, crouching low for the last few paces before he lay down beside the point man. Round the bend of the river was a small weir, part natural obstacles and part manmade to act as a crossing point. The sound of the water tumbling down the far side in a muffled roar reached their ears. But what had attracted the point man's attention was the group of horsemen well beyond the weir. As they watched, one of the Britons detached himself from the group and headed upriver directly towards them, hands cupped as he shouted something barely audible above the din of the weir.

'They're looking for our man,' Cato decided. 'Checking if he's seen anything.'

'And if they don't find him?'

'Then they'll get suspicious and start searching. We can't let that happen.'

The point man glanced towards the Britons. 'We can't take that lot on. Too many.'

'Of course we can't take them on. In any case, I doubt they'd fight. They're doing the same job as us. Find the enemy and report in, nothing more. But we mustn't let them start worrying about one of their scouts.' Cato watched as the Briton slowly walked his horse nearer, still calling out. 'Wait here, and stay out of sight.'

Cato scrambled back to the rest of the patrol. He examined the dead Briton and then looked round at his men. 'Pyrax! Can you ride a horse?'

'Yes, Optio.'

'Right then, get this man's cloak and helmet on, quick as you can.'

Pyrax looked puzzled.

'Don't think, just do it!'

Pulling the javelins out of the corpse, the patrol hastily stripped off his cloak and leggings and passed them to Pyrax. With grim distaste the veteran pulled on the Briton's crude garments and tied the straps of the bronze helmet. Then he climbed onto the horse. The animal shied about a bit at first, but a firm hand on the reins and a steadying pressure to its flanks somewhat reassured the beast.

'Now get down to the river bend and wait there.'

'Then what?'

'Then you do exactly as I say.'

The patrol followed as Pyrax walked the horse downriver, and then they ducked into the undergrowth along the bank.

From his vantage point Pyrax could see the Briton approaching, calling out for his comrade no more than a hundred and fifty paces away, almost level with the weir.

'What do I do?' he asked quietly.

'Just wave your arm and make out that you haven't seen anything.'

'How do I do that?' Pyrax asked.

'How should I know? I'm not a bloody theatre director! Improvise.'

'And if that doesn't satisfy him?'

'Then the legion gets into battle a bit earlier than we bargained for.'

'He's seen me!' Pyrax stiffened nervously, before he remembered to raise an arm in greeting.

Cato eased himself forward until he could glimpse the approaching Briton through the sun-dappled ferns and stinging nettles. The man had reached the weir and reined in his horse. He called out again, the words still indistinct above the faint roar of tumbling water. Pyrax waved his hand, and followed it with a slow, elaborate shake of the head. The Briton turned downriver and shouted something to his comrades, a short distance beyond. After a brief exchange the Briton dug his heels into his horse and continued approaching the river bend.

'What now?' Pyrax asked softly.

'When I say "now" you beckon him and steer the horse back round the bend until you are out of sight of the others. We'll jump him.'

'Great. And then?'

'One thing at a time.'

As Cato continued to watch from cover, the horseman walked his mount closer, his demeanour casual and unconcerned as he enjoyed the early summer morning. Cato wriggled back a short way and gently drew his sword. Taking his cue, the other men braced themselves to spring once the Briton had passed beyond them. Then when the man was no more than a hundred feet away, close enough for Cato to see beneath his helmet he was just a youngster, the shrill cry of a Celtic war horn carried up the river. The Briton checked his horse and turned back towards the band of horsemen. They were wheeling round, arms waving frantically, gesturing for him to come at once. With a final shout towards Pyrax, the young Briton turned his horse and kicked it into a trot towards his comrades who were already surging up the slope in the direction of the fortified river crossing.

'What shall I do?' asked Pyrax.

'Nothing. Stay still until they're out of sight.'

As Cato had expected, the Britons were in too much of a hurry to spare their lone scout any attention and the horsemen disappeared without a backward glance at Pyrax. When the youngster had disappeared into the trees, Pyrax relaxed his grip on the reins and slumped forward.

'Shit! That was close.'

'Nice work!' Cato smiled as he rose up and patted the horse on the side of its head.

'What was all that about? That blast on a horn.'

'I guess they've discovered the Batavians. You'd better get back to Vespasian at once and let him know what's happened. We'll continue down the river but I doubt we'll encounter any more of their scouts now. You get going.'

'Right!' Pyrax yanked the reins round and kicked in his heels.

'Pyrax!' Cato called after him. 'You'd better lose the helmet and cloak before you go if you want to survive long enough to make the report!'

Chapter Ten

A distant mass of infantry and cavalry was forming up behind the British fortifications as Vitellius looked anxiously towards the north-east. It was almost midday, the sky was a deep blue and the sun beat down on the two armies facing each other across the river. From where he stood he had a glorious view across the gently rolling landscape, much of it cleared for the cultivation of cereal crops, gently rippling like sheets of green silk in the light breeze. This land would make an excellent province for the empire, he decided, once its inhabitants had submitted to Rome and adapted to civilised ways. But that submission was not forthcoming. Indeed these people were proving to be a somewhat tougher nut to crack than the army had been led to believe. Their technical knowledge of modern warfare was sadly lacking but they fought with an élan that was most impressive.

As soon as the Roman warships had expended their incendiary ammunition, the Britons had scurried out from behind their earthworks and thrown up a screen of rubble-filled wicker baskets to protect them from the bolt-throwers as they repaired the fire damage. Many more men had been cut down in the process, but the Britons had simply heaved the corpses up onto the earthworks. One particular warrior had proved extremely aggravating for the Roman artillery crews. He was a huge man, with a winged helmet over his blond hair, and he stood naked at the water's edge, shouting abuse at the Roman warships as he defiantly waved a double-headed axe. Every so often he would turn round and thrust his backside towards the enemy, defying them to do their worst. The navy were piqued by this haughty challenge, and the bolt-throwers on the nearest trireme had swung round towards the British warrior. He was proving to be remark-ably agile and so far he had managed to avoid the bolts being fired at him. Indeed, the more insulting he got, the worse the crews' aim became in their desperation to nail him.

'Fools!' muttered General Plautius. 'Can't those idiots see what he's doing?'

'Sir?'

'Look, Vitellius.' The general pointed. The ship that was concentrating its fire on the blond warrior was also shielding the Britons from the other triremes, and their repair work continued apace. 'Bloody navy! Letting pride come before brains, as usual.'

'Shall I send a man to the fleet prefect, sir?'

'No point. By the time we reach him, and he gets a message to the captain of that ship, the bloody Britons will have finished their work and be settling down for an afternoon nap. All because some touchy naval officer can't cope with a barbarian waving his bloody arse in his face.'

Vitellius picked up the strained note in the general's voice and realised that the previous evening's plan was beginning to unravel. Not only had the navy failed to destroy the defences, they had failed even to damage them enough to clear the way for the subsequent infantry assault. And far from demoralising the Britons the navy had made the Romans look foolish by turning their wrath on one naked warrior. When the Ninth crossed the ford they would be facing an emboldened enemy fighting from behind fortifications. The success of the attack was no longer a foregone conclusion. To add to this problem, there had been no report on the progress of the Second Legion since it had crossed the river at first light. If Vespasian was manoeuvring according to plan, he would almost be in position now, ready to launch an attack on the Britons' right flank.

At the other end of the battlefield word had come back from the prefect in charge of the Batavian cohorts that the river crossing had been successful. The enemy had been caught on the hop, and all the men had formed up on the far bank before any serious counterattack could be launched by the Britons. Better still, the Batavians had run into a large unit of chariots. Undaunted by these impressive but outdated weapons, the Batavians had ploughed into them, attacking the horses first, as General Plautius had ordered. Without horses the chariots were useless, and all that remained to be done was the mopping up of the unmounted spearmen and their drivers.

So far so good.

But now Caratacus was wise to the weakness of the Roman force on his left flank and was rapidly moving to surround the Batavians and throw them back against the river. If that could be done quickly enough he would be able to redeploy his forces to meet the next attack Plautius had prepared. Now was the time for the Ninth Legion to make their move, to take the pressure off the Batavians and suck more Britons into the defence of the fortifications around the ford. And when Caratacus' last reserves had been committed then the Second Legion would emerge from the woods to the south-west and crush the enemy in an iron vice.

'Oh, sir!' Vitellius suddenly laughed. 'Look there!'

The naked warrior had finally paid the price for his bravery, and was sitting down, legs open and stretched out before him as he struggled with a bolt that had smashed into his hip. From the amount of blood that was flowing into the churned mud around him, a major artery must have been severed by the bolt. Even as they watched he was struck in the face by another bolt, and helmet and head burst into bloody fragments as the torso was hurled back by the impact.

'Good!' The general nodded. 'That should please the navy. Tribune, it's time for the main assault. Better get yourself a shield from someone.'

'Sir?'

'I need a good pair of eyes on the ground, Vitellius. Go in with the first wave and make a note of all the defences you encounter, the nature of the ground you pass over, and any terrain we might be able to exploit if we have to go through it all over again. I'll have your report when you get back.'

If I get back, Vitellius reflected bitterly as he sized up the task facing the Ninth Legion. It would be dangerous down there, far too dangerous. Even if he survived, there was always the chance of suffering an injury so disfiguring that it would cause people to avert their gaze. Vitellius was vain enough to want affection and admiration as well as power. He wondered if the general might be persuaded to send a more expendable officer instead, and looked up. Plautius was watching him closely.

'There's no reason to delay, Tribune. Off you go.'

'Yes, sir.' Vitellius saluted and immediately comman- deered a shield from one of the general's bodyguards, before making his way down to the two cohorts of the Ninth Legion earmarked for the first assault. The other eight cohorts were sitting down in the trampled grass that sloped towards the river. They would be afforded a spectacular view of the attack and would cheer their comrades on at the top of their voices when the time came – mostly out of a sense of self-preservation, for if the first wave failed, it would be their turn to face the Britons soon enough. Vitellius picked his way through the unit and made for the even lines of the First Cohort – every legion's teeth arm, a double-strength unit trusted with the most dangerous tasks on any battle-field. Over nine hundred men stood to attention, spears grounded, silently surveying the dangers ahead of them.

The legate of the Ninth, Hosidius Geta, was standing immediately behind the First Century. At his side stood the legion's chief centurion and behind them the colour party surrounding the eagle standard.

'Afternoon, Vitellius,' Geta greeted him. 'You joining us?'

'Yes, sir. The general wants someone to analyse the ground as the attack goes in.'

'Good idea. We'll do our best to see you get to make your report.'

'Thank you, sir.'

Heads turned at the heavy irony lacing the tribune's reply but the legate was gentleman enough to let it pass.

Just then the headquarters trumpets blasted out a unit signal, followed by a short pause and then the call for advance.

'That's us.' The legate nodded to the chief centurion. Geta tightened the strap on his gaudily decorated helmet and drew in a deep breath to bellow out his orders.

'The First Cohort will prepare to advance!' A beat of three, and then, 'Advance!'

With the chief centurion calling out the pace, the cohort moved off in a rippling mass of bronze helmets, chinking links of mail and gleaming javelin tips, line after line of men marching straight down to the edge of the river where the water ran over a bank of shingle and weed.

Vitellius took his position just behind the legate, concentrating on keeping in step with the colour party. Then he was in the river, splashing into the brown churned-up water swirling in the wake of the First Century. To his right the nearest trireme seemed to be a vast floating fortress, towering up only fifty paces away. The faces of the crewmen were clearly visible on deck as they stepped up the bombardment of the far bank, softening up the defenders as much as possible before their army comrades struck home. The whack of the catapults and sharper cracks of the bolt-thrower arms carried clearly across the water, and were audible even above the infantry thrashing through the river.

The water quickly rose to his hips, and Vitellius glanced up in alarm to see that they were less than a third of the way across. The increase in depth slowed the advance and already the foremost lines were beginning to bunch up. The centurions in the following units slowed the pace and the cohort floundered on, water rising steadily until it was halfway up their chests. Vitellius saw that they were approaching the far bank, fifty paces away, and beyond that the looming mass of the British earthworks guarding the ford.

Suddenly there was a sharp cry ahead, then a few more, as the front rank encountered the first series of underwater obstacles – several lines of sharpened stakes driven into the river bed.

'Break ranks!' shouted the chief centurion at the top of his voice. 'Break ranks and watch out for them fucking spikes! When you've got 'em, pull 'em up and move on!'

The advance faltered and then halted as the men of the First Cohort felt their way through the water, pausing to heave the stakes up, two and three men at a time. Gradually a path was cleared through to the far bank, and the advance continued past the handful of injured men being helped to the rear. The First Century had already climbed out of the river and was dressing its ranks on the muddy bank when the following units passed through the gap in the stakes.

Geta turned back to Vitellius with a wry smile. 'I'm afraid things are about to get hot, so keep that shield up!'

The triremes stopped firing and the noise of bolts and rocks flying through the air ceased. The flat trajectory was now too close to the heads of the infantry to continue. As soon as the barrage stopped, there was a great roar and braying of war horns from the Britons behind the earthworks. All along the palisade the enemy rose up and prepared to meet their attackers. A strange whirring sound filled the air, and before the Romans could react, the first volley of slingshot slashed into the foremost ranks of the cohort, knocking men to the ground as the vicious mixture of lead shot and stones cracked into their targets. Vitellius raised his shield just as a shot struck the boss, the numbing impact jolting every bone and nerve as far as his elbow. Glancing about he saw that the First Cohort had gone to ground, covering themselves as best they could against the fusillade. But the curved line of the fortifications meant that fire was coming in on three sides and continued to whittle down the attackers. At the same time the Second Cohort was emerging from the river. Unless something was done immediately, the attack would crumble into a heaving mass that would provide the British slingers with the best possible target.

Geta was squatting beside Vitellius in the middle of the colour party. He checked the strap on his helmet, held his shield close and rose to his feet.

'First Cohort! Form testudo by centuries!'

The order was relayed at top parade-ground volume by the chief centurion and the men of each century were bullied back onto their feet by their centurions. The men realised that the testudo was their best chance of surviving the assault, and they quickly formed the wall and roof of protecting shields. The colour party sheltered behind the shields of Geta's bodyguards and watched the testudo tramp towards the earthworks, under constant, but largely ineffective, fire. As the following centuries mounted the bank, the same order was given, and each formation was ordered to make for a different section of the defences. The muddy ground between the river and the fortifications was littered with dead and injured. Those who could kept themselves covered with their shields against the British missiles whirling through the air. Vitellius was filled with a sickly sense of fear and excitement as the First Cohort reached the outer ditch and, struggling to retain their formation, slowly rippled over its edge.

When the testudo reached the slope up to the palisade a sharp order was given. The formation dissolved and each man scrambled up the earthworks towards the British warriors screaming war cries beneath their flowing serpent standards. With the steep incline against them and laden down with heavy equipment, the legionaries fared badly. Many were swept from their feet by the slashes of the Britons' long swords and axes, to tumble down into the ditch, bowling over their comrades as they fell. Here and there a handful of men forced a way through or over the palisade, but the weight of numbers was against them and these brave pockets were quickly overwhelmed and hurled back down the slope.

The fighting spread all along the wall but the other

cohorts fared no better and the number of Roman bodies sprawled across the slope of the earthworks steadily grew.

'Sir, should we pull back?' Vitellius asked the legate.

'No. The orders were clear. We keep going at them until Vespasian can attack their rear.'

The legate's staff officers exchanged worried glances. The Ninth were being cruelly punished for their headlong assault; they were bleeding to death while they waited for the Second Legion to attack. Looking round, Geta sensed the doubt in his men.

'Any moment now. Any moment the Second will attack. We just hold on until then.'

But already Vitellius could detect a change in the fight along the palisade. The legionaries were no longer rushing up the slopes, they were being driven to it by their centurions, bullied into attack by the blows from vine sticks. In several places the men were actually falling back from the wall, worn down by the effort and slowly but surely losing the will to continue the fight. The signs were unmistakable to everyone in the colour party. The assault was crumbling before their eyes.

If Vespasian did not launch his attack immediately the costly efforts of the Ninth would have been in vain.

Chapter Eleven

'Why don't we attack?'

'Because we haven't been ordered to,' Macro replied harshly. 'And we sit tight until told otherwise.'

'But, sir, look at them. The Ninth are getting massacred.'

'I can see what's happening well enough, boy, but it's out of our hands.'

Lying on their stomachs in the long grass growing along the crest of the low ridge, the skirmish line of the Sixth Century watched helplessly as the Britons smothered the Ninth's attack. The last of the Ninth's remaining cohorts were already being fed into the desperate fight. For the inexperienced optio this was an unbearable agony. Barely a mile away his comrades were being slaughtered as they attempted to storm the earthworks. And yet not a hundred yards behind him the men of the Second Legion sat in silent concealment in the shadows of the trees. With one simple order they could sweep down the slope, catching the Britons between the two legions, and crush them totally. But the order had not been given.

'Here comes the legate.' Macro nodded back down the slope towards the trees. Vespasian came running up towards them, helmet tucked under his arm. A few yards short of the skirmish line the legate dropped down and crawled up beside Macro.

'How's the Ninth doing, Centurion?'

'Doesn't look good, sir.'

'Any signs of movement from the enemy's reserves?'

'None, sir.'

Behind the British lines sat several thousand men, calmly waiting to be called into action. Vespasian smiled with grim admiration of the enemy general's coolness. Caratacus knew the value of keeping a fresh reserve in hand and had firm control over his coalition of tribal levies. The selfish pursuit of tribal glory had led to the destruction of more than one Celtic army in the past. Caratacus had even resisted the Batavian bait offered up by Plautius. Just enough men had been released to repulse the Roman auxiliaries and hold them back against the river. There, in the distance, well beyond the earthworks defending the ford, a loose milling of men and horses revealed the plight of the Batavians.

Vespasian turned away from the spectacle. Compassion for his comrades urged him to order his legion to charge to the rescue. But that temptation had been foreseen by Aulus Plautius, and the general had stressed that his orders must be followed to the letter. The Second was to remain concealed until Caratacus had committed his reserves to the defence of the fortifications. The order to move would be signalled by the massed trumpeters from the general's headquarters on the Roman bank. Only when the Britons were fully engaged would Vespasian be permitted to launch his attack. Only then.

Vespasian noticed that the optio was giving him a bitter look, and to emphasise the point the boy gave an almost imperceptible nod down the slope. The insubordinate gesture was quite deliberate, but it was understandable and Vespasian forced himself to let it pass.

'Keen to get stuck in then, young Cato?'

'Yes, sir. As soon as we can, sir.'

'Good lad!' Vespasian clapped him on the shoulder before turning to the centurion. 'The command post is just inside the woods there.' He pointed to where the legion's colour party was failing to look inconspicuous at the edge of the trees. 'If anything develops down by the river, send a runner to me immediately.'

As the legate scrambled back down the slope, he felt the eyes of the entire Sixth Century follow him with the resentment all common soldiers feel for senior officers who seem to sacrifice their men needlessly. Of course it was unfair – Vespasian was under orders and could not do anything about the situation. He shared Cato's angry helplessness and would dearly have liked to explain the general's battle plan and demonstrate why the men of the Second had to sit and watch while their comrades died. But to share such confidences with a mere optio was unthinkable.

The colour party moved even more indiscreetly towards the edge of the trees as their legate approached.

'What the bloody hell are you doing?' he shouted angrily. 'I gave orders for you to stay out of sight!' When they were once more among the trees, the legate called the senior officers of the legion over to him.

'I want the legion moved up to within twenty paces of the ridge there. They're to be formed up ready for battle, and to move forward the instant I give the order. Colour party with me.'

As the tribunes and senior centurions dispersed to pass the word to the rest of the legion, Vespasian led the colour party up to the spot indicated and a battle line was quickly marked out with the small red pegs designed for the task.

Leaving the staff officers to their duties, the legate rejoined the Sixth Century and was horrified to see the new mounds of Roman bodies littering the wrong side of the ford's defences. On the far bank of the river another legion, the Fourteenth, was quickly marching down towards the shallows to support the Ninth. As its First Cohort plunged into the slack current, passing the column of wounded streaming back to the Roman lines, Cato stirred in the long grass beside the legate, craning his neck to see better.

'Down, you fool!'

Cato instantly obeyed, and then turned to his legate. 'Sir! Did you see? The river's getting deeper.'

'Deeper? Nonsense! Unless the tide . . .'

The legate quickly looked up and stared hard at the river. The optio was right, it was deeper. Vespasian could see that the incoming tide was threatening to make the ford impassable. By the time the Fourteenth had crossed, the water would be too deep to permit a retreat. With cold dread he realised that this was something no one had considered the previous night when the general had gone over his plan. Surely he must see it now. Surely he must order the recall before two Roman legions were caught in the killing ground on the British-held side of the river. But there was no trumpet call, no shrill blaring of the bucinas to save the men of the Fourteenth from sharing the fate of the Ninth. Instead, the legion waded on, chest-high in the quickening current.

'Poor bastards!' muttered Macro. 'They'll be crucified.'

The uneven ranks of the Fourteenth struggled across the river. Men were almost up to their necks in the churning water now, and the watchers on the hill could well imagine the fear of the men crossing. And still no recall.

Behind the enemy line word had been passed of the new

threat approaching their fortifications and the tribes surged forward to the crest of the ridge to watch the approach of another legion. Any sense of order their chiefs had struggled to maintain quickly dissolved as the Britons poured through the crude gateways, making for their comrades defending the palisade.

Vespasian watched as dense columns of his men emerged from the forest and moved into position. A few more moments and all would be ready. His ears strained for the first sound of the trumpets ordering the Second into action. But the air remained thick with the sounds of the battle below, unbroken by any trumpet call. By the time the Second Legion was formed up and ready to advance, the defenders on the palisade had been swelled by thousands more screaming to get their share of the promised blood-bath. And still no trumpets.

'Something's wrong.'

'Sir?' Macro turned to him.

'We should have heard the headquarters trumpets by now.'

Then a dreadful thought occurred to Vespasian. Maybe he had missed the signal. Maybe the order had been given already and the men down by the river were desperately searching the ridge for any sign of relief.

'Did either of you hear anything while I was back at the command post? Any signal?'

'No, sir,' Macro replied. 'Nothing.'

Chapter Twelve

'Where the hell is the Second?' Vitellius asked bitterly, not for the first time. Legate Geta exchanged a look with his chief centurion and briefly raised his eyes before drawing closer to the tribune crouching beneath his shield.

'A quiet word of advice: officers should always consider how their demeanour affects the men around them. If you want to make a career out of the army you must set a good example. So let's have no more of this nonsense about the Second, all right? Now get off your belly and stand up.'

At first Vitellius was incredulous. Here they were, right in the middle of a first-class military disaster, and Geta was more concerned about etiquette. But the contemptuous looks he was getting from the veterans who made up the command party shamed him. He nodded, swallowed, and rose to his feet, taking his place with the rest of the officers and standard bearers. The fire they had at first attracted from the British slingers had slackened as soon as the cohorts charged the palisade and now only the occasional quick shot could be spared in their direction.

Even so, two of the Ninth's tribunes had been downed. One lay dead at the foot of the eagle standard, his face shattered by the impact of a lead shot. The other had just been struck on the shin. The bone was smashed. The young officer was white-faced with the effort not to let out a cry as he looked at the bone protruding from his skin. Vitellius was relieved when a burly legionary heaved the tribune up onto his shoulders and headed back across the river.

And there, surging down the slope and into the water came the Fourteenth Legion. For an instant Vitellius' spirits soared at the prospect of reinforcements, a feeling shared by the rest of the colour party, until they saw how the tide was slowly covering the ford. Vitellius turned back to the legate, unable to conceal his alarm.

'What's the general up to?'

'It's all in the plan,' Geta replied calmly. 'You should know, you were at the briefing. The Fourteenth are to reinforce us if we need them. Seems we do.'

'But the river! We won't be able to get back across unless we withdraw now, sir.' Vitellius looked round the colour party despairingly. Surely someone would agree with him, but the contempt in their expressions only deepened. 'We can't just sit here, sir. We must do something. Before it's too late.'

Geta regarded him silently for a moment, then pursed his lips and nodded. 'You are right, of course, Vitellius. We must do something.' Turning to the colour party, he drew his sword. 'Raise the eagle. We're going to advance.'

'What?' Vitellius stared at him in disbelief, and shook his head, desperately trying to think of a way to talk the legate out of the crazy decision. 'But, sir. The eagle – what if it's lost?'

'It won't be, once the men see it right at the front. Then they'll fight to the last drop of blood to follow it to victory, or die in its defence.'

'But it'd be safer where it is, sir,' Vitellius countered.

'Look here, Tribune,' Geta said sternly. 'That's an eagle up on the standard, not a bloody chicken. It's supposed to inspire men to valour, not to save their skins. I've had just about enough of your whining. You're supposed to be a hero. I thought you'd saved the Second Legion's bacon! Now I wonder . . . But you're with us right now, and I need every man I can get hold of. So shut your mouth and draw your bloody sword.'

The steel in the legate's tone was chilling. Without another word Vitellius drew his weapon and fell in behind the colour party. Geta led them at a trot over to where the First Cohort was battling to secure a foothold on the palisade. The wounded and dead carpeted the slope of the earthworks. As the colour party pressed through the throng towards the palisade, the British warriors hacked and slashed at them, their war cries deafening. At last the Ninth's eagle rose above the crush and the legionaries returned the British cries with a great roar of their own.

'Up the Hispania!'

The Romans fell upon their enemy with renewed energy and aggression and the flashing blades of the Roman short swords stabbed forward with deadly efficiency as all along the palisade the battle cry was taken up.

'Up the Hispania!'

Vitellius kept his silence as with gritted teeth he pressed on with the colour party up the slope. Suddenly he found himself hard up against the palisade – a line of rough-hewn posts driven into the ground. Overhead loomed a yelling British warrior, black against the brilliant blue of the sky, axe raised for the kill. Instinctively Vitellius thrust his sword at the man's face and ducked behind the rim of his shield. There was a sharp scream of agony an instant before the axe cracked into the reinforced trim along the top of the shield. Vitellius' legs buckled for a moment and then he was up again. A huge centurion was at his side, great arms wrapped round a wooden stake which he was wrestling free of the soil.

'Pull the palisade down!' the centurion bellowed, grabbing hold of the next stake. 'Pull it down!'

Other men followed suit and soon a number of small gaps had been wrenched in the palisade, and the Ninth began to force their way through to the flattened earth rampart beyond. To Vitellius' left the eagle rose, and Britons swarmed towards it, drawn on by a savage desire to seize the legion's standard and crush the resolve of their enemy. The fighting round the eagle was conducted with a terrible intensity that Vitellius could not have imagined possible from human beings. He turned away from the ghastly scene and urged the legionaries round him to press on through the palisade, jabbing his sword in the direction of the Britons.

'On, lads! On! Kill them! Kill them all!'

Hardly a man spared him a glance as they charged through. Only when he was sure that there were enough Romans on the rampart to form a living barrier between himself and the enemy did Vitellius climb through the ruined palisade and onto the rampart. From this height he had a quick chance to survey the immediate battlefield. On both sides the fighting line stretched out along the curved fortifications. Behind the Ninth Legion the First Cohort of the Fourteenth was emerging from the river and would shortly add its weight to the assault. Even now it might not be needed. Geta's desperate attempt to force the defences was succeeding and all the while more and more Romans were packing the rampart and pushing the Britons back, down the reverse slope and into their camp. Sensing that victory was at last in their grasp, and driven on by a blood-crazed desire to avenge the torment they had suffered on the killing ground by the river, the men of the Ninth savagely hacked their way forwards.

Vitellius went with them, urging the legionaries on as he sought to rejoin the colour party. He found them in a ring of bodies – Roman and Briton alike sprawled at the foot of the eagle. Most of the officers bore wounds from the desperate fight on the rampart and Vitellius saw that fewer than half of the original party were still on their feet. Geta was busy issuing orders to be carried to the cohort commanders to prevent their units from dispersing in a general pursuit of the enemy. The fresh troops of the Fourteenth would be permitted that duty while the Ninth secured the fortifications they had given so many lives to take.

'There you are, sir!' Vitellius called out cheerfully. 'We did it, sir! We beat 'em!'

'We?' Geta arched an eyebrow but Vitellius ploughed on. Sheathing his bloodied sword he grabbed the legate's hand and pumped it warmly.

'A brilliant action, sir. Quite brilliant. Wait until Rome hears about this!'

'I thought we'd lost you, Tribune,' Geta said quietly.

'Got separated in the crush, sir. I helped some lads break onto the rampart over that way.'

'I see.'

The two men faced each other for a moment, the tribune smiling effusively, the legate's expression cold and restrained. Vitellius broke the silence.

'And no sign of the Second Legion! This is the Ninth's victory alone. Your victory, sir.'

'It's not over yet, Tribune. For any of us.'

'It's over for them, sir.' Vitellius waved an arm in the direction of the enemy camp through which the erstwhile defenders were streaming back towards the rear gateways.

'For them, maybe. Excuse me.' Geta turned towards his trumpeters. 'Sound recall and re-form.'

The bucinas each drew in a lungful of air and pursed their lips to the mouthpieces. The brassy notes blasted out a brief melody and then continued repeating it. Slowly the men of the Ninth disengaged and looked for their cohort standards. But before he could give the order for the signal to cease, Geta was aware of a new noise, a rippling roar of war cries welling up from behind the enemy camp. As the other members of the colour party became aware of the sound they looked to the low ridge behind the camp. All along the battle line men stood still and listened, Roman and Briton alike. Then as an icy dread gripped the exhausted Romans, Caratacus' carefully husbanded reserves burst into the camp.

'Oh shit!' Vitellius whispered.

Legate Geta smiled and drew his sword again. 'I rather think your earlier report of our triumph was greatly exaggerated. If we're going to make the columns of the Rome gazette, I'm afraid it may be the obituaries.'

Chapter Thirteen

Vespasian watched with unabashed anguish as the British reserves rolled forward like a great wave threatening to dash the thin line of the Ninth to pieces. The Fourteenth Legion would not be in a position to lend any support until the fight on the rampart was over, and then it would be their turn to be thrown into the grinder, with no possibility of retreat.

Beside the legate, Cato realised that the fate of the entire army was bound up in what happened in the very next moment. The Britons were on the verge of a decisive victory over the Roman invaders, and the mere thought of such a calamity filled him with bleak despair, as if the world itself was on the brink of extinction. Only the Second Legion stood in the way of disaster now.

Amidst the muffled din of the battle Cato thought he could hear the faint falling note of a trumpet, and he strained his ears to try and pick out the sound again. But whatever the sound may have been, it was lost now. Might it have been some trick of acoustics? he wondered. Or a stray note from a British war horn? Then it came again, more distinctly this time. Cato quickly turned to his legate.

'Sir! Did you hear it?'

Vespasian raised himself up and listened intently before he shook his head. 'I can't hear them. Are you sure? You'd better be sure.' In a mad instant Cato knew that it was down to him. On him alone hung the fate of the army.

'It's trumpets, sir! Ordering us to advance.'

Vespasian exchanged a long look with the optio and then nodded. 'You're right. I can hear them. Sound the advance!' Vespasian bellowed over his shoulder and before the first notes of the signal had died, the Second Legion were advancing up the slope. Vespasian turned to his messengers. 'Pass the word, I want us to arrive in formation. If any man feels inclined to grab all the glory for himself and breaks ranks I will personally see to it that he's crucified. Centurion Macro!'

'Yes, sir.' Macro stood to attention now that there was no longer any need for concealment.

'Get your century formed up and rejoin your cohort.'

'Yes, sir.'

'Good luck, Macro.' The legate nodded grimly. 'We'll need all the luck we can get.'

Then he turned and fell in step with the colour party as it crested the ridge and the full scale of the task was revealed to them. Even the veterans sucked in their breath and exchanged surprised looks. It was too late to go back on his decision now, Vespasian reflected. In a short time the Second Legion would earn a footnote in the pages of history for itself, and if the gods were kind this day, the reference would not be immediately posthumous.

The centurions called the pace in steady parade-ground tones and the legion marched down the slope in two lines of five cohorts. At the front of the Sixth Century Cato did his best to keep in step with his centurion. Ahead he saw that the British reserves had reached the rampart and were swarming up the reverse slope against the thin wall of shields presented by the men of the Ninth. Down by the river the cohorts of the Fourteenth were hastily re-forming as they reached the bank. But the rising tide made their progress across the ford terribly slow and even now most of them would arrive too late to be of any use.

The sudden threat from the Second Legion on their right flank threw the nearest British warriors into a panic; many just stopped in their tracks to stare at the new danger. The distance closed steadily and Cato began to make out individual features in the men he would soon be fighting hand-to-hand. He could see the lime-washed hair, the elegantly swirling tattoos covering their woad-stained torsos, the brightly dyed woollen breeches and the wicked long blades of their swords and war spears.

'Steady there!' Macro bellowed as the uneven slope caused his century to fall out of alignment with the rest of the cohort. 'Keep to the pace!'

The ranks hurriedly dressed themselves and the Sixth Century continued rolling forwards, less than half a mile from the fortifications now. A small band of slingers ran out of the nearest gateway and moved into range. Then a light but deadly volley of slingshot rattled down on the large rectangular shields of the legionaries. Something whirred over Cato's head and a man at the rear of the century cried out as the shot shattered his collarbone. He fell out and slumped into the long grass, dropping his javelin. But there was no time to spare for the man as a fresh volley clattered down.

A quarter of a mile to go, and the slope levelled out. Now the Second Legion could no longer see the desperate fight along the palisade. A large gateway lay to the front of Cato's cohort, and the senior centurion pointed it out with his vine staff, giving the order for the cohort to wheel towards it. With a carelessness typical of the Celtic temperament, the gates lay wide open and the Fourth Cohort had brushed the slingers aside and was only a scant few feet from the fortifications before the first of the British heavy infantry appeared. With a defiant roar the Britons, in ornate helmets, kite shields and long swords, charged the Roman line.

'Javelins! Release at will!' Macro just had time to shout and the lead centuries of the cohort hurled an uneven volley that arced in a low trajectory straight for the British swordsmen. As always there was an instant of silence as the javelins swept down and their targets braced themselves for the impact. Then came a sharp crack and clatter followed by screams. Many of the javelins had lodged firmly in the British shields. Their soft iron shafts bent on impact and made it impossible for the recipients to throw them back or dislodge them from their shields, which then had to be discarded. After the javelin volley the legionaries quickly drew swords and closed with the Britons who were still reeling from the javelins. No amount of courage could withstand the ruthless efficiency of vigorous training and equipment specifically designed for such confined fighting conditions, and the Roman cohorts steadily pushed their way inside the fortifications. The superior numbers of the enemy, which might have made all the difference in an open battlefield, were here a handicap. The Britons were herded together in a tight press and cut down by the short swords stabbing out from between a line of large rectangular shields.

The Sixth Century moved out to a flanking position once the cohort had fought its way through the gateway into a vast area of crude tents and other shelters erected by Caratacus' army. Between the Second Legion and the two other legions now fighting all along the earthworks, thousands of Britons were massed. There was a momentary lull as the enemy suddenly realised the grim reality of their predicament, caught between two Roman forces with no easy escape route. Their chiefs realised the danger they were in and strove to bring some semblance of order to their men before the battle turned into a massacre.

In the middle of the Second Legion's battle line Cato stood shoulder to shoulder with his centurion in the dense ranks of men waiting for the order to finish the fight. On the extreme right of the Roman line Vespasian gave the order to advance; the command was quickly passed along to each cohort and moments later, behind a wall of shields, the legion moved forward at the slow, even pace of the unit advance. Those slingers and archers still supplied with ammunition kept up their fire on the Roman ranks, but the shield wall proved to be all but impenetrable. In desperation the British warriors started to hurl themselves forward, directly into the shields, to try and break up the line.

'Watch it!' Macro shouted as a huge man lumbered in towards Cato at an oblique angle. The optio swung his shield left and thrust the boss towards the man's face. He felt something connect and then automatically thrust his short sword into the man's guts, twisted and withdrew the blade. The Briton groaned and collapsed to one side.

'Nice kill!' Macro smiled, in his element, as he stuck another Briton in the chest and kicked the man free of his weapon. Two or three men of the Sixth Century, overcome by the desire to get at the enemy, burst forward, out of the Roman line.

'Get back in the ranks!' Macro bellowed. 'I've got your names!'

The men, instantly stilled by his voice, slunk back and rejoined the formation, not daring to meet the centurion's withering gaze, for the moment more concerned about the inevitable disciplinary punishment than the present fight.

The battle on the palisade was over and the men of the Fourteenth Legion were pushing the Britons back down the reverse slope into their encampment. Caught between the two forces, the Britons fought for their lives with a wild desperation that Cato found truly terrifying. The savage faces, flecked with spittle from their hoarse screams, confronted him like the spirits of devils. The Roman army's training took over and the sequence of advance-thrust-disengage-advance was carried out automatically, almost as if his body belonged to another entity altogether.

As the dead and dying fell beneath the blades of the Romans, the line slowly moved forward over a field of bodies, wrecked tents and scattered equipment. Suddenly the Sixth Century came upon an area the Britons had set aside for cooking; the turf ovens and open fires still crackled and burned with an orange brilliance in the failing light, bathing those nearby in a lurid red that only accentuated the horror of battle.

Before Cato could see it coming, a massive blow to his shield caught him off balance and he tumbled into a large steaming pot suspended over a fire. The flames seared his legs and before the water spilled and dowsed the fire, it scalded him down one side of his body. He could not help screaming at the sharp, nerve-searing agony of his burns and nearly dropped his shield and sword. Another blow landed on his shield; looking up, Cato saw a thin warrior with long pigtails looming over him, feral hatred twisting his features. As the Briton raised his two-handed axe for the kill, Cato thrust Bestia's sword up to cover the blow.

It never landed. Macro had rammed his blade in under the Briton's armpit almost up to the hilt and the man died instantly. Biting back the pain from his burns, Cato could only nod his thanks to the centurion.

Macro flashed a quick smile. 'On your feet!'

The front rank of the century had passed them and for a moment Cato was safe from the enemy.

'You all right, lad?'

'I'll live, sir,' Cato hissed through gritted teeth as a river of pain raged down the side of his body. He could hardly focus his mind through the agony. Macro was not fooled by the bravado, he had seen it enough times in the fourteen years he had served in the army. But he had also come to respect an individual's right to deal with it as he chose. He helped the optio back to his feet, and without thinking gave Cato an encouraging slap on the back. The youngster stiffened, but after only a moment's trembling he recovered enough to take a firm grasp of his sword and shield, and pushed his way towards the front rank. Tightening his grip on his own sword handle, Macro waded back into the fight.

For Cato the rest of the battle for the Britons' camp was a blur in his mind, so much effort was required to keep the terrible pain of his burns at bay. He might have killed any number of men but later he could not recall a single incident; he stabbed with his sword and countered blows with his shield oblivious to any sense of danger, aware only of the need to control the agony.

The battle flowed remorselessly against the Britons, crushed between the relentless pressure of the two legions. Desperately they looked for the point of least resistance and began to rush for the gaps between the closing lines of legionaries. First dozens then scores of Britons broke away from their comrades and ran for their lives, scrambling up the reverse slopes of the ramparts and running off into the gathering dusk. Many thousands escaped before the two lines of legionaries met and encircled a doomed band of warriors determined to fight to the last.

These were no ordinary levies, Macro realised as he exchanged blows with an older warrior whose sweat glistened on the skin of his well-muscled body. A heavy gold torc hung round the Briton's neck, similar to the trophy taken from the corpse of Togodumnus, which Macro now wore. The Briton saw it; recognition flashed across his features and he hacked at Macro with renewed frenzy in his desire for revenge. His wrath did for him in the end; the cooler-headed Roman let the man's fading energy use itself up on his shield before a swift strike settled the matter. A legionary, one of the previous autumn's recruits, knelt down and laid a hand on the dead Briton's torc.

'Take that and you're dead,' warned Macro. 'You know the rules on looting.'

The legionary nodded quickly and threw himself at the dwindling knot of Britons, only to impale himself on a broad-bladed war spear.

Macro swore. Then he pushed on, and found Cato at his side once more, teeth clamped together in a snarl as he fought on with vicious efficiency. As the setting sun's afterglow of orange and red stained the sky, a Roman trumpet blasted out the signal to disengage and a small space opened up around the surviving Britons. Cato was the last one to give way; he had to be physically hauled back from the fight by his centurion and shaken into a more stable frame of mind.

In the dusk, a small ring of no more than fifty of the Britons glared silently at the legionaries. Bleeding from numerous wounds, blood-smeared bodies heaving with spent breath, they leaned on their weapons and waited for the end. From the ranks of the legions a voice called out to them in a Celtic tongue. A call for surrender, Macro guessed. The call was repeated and this time the surrounded Britons gave vent to a chorus of shouts and defiant gestures. Macro shook his head, suddenly very weary of killing. What more had these men to prove by their deaths? Who would ever know of their last stand? It was axiomatic that history was written by the victors in war. He had learned that much from the history books Cato had used to teach him to read. These brave men condemned themselves to die for nothing.

Gradually the defiant words and gestures petered out and the Britons faced their foes with fatalistic calm. There was a moment's silence, then without need of any word of command the legionaries surged forward and wiped them out.

By torchlight the Romans took stock of their victory. The gates were guarded against counterattack and the work of searching the bodies strewn across the British encampment for Roman injured commenced in earnest. With torches held aloft, the patrols of legionaries located their wounded comrades and carried them to the forward casualty station hurriedly erected on the bank of the river. The wounded Britons were mercifully dispatched with quick sword and spear thrusts and heaped into piles for later burial.

Macro sent a forage party out to find provisions for the Sixth Century and dismissed Cato. Only one thing was on the optio's mind. The desperate need for some kind of relief from the pain of his burns. Leaving the century by the rampart, he climbed over the remains of the palisade and scrambled down the far side. He made his way across the ditch and up onto the river bank, eerily lit by the flickering torches and braziers of the casualty clearing station. Rows of injured, dying and dead had been arranged all along the river bank and Cato had to pick his way through them to reach the river. At the water's edge he laid down his shield and carefully unfastened the straps of his helmet, mail corselet, and weapons belt. He felt a palpable sense of lightness seep into his exhausted body as he gingerly stripped off his equipment and felt himself for injuries. There were some cuts, now crusted over with dried blood, and the burns were starting to blister. They were agony to the lightest touch. Naked, and shivering more from tiredness than the cool evening air, Cato waded out into the gentle current. As soon as he was deep enough, he slumped down and gasped as the cold water enclosed his body. A moment later he was smiling in pure bliss at the numbing relief it brought to his burns.

Chapter Fourteen

'Bet that hurts!' Macro grinned as the surgeon spread salve over the blistered skin that ran up Cato's right side from his hip to his shoulder. The blazing look the optio shot back at him was eloquence itself.

'Keep still,' the surgeon tutted. 'It's hard enough working by this light without you twitching all over the place. Here, Centurion, hold that torch steady.'

'Sorry.' Macro raised the pitch torch higher, and by its flickering orange glare the surgeon dipped his hand in the small jar of salve between his knees and gently smeared it over Cato's shoulder. Cato flinched, and had to clench his teeth as the surgeon continued the application. The cool air of the hour before dawn made him shiver, but it provided some small relief from the intensely painful injury that was sending waves of nerve-searing agony up and down his side.

'Is he going to be able to rejoin the unit?' asked Macro.

'Do me a favour, Centurion!' The surgeon shook his head. 'When will you officers learn that you can't expect wounded men to jump up and dash right back into a fight? If the optio here goes off and opens up the blisters, and they get infected, he'll be far worse off than he is now.'

'How long then?'

The surgeon examined the mass of angry blisters and cocked his head on one side. 'A few days for the blisters to come and go. He'll have to keep his side open to the air, and rest as much as possible. So he's excused duties.'

'Excused duties!' Macro scoffed. 'You might not have noticed but there's a bloody battle on the go. He has to return to the unit. I need every man I've got.'

The surgeon rose to his full height and confronted the centurion. For the first time Macro realised what a giant of a man the surgeon was, nearly a foot taller than him, and built like a bull. He was in his mid-twenties, with dark features and tightly curled black hair that suggested African origins. Big as he was, there didn't appear to be any fat on his muscled body.

'Centurion, if you value this man he has to be allowed to recover from the burns. He is excused duties – and my decision has the backing of the senior surgeon and the legate.' His tone and expression made it quite clear that he was in no mood to listen to any arguments about his decision. But that didn't change the fact that the Sixth Century was badly undermanned and needed the presence of everyone who could still wield a weapon.

'And I said I want him back with the century.'

The confrontation between the surgeon and the centurion in the flickering pool of torchlight was turning nasty. Cato gritted his teeth and struggled to his feet to intervene.

'I'm sorry, sir. He's right – I can hardly move this arm. I'd be no use to you right now.'

'Who asked you?' Macro glowered at the optio. 'Anyway, what are you taking his side for?'

'I'm not taking sides, sir. I want to get back into action as fast as possible, but I won't be doing any good until I can use this arm.'

'I see.' Macro was not unsympathetic, in principle, to those bearing injuries, but short of having a limb lopped off or being beaten unconscious, he found it difficult to see why a man should not take part in battle. The Britons may have lost their camp but there were still plenty of them milling about outside the earthworks; the injured might well have to fight for their lives before much longer.

'All right then, lad,' he said, relenting slightly. 'But you get back to the century as soon as you can, understand? No malingering.'

'Sir!' Cato was indignant. But Macro had already turned away and was marching off through the lines of Roman injured lying beside the river. Cato's gaze followed the centurion's torch for a while, before it was lost amid the other torches and the flare of campfires.

'Nice one, your centurion,' muttered the surgeon.

'Oh, he's all right. Just a little lacking in empathy and tact at times. But an excellent soldier.'

'And you'd be a good judge of such soldiers, would you?' The surgeon dipped into his pot for some more salve. 'Ready for this?'

Cato nodded, bracing himself for more pain. 'I think I've seen enough of army life.'

'Really? And how long have you served in the Second?'

'Getting on for a year.'

The surgeon paused in his application of salve. 'A year? Is that it? And this is your first legion?'

Cato nodded.

'You're hardly more than a boy.' The surgeon shook his head in amused bewilderment, then he noticed Cato's tunic and armour lying on the ground. The dull glow of the phalera on Cato's body harness caught the surgeon's eye. 'Yours?'

'Yes.'

'How'd you come by it?'

'I saved my centurion's life, before we left Germany last year.'

'You mean you're *that* optio? The one everyone was talking about back at base?' The surgeon looked at Cato with fresh eyes. 'The optio from the palace?'

'That's me.' Cato blushed.

'And you volunteered for the army?'

'No. I was born a slave. I was freed on condition that I joined the eagles. A reward for my father's services to the palace.'

'And he was a slave too?'

'Freedman. He was given his freedom after I was born so I stayed a slave.'

'That's tough.'

'That's the way it is.'

The surgeon laughed, a rich, deep laugh that drew glances from those nearby. 'Well, you really have made your mark, haven't you? From slave to raw recruit to decorated veteran in less than a year. At this rate you'll probably make centurion – no, what am I saying? You'll make legate by this time next year!'

'Can we get on with the salve?' Cato asked, embarrassed by the sudden attention they were attracting.

'Sorry. No offence intended, Optio.'

'None taken. And let's keep it that way, please.'

The surgeon continued with his work, applying the sweet-smelling salve to the raw flesh down the side of the optio's skinny body. Cato tried to occupy his mind, to keep the pain at bay as much as possible. He looked along the rows of injured men, some moaning and crying out as they writhed feebly on the ground. The medical staff of all three legions were busy ferrying the injured back across the river in several small skiffs that had been brought up from the engineers' baggage train. A two-way traffic of wounded men and empty stretchers struggled past each other down towards the river.

'How bad have our casualties been?' Cato asked.

'Bad. Hundreds dead. We've placed them in the centre of the camp. Word is that the general is going to flatten the earthworks when the army moves forward. Should be enough for a sizeable mound over the ashes.'

'And the wounded?'

'Thousands.' The surgeon looked up. 'Mainly from the Ninth, thanks to those bloody slingers. I've never treated so many broken bones. Here, let me find you a souvenir.'

The surgeon scanned the ground for a moment and then pounced on something in the trampled turf. He straightened up and popped it into Cato's hand. It was small and heavy and in the dim light Cato could see an oval lump of lead the size of his thumb, but thickening in the middle.

'Nasty, isn't it?' The surgeon nodded at it. 'You'd be surprised just how much damage one of those can do in the hands of a good slinger. The impact will break bone, even through chain mail, or a helmet. I had to cut one out of a tribune tonight. Went right into his leg, smashing the thigh bone to pieces. Poor sod died from loss of blood before I could finish.'

'From one of these?' Cato tossed the lead shot up and felt the stinging impact as he caught it. Travelling many times faster, he shuddered to think of the damage it would do to a human being. As he rolled the shot in his hand he noticed an irregularity on its surface, and raised it to his eyes for a closer look. Even in the poor light he could see that something had once been stamped on the side of the shot and that someone had tried to erase the markings, rather too hurriedly.

'Can you see some letters there?' he asked, holding up the shot.

The surgeon gazed at it a moment, then frowned. 'Well, it looks like an L, then an E, but that's all I can make out.'

'That's what I thought.' Cato nodded. 'But what is Latin script doing on British shot?'

'Maybe it's one of ours being returned.'

Cato thought for a moment. 'But slings haven't been issued to the legions yet. So where can this have come from?'

'Someplace beginning with LE,' suggested the surgeon.

'Perhaps,' Cato said quietly. 'Or maybe the LE stands for LEGIO, in which case it really is one of ours. You see any more like this?'

'Look around.' The surgeon waved his hand. 'They're all over the place.'

'Really?' Cato tossed the lead shot up in the air again. 'That's interesting . . .'

'Right! That's you finished.' The surgeon stood up and wiped his hand on a rag tucked into his belt. 'Get down to the river and take a boat back to your unit's camp. You're to rest up and keep the arm as still as possible. If there's any sign of pus in the burns, go and see the nearest surgeon immediately. Clear?'

Cato nodded. He tucked his tunic into his belt and picked up his equipment in his good hand. The salve and the cool air on the naked skin of his upper torso combined to take some of the sting out of his burns and he smiled gratefully.

'If you pass our way in the next few days I'll stand you a drink.'

'Thanks, Optio. That's very kind. I don't usually make house calls, but given your offer I'll be happy to make an exception. Who shall I ask for?'

'Cato. Quintus Licinius Cato, Optio of the Sixth Century, Fourth Cohort of the Second Legion.'

'Well met then, Cato. I'll look forward to it.' The surgeon placed the salve jar into his leather dressing bag and turned to leave.

'Er, might I have your name?' Cato called out.

'Nisus. At least that's my known name.' The surgeon replied bitterly and strode off between the lines of wounded.

Chapter Fifteen

As dawn flooded over the rolling British landscape, the Britons launched a desperate counterattack to regain control of the ford. It was a vain effort since the same boats that had been used to shuttle the wounded back to the eastern bank of the river had returned with bolt-throwers from the army's artillery train. Long before dawn, many of these weapons had been mounted on the western ramparts of the British fortifications, and covered all the approaches.

As the hapless Britons rose up from the mists wreathing the low ground behind the fort and roared their battle cry, many were cut down before they had a chance to draw a second breath. With reckless courage they charged forward, urged on by the braying of their war horns and the example of their standard bearers leading the way beneath their billowing serpents. The Romans had sealed up the gateways and had formed a solid line along the length of the rampart. Disciplined and determined, the legionaries did not yield one foot of ground, and the wave of Britons dashed themselves to pieces on the defences.

Cato was being helped aboard one of the engineers' shallow-bottomed craft when the peal of British war horns sounded on the dawn air, somehow muffled and distant, as if they belonged to a different world. The sounds of battle drifted down to the grey glassy surface of the river but there was little sense of excitement amongst those in the boat. For a moment Cato sat up and strained his ears to listen. Then he glanced down at the weariness and pain etched into the faces of the men around him, too tired to pay heed to the desperate battle being fought, and Cato realised that it was no longer his affair. He had done his duty, he had felt the fire of battle coursing through his veins and shared in the exultation of victory. Now, more than anything else, he needed rest.

The other men's heads nodded and lolled as the engineers steadily paddled the craft over the water, but Cato concentrated on the activity around him to divert his mind from the pain of his burns. The small boat was passing close by one of the warships and Cato looked up to see a bare-headed marine leaning on the side, a small wineskin in his hands. The man's face and arms were blackened from the soot of the incendiary fire the ships had been pouring down on the British the previous day. He raised his head at the sound of the engineers' paddles splashing into the smooth surface of the river, and raised a finger to his forehead in casual greeting.

Cato nodded back. 'Hot work?'

'You said it, Optio.'

Cato fixed his eyes on the wineskin, and instinctively licked his lips at the thought of its contents. The marine laughed. 'Here! You seem to need it more than I do, Optio.'

Cato, clumsy in his exhaustion, fumbled to catch the thrown wineskin. The contents sloshed heavily inside. 'Thanks!'

'Typical bloody marine,' grumbled an engineer. 'Those tossers have got nothing better to do than drink all day long.'

'While the likes of us do all the bloody work,' complained his comrade on the other paddle.

'That's your problem, mate!' the marine called out. 'And watch what you're doing with them paddles, or you'll foul the anchor chain!'

'Piss off,' one of the engineers replied sourly, but increased his efforts on the paddle to steer the craft away from the stem of the warship.

The marine laughed and raised a hand in mock salute. Cato pulled out the wineskin stopper and took a deep draught of wine. He almost choked when a sudden whoosh and crack broke the stillness. A catapult on the deck of the ship had just hurled a flint-filled casket high into the air towards a small force of chariots downstream from the fortifications. Curious about the accuracy of the weapon, Cato watched as the casket arced up into the air in the general direction of the spectral shapes of the distant enemy. All eyes must have been fixed on the fight for the fortifications as there was no sign of any reaction to the black speck pitching down towards them. The casket disappeared into the faint shapes of men, horses and vehicles. Moments later a dull crash carried across the water, followed by cries of surprise and pain. Cato could well imagine the devastating impact of the casket and the wounds inflicted by the flints flying out in all directions. Moments later the British had vanished and only the dead and injured remained where the chariots had stood.

As the hulk of the warship fell away in the milky light, Cato slumped back against the hard side of the boat and closed his eyes, despite the agony of his burns. All that mattered now was snatching a moment's rest. Helped by the wine, the young optio fell into a deep sleep. So deep that he barely murmured as he was lifted from the boat and transferred to one of the Second Legion's hospital carts for the jolting journey back to the camp. He stirred only briefly when the legion's surgeon had him stripped and prodded the burns to assess the damage. A fresh application of salve was ordered and then Cato, having been entered in the walking wounded lists, was carried back to the Sixth Century's tent line and gently transferred to his coarse sleeping roll.

'Hey! . . . Hey! Wake up.'

Cato was abruptly wrenched from his sleep as a pair of hands roughly shook his leg.

'Come on, soldier! This is no time for malingering – there's work to be done.'

Cato opened his eyes, squinting against the brightness of a midday sun. Squatting at his side, and smiling, Macro shook his head in despair.

'Bloody younger generation spends half its time on its back. I tell you, Nisus, it's a sorry lookout for the empire.'

Cato looked over his centurion's shoulder and saw the looming form of the surgeon. Nisus was frowning.

'I think the lad needs more rest. He's in no shape for duty right now.'

'No shape for duty? That's not what the chief quack seems to think. The optio's walking wounded, and right now we need all the men we can get back into the fighting line.'

'But—'

'But nothing,' Macro said firmly, and hauled his optio up. 'I know the regulations. The boy's fit enough to fight.'

Nisus shrugged; the centurion was in the right about the regulations, and there was nothing he could do about that. Still, it would not look good for the record if one of his patients died of some infection because he had not been allowed sufficient time for recovery.

'The lad just needs a quick drink and a decent meal inside him and he'll be ready to take the Britons on all by himself. Ain't that right, Cato?'

Cato was sitting up, still not quite awake, and badly irritated by the way the other two were continuing their earlier argument. In truth, Cato felt very far from being able to take on the enemy at the moment. Now that he was awake again, the pain from his burns seemed worse than ever, and glancing down he could see that the side of his body was a mass of red skin and blisters beneath the glistening salve.

'Well, lad?' asked Macro. 'You up for it?'

Cato just wished himself back asleep, and the centurion and the rest of the bloody army as far from his mind as possible. Behind the centurion Nisus was gently shaking his head, and for a moment Cato was tempted to agree with the surgeon's advice and take as long a break from his duties as possible. But he was an optio, with an optio's responsibilities to the rest of the men in his century, and that meant he could not afford to indulge any private weakness. Whatever pain he was in right now was no worse than his centurion had suffered from any one of his innumerable wounds in past campaigns. If he was to win the respect of the men he commanded, the same respect that Macro wore so easily, then he must suffer for it.

Gritting his teeth, Cato pushed himself up, and rose to his feet. Nisus sighed at the obstinacy of youth.

'Well done, lad!' Macro barked and slapped the boy on the shoulder.

A sheet of pain scoured the nerves down the side of the optio's body and he grimaced, locking his body still for a moment. Nisus started forward.

'You all right, Optio?'

'Fine,' Cato managed between gritted teeth. 'Fine, thank you.'

'I see. Well, if you need anything, get down to the field hospital. And if there's any sign of infection, come and see me at once.'

The last remark was directed at the centurion as much as the optio, and Cato nodded his understanding.

'Don't worry. I'll be sensible.'

'All right then. I'm off.'

As Nisus walked away, Macro tutted with disapproval. 'What is it with surgeons? They either refuse to believe you're ill until you croak on them, or they treat the lightest scratch as some kind of mortal wound.'

Cato was tempted to say that his burns were somewhat more serious than a light scratch, but managed to bite his tongue. There were more important issues. The presence of his centurion on this side of the river was worrying and required an explanation.

'What's happening, sir? Why's the legion back here? Have we retreated across the river?'

'Relax, lad. Things are going well. The ford's in our hands and the Second's been relieved by the Twentieth. The boys are having a rest before General Plautius moves the army over to the far bank.'

'Have the Britons gone?'

'Gone?' Macro laughed. 'You should have seen them this morning. I tell you, that British general must have a pretty impressive hold over his men. They came at us like madmen, screaming and shouting as they threw themselves onto the shield wall. It was a close call, we very nearly lost it at one point. Bunch of them burst through by one of the gates and would have opened a sizeable breach in our line if it hadn't been for Vespasian. Bloody legate's a game lad, all right.'

Macro chuckled. 'Took the colour party and the staff officers by the scruff of the neck and threw them into the fight. Glorious stuff. Even the trumpet-blowers got involved. I saw one of the beggars take his horn and lay into the Britons, swinging it round like a bloody battle-axe. Anyway, once the line had been closed again, the Britons lost heart and pulled back.'

'The general's just letting them escape?' Cato was appalled. What was the point of so much loss of life the day before if the enemy was allowed to pull back and fortify the next river?

'He may be a general but he's not that stupid. He's sent the auxiliary cavalry after them. Meanwhile, the Twentieth are finally off their arses and doing something and we're back here for a day's rest. Then we push on again.'

'A whole day's rest?'

'Don't be sarcastic, lad. We've got the buggers knocked off balance and if we can keep pushing forward then Caratacus won't have the chance to re-form his army. It's all a question of time. The more he gets, the stronger his army will be. We march hard now or we fight a lot more of them later. Either way, we're in for a tough time of it.'

'I can't wait.'

They both fell silent for a moment as all too vivid memories of the previous day flooded back. Cato felt a chill of horror ripple up his spine into the nape of his neck. It took an effort to order the jumble of impressions into sequence, and make sense of what had happened. The ferocity of battle had a way of altering one's perception and it seemed to Cato that an impossible intensity of life, in all its terror and ecstasy, had been experienced the day before. He was filled with a deep sense of being far too young for the things he had witnessed. Indeed, far too young for the things he had done. A wave of disgust washed over him.

Macro, glancing over at his optio, saw the grim expression on the youngster's face. He had seen enough young soldiers in his time to guess what Cato was thinking.

'It isn't all glory being a soldier, my lad, not by a long way. And those who ain't been soldiers never realise that. You're new to the game, still adjusting to our ways. But it'll come to you.'

'What'll come to me?' Cato looked up. 'What will I become?'

'Hmmm. Tough question.' Macro grimaced. 'What you will become is a soldier. Even now I'm not quite sure what that means. It's just a way we have. A way we *have* to have – to get through each day. I guess you must think me and the others a bit hard sometimes. No, hard's not the right word. What about that word I came across the other day? I asked you about it, remember?'

'Callous,' Cato replied quietly.

'That's it! Callous. Good word.'

'And are you, sir?'

Macro sighed, and sat down beside his optio. Cato noticed the weariness in his movements, and realised that Macro had had no rest for the best part of two days. He wondered at the marvellous resilience of the centurion, and the way in which he made the well-being of the men in his command his priority in all things, as the present situation proved.

'Cato, you've got eyes. You've got a good brain. But you ask the most daft bloody questions at times. Sure, some soldiers are callous. But aren't some civilians? Didn't you meet any callous men when you were living in the palace? The kind of men who would kill their own children for political advancement? When Sejanus fell, didn't someone order the executioner to rape his ten-year-old daughter because the law doesn't allow the execution of virgins? Doesn't that smack of callousness? Look around you.' Macro waved at the lines of tents stretching out on all sides, the hundreds of men quietly resting in the warm summer's day, a handful playing at dice, one or two reading, some cleaning their equipment and weapons.

'They're just men, Cato. Ordinary men with all their vices and virtues. But where other men live their lives with death as a side issue, we live ours with death as a constant companion. We have to accept death.'

Their eyes met, and Macro nodded sadly. 'That's how it is, Cato. Now look here. You're a good lad, and have the makings of a fine soldier. Think on that.'

'Yes, sir.'

Macro rose to his feet and tugged his tunic straight under his chain mail. With a quick smile of encouragement he turned to leave, and then clicked his fingers in irritation.

'Shit! Almost forgot the reason I came to see you.' He reached under his harness and pulled out a small, tightly wound and sealed scroll. 'For you. Some letters have arrived with the supply column. Here. Read it and get some rest. I'll need you back on duty this evening.'

As the tired centurion walked stiffly towards his tent, Cato examined the scroll. The address on the wafer that bound the scroll had been written in a neat, tidy hand. 'To Quintus Licinius Cato, Optio of the Sixth Century, Fourth Cohort, Second Legion.' Curiosity turned to delicious anticipation as he read the name of the sender: Lavinia.

Chapter Sixteen

To fighting men on campaign, any opportunity to rest represented a luxury to be savoured, and the men of the Second Legion dozed happily in the sunlight. The heat of the afternoon sun soaked into the world below, and induced a still, warm haze that floated across the landscape and filled them with a sense of calm and contentment. The legate had seen to it that his men were well fed on their return to camp, and a generous allowance of wine had been sent to all the field kitchens. As usual some of the legionaries had gambled their wine ration in games of dice in a bid to win more. Accordingly, some were sullenly sober as they glared at their insensible comrades snoring off their winnings in a drunken stupor.

Wandering down the quiet lines of men, the legate of the Second Legion could not help but be conscious of the abrupt changes that life wrought. This time the day before, these same men had been preparing to assault the British fortifications and kill or be killed in the attempt. Yet here they were sleeping like babes. And those who weren't asleep were quietly contemplative. So lost in their thoughts were some of the men that they failed to notice him passing, but Vespasian made no issue of this breach of discipline. They had fought hard. Fought hard and won through at some cost, and it was good that they rested and recovered some sense of inner well-being. Tomorrow they would be hard at it again, as the army shifted its position across the Mead Way and continued to push the Britons back.

But military matters were a side issue at the moment. Tucked inside his belt purse was a letter he had found with the dispatches on returning to his headquarters tent. The handwriting was instantly recognisable, and the legate had seized it eagerly. A message from his wife was what he needed more than anything else in the world at this moment. Something to occupy his thoughts for a brief while and remind him that he was human; something unrelated to the press of duties that surrounded him. He had curtly ordered his staff officers to deal with the paperwork, removed his armour and left the tent in a light linen tunic in search of some privacy. The decurion in charge of the legate's body-guard had snapped to attention, and prepared to order his men to their feet, but Vespasian had managed to stop him in time. He ordered the decurion to stand the men down and let them rest. Then he strolled off, alone and unprotected.

Beyond the picket lines rose a small knoll, on top of which stood a copse of birch trees. An animal track traced a more or less straight line up the slope through a dense mass of cow parsley and stinging nettles. No breeze disturbed the air; butterflies, bees and other insects wafted above the unmoving greenery, oblivious of the great force of men, their horses and oxen stretched out across the ridge above the placidly flowing river. Up here on the knoll it was silent, and quite still. Vespasian slumped down with his back against the rough bark of a tree.

Even in the shade the air felt warm and close. Sweat trickled from under his arms, and felt cold as it slid down his sides under the tunic. Below, by the river crossing, a glittering spray amid tiny figures caught his eye. Some legionaries were swimming in the river, no doubt delighted at the chance to enjoy the cool water. Vespasian could think of nothing more he wanted than a swim, but the walk down to the river would take up too much time. In any case, the walk back up to the camp on the ridge would only make him uncomfortably hot once again.

A quite wonderful sense of anticipation had been building up inside him; the letter could be savoured now, rather than slotted into a convenient break between sifting the paperwork back at headquarters. He broke the wafer, imagining as he did so Flavia's hands holding this very scroll not so long ago. The parchment was stiff, and he smiled as he recognised it as part of the writing set he had bought Flavia nearly a year ago. The handwriting was as elegant as ever. Resisting the impulse to scan ahead, as he did with most documents, Vespasian settled to read his wife's letter. It began with customary mock formality.

Written on the Ides of June, from the headquarters of the governor at Lutetia.

To Flavius Vespasianus, commander of the Second Legion, and incidentally beloved husband of Flavia Domitilla, and absent father of Titus.

Dear husband, I trust that you are safe, and doing your very best to keep safe. Young Titus begs you to be careful and threatens that he won't ever speak to you again should you fall in battle. I rather think he takes the euphemism literally and wonders at the clumsiness of you army types. I haven't the heart to explain what really happens. Not that I could; nor would I ever want to discover what a battle is like. You might explain it all to him one day when, not if, you return.

111

I expect you want to know about our journey to Rome. The roads have been difficult to negotiate since there is all manner of military traffic pouring towards the coast. It seems that no effort is being spared to ensure that your campaign succeeds. We even passed a convoy of elephants heading for Gesoriacum. Elephants! Quite what the Emperor thinks General Plautius will do with the poor creatures is anybody's guess. I hardly think a bunch of ignorant savages will be able to put up much of a fight . . .

Vespasian gently shook his head; so far the ignorant savages were doing rather better than had been anticipated, and the reinforcements being rushed to support Plautius were desperately needed. The Second Legion badly needed replacements to bring them up to full fighting strength.

The more optimistic of the officers' wives are saying that Britain will be a part of the empire by the end of the year – just as soon as Caratacus is crushed and their tribal capital at Camulodunum taken. I tried to explain to them what you told me about the island's size, but such is their belief in the invincibility of our troops that they insisted that every one of the native tribes would wilt at the mere mention of Rome. I hope they are right, but I have my doubts given what you once told me about the Briton's penchant for guerrilla fighting. I just pray that the gods deliver you back to me in Rome older and wiser, and in perfect health, so that you can put the army behind you and concentrate on your future in politics. I have sent word ahead that we are returning to Rome, and I will get to work on building up our social connections as quickly as possible.

Vespasian frowned at the mention of politics, and his expression deepened as he reflected on Flavia's mention of connections. If she misjudged them in the current political climate in the capital, she might well jeopardise his chances and, worse, might actually endanger them all. Vespasian had only recently discovered that Flavia had been linked to an attempt to unseat Claudius. Scores of conspirators had been rounded up and executed in Rome, but Flavia had not been directly implicated. So far. Vitellius had uncovered her involvement, and it was only the threat of his own disgrace over his attempt to steal a fortune in imperial gold and silver, about which Vespasian had evidence, that kept Vitellius from exposing Flavia's treachery. It was an acutely uncomfortable state of affairs, Vespasian reflected before turning back to the letter.

Dear husband, I must tell you that I have had word from Rome that the Emperor is still hounding the survivors of the Scribonianus plot. It seems that there is a rumour going round about a secret organisation conspiring to overthrow the empire and return Rome to its republican glory. Everyone here in Lutetia is talking, or rather whispering, about it. It seems this gang refers to itself as 'The Liberators', a rather presumptuous nomenclature – but shrewdly evocative of a more egalitarian age, don't you think? I believe the days of the republic are long gone, and we are in an age where the winner takes all. Great men must play by whichever rules help them most efficiently to achieve their ends. Dearest husband, in this, as in all things, I am your ardent servant.

Despite the day's warmth, and his earlier contentment, Vespasian suddenly felt a nerve-tingling chill rise at the back of his neck and glide slowly down his spine. Was Flavia trying to sound out his feelings about the Liberators? If, indeed, she was linked to them at all, as Vitellius claimed. Flavia did not yet know that her husband knew of her role in Scribonianus' plot. What was Flavia saying to him between the words written there on the page?

Suddenly, he felt an intense longing to have Flavia with him right at this moment, here in the warm shadows of the sun-dappled birch trees. He wanted to hold her, to look her in the eye and demand the truth, to be reassured of her innocence, to see no trace of guile in those wide brown eyes. And then to make love. Oh yes, to make love! He could almost believe she was with him as he conjured up the sensation of holding her naked in his arms.

But what if she was part of the conspiracy? She might deny it even then, even while gazing into his face, with an expression of injured innocence, and he would never be able to prove it – or disprove it. He cursed out loud at the wedge Vitellius had driven between them. The smouldering distrust that the imperial agent had planted in his heart now ignited into a raging despair at the situation he faced. Flavia must be confronted with the accusation and made to relinquish any link she might have to the Liberators. And if she was innocent, then Vitellius must be made to suffer for the damage he had caused by fracturing the sacred trust that exists between man and wife. Vitellius would pay dearly, most dearly, Vespasian promised himself as he stared bitterly down the slope to where the legionaries still splashed about in the river.

For a moment he continued staring, an icy glint of hatred in his eyes, his fist unconsciously clenching the scroll. A vague pain finally registered in his mind, and he looked down and saw that the scroll was tightly crushed, and that his fingernails were biting deeply into the palm of his hand. It took a moment to refocus his mind, relax his grip and uncrumple Flavia's letter. There was more to read; a few more lines about their son Titus, but the words blurred into meaninglessness and so Vespasian abruptly rose to his feet and strode off down the slope back towards his head-quarters.

Chapter Seventeen

'You're in a good mood!' Macro stopped whetting the blade of his sword and grinned at Cato. Normally he would send his weapon to be sharpened by one of the legionaries on fatigues, but they were at war now, and Macro had to be confident his weapons were honed to their sharpest. He ran his fingers gently back from the point along each edge. 'That letter, I guess.'

'From Lavinia.' Cato gazed dreamily towards the fading bronze sky in the west. The sun had set, and faint fingers of light gilded the underside of scattered clouds. After the beating heat of the day, the air felt cooler at last. Even the wood pigeons in the nearest trees sounded more comfortable in the dull haze of the closing dusk. 'First letter I've had from her.'

'Still burning a lamp for you, eh?'

'Yes, sir. Seems that way.'

The centurion regarded his optio for a moment and slowly shook his head with pity. 'Not even a man yet and you're straining at the leash to get hitched to the girl. At least, that's how it looks. Haven't you got some wild oats to sow?'

'If it's all the same to you, sir, that's my business.'

Macro laughed. 'All right, boy, but don't say I didn't encourage you when some day you look back on all the lost opportunities. I've met some odd types in my time, but you must be the first lad I've met who's been so smitten that he's not looking forward to getting his leg over the first of the local women we get to grips with.'

Cato looked down, ashamed and bitter. Try as he might, he could not slip into the role of the legionary that Macro was so comfortable with. He was plagued by a painful and perpetual self-consciousness whenever he approached a new challenge.

'Now then, how are those burns? Can you cope?'

'Do I have a choice, sir?'

'No.'

'They hurt like hell, but I can do my duty.'

'That's the spirit! Spoken like a true soldier.'

'Spoken like a true fool,' muttered Cato.

'But you are up to it? I mean, seriously?'

'Yes, sir.'

The centurion cast an eye over the glistening mass of blisters covering Cato's arm then nodded. 'All right then. The legion's moving off at first light. We leave our packs here, and the army's baggage train will bring everything up once we cross the Tamesis. When we're on the far side, the orders are that we dig in and wait for the Emperor to arrive with reinforcements.'

'The Emperor's coming here?'

'In person. Least that's what the legate said at the briefing. Seems he wants to be in on the kill so that he can present himself as triumphant general to the mob in Rome. We get across the Tamesis, and then we're nicely poised to strike west into the heart of Britain, or go east and take the Catuvellauni capital. Either way we keep the natives guessing and meanwhile get ourselves fully rested and ready for the next stage of the invasion.'

'Wouldn't it be better to keep our swords in Caratacus' back, to keep him from re-forming? If we just sit there and wait he can only grow stronger.'

Macro nodded. 'That's what I'd have thought. Still, orders is orders.'

'Are we going to get any replacements, sir?'

'Some cohorts of the Eighth are being sent over from Gesoriacum. They should catch up with us by the time we cross the Tamesis. Thanks to our losses the Second's been promised the biggest share of the replacements. You up to date with the century's strength returns?'

'Just sent them over to headquarters, sir.'

'Good. Let's hope those bloody clerks see fit to send us our quota. Not that those idle buggers in the Eighth are up to much. They've spent too long on garrison duty and most will be soft as rotten fruit. You can count on it. Still, a live idle bugger is more use than a dead one.'

Cato could only nod in agreement with such flaw-less wisdom. Particularly since all the men who had died were now generating a distastefully large amount of paperwork.

'So how are we doing?'

'Sir?'

Macro raised his eyes. 'What's our current strength?'

'Oh. Forty-eight effectives, including us and the standard bearer, sir. We've got twelve in the hospital; three of those have lost limbs.'

Macro spared the last three a moment's thought, well aware of the fate waiting those who were discharged from the legions. 'Those three, any of them veterans?'

'Two, sir. The third, Caius Maximus, only joined the legion two years ago. Took a sword blow to the knee, nearly cut right through. Surgeon had to amputate.'

'That's tough. Very tough,' Macro murmured, his face all but hidden in the gathering shades of night. 'Two twenty-fifths of his gratuity is all he'll get. Not much for a man to survive on.'

'He's from Rome, sir. He'll be eligible for the corn dole.'

'Corn dole!' Macro sniffed contemptuously. 'That's a bloody humiliating prospect for an ex-legionary. No, I can't let him depend on that. He has to have some money to set up in trade. A cobbler wouldn't miss a leg or two. He can do that, or some similar trade. We'll have a collection for Maximus. You do the rounds before everyone turns in tonight. And do him a refund from the funeral club. I doubt if the lads will protest about that. See to it.'

'Yes, sir. Anything else, sir?'

'No. You can pass the word about tomorrow's advance while you note the contributions for Maximus. Let the lads know we'll be up before dawn. Breakfasted, assembled and ready to move off. Now go to it.'

As he watched the optio's dark form move down the tent line, Macro's thoughts returned to Caius Maximus. He was barely older than Cato, but not nearly as bright. Quite stupid in fact. A big, gangling youth from the slums of the Subura in Rome. Tall, ponderous, with large ears between which a maddening lopsided smile split his face. From the moment Macro had taken charge of the century he had seen Maximus as a casualty waiting to happen, and he had shaken his head in pity at the boy's attempts to cut it in the legion. It gave Macro no satisfaction to be proved right about the lad, and the thought of the thick young invalid trying to survive in a teeming metropolis populated by thieves and rogues of the very worst kind was painful. But the sword that had cut short the lad's career, not to mention his leg, could just as easily have landed on any other man in the century, Macro reflected. It could just as easily have been him or young Cato.

The centurion folded up his tunic and placed it between his harness and his armour so that the dew would not soak it. Satisfied that his weapons were to hand, Macro pulled his wool cape across his body and lay back on the grass staring up into the star-pricked blackness. All around, the night was filled with the sounds of an army bedding down. The distant blare of a horn from headquarters announced a change of watch, and then, in the gathering quiet of rows of slumbering men, the centurion fell asleep.

Chapter Eighteen

'Why?'

'Sir?' Vitellius smiled innocently at the legate.

'Why have you been posted back to the Second Legion? I thought you'd been promoted to the general's staff permanently. A reward for your heroic efforts. So what's changed?' Vespasian eyed him suspiciously. 'Were you ordered back here, or did you request it?'

'It was my request, sir,' the tribune replied easily. 'I told the general that I wanted to be back in the thick of it when the legion next goes into battle. The general said he admired my pluck, wished there were more like me, asked me once if I wished to change my mind, and then sent me on my way.'

'I can imagine. No one in his right mind would actually want an imperial spy camping on his doorstep.'

'He doesn't know, sir.'

'Doesn't know? How can he not know what you are?'

'Because no one has told him. Our general assumes that my preferment is entirely down to my palace connections. When I asked to be returned to the Second he wasn't that sorry to see me go. If I can be honest, sir?'

'Please go ahead.'

'I'm not sure I have the right temperament to be on the general's staff. He works them too hard and exposes them to too many risks, if you understand me.'

'Perfectly,' Vespasian replied. 'I heard you had gone in with the Ninth on the river assault.'

Vitellius nodded, the terror of the attack still fresh in his mind; the mind-searing certainty that he would never survive the savage fusillade of arrows and slingshot poured down on the Romans by the desperate defenders.

'I heard you acquitted yourself well enough.'

'Yes, sir. All the same, I'd rather not have been down there.'

'Possibly, but perhaps there's some hope for you yet. Start behaving like a tribune, forget the espionage, and we might just survive each other's company.'

'That would be nice, sir. But I am the Emperor's servant, and will remain so until I die.'

Vespasian regarded his senior tribune closely. 'I thought the only thing you served was your ambition.'

'Is there anything more worthy of a man's service?' Vitellius smiled. 'But ambition has to work within the boundaries of the possible and the whim of fate. No one knows the will of the gods. Given the prospect of his imminent deification, I expect that only Claudius can know how things will turn out.'

'Hmmm.' The imperial predilection for immortality was something that had troubled Vespasian over the years. He found it hard to believe that a motion voted for on the floor of the senate house could determine the divine status of a man. Especially such an unprepossessing creature as the present Emperor. Being declared a god had not protected Caligula from the wrath of those who had assassinated him. It seemed that those mad emperors whom men would destroy they first made gods. Vespasian looked up into the eyes of his senior tribune.

'Look here, Vitellius, we're in the middle of a major

campaign. The last thing I need to worry about is you spying on me and my men behind our backs.'

'Can you think of a better time to spy, sir? When men's minds are preoccupied with battle they're inclined to guard their tongues less. Makes my task that much easier.'

Vespasian regarded him with open contempt. 'There are times when you make me feel quite sick, Tribune.'

'Yes, sir.'

'If you come between my legion and its responsibilities to the rest of the army, I swear I will kill you.'

'Yes, sir.' If there was any sense of either smugness or surrender to a higher authority in the tribune's expression, it was unreadable to Vespasian. Neither man spoke, or even moved, as they watched each other closely. Eventually Vespasian eased himself back in his chair.

'I'm sure we understand one another, Vitellius.'

'Oh, I'm quite sure that we do, sir. And may I assume that the arrangement we came to over your wife's extracurricular politics and my treasure-hunting still stands?'

Vespasian clasped his hands together tightly and nodded. 'As long as you keep to your side of the bargain.'

'Don't worry, sir. Your wife is quite safe, for the moment.'

'Assuming there's a shred of truth in what you have said about her.'

'Shred of truth?' Vitellius smiled. 'I think you'd be quite surprised at the lengths Flavia would go to pursue her political ends. Far more than is discreet for one whose husband has a promising future . . . in the service of the Emperor.'

'So you say.' Vespasian nodded slowly. 'But you have yet to provide me with firm evidence of your allegations. Nothing you have told me so far would be provable in a court of law.'

'Court of law!' Vitellius chuckled. 'Such a quaint notion. What makes you think for a moment that any charges against Flavia, or yourself, would be brought before any court at all? A quiet word from the Emperor and a small squad of Praetorians would pay you a visit with orders not to leave until you were both dead. The best you could hope for is a polite little obituary in the Rome gazette. That's how the world works, sir. Best get used to it.'

'I'll get used to it. Just as you had better get used to the fact that I can implicate you in a little treason of your own.'

'Oh, I haven't forgotten, sir. That's why we're having this discussion. I assume you have made sure that your side of the agreement is safely documented?'

'Of course,' lied Vespasian. 'I have sent a message to Rome to be lodged with my lawyer until either I reclaim it or I perish. Whichever comes first. At which point the letter will be opened and read before senate and Emperor. I should imagine that your death would follow swiftly upon my own. So swiftly that we might even cross the Styx in the same vessel.'

'I would count that an honour, sir.' Vitellius permitted himself a wry smile. 'But there really is no need for things to go that far, wouldn't you agree?'

'I would.'

'Then there's nothing more to be said, sir.'

'Nothing.'

'Am I dismissed?'

Vespasian paused a moment and then shook his head. 'Not quite yet, Tribune. I need you to answer a question before you leave.'

'Oh yes?'

'What do you know of the Liberators?'

Vitellius raised an eyebrow, seemingly surprised by the

question. He tightened his lips and frowned before the answer came to him. 'She's been in touch with you, hasn't she?'

Vespasian refused to satisfy the tribune with a response and tried to hide his irritation at the informal reference to his wife.

'I thought so.' Vitellius nodded. 'The Liberators. Now there's a name that's been cropping up more and more in recent months. Well, well. Our Flavia is a darker horse than I realised, sir. You'd best guard her well before she does something your family line might have cause to curse her for.'

'You know of this organisation then?'

'I have heard of them, you might say,' the tribune replied smoothly. 'Rumour has it that the Liberators are a secret organisation with ambitions to overthrow the Emperor and restore the republic. They're supposed to have existed since the time of Augustus, and were vain enough to name themselves after the assassins of Julius Caesar.'

'A rumour?' Vespasian mused. 'Is that all?'

'It's still enough to get you executed, sir. Narcissus has men crawling all over Rome, and the provinces, searching for people connected to the organisation. Those involved with Scribonianus' plot are supposed to have links with the Liberators. I wonder how much your wife knows about them. I imagine Narcissus would be keen to ask her, given the chance.'

Vespasian refused to respond to the scarcely veiled threat; neither of them had anything to gain from exposing the other. He focused instead on Flavia, and her possible connection to this conspiracy hiding in the shadows of history. From what he knew of Narcissus, the imperial chief of staff would be relentless, and quite ruthless, in his pursuit of any who threatened the Emperor. However long it took, however many suspects were tortured for information, the conspiracy would be tracked down and its members quietly eliminated.

Yet if Vitellius was right, the Liberators had been quietly plotting for decades and that spoke of an extraordinary commitment to secrecy and patience. Vespasian could guess at the motivation of those who had joined the Liberators. Rome had been ruled by the emperors for over sixty years, and while Augustus had ended the terrible era of civil strife that had torn the Roman state asunder for generations, it was a peace bought at the cost of denying the aristocrats the political powers their families had wielded for hundreds of years. A social class imbued with such a sense of its own destiny does not easily accept its subordination to a dynasty that produced a madman like Caligula and a fool like Claudius.

But, wondered Vespasian, what other way was there for Rome now?

Returning control of the empire to the senate would once again transform the civilised world into a battlefield, over which roamed the vast armies of power-crazed senatorial factions. They would leave devastation in their wake, while the barbarian hordes watched in glee from beyond the wild frontiers of the empire. Whatever their faults, the emperors stood for order. They might thin out the ranks of the aristocrats from time to time, but for the heaving masses of Rome, and everyone else who lived within the empire, the emperors stood for some measure of order and peace. Even though Vespasian was a member of the senatorial class, whose cause the Liberators claimed to represent, he knew that the consequences of the return to senatorial control offered by the Liberators were too terrible to contemplate.

'Sir?'

Vespasian looked up, irritated by the interruption to his train of thought. 'What is it?'

'Is there anything else for us to discuss? Or can I return to my duties with the Second?'

'We've said all that need be said. You'd better let Plinius know that he's to step down from the senior tribune's post. Get him to brief you on tomorrow's advance. And there's still some supplies admin to sort out. See to it before you turn in.'

'Yes, sir.'

'Bear in mind what I said, Vitellius.' Vespasian fixed the tribune with a stern expression. 'Regardless of your duties as an imperial agent, you are still *my* senior tribune and I expect you to act the part. One step, or word, out of line and I'll see you suffer for it.'

Chapter Nineteen

Early next morning the army advanced across the Mead Way. As the dense column of soldiers reached the ford, the pace slowed. Most had served long enough to know the discomfort of marching with a waterlogged shield, and kept their equipment held high as they waded into the churning water in the wake of the thousands of men crossing to the far side. Despite the previous afternoon's rest, the men still felt weary, and those with injuries light enough to classify them as walking wounded bore the strained expressions of men who fought their pain. All along the column were men with dressings to head or limbs, some still soiled by their blood, and the blood of others. But despite the ravaged look of the legion it still marched to the front fully prepared and willing to engage the Britons once more.

The success of yesterday's attack had rekindled the Second Legion's confidence in a way that heartened its commander. He watched the column on the far bank rise up from the river and drip through the muddy shallows before climbing the earthworks and disappearing inside the fortifications beyond. In the dim light Vespasian was reminded of a giant centipede he had once seen as a child at his family's estate near Reate; a shining mass with dark limbs struggling up the slope.

At his side Vitellius sat silently on his mount, staring at the ground before the earthworks. The memory of the harrowing assault across this very ground contrasted sharply with the early morning serenity of the river. The blood that had stained the river red had been washed away, and the bodies that had littered this shore had been carried away for cremation. Little indication of the savage fight remained beyond the memories of those who had fought and survived. With a vague sense of the depressing unreality of it all, Vitellius turned his mount and dug his heels into its flanks, trotting up the incline prepared by the engineers. He passed alongside the men of the Fourth Cohort, unaware of the hostile looks directed at him from the two men marching at the head of the Sixth Century.

'Thought we'd seen the last of that bastard,' Macro grumbled. 'Wonder what he's doing back in the legion.'

Cato was not unduly bothered by the tribune's return to the Second Legion. His mind was on other things. The pain from his burns seemed to be worse than ever this morning, and he longed for the inactivity of the previous day. Already the chafing of his equipment had burst some of the blisters and his raw flesh was agony against the rough material of his tunic. He gritted his teeth and concentrated his mind on following the rear of the century ahead.

He was shocked by the scene that met his eyes as the Sixth Century passed through the remains of the British fortifications. The enclosed area was fire-blackened, and while the bodies of the Romans had been respectfully cremated, no such treatment had been accorded the dead natives who lay heaped in sun-ripened piles of decay. The still air was heavy with the sickly sweet stench of dead men, and their stiff limbs, blank eyes and sagging open mouths filled the young optio with a nauseous disgust. Cato could feel the bile rising up the back of his throat and he quickened his pace, as had all the men passing through the fortifications ahead of him. Scores of prisoners were being kept busy digging burial pits for their fallen comrades, under the watchful gaze of men from the Twentieth Legion detached for guard duties. They must be grateful for the chance to keep out of the coming fight, Cato reflected, momentarily envious of their lot before a fresh waft of rotting flesh filled his nostrils, causing him to retch.

'Easy, lad!' Macro comforted. 'It's just a smell. Try not to think about what's making it. We'll be out of this place soon enough.'

Cato wondered that Macro could be so unmoved by the charnel chaos surrounding them. But then he saw his centurion swallow nervously and realised that even this hardened veteran was not unaffected by the foul consequences of battle. The column hurried through the ruined camp in silence, broken only by the jingle of equipment and the nervous coughs of those most afflicted by the unholy stench. Once over the far ramp and back into the open countryside Cato breathed deeply to expel every last breath of the foetid air from his lungs.

'Better?' asked Macro.

Cato nodded. 'Is it always like that?'

'Pretty much. Unless we fight in winter.'

The British camp was behind them now and the air was filled with fresh country scents that brushed away the memory of the stench of the dead. Even so, traces of the running fight between the Britons and their pursuers littered the track as far as the eye could see in the direction of the Tamesis. Spent weapons, dead horses, overturned chariots and sprawling bodies lay strewn across the trampled ground. The air hummed with the sound of flies whirling in small speckled clouds over the dead. A dull haze hung above the track, kicked up from the passage of the legions marching to join the auxiliaries and the cavalry in their pursuit of the enemy.

Cato felt the first of the day's warmth flow over him. Later, he knew, the growing heat would make conditions intolerable under the load of cumbersome equipment that was designed for efficiency in battle, with little thought to the wearer's comfort on the march. Already his exposed burns were causing him torment beyond imagination. But he knew the pain would last for some days yet and since there was nothing to be done about it, he would just have to bear it, Cato reflected with a grimace.

As the sun eased its way high into a clear azure heaven the shadows of the tramping legionaries shortened, as if themselves withering in the growing heat, and the cheerful conversation of dawn dwindled to the odd murmured comment. As noon drew near, the legion approached the crest of a low ridge and the legate ordered a halt. Shields and spears were laid down at the side of the road before each legionary slumped down and gratefully sipped from the leather canteens filled before first light.

The Sixth Century found itself near a small circle of bodies, some Roman, most Britons, silent testament to a bitter skirmish fought the day before. Today, no sound of fighting disturbed the muted talk of the men of the Second Legion, not even a far-off trumpet or horn. It was as if the battle of the previous two days had withdrawn like some fleeting tide and left the land strewn with its broken and bloody flotsam. Cato felt a sudden desire, tinged with panic, to know more about how things lay between the legions and their enemy. He stilled the urge to ask Macro what was unfolding since the centurion knew as little as he did and could only offer a veteran's best guess at the situation. As far as Cato could work out, the legion had marched eight or nine miles beyond the Mead Way, and that meant a similar distance lay ahead before they encountered the Tamesis. Then what? Another bloody river assault? Or were the Britons retreating too quickly to form an organised defence this time?

The grassy downs gave way to dense gorse thickets that crowded the track on both sides and through which little runs twisted out of sight. If this was the nature of the terrain ahead, reflected Cato, then the next battle was going to be a very different affair, a mass of skirmishes as both sides negotiated their way through the tangled undergrowth. The kind of battle that a general could do little to control.

'Not the best of battlefields for us Romans, eh?' Macro had seen his optio glancing anxiously into the gorse thickets.

'No, sir.'

'I shouldn't worry, Cato. This stuff's as likely to hamper the Britons as it is us.'

'I suppose so, sir. But I'd have thought they'd know their way about the local tracks. Could cause us problems.'

'Maybe.' Macro nodded without too much concern. 'But I doubt it will count for much now they haven't got a river and a rampart between them and us.'

Cato wished he could share his superior's equanimity about the situation, but the tactical claustrophobia of the soldier at the very end of the chain of command preyed upon his imagination.

A shrill blast on several trumpets abruptly split the air, and Macro was on his feet in an instant. 'Up! Up, you lazy bastards! Get your kit and form up on the track!'

The orders echoed down the line and moments later the

men of the Second Legion had formed a long, dense column with every shield and javelin held ready for action.

Where the track rose ahead of the century, Cato could see the command party on the crest of the ridge. A mounted messenger was addressing the legate and waving his arm over the terrain on the other side of the ridge. With a quick salute the messenger wheeled his horse and galloped out of sight, leaving the legate to turn to his staff officers and issue the necessary orders.

'What now?' grumbled Macro.

Chapter Twenty

The advance to the Tamesis was rapidly running out of control, Vespasian decided. The pursuit of the Britons had been badly mishandled by the Batavian cohorts. Rather than concentrate on clearing the line of march through to the next river, the auxiliaries had fallen victim to the blood lust so typical of their race. And so the cohorts were dispersed over a wide front, running down every Briton that came in sight, as if the whole thing was just some great stag hunt.

Below the hill crest, the dense undergrowth dipped down to merge with yet another of the marshes that seemed to comprise rather too much of this landscape. Dotted among the gorse thickets were the crests of helmets and the odd standard as the Batavians, their thirst for blood evidently not yet slaked, pushed their way through the gorse, struggling along narrow paths in pursuit of the hapless Britons. The marsh stretched out, dull and featureless, before it gave way to the wide gleaming expanse of the great Tamesis coiling its way into the heart of the island. The track the Second Legion was marching along went straight down the slope, and on to a crude causeway that ended in a small jetty. A matching jetty lay on the far side of the river.

Vespasian slapped his thigh in frustration at the nature of the task ahead. His battle-trained horse ignored the sound and grazed contentedly at the luscious grass growing alongside the track. Irked by the beast's ignorant complacency, Vespasian yanked on the reins and wheeled the animal round to face back down the line of the legion. The men stood still and silent, waiting for orders to move. A dark writhing mass some miles off revealed the progress of the Fourteenth Legion approaching the Tamesis from a roughly parallel track a few miles upstream.

According to Adminius there should have been a bridge lying before the Fourteenth but Vespasian could see no sign of it. Caratacus must have had it destroyed. If there were no other bridges or crossing points, the legions would have to march upstream in search of an alternative way across, all the while extending the tenuous lines of supply back to the depot on the coast. Alternatively, Plautius might chance an opposed landing. Away to the east where the Tamesis broadened towards the distant horizon the distinct forms of ships were visible as the fleet strove to retain contact with the advancing legions. Even though Adminius claimed that the Britons had no fleet to oppose the Romans, General Plautius was not taking any chances. The sleek silhouettes of triremes shepherded the low broad-beamed transports struggling to keep in formation. Only when these ships had rejoined the army could a river assault begin.

But all these considerations were academic for the moment. The orders in hand were simple enough: the Second was to fan out and clear this stretch of the south bank of any remaining enemy formations. Simple orders. Simple enough to have been written by a man who had not seen the lie of the land for himself. Vespasian knew that the legion would not be able to retain a battle line as it negotiated the gorse thickets. Worse still was the marsh which would suck the men down unless they were fortunate enough to stumble upon the paths used by the natives. By nightfall Vespasian expected to find his legion completely dispersed and bogged down, stuck in the vile marsh until daylight gave them a chance to re-form.

'Give the signal!' he called out to the headquarters trumpeters. A chorus of spitting ensued as the men cleared their mouths and pursed their lips to their instruments. A barely discernible nod from the senior trumpeter was instantly followed by the harsh notes of the execute instruction. With well-trained precision the First Cohort marched past their legate. The senior centurion marked the turn point and barked out the order to change formation and the front ranks marched to the right, perpendicular to the track. Immediately they encountered the first patch of gorse bushes, the cohort broke formation to negotiate the obstacle and the steady marching pace slowed to a stumbling shuffle as the succeeding cohorts tried not to pile into the rear of the cohort in front. Vespasian met the eyes of Sextus, the Second Legion's grey-haired camp prefect, and grimaced. The most senior career soldier in the legion inclined his head in full agreement about the idiocy of the orders emanating from army headquarters.

A manoeuvre that could be executed so efficiently on the parade ground rapidly degenerated into an unsightly tangle of cursing men that struggled across the wild terrain for the best part of an hour before the Second Legion had shifted its facing and was ready to advance down the slope towards the distant Tamesis. Once the cohorts were in position Vespasian gave the order to advance and the line moved forward, overseen by the centurions holding their canes out and cursing at the men to keep the line straight.

Once again, the thick patches of gorse opened up gaps in the line and in very little time the legion disintegrated into clusters of struggling men. Here and there the line halted as men encountered Britons, mostly wounded, and disarmed them before sending them to the rear under guard. Those that were too badly injured to walk were quickly dispatched with a sword thrust to the heart, and the legionaries struggled forward again. Often the Britons would attempt to bolt for it and with excited cries the legionaries would tumble after them to add yet more spoils to the campaign pot. In the partially clear ground before the dense growths of gorse a motley crowd of prisoners grew in size, while off to one side a small group of injured men bore witness to the trickle of casualties returning from the clashes being fought out of sight in the wilderness beyond. These were the only indication of the way the fight was going.

By mid-afternoon, under the despairing eye of the legate and his staff officers, the Second Legion had been reduced to small bands hacking their way towards the river with little or no sense of where the rest of their comrades were. Mingled in among them were occasional small knots of Britons also trying to make the river in the hope of escape, and faint war cries and the ringing clash of blades wafted up the slope. Vespasian and his staff had dismounted and sat in the shade of a small copse not far from the track, watching the chaotic mêlée in silent frustration.

By late afternoon most of the men of the legion were lost to view and only the legate's guard century stood formed up in a thin line a hundred paces down the slope. Beyond them sat the pathetic huddle of prisoners, surrounded by gorse briars hacked down and piled up in a circle to form a crude stockade. Beyond the briars a scattered line of legionaries stood watch. Tribune Vitellius rode down to inspect the captives. When he had finished interrogating their leader, he gave a last cuff to the man's head and swung himself up onto his mount and spurred it back up the slope.

'Discover anything useful?' asked Vespasian.

'Only that some of the better educated among these savages have a little Latin, sir.'

'But no fords or bridges nearby?'

'No, sir.'

'It was worth a try, I suppose.' Vespasian's gaze flickered back to the legate's guard century baking in the sun.

'Tell them to sit down,' Vespasian muttered to the camp prefect. 'I doubt the Britons will be springing any surprises on us now. No point in keeping the men on their feet in this heat.'

'Yes sir.'

As Sextus bellowed the order down to the guard century, tribune Vitellius caught the legate's eye and nodded back towards the track. A messenger was galloping up. When he spotted the legate's command party he spurred his horse along the ridge towards them.

'What now?' wondered Vespasian.

Breathless, the messenger slid from his horse and ran to the legate, dispatch already to hand.

'From the general, sir,' he panted as he raised his arm in a salute.

Vespasian acknowledged him with a curt nod, took the scroll and broke the seal. His staff officers sat impatiently waiting for their legate to read it. The message was brief enough and Vespasian immediately handed it on to Vitellius.

Vitellius frowned as he read it. 'According to this, it appears we should already be down on the river bank and be preparing for a river assault this evening. The navy will be carrying us across and providing fire support.' He looked up. 'But, sir.' He waved a hand down the slope towards the gorse and the marsh which had swallowed up the Second Legion.

'Quite, Tribune. Now read out the last bit.'

Vitellius did so. 'Further to earlier orders it should be noted that the Batavian cohorts have encountered problems dealing with the marsh terrain and you are advised to limit your advance to established tracks and paths only . . .'

One of the junior tribunes hooted with derision and the rest laughed bitterly. Vespasian held up his hand to quieten them before he turned back to Vitellius.

'Seems the lads back at army headquarters haven't quite grasped the practical difficulties attached to the orders they are so quick to dish out. But with your recent staff experience I'm sure you'd know all about that.'

The other tribunes struggled to hide their grins and Vitellius blushed.

'Still, we can't carry this order out. By the time the legion reassembles on the river it'll be well into the night. And the navy are still some miles downriver. There's no chance of an assault until tomorrow,' concluded Vespasian. 'The general had better be told. Tribune, you know the ropes at headquarters and you know our situation here. Go back to Aulus Plautius with the messenger and let him know our position and tell him that I will not be able to carry out the assault until tomorrow. You might also describe the terrain in some detail so that he understands our position. Now go.'

'Yes, sir.' Vitellius saluted and strode across to his horse, angry at the prospect of a long hot ride, and bitter at the legate's sarcastic treatment of him in front of the junior tribunes.

Vespasian watched in amusement as the tribune snatched the reins from the hands of a horse holder and threw himself onto his horse's back. With a savage kick to the animal's ribs he galloped off in the direction of army headquarters. It had been impossible to resist teasing Vitellius, but any elation he might have derived from deflating the smug tribune quickly evaporated, and he cursed himself for indulging in behaviour that was far below the dignity of his rank. Fortunately, the camp prefect had missed the exchange; as the tough old veteran strode back up the slope from the legate's guard he frowned at the amused expressions on the faces of the young tribunes.

'Fresh orders, sir?'

'Read it.' Vespasian held out the scroll.

Sextus quickly scanned the document. 'Some young gentleman on Plautius' staff is going to get a few harsh words when I catch up with him, sir.'

'Glad to hear it. In the meantime we need to reassemble the legion. There's no point in sounding the recall. They're far enough into the marshes by now to make it easier to continue forward than march back.'

'True enough,' muttered Sextus, stroking his chin.

'I'll take the command party and the guard century along the causeway to that jetty.' Vespasian pointed down the slope. 'Once we get there I'll start sounding the recall. Meanwhile, you and the junior tribunes mount up and find as many of our men as possible and let them know what's going on. We need the main body of the legion gathered on that rise by the jetty before nightfall if we're going to have enough men for the assault in the morning.'

'Fair enough, sir,' said Sextus. He turned to the junior tribunes who had all heard the legate's orders and were not looking forward to the discomfort of their task. 'You heard the legate! Off your arses and on your horses, gentlemen. Quickly now!'

With a barely tolerable display of reluctance the young tribunes dragged themselves to their horses, trotted down the slope and separated along the myriad paths and ways that crisscrossed the dense mass of gorse and marsh. Vespasian watched them disappear from sight. Then he turned to his own mount and led the legate's guard and the rest of the command party towards the track leading down to the causeway.

This was no way to fight a battle, he reflected angrily. No sooner had the Second Legion won back its self-respect than some bloody careless order plunged the men into an unholy mess, dispersed and leaderless across the wretched wilderness of this wretched bloody island. By the time he managed to regroup the legion they would be exhausted, filthy, and hungry, their flesh and clothing torn to shreds by the gorse bushes. It would be a wonder if he managed to get them even to contemplate anything half so dangerous as the general's order for an amphibious assault on the opposite river bank.

Chapter Twenty-One

'This is a complete fucking nightmare!' Centurion Macro growled as he slapped at a large mosquito feeding on his forearm. No sooner had it become a smear of red and black amid the dark hairs below the hem of his sleeve than several more insects from the swirling cloud hovering above him decided to take their chance, and landed on the nearest patch of exposed skin. Macro slapped away at them with one hand and swiped at their airborne comrades with the other. 'If I ever get my hands on the man responsible for this fucking fiasco he'll never draw another breath.'

'I suspect the order came from the general, sir,' Cato responded as mildly as he could.

'Well then, I'll take up the issue in Hell, where we'll be on a more equal footing.'

'By then the general will be well past drawing another breath, sir.'

The centurion paused in his war against the native auxiliaries and rounded on his optio. 'Then I might just satisfy myself with someone else right now. Someone a little lower on the pecking order. Unless that's the very last of your helpful comments.'

'Sorry, sir,' replied Cato meekly. The situation was intolerable, and levity did nothing to ease the situation.

For the last hour the Sixth Century had been following a

twisting path through the clumps of gorse bushes, clinging to the more solid patches of ground in the marsh that stretched out all round. The path was wide enough for one man and had, in all likelihood, been made by wild beasts. Contact had been lost with the rest of the cohort, and the only other indications of human presence were far-off shouts and sounds of small-scale skirmishes from elsewhere in the marsh. The only Britons they had encountered had been a bedraggled handful of light infantry armed with wicker shields and hunting spears. Outnumbered and outclassed by the legionaries, they had given in without a fight, and were escorted to the rear by eight men Macro could ill afford to release from his shrinking command. Once the escort had left, the century struggled on.

As the sun declined towards the horizon, the still, hot air closed in on the century like a smothering blanket and sweat trickled from every pore. Macro had called a halt to try to get some sense of where they were in relation to the river and the rest of the legion. If the sun lay to their left then the river had to be more or less straight ahead, but the track seemed to be taking them to the west. The river ought to be near by now. It would be easier to go on and find it rather than face the prospect of retracing their steps for several hours through the coming night.

As he considered his options, the men sat in sullen, sweaty silence, plagued by the thousands of insects gathering over them. At length Cato could stand the insects no more, and crept further along the path to spy out the way ahead. A warning glance from Macro ensured that he remained in sight as he moved stealthily along the path. A short distance on, it dog-legged to the right. Cato squatted down and peered round the corner. He had hoped to see further along the track but almost immediately it swung back to the left out of sight. Mindful of the centurion's expression, Cato stayed where he was and strained his ears for any sound of movement. A distant skirmish was just audible above a dull background buzzing from what sounded like a large swarm of flies and their kin. The immediate vicinity seemed to be clear of the enemy, but Cato felt little sense of relief. The discomfort caused by the heat and the insects was such that any diversion would have been welcome, even the enemy.

That buzzing from the insects was unusually loud, and Cato's natural curiosity was aroused by the sound.

'Pssst!'

He turned and looked back down the track to where the centurion was trying to attract his attention. Macro raised his thumb with a questioning expression. Cato shrugged his shoulders and pointed his javelin round the corner. Moments later Macro squatted quietly at his side.

'What is it?'

'Listen, sir.'

Macro cocked his head. He frowned. 'Can't hear a thing. Not from nearby, at least.'

'Sir, that buzzing – the insects.'

'Yes, I hear it. So?'

'So, it's a bit too loud, wouldn't you say, sir?'

'Too loud?'

'Too many of them. Too many, too close together, sir.'

Macro listened again, and had to admit that the lad had a point. 'Stay here, Cato. If I call for you, get the century up here double quick.'

'Yes, sir.'

The sun was low enough to throw much of the track into shadow, dark against the burnished halo rimming the tops of the gorse thickets. Crouching low, Macro padded softly down the track, round the corner and out of sight, while

Cato squatted, tense and ready to spring to his centurion's aid the instant he called out. But there was no call, no noise of any kind above the droning of insects. The suspense was dreadful and, in his effort to remain quite still, the prickling heat and sweat on his body became almost unbearably uncomfortable on top of the pain of his burns.

Suddenly Macro strode back into view, no sign of the previous caution in his posture, merely a resigned grimness in his features.

'What is it, sir?'

'I've found some of the Batavian auxiliaries.'

Cato smiled. 'Good. Maybe they can tell us where we are, sir.'

'I think not,' replied Macro quietly. 'They're past caring.'

In a flat voice Macro ordered the Sixth Century to rise, and led them down the track, past the double bend and into a clear area formed by a slight rise in the ground. The path and trampled grass were littered with the remains of auxiliary troops from one of the Batavian cohorts. Most had been killed as they fought, but a good number had had their throats cut and lay in a heap to one side of the track. The bodies were swarming with flies and the sickeningly sweet stench of blood filled the still air. A handful of British warriors had been laid in a straight line, shields across their bodies and a spear resting at their sides. These men were helmeted and wore chainmail corselets.

Macro paused by one of the Batavian bodies which had a cut throat, and nudged it with his toe. Then he spoke in a voice loud enough to be heard by all his men.

'This is what you can expect if ever you feel the temptation to surrender to the natives. Make sure you all take a good long look, and thank the gods that it isn't you. Then swear you'll never die the same way. These Batavians were fools, and if I catch any of you being as foolish, I'll have my revenge in this life or the next. Count on it.' He glared round at the century, determined that they should be more afraid of their centurion than the enemy. 'Right, let's get this lot cleared up then! Cato, have our lads lined up alongside the Britons. Help yourself to anything you find on them.'

While the legionaries carried out the distasteful task, Macro posted a watch at each end of the clearing and then sat down on the grass, avoiding the areas still dark with blood. He undid the strap of his helmet and took it off, happy to be relieved of its weight. His hair, drenched with sweat, lay plastered to his scalp and rucked up in matted clumps when he tried to run his fingers through it. He looked up and saw Cato standing nearby. The optio was staring at the bodies of the Britons.

'Impressive-looking lot, aren't they?'

Cato nodded. These were clearly not the ordinary rank and file of the enemy. They were men in their prime, well-muscled and tough. The finery of their dress and equipment indicated some special status. 'Someone's bodyguard?'

'That'd be my guess,' agreed Macro. 'And judging from the rather unequal outcome in bodies, they're a pretty tough bunch. Hope there aren't too many of them out there.'

Cato glanced at the impenetrable gorse surrounding the clearing. 'Do you suppose they're still around, sir?'

'I'm a centurion, lad, not a bloody soothsayer,' Macro responded sharply. And instantly regretted it. The young optio was merely giving voice to the fears of them all, but the heat and exhaustion of fighting through this tangled landscape exacerbated Macro's growing anxiety about being separated from the rest of the legion. 'Don't worry, Cato, there's more of our lot out there than there is of them.'

Cato nodded but was not convinced. Numbers didn't matter in a situation like this, only local knowledge. The thought of a large party of elite British warriors hunting down isolated units of Romans was terrifying, and he felt ashamed of the fear that the prospect aroused in him. What made it worse was the imminent approach of night. The idea of spending any time in this ghastly wilderness during the hours of darkness appalled him. Already the sun had passed beyond the dense horizon of foliage and the sky blazed in its molten bronze afterglow. Against this the dark shapes of swallows flitted through the air as they fed on the insects above the marsh. The insects in turn were looking for the warm decay of the dead and the blood of the living to feed on, and today the marsh was positively crawling with sustenance.

Cato slapped at his cheek and caught a knuckle on his cheek guard. 'Shit!'

'Nice to see the little buggers go for a younger vintage once in a while,' commented Macro and waved a swarm of midges away from his face. 'Won't be sorry to be shot of this lot and have a swim in that river.'

'Yes, sir,' replied Cato with feeling. He could think of nothing more he would like to do than cast off his heavy, uncomfortable equipment that chafed so badly on his weeping burns and plunge into the cool flowing current of a river. The image conjured up was so desirable that for a moment Cato was quite transported from his immediate troubles, and the mental return to them was that much more painful as a consequence. 'Should we try and reach the river tonight, sir?'

Macro rubbed his eyes with the palms of his hands as he mentally debated the available courses of action. The prospect of staying put in this clearing overnight with the spirits of the newly dead creeping about the place made his flesh tingle with revulsion and horror. The river could not be that far, but in this marsh any progress along the narrow paths would be dangerous in the dark. A sudden thought struck him. 'Isn't there a moon tonight?'

'Yes, sir.'

'Right. Then we rest here until the moon rises enough to let us see where we're going. We'll take our chances on this path. It seems to be heading in the right direction for now. Detail two sentry watches and pass the word to the lads to try and get as much sleep as they can.'

'Yes, sir.' Cato saluted and strode off to give the orders. On his return he discovered his centurion lying on his back, eyes closed, snoring with the raucous grumble of a man deeply asleep. With an affectionate smile Cato slumped down on the opposite side of the path, removed his helmet and laid it with his other equipment. For a while he watched the sunset paint the sky in lurid shades of orange, red, violet and finally indigo. Then, after he had changed the watch, he also lay down, and tried to surrender to his own exhaustion. But the pain down his side, the merciless whine of insects, the droning from the flies, the rumbling snores of the centurion and the prospect of encountering any comrades of the dead Britons opposite ruined any immediate prospect of sleep. And so Cato lay uncomfortable, exhausted and angry at himself for not sleeping. The snoring from nearby had long since ceased to have any endearing quality and the young optio could quite happily have smothered his centurion long before the moon made its first appearance amidst the scattered clouds of the night sky.

Chapter Twenty-Two

'Optio!' hissed a voice.

Cato's eyes flickered open. A dark shape loomed against the star-pricked night sky. A hand was grasping his blistered arm, shaking him, and Cato nearly howled with agony but just managed to bite it off in time. He snapped upright, fully awake.

'What is it?' Cato whispered. 'What's happening?'

'Sentry reports movement.' The shape pointed to the end of the clearing near the track by which they had entered at dusk. 'Should we wake the centurion?'

Cato looked over towards the source of the snoring. 'I think we'd better. Just in case they hear us before we see them.'

As Cato hastily strapped his helmet on and picked up his equipment, the legionary woke Macro as quietly as he could. Not an easy task due to the depth of the centurion's slumber, and even when Macro came round he seemed to be breaking out of a fairly powerful dream.

'Because it's MY fucking tent!' grumbled the centurion. 'That's why!'

'Sir! Shhh!'

'W-what? What's up?' Macro jerked upright and immediately reached for his sword in a swift reflex action. 'Report!'

'We've got company, sir!' Cato called out softly as he crept over to the centurion. 'Sentry says he can hear movement.'

Macro was on his feet in an instant, his other hand automatically fastening his helmet strap. 'Get the lads formed up across the clearing, but keep 'em as quiet as you can. We might want to avoid this one.'

'Yes, sir.'

Cato crept off towards the sleeping legionaries and Macro quietly lifted his shield and made his way past the line of bodies, grateful that the drone from the flies had diminished with the coming of night. He almost missed the sentry in the darkness as the man was standing to one side of the track, completely still, straining to detect sounds from further down the narrow path.

'Sir!' the sentry whispered so quietly that had Macro not been listening so intently he might have missed it. As it was, the sudden sound caused him to flinch in surprise. He recovered in an instant, and silently crouched down beside the sentry.

'What is it, laddie?'

'Please, sir, there's nothing now. But I swear I heard something just a moment ago.'

'What did you hear, exactly?'

'Voices, sir. Very low, but not far off. Talking very quiet like.'

'Ours or theirs?'

The sentry paused for a moment before replying.

'Spit it out!' Macro whispered angrily. 'Ours or theirs?'

'I-I can't be sure, sir. It was mostly something I couldn't quite make out. But then again there was something that sounded like Latin.'

The centurion sniffed dismissively. He squatted in silence, straining his ears to detect the slightest sound from the direction of the path which bent out of sight a scant thirty feet from his position. The sounds from the clearing were all too audible even though the men tried to form up as quietly as possible. But, at last, they were still, and Macro renewed his concentration. But there was nothing out of the ordinary, just the occasional sound of frogs croaking. A dark shape drew close from the direction of the clearing.

'Psst!' hissed Macro. 'Over here, Cato.'

'Any sign of them, sir?'

'Fuck all. Seems our boy here just got a little too carried away with his imagination.'

It was a common enough fault in sentries, particularly on active service. Darkness heightened a man's reliance on one sense, and imagination went to work on even the slightest noise for which there was no immediate interpretation.

'Shall I stand the century down, sir?'

Macro was about to reply when a sudden rustle, as of a bush caught and quickly released, turned their blood to ice. There was no question about the sentry's report now, and they squatted motionless in the warm night air, muscles tensed and ready for action. A faint orange glow flickered from round the corner of the track, and sparks pierced the gaps in the foliage as someone bearing a torch approached down the track.

'Ours?' Cato asked.

'Quiet!' Macro whispered.

'Who's there?' a voice suddenly called out from the direction of the torch. Cato felt a wave of relief sweep over him, and nearly laughed at the abrupt easing of tension. He made to rise but Macro grabbed his wrist.

'Keep still!'

'But, sir, you heard him. It's one of ours.'

'Shut up and keep still!' Macro hissed.

'Who's there?' repeated the voice. There was a pause,

followed by what might have been a quick exchange of words in low whispers. Then the voice continued, 'I'm Batavian. Third Cohort of horse! If you're Roman, make yourself recognised!'

There was no denying the accented Latin sounded right for the Batavians, and Macro knew the Third mounted were in the area. And yet there was something in the man's tone that prevented him from risking a reply.

There was another brief silence before the voice came again, this time with a quavering edge to it. 'For the love of the gods! If you're Roman, reply!'

'Sir!' Cato protested.

'Shut up!'

With a sudden crackle, the glow from the torch grew bright and flames licked up above the gorse bushes. An inhuman scream cut through the thick, hot air hanging over the marsh.

'What the?' The sentry reeled back in shock.

Macro made to grasp him when suddenly a blazing figure burst from round the corner of the path and ran shrieking into the clearing, illuminating the ground about him in a lurid flickering glow. The air reeked of pitch and burned flesh, and the figure tripped and rolled on the ground, still screaming.

Macro grabbed the sentry and his optio and thrust them back towards the rest of the century. 'Run!'

Just behind them the night was rent with savage war cries, followed by the shrill braying of a war horn. Down the track, in the wake of their Batavian captive, poured the Britons, dreadful in the blazing light of the torch raised high by the man at the head of their charge. Cato had time for just one glance, enough to see the Batavian mercifully still on the ground, before he bolted after his centurion. They burst through the silent line of legionaries waiting beyond the red loom of the torch and turned to face the Britons, ready to fight on the instant. But their pursuers had halted momentarily to lay into the line of bodies arranged alongside the track, hacking and slashing at the corpses.

'What the hell?' wondered Macro.

'They think it's us, sir! They think they've caught us asleep!'

With a savage shout of dismay the Britons realised their error and turned towards the legionaries lined up across the middle of the small clearing.

'Release javelins at will!' roared Macro.

The dark shafts arced in a shallow trajectory straight into the foremost Britons. Hidden by the night, the javelins tore into their victims before they were even aware of the danger; several of the attackers fell and were trampled by the feet of their comrades desperate to get at the Romans. There was barely time for the second volley to be released before the Britons were upon them, screaming their savage war cries. A sharp clatter and clash of weapons and shields rang out, accompanied by the shouts, grunts and cries of men fighting wildly in the darkness.

'Close up! Close up!' Macro shouted above the din. 'Keep together!'

Unless the legionaries could remain distinct from their enemies, there was every chance that Roman would attack Roman.

Just then the moon began to appear from behind a dark bank of clouds and a thin grey light was thrown on the scene. Macro saw to his relief that his men were managing to keep close enough together to hold off the wave of Britons hacking and slashing at the shield wall. But even as he looked round, a large warrior threw himself between the shields of the men, nearly knocking them to the ground, and hurled himself on the centurion. Macro had only an instant to react and began to roll back to absorb the impact.

'Sir!' Cato shouted from one side, and swung his weight behind his shield and slammed the boss into the Briton's side. It was enough and the man crashed to the ground at Macro's side, badly winded. Macro drew back his sword arm and smashed the pommel up into the Briton's chin. The man went down with a single grunt, out cold.

Cato quickly helped his centurion back to his feet and then, shield to the fore, thrust his short sword into the mass of warriors confronting him. The tip of the blade struck home, a man cursed at the injury, and Cato pulled the sword free and struck again.

The moon was now clear of the clouds and beamed its melancholy light down on the writhing mêlée, reflecting dully on flickering blades, polished helmets and armour. Macro could see that he and his men were badly out-numbered and that even more of these fierce warriors were emerging from the path at the head of the clearing. The legionaries could not hope to last long against these odds and seemed doomed to the same gruesome fate that had befallen the Batavians.

'Fall back! Fall back to the far end of the clearing!' Macro bellowed above the din of the vicious skirmish. 'With me!'

He parried a blow to one side and retreated a step. To both sides his men rippled back and gave ground, slowly moving into the neck of the clearing. It was just as well, since they could not have held the full width of the clearing for much longer. Slowly, slowly they inched back either side of the path, forming a tight knot, three, then four, ranks deep, against which the superior weight of the Britons ceased to have a significant impact. Now it became the kind of dense hand-to-hand fighting in which Roman equipment and training excelled, and the thrusts of the short swords began to claim more victims than the unwieldy blades favoured by the natives. Even so, the sheer volume of enemy numbers would eventually guarantee that the legionaries would be overwhelmed. Macro glanced anxiously about the dwindling ranks of his men.

'Keep falling back! Back!'

By the time they reached the edge of the clearing the skirmish was being fought on a narrow front, and the surviving Romans instinctively compacted three shields across the path to provide a solid obstacle to the pursuing Britons.

'Rear five men stay with me!' shouted Macro. 'Cato! Get the others along that track as fast as you can. Head for the river and go downstream.'

'Yes, sir. But what about you?' the optio called out anxiously. 'Sir?'

'We'll be along, Optio. Now go!'

As the rest of the century ran off down the path, Macro looked round at his companions' pale faces and grinned. He thrust his sword out into the mass on the other side of his shield. 'Right, lads! Let's make this one count. They'll not forget the Second Legion in a hurry.'

As he raced down the track, Cato tried not to step on the last man's heels. Every instinct drove him to flee as fast as he could from the sounds of the fight behind. Yet he burned with shame as well, and would have turned and run back to his centurion's side were it not for Macro's express order and the responsibility he now carried for these survivors of the Sixth Century. When the sound of the fighting had grown faint, Cato shouted out an order to halt, and quickly pushed through to the front of the century. He could not trust the man in the lead to pay heed to the location of the moon in relation to the river; he might just blunder off into the marsh.

Having got his bearings, and now no longer able to hear any sound of the centurion's last stand at the clearing, Cato ordered the century to follow him at the trot. It was dangerous to run in the dark, there were too many irregularities in the path and too many twisted roots. Far better to move at a pace they could sustain for a while yet. Jangling and chinking, the legionaries wound their way along the path in the pale moonlight and Cato was relieved to find that the track grew steadily wider and followed a generally straight line – evidence that the track was now manmade and therefore led somewhere.

A distant shout from behind them revealed that the Britons had taken up the chase. Cato extended his stride, snatching at breaths as he pounded along. He frequently glanced back to make sure the men were still with him. All at once he thought he heard what he was searching for: the sound of water rippling along the banks of a river. Then he was sure of the sound.

'The river, lads!' he shouted, gasping hard to draw in enough breath to be heard. 'We've made the river!'

The track twisted slightly to one side and then there it was, the great Tamesis, flowing seaward and glistening with reflected moonlight. The track abruptly spilled out on to a smooth expanse of mud and Cato felt it giving way beneath his feet, sucking at his boots.

'Halt! Halt!' he cried out. 'Stay on the track!'

As the century waited, gasping in the warm air, Cato poked the ground ahead with his sword tip. The blade passed into it with almost no resistance. The shouts on the track were drawing nearer and Cato looked up in terror.

'What the fuck're we going to do, Optio?' someone called out. 'They'll be on us in a minute.'

'Swim for it!' someone suggested.

'No!' Cato replied firmly. 'There's no question of swimming anywhere. It'd be useless. They'd pick us off easily.'

He was gripped by a moment of paralysing indecision, before fresh shouting from the Britons stirred him. This time the shouting came not from the track but much closer, just along the river. He scanned the river bank until he saw a man shouting and jabbing a spear at them. Two more men squelched through the mud to join him. Beyond them, not fifty paces away, was a mass of large shell shapes hauled up from the river's edge.

'There! Boats! Let's go!' Cato shouted. He dragged his foot from the mud and planted it ahead of him where it sank past the ankle and into the grip of the foul, stinking mud. The rest of the century plunged after him and, grunting with desperate exertion, struggled towards the vessels Cato had seen. The slime squelched and sucked at their legs, and the more exhausted stumbled and were almost immersed in the filth. The three Britons watched their approach, shouting out for their comrades at the top of their voices. Glancing back, Cato saw the red glow of the torch weaving towards them and dragged himself on, forcing his legs to push their way through the mud.

Then there was a shout of triumph from behind as their pursuers reached the end of the track and caught sight of their prey stuck in the river mud. Without an instant's hesitation the Britons plunged after them, the torch bearer leading the way. The flickering red glow glimmered off the slick surface of the mud and threw the wavering shadows of Romans and Britons alike far and wide. Every sinew of his heart and body strained as Cato urged himself and his men on, calling on them to hold their shields to the rear in case their pursuers had any throwing spears.

The mud became more shallow and solid underfoot as they reached the three Britons guarding the boats. Cato struggled to get a firm footing in the slippery mud and he made for the nearest of them – an old man in rough clothes and carrying only a hunting spear. He made a two-handed thrust at Cato's body and the optio swiftly parried, deflecting the tip down into the mud, allowing the impetus of the thrust to overbalance the Briton, who was then perfectly positioned for a swift strike to his back. With a deep groan as the air was forced from his lungs, the man went face down into the mud and Cato slithered over the top of him towards the two remaining guards. They were only boys, and one look at the filthy Roman making for them with lips unconsciously drawn back in a snarl was more than enough. Clutching their spears they turned and ran, past the ranks of boats they were supposed to protect and off into the night. For the first time Cato could see the vessels clearly; they were small, wood-framed and skin-covered, and might hold three or four men each. They looked light and flimsy, but they were now the only chance the Sixth Century had of escaping annihilation.

Cato turned round, gasping for breath, and saw that his men were emerging from the deeper mud behind him. A short distance beyond, the British warriors came on, struggling almost knee-deep through the disturbed morass left by their quarry. The torch bearer was doing his best to keep his torch held high, and the flickering glare lit up the faces of the Britons in a terrifying red glow. One of the Romans had waded into deeper mud than his comrades and was being rapidly overhauled by his pursuers.

'Slash the sides of those boats,' Cato shouted to his men. 'But save ten for us!'

The legionaries pressed past him and set about the skin sides of the nearest boats, working quickly along the river bank. Cato stepped back towards the last Roman still struggling through the river mud, now identifiable in the mix of moonlight and the glow of the torch.

'Pyrax! Hurry, man! They're right behind you.'

The veteran glanced quickly over his shoulder as he strained to pull his leg from the mud, but the suction was too great and his last reserves of energy were nearly spent. He tried once again, cursing in accompaniment to his efforts, and with a loud sucking plop the foot came free and he planted it as far ahead of him as he could, shifted his weight and tried to extract his rear foot. But the effort required to make any further progress was too much for him and he stood for a moment, an expression of dread and frustration etched on his face. His eyes met Cato's.

'Come on, Pyrax! Move!' Cato screamed at him in desperation. 'That's an order, soldier!'

Pyrax stared a moment before his face relaxed into a grim smile. 'Sorry, Optio. Guess you'll just have to put me on a charge.'

'Pyrax . . .'

The legionary braced himself as firmly as he could in the mud, and twisted round to face the Britons who were several feet away but struggling forward ferociously to get at him. Appalled, Cato watched from a short distance, quite helpless to intervene, as Pyrax fought his last battle, stuck in the foul-smelling mud, screaming out his defiance to the end. In the orange cast of the torch, Cato saw the first Briton swing his sword at Pyrax's head. Pyrax blocked it with his shield, before thrusting back with his own sword. But the difference in reach between the weapons meant that he could not strike his opponent.

'Come on, you bastards!' Pyrax shouted. 'Come and get me!'

Two spearmen waded in range and thrust at the trapped legionary, aiming for the gaps between his shield and his body. On the third attempt one succeeded and Pyrax cried out as the tip was buried deep in his hip. His guard slipped, the shield dropped to one side and instantly the second spearman thrust into his armpit. Pyrax stood quite still for a moment, then his sword dropped from his hand and he slumped into the mud. He looked towards Cato one last time, head drooping, and blood spurted from his open mouth.

'Run, Cato . . .' he choked.

Then the Britons closed in, hacking and stabbing at Pyrax's body as Cato stood frozen in horror. Then, recovering himself, he turned and ran for his life, slithering over the treacherous mud towards the handful of boats that the rest of the century had pushed into the river. He made for the nearest one, and splashed into the shallows as the first of the Britons pursuing him emerged from the deeper mud, screaming his war cry. Cato dropped his shield and reached for the side of the boat. He gripped it firmly, causing the flimsy craft to tilt dangerously.

'Careful, Optio! You'll have us over.'

He struggled to clamber over the side. The three men already in the boat leaned the opposite way to keep it level and only a little water spilled in as Cato rolled into the bottom, causing the craft to rock alarmingly. Suddenly another pair of hands grasped the side and the boat tipped again, revealing the snarling face of a British warrior, a triumphant gleam in his wild wide eyes. There was a swish through the air and a glint of moonlight on Cato's blade, followed by a soft crunch as the sword cut through the

Briton's hand just below the wrist. The man bellowed with pain; the severed hand splashed into the river and he fell back with it.

'Get us out of here!' shouted Cato. 'Move!'

The legionaries thrust their paddles into the river, straining awkwardly to move the unfamiliar craft away from the river bank. Cato knelt in the stern, watching as the Britons plunged into the river behind him, but the gap between them widened and eventually the enemy gave up, shouting with enraged frustration. Some of the quicker-witted made for the remaining boats, before discovering the tears and rents in the sides that rendered them useless. The gap between Cato's small flotilla and the river bank steadily grew until the Britons were small figures milling about in the shrinking loom of their torch which cast a glittering trail of dancing reflections out towards the Romans.

'What now, Optio?'

'Eh?' Cato turned round, momentarily dazed by their terrible flight.

'Which way should we head, sir?'

Cato frowned at this formal mode of address, before it dawned on him that he was now in command of the century, and it was to him the men would look for order and salvation.

'Downriver,' he muttered, then raised his head towards the other craft. 'Head downriver! Follow us.'

By the light of the moon the string of little craft steadily paddled with the slow current. When the torch on the river bank was finally lost from view round the first bend they came to, Cato slumped down against the side of the boat and let his head roll back, wearily gazing up at the face of the moon. Now that they were out of immediate danger, his first thought was for Macro. What had happened to him?

The centurion had stayed and fought to save his men without a moment's hesitation, as if it was the most natural thing in the world to do. He had bought Cato and the others enough time to escape, but was that at the cost of his life? Cato looked back upriver, wondering if there was any way Macro might have escaped as well. But how? His throat tightened. He cursed himself and struggled to contain his emotions in front of the other men in the boat.

'Hear that?' someone said. 'Stop paddling.'

'What's the matter?' Cato shook himself free of his thoughts.

'Thought I heard trumpets, sir.'

'Trumpets?'

'Yes, sir . . . There! Hear it?'

Cato heard nothing above the lapping of the water and the splash of paddles from the boats behind them. Then, carried upriver on the warm night air, came the faint sound of brass notes. The melody was quite unmistakable to the ears of any legionary. It was the assembly signal of the Roman army.

'They're our trumpets,' muttered Cato.

'Hear that?' the legionary called out to the other boats. 'It's our side, lads!'

The men of the century cheered the sound and bent themselves to their paddles with renewed strength. Cato knew that he really should order them to still their tongues, for the sake of discipline as much as any danger posed by other craft on the river tonight, but a great weight clamped down on his heart. Macro was dead. He could not stifle his feelings and tears rolled down his cheeks, dripping onto his filthy armour. He turned away to hide his grief from the men.

Chapter Twenty-Three

The legion slowly re-formed during the night as men responded to the trumpet calls. They arrived in small groups, centuries and even complete cohorts led by the few senior centurions who had grasped in time the danger the terrain had posed to unit cohesion. Most of the legionaries were dog-tired and covered in mud. They slumped down and rested in the areas marked out for them by the command party. Vespasian had arrived at the crudely built jetty just after sunset, and his small body of officers and guards had waited anxiously beside a large signal fire. At regular intervals through the night the legion's trumpeters had been blasting out the recall and the strain to lungs and lips told in the signal's gradual deterioration.

Separated from the rest of the army and without any auxiliary support, Vespasian felt terribly exposed. Any sizeable enemy force that emerged from the marsh could easily wipe out the command party and his guard century. Every sound from the skirmishes being fought out in the darkness caused him to dread the worst. Even when the men began to trickle back to the legion, the fear that they might be British warriors ratcheted up the tension until the moment that the official challenge was responded to with the correct password. Slowly the bedraggled legionaries emerged from the night and, having found their harbouring area, dropped where they stood and fell asleep.

There was no question of asking the men to erect a marching camp in their present state of exhaustion, and Vespasian had to satisfy himself with a screen of sentries drawn from the legate's guard. The men had to be permitted to rest if the Second was to go back into action on the morrow. Moreover, they must have food, and be re-armed with javelins and other items lost in bitter fighting in the marsh. The baggage train had been sent for, and a detachment of the legion's cavalry was escorting it along the track. Heading back the other way was a column of prisoners guarded by another cavalry squadron. Vespasian had handed this task to Vitellius with orders to proceed directly from the encampment on the far side of the Mead Way to the headquarters of Aulus Plautius. The general needed to be updated on the situation so that he might rethink the attack planned for the following morning. It was an onerous duty for the tribune and not without danger, but Vitellius had, surprisingly, seemed willing enough when the legate had given him his orders, even though he had only just returned from his previous errand. It crossed Vespasian's mind that his senior tribune might well be pleased to be as far from the front line as possible, whatever discomfort that entailed.

As the moon emerged from a low cloud bank, the landscape was bathed in its baleful glow, revealing to the legate the full extent of the legion's poor condition. The exhausted soldiers asleep on all sides gave the appearance of a vast casualty clearing station rather than a legion. Vespasian was momentarily shocked to recall that this was the same unit that so recently had a sparkling parade ground gleam to all its equipment, and an eagerness to get stuck into the enemy radiating from every single man. Though they still numbered in their thousands, it was painful to see how far the ranks of each resting century had been whittled down over the last few weeks of campaigning.

The grinding passage of wagon wheels eventually heralded the arrival of the baggage train, and the headquarters staff moved swiftly into action. The tents of the field hospital were quickly rigged, and the field kitchen set up to make sure that warm food was in the belly of every man as soon as possible. Around Vespasian the clerks hurriedly assembled a headquarters tent, lit numerous oil lamps mounted on great bronze stands, and erected the campaign desks. All the centuries that arrived were ordered to submit strength reports and requests for replacement of expended weapons and lost equipment, before being led to their assigned assembly areas. From his campaign desk the legate watched as the dark files of men slowly passed by. No one saluted, no one looked up. The legion seemed spent as an offensive formation for the immediate future. The only compensating factor was that the enemy were in no state to counterattack, having been thrown back from the last river and forced to scramble into defensive positions on the other side of the Tamesis. However, the time needed by the legionaries to recover their momentum would be well spent by the Britons in preparing for the next bloody phase of the campaign.

These were factors the legate had no influence over, and the best he could do under the present circumstances was to get the Second rested, fed and re-equipped as soon as possible. The men deserved better from the general after their spectacular performance two days ago. Two days? Vespasian frowned. Was that all? Even time itself seemed to have been sucked down into this infernal marsh stretching out around him in the dark . . .

Vespasian's eyes flickered open just in time as he started to slip from his stool, and he recovered his balance with a cold shock of surprise. Instantly he reproached himself, then glanced about to see if anyone had noticed this all too human failing in their commander. The clerks were bent to their work in the glow of their oil lamps, and his bodyguards stood rigidly to attention. Another instant's slumber and he would have fallen from his stool and ended up sprawled on the ground. The image made him burn with shame, and he forced himself to stand.

'Bring me some food!' he snapped to an orderly. 'And quick about it.'

The orderly saluted and ran off towards the field kitchen. Vespasian turned his mind to another worrying detail of the campaign. One of the centurions emerging from the marsh had presented him with a short sword. Nothing remarkable in that, but the centurion had encountered a large formation of Britons armed with identical swords.

'See there, sir.' The centurion held the blade up so that it was more clearly visible in the moonlight. Vespasian looked closely and saw the manufacturer's stamp.

'Gnaeus Albinus,' he muttered. 'That's a firm in Gaul, I believe. This sword's a long way from home.'

'Yes, sir. That's right.' The centurion nodded politely. 'But that's not all, sir. The Albinus forge is one of the main suppliers to the Rhine legions.'

'And the arms contracts are exclusive. So what is this doing here?'

'And not just this one sword. I saw scores of them back in the marsh, sir. And since we're the first Roman army on these shores since Caesar's day, they can hardly have been captured.'

'So, what are you suggesting, Centurion? That the Albini

are moonlighting on an imperial arms contract?'

'Doubt it, sir.'

The grievous penalties for such an act made this very unlikely. The centurion shrugged, then continued in a meaningful tone, 'But if not the manufacturers, then it has to be someone further down the line.'

'You mean someone in the army, or in the civil service?'

'Maybe.'

Vespasian looked at him. 'That's as far as you want to pursue the matter, I presume.'

'I'm a soldier, sir,' the centurion replied firmly. 'I do what I'm ordered to do, and I'll fight who I have to. This is nothing to do with soldiering. It stinks of politics and plots, sir.'

'Meaning you think I should be the one to look into it.'

'Goes with the rank, sir.'

The reference to rank implied social class as well as military title, and Vespasian had to bite back the bitter retort that had been his first response. The centurion was speaking no more than the truth. The man had served for most of his life under the eagles and no doubt had a healthy disdain for the deviousness of the political class from which the legions' legates were drawn. Vespasian, peculiarly driven to win the acceptance and admiration of those under his command, was wounded by the professional soldier's slight. He had hoped to have won their trust by now, but some of the men clearly still had their misgivings. Today's fiasco in the marsh had been the result of orders received from the general, but it would be the legate the soldiers blamed first.

There was nothing to be done about this. It would be an unconscionable display of personal weakness to explain to any of his subordinates the limits of his authority, that he was compelled to obey orders, just as they were. High command placed a man at the heart of an irresolvable dilemma. To his general he was responsible for the actions of his men. To the men he was responsible for the orders he was compelled to pass on to them. No excuses would be tolerated by either side, and any attempt at self-justification would arouse only humiliating contempt and disgust from superiors and subordinates alike.

'I'll see to it then, Centurion. You're dismissed.'

The centurion nodded his satisfaction, saluted and strode off back to his men. Vespasian watched him disappear into the gloom, reproaching himself for letting the man witness his distraction. He must be stoical about such things. Besides, there was a far more important issue to be considered. Far more important than the self-pity of a legate, he chided himself. The presence of these swords and the earlier discovery of army issue slingshot amongst the ammunition used by the Britons formed a disturbing pattern. The odd weapon might be accounted for by the looting of dead Romans but what the centurion had told him indicated something more. Someone was supplying the enemy with arms that had been destined for the legions. Someone with money, and a network of agents to handle the movement of substantial cargoes. But who?

'This will do nicely,' Vitellius said to the decurion. 'We'll rest here for a moment. You can water the horses.'

The column of prisoners and their mounted guards had reached a point on the track where it dipped into a small copse beside a narrow stream.

'Here, sir?' The decurion glanced about at the dark undergrowth hemming them in. He continued as tactfully as he could. 'Do you think that's wise, sir?' Ordinarily no officer in his right mind would ever consider stopping a column of prisoners in surroundings that were so conducive to escape.

'Do you think it's wise to question my order?' Vitellius replied curtly.

The decurion quickly turned in his saddle and filled his lungs. 'Column – halt!'

He ordered the prisoners to sit and arranged for the guards to see to their horses in a hurried rota, while Vitellius dismounted and tethered his beast to a tree stump at the head of a trail that ran alongside the stream.

'Decurion!'

'Sir?' The decurion trotted back towards the stream.

'Get me that chieftain. I fancy it's time I tried having another quiet word with him.'

'Sir?'

'You've been warned about questioning my orders, Decurion,' Vitellius said coldly. 'Once more, and you won't forget it. Now get me that man, and tend to your other duties.'

The gaudily attired Briton was hauled to his feet and thrust towards the tribune. He stared at the Roman officer with an arrogant sneer. Vitellius stared back, then suddenly whipped the back of his hand across the Briton's face. The man's head snapped to one side, and when he brought his face forward once again, a dark trickle of blood, black in the moonlight, was dripping from a cut lip.

'Roman,' he muttered in a coarse accent. 'If I ever get rid of these chains . . .'

'You won't,' sneered Vitellius. 'Consider them an extension of your body, for whatever is left of your life.' He struck the prisoner again, slamming his fist into the man's midriff, causing him to double over and gasp for air.

'I don't think he's going to cause me any trouble now,

Decurion. Continue watering the horses until we get back.'

'Back from . . . Yes, sir.'

Vitellius grasped the leather thongs between Briton's iron wrist collars and roughly hauled him down the trail, dragging him savagely when he stumbled. When they had turned a corner and were out of sight and earshot of the column of prisoners, Vitellius stopped and pulled the man upright.

'You can stop the acting now, I didn't hit you that hard.'

'Hard enough, Roman,' the Briton grunted. 'And if we ever meet again, you'll pay for that blow.'

'Then I must make sure we don't meet again,' replied Vitellius, and drew his dagger. He raised the tip so that it was poised barely a finger's breadth from the Briton's throat. The Briton showed no sign of fear, merely a cold contempt for an enemy who would do such an unmanly thing as threaten a bound prisoner. Vitellius sniffed at the other's expression. Then the blade dropped and he sawed briefly at the thongs until they parted. He stepped back from the freed Briton.

'You're sure you remember the message?'

'Yes.'

'Good. I'll send a man to you when I'm ready. Now then.' Vitellius flipped the dagger and caught it by the blade, handle towards the other man. 'Make it look good.'

The Briton took the knife and slowly smiled, then suddenly smashed the tribune in the face with his spare hand. With a grunt the tribune dropped to his knees, only to be hauled up, spun round and have the tip of the blade jabbed into the small of his back.

'Easy there!' he whispered.

'This has to look convincing, remember?'

With one arm locked round the tribune's throat and the other holding the dagger to the back of his erstwhile captor, the Briton pushed him back up the trail towards the column.

As soon as the decurion was aware of his superior's plight, he scrambled to his feet.

'To arms!'

'Hold back!' Vitellius managed to choke out. 'Or he'll kill me!'

The decurion waved his arms at the cavalrymen rushing up with spears levelled for action. 'Stop! He's got the tribune.'

'The horse!' shouted the British chieftain. 'Get me his horse. *Now!* Or he dies.'

Vitellius yelped as the point bit into his flesh. At the sound the decurion hurried across to the horse and untethered it, offering the reins to the Briton.

The other Britons had risen to their feet at the sight of the confrontation and were surging forward for a better view, some shouting encouragement.

'Get them back on the ground!' bellowed the decurion and after a moment of hesitation the cavalrymen herded their prisoners back.

The chieftain didn't waste the chance. With a kick and a thrust he hurled Vitellius on top of the decurion, grabbed the reins and leaped onto the horse. He folded low on the animal's back and with a savage kick spurred it back down the trail. By the time the decurion had returned to his feet, the Briton had rounded the corner and was gone, only the fading sound of the horse's hoofbeats lingering. The other Britons cheered.

'Shut that lot up!' roared the decurion, before turning to help Vitellius back to his feet. He seemed shaken and scared, but unharmed beyond that.

'Close escape, sir.'

'For him or for me?' Vitellius responded bitterly. The decurion was just smart enough not to reply.

'Want me to go after him, sir?'

'No. No point. He probably knows his way in the dark better than us. Besides, we can't afford to send any of the guards off on some wild chase. No, I'm afraid he's got clean away.'

'Perhaps he'll run into some of our men,' the decurion said hopefully.

'I doubt it.'

'Shame about your horse, sir.'

'Yes, one of my better mounts. Still, there's no need to worry about me, Decurion. I'll have your horse until we reach the camp.'

Chapter Twenty-Four

Macro . . .

Cato had been trying to avoid all thought of the centurion's fate. Macro was probably dead. Pyrax was dead. Many of his comrades in the Sixth Century were dead. But the thought of Macro lying cold and still out there in the marshes was impossible to accept. Although a cold, logical part of his mind reiterated that Macro could not have escaped death, Cato found himself imagining all kinds of ways in which he could have survived. He might be out there now, injured or unconscious, helpless, waiting for his comrades to come and find him. He might even have been taken prisoner. But then, the image of the slaughtered Batavians flashed before Cato's mind. There would be no prisoners, no sparing of the wounded.

The optio sat up and rested his arms on his knees. He gazed at the remains of the century sleeping around him. Of the eighty men who had disembarked from the invasion fleet, only thirty-six remained. Another dozen were injured and might be expected to return to duty over the next weeks. That meant the century had lost over thirty dead in the last ten days.

Cato was acting centurion for the moment – until the headquarters staff merged the century with another, or received replacements to bring it back up to strength. Either way Cato would not be in command for more than a few days. For that he was thankful, even as he despised himself for feeling relieved by the prospect of surrendering his authority. Though he felt he had grown into manhood over this last year, there was still a residual anxiety that he had not developed the special qualities that qualified a man for command. He would be a poor replacement for Macro, and he knew that the men would share that view. Until he reverted to the status of optio he would try his best to lead them as well as he could, following in the bold striding footsteps of Macro.

Earlier that night, when Cato and his small flotilla had emerged from the river, they had alarmed the sentries who had not been expecting any Romans to arrive from that direction. Anticipating such a reaction, Cato had responded quickly and loudly to the sentry's challenge. After the bedraggled soldiers had clambered from the muddy shore-line into the camp, safe at last, Cato had been escorted to the headquarters tent to make his report.

A mass of lamps and small fires marked the location of the Second Legion's headquarters, while all around stretched the long dark lines of the resting soldiers. Cato was shown into a large tent within which clerks pored over their paperwork on long trestle tables. One of them beckoned to him and Cato stepped forward.

'Unit?' The clerk looked up from his scroll, pen poised above the inkwell.

'Sixth Century, Fourth Cohort.'

'Ah! Macro's lot.' The clerk dipped his pen and started to write. 'Where is he?'

'I don't know. Still somewhere in the marsh.'

'What happened?'

Cato tried to explain in a way that left open the question of Macro's fate, but the clerk shook his head sadly as he regarded the youngster standing before him. 'Are you his optio?'

Cato nodded.

'Well, you aren't any more then. You're acting centurion until further notice. What's your strength?'

'Thirty odd of us left, I think,' replied Cato.

'Exactly, please,' said the clerk. Then he looked up and saw that the young soldier was at the end of his tether, eyes red and head drooping even as he stood there. The clerk continued in a more kindly tone, 'Sir, I need the exact number, please.'

This gentle reminder of his new responsibility caused Cato to straighten up and focus his mind.

'Thirty-six. I've got thirty-six men left.'

As the clerk took down the details, a flap at the rear of the tent parted, and the legate entered. He handed a small scrap of parchment to a staff officer and was turning to leave when he caught sight of Cato and paused.

'Optio!' he called out as he made his way over. 'How goes it? You just rejoined us?'

'Yes, sir.'

'It's been quite a night, hasn't it?'

'Yes, sir, quite a night.'

Something in the lad's tone went beyond weariness, and looking more closely Vespasian could see that Cato was struggling to control his emotions. And to bear the pain, Vespasian thought, as he caught sight of the terrible blisters running down the lad's arm.

'It's been a hard day for us all, Optio. But we're still here.'

'My centurion isn't . . .'

'Macro? Macro's dead?'

Simon Scarrow

'I don't know, sir,' Cato replied slowly. 'I think so.'

'That's too bad. Too bad.' Vespasian shifted uneasily at the news, torn between expressing genuine regret and maintaining the image of imperturbability he was trying so hard to project. 'He was a good man, a good soldier. Would have been a good senior centurion in time. I'm sorry. You admired him, didn't you?'

'Yes, sir.' Cato felt his throat tighten.

'See to it that your men get some food and rest. Off you go.'

The young man saluted and was about to turn and leave when Vespasian added quietly, 'Don't let grief cloud your judgement, son. We've got hard days ahead of us, and I don't want you throwing your life away on some quest for revenge. Your men will be looking to you now.'

Chapter Twenty-Five

'Are you sure about this?'

Vitellius nodded.

'And you briefed him fully on our condition?'

'Yes, sir. I told him everything.'

Vespasian read the dispatch from Aulus Plautius again, in case he had missed some nuance that would allow him to make a case for rescinding the order. But there was nothing. For once, the clerks at the general's headquarters had expunged every ambiguity and produced a set of orders with the kind of terse elegance that would have compared favourably with Caesar's commentaries. In a brief paragraph the Second Legion was ordered to board transports provided by the navy and make a landing on the far side of the Tamesis. One warship was deemed all that was necessary to provide fire support for the operation. The Second Legion was to seize control of the river bank and establish a bridgehead. If successful, Vespasian would be reinforced by elements of the Ninth Legion.

'Madness!' Vespasian grumbled and tossed the dispatch onto his travel desk. 'Complete madness. We're not in any fit condition to carry this out. Some of the men are still out there in the marsh, and those who have returned to the eagle . . . What the hell does Plautius think we're made of?'

'Do you want me to ride back and try and change his mind, sir?'

Vespasian looked up sharply. He was about to launch into an attack on the tribune for taking every opportunity to undermine him when he noticed Vitellius' exhausted stoop. The tribune was worn out and seemed well past exercising his usual guile. The man needed a rest and in any case it would be pointless sending him back to argue the case with the general. The orders had been issued and Vespasian was obliged to carry them out with whatever resources he had available to him. Any attempt to prevaricate or delay would damage his reputation. He could well imagine the senators in Rome tutting if word reached them that he had been reluctant to throw his troops across the river. Those who had experience in the field would exchange knowing looks, and mutter darkly about his lack of resolve; they might even go so far as to quietly attribute it to cowardice. Vespasian flushed angrily at the thought.

There would be bitter feeling among the men when they were told about the proposed assault. After the battle on the Mead Way, yesterday's deadly games of cat and mouse in the marshes, and now this forlorn hope against yet another defended shore, memories of the recent mutiny back in Gesoriacum were bound to be stirred up. If it had not been for Narcissus' ruthless elimination of the leaders of the mutiny, the invasion of Britain would never have been launched and, worse, the authority of the Emperor would have been fatally undermined. It was bad enough having the likes of the Liberators working against Claudius without his army commanders unwittingly fuelling the dissent of the lower ranks. If the Second Legion refused the order to cross the Tamesis, how long would it take for news of it to spread to the other legions? No more than two days at the very most.

And the orders were clear. There was no leeway for interpretation at all. Vespasian would just have to trust the judgement of his superior even as he feared the consequences of doing so. With a bitter sigh of resignation he glanced up at this senior tribune, determined to restore his reputation as the kind of commander who stopped at nothing in the pursuit of his orders.

'Inform the staff officers first. They're going to be busy for the next few hours. I'll speak to the centurions once the plan is ready. I want the men to be well fed – if the landing succeeds, it might be a while before they next get a proper meal. See that the field kitchen issues double rations; any more than that and they'll sink the transports.'

It was a feeble joke but Vitellius managed a brief smile before he saluted and left the legate's tent. Vespasian slumped down onto his stool and cursed Plautius with all the vehemence that his frustration and despair could muster. He was well aware how much his mood was determined by his exhausted state: when was the last time he had slept? Two days ago, and then only a brief rest between the attack on the river fortifications and giving the orders for this latest phase of the advance. His body ached, his eyes stung, and it took some force of effort to focus his mind. From some insidious recess of his brain emerged the desire to shut his eyes for just a moment, no more. Just a moment to clear the stinging sensation. The suggestion was no sooner made than his eyelids closed and his body surrendered to the warm wave of relaxation that he permitted it. A few moments, no more, he reminded himself dimly.

'Sir!' Someone was shaking his shoulder gently. In an instant Vespasian was fully awake, and aware of what had happened. He silently raged against himself. The orderly who had woken him backed off respectfully before his thunderous expression. How long had he been asleep? He dare not ask the orderly, who would suspect an all too human weakness in his legate. Looking beyond the fellow, Vespasian saw a dull glow rimming the bottom of the tent and filtering through the chinks in the closed tent flaps. Not so long after daybreak then. By that much his shame was assuaged.

'Are my officers assembled?'

'Yes, sir. They're waiting for you in the staff tent. Some still haven't returned from the marsh, but I'll send them to you as soon as they reach the legion, sir.'

'Very good. Now leave me.'

The orderly saluted and silently disappeared between the tent flaps. Vespasian instantly slammed his fist down on his leg and swore at himself in bitter self-reproach. To fall asleep at such a moment! To have given in to such a weakness when his reputation and that of his legion was to be tested to the utmost. It was unforgivable, and he fervently resolved never to let it happen again. He stood up, straightened his tunic, and crossed to the small pitcher and bronze bowl in the corner. He emptied the contents of the pitcher over his head. The water had been refilled directly from the river during the night and was still refreshing enough to help his senses return to a more conscious state. He straightened up and dried himself, smoothing the wet hair back into place with his hands. A quick glance in the polished bronze mirror revealed a three-day growth of stubble that rasped on his palm as he rubbed his cheek. The stubble, the hollow eyes and his drawn expression combined to make him look like one of the poor wretches that begged from the gutters outside the Circus Maximus in Rome. But there was no time for cosmetic adjustment, and he consoled himself with the thought that his staff officers would look just as unkempt.

Lifting the flap of his tent, Vespasian saw that the sunrise was well advanced; the pale orange disc hung just above the horizon, faintly shrouded by wisping smoke from the dying campfires. Some of the men were already talking and coughing in the cool dawn air, while the centurions and their optios began to rouse the rest. The reluctance of the men to bestir themselves and begin the daily routine of legionary life was palpable, and Vespasian made himself greet the men cheerfully as he passed by.

The assembled centurions and tribunes of the legion rose stiffly to their feet as Vespasian entered the headquarters tent. He waved them back to their stools. It was then that he noticed Vitellius, clean-shaven and dressed in a crisp new tunic. Although the man looked tired, the contrast with the other officers and himself was striking and the old antagonism for Vitellius bloomed in his heart.

'No time for ceremony, I'm afraid, gentlemen,' Vespasian said as he leaned across the map table, resting on spread fingers. 'The general's decided to keep the battle rolling forward, and we get to play the leading part once again.'

Although the tribunes had suspected bad news they still could not help groaning with dismay at the prospect of further action.

'Before anyone asks, the general is aware of our condition, and the order to attack stands.'

'Why us, sir?' asked Tribune Plinius.

'Because we're here, Plinius. Simple as that.'

'But the Twentieth have hardly been scratched,' Plinius persisted with a bitter tone that evidently reflected the mood of the other officers, many of whom nodded and muttered in agreement. Vespasian heartily shared their grievance, especially after what the Second Legion had been through recently, and everything they had achieved.

181

But his rank demanded a stoic acceptance of orders.

'The Twentieth are being held in reserve. Plautius wants to keep one unit intact to meet any counterattacks, and to spearhead any advance we might make.' That was true enough, Vespasian reflected: he did not mention that the Second was being used to wear the enemy down. Attrition was a hard tactic to stomach when the numbers being whittled down were your own men.

Tribune Plinius was not yet mollified. '*If* there is an advance,' he said angrily. 'At this rate, sir, we'll all be dead before the Twentieth loses a man.'

'Maybe. Maybe not. But the orders will be obeyed, Tribune,' Vespasian replied firmly. 'If there's any man here who wants no part in this I'll willingly accept his resignation . . . after the assault.'

Subdued laughter rippled round the tent, and the tribune blushed.

'Right then, gentlemen. Down to details.'

The light mood quickly died away and the centurions and tribunes focused their attention on Vespasian.

'We should be joined by the navy early this morning. The general has supplied a trireme to provide covering fire for the landing, and ten transports to convey the legion across the Tamesis. As the sharper ones among you will have calculated, it's going to take us three journeys to get what's left of the legion across. And that means the first wave must hold the landing ground until the other waves can be fed into the fight. There will be no chance of retreat if things go badly – the transports will be heading back for the next wave.' Vespasian paused to let the point sink in. 'As you gentlemen will appreciate, the first wave might well be wiped out. Now, I don't want to order anyone into the first transports to cross, so I'll ask for volunteers.' He looked up and quickly glanced round the room. Some officers avoided his gaze while others shuffled nervously. Vespasian's eyes came to rest on an arm raised at the rear of the tent, held straight in the air. The light inside the tent was still dim and the legate's tired eyes could not make out the identity of the officer.

'Stand up!'

The officer rose to his feet, amidst the astonished murmurs of the others.

'Are you volunteering for the first wave?' Vespasian asked, barely keeping the surprise from his voice.

'Yes, sir. First vessel of the first wave.'

'And you think your men are up to it?'

'Yes, sir. They're ready, and they want revenge.'

'Then they shall have it, acting Centurion. But do you think you are the man to lead them on this assault?'

Cato flushed angrily. 'I am, sir.'

Vespasian smiled grimly at the youngster's determination to avenge his centurion. There was no doubting his courage, but leaders needed to be above personal motivation in the heat of battle. Could this boy be relied upon to put duty before revenge? Or would he just hurl himself upon the enemy and fight like a fury until he was killed, heedless of his responsibility to the men under his command? Vespasian weighed up the situation and came to a quick decision. The first wave would have little time to co-ordinate a defence of the landing point and he might as well make best use of whatever battle frenzy came his way.

'Very well, acting Centurion. And good luck. Any others ready to join him?'

Cato's instant response had shamed the veterans, and almost to a man they raised their arms.

'Good,' said the legate. 'Your final orders will be with you after the legion has been fed. Now you'd best ready your men and let them know what Rome wants for its money today.'

As the officers filed out of the tent, Vespasian caught Cato's eye and raised a finger to beckon him over.

'Sir?'

'Are you sure about this?'

When Cato nodded, Vespasian leaned closer so that his words would not be overheard by the men leaving the tent. 'It's not necessary for you to lead the attack. You and your men must be exhausted, and you're injured.'

'I'll live,' Cato muttered. 'We are tired, sir. And there aren't many of us left in the century. But that's no different to any other century, sir. The difference is we've got more reason to fight than most. I think I can speak for Macro's men on this.'

'They're your men now, son.'

'Yes, sir.' Cato stiffened and raised his chin.

'Good man!' Vespasian said approvingly. 'And make sure you look after yourself, young Cato. There's the promise of great things in you. Survive this and you can survive anything.'

'Yes, sir.'

'Now go. I'll see you later, on the other side of the river.'

Cato saluted and followed the other officers out of the tent.

As he watched the young man leave, Vespasian felt a pang of guilt. It was true the lad showed promise, and the cheap rhetoric he had offered had worked, as he knew it would. The optio – the acting centurion, Vespasian corrected himself – would feel fired by his superior's confidence in him. But it would probably get him killed that much more quickly. It was too bad. The lad was likeable and had performed well enough in the short time he had served with the eagles. But that was the nature of command. Regardless of one's feelings, the battle had to be won, the enemy defeated, and both had their price – measured in the blood of the men in his legion.

Chapter Twenty-Six

The sun beat down on the men packed into the wide-beamed transport. The wool tunics under the heavy armour made the men sweat and the damp material clung uncomfortably to their skin. The resulting odour, combined with the residue of the marsh, made the air aboard the transport foetid to the point of nausea. The heat, the fear and nervous exhaustion had combined to make some of the men throw up, adding the stink of their vomit to the other odours.

Over the side, the Tamesis drifted glassily by, disturbed only by the monotonous splash and gurgling churn from the long sweeps at the bow and stern of the transport as the crew strained to keep the vessel in line with the warship directly ahead. In perfect unison the great oars of the trireme rose from the surface of the river, shedding glistening cascades of water, then swept forward before plunging back into the river to lever the beaked prow on towards the far bank.

From the small foredeck of the transport Cato scanned the massed ranks of the enemy waiting to receive them. All morning the Britons had been gathering in response to the assault being prepared in their full view on the Roman side of the Tamesis. The assembling of the transports and the warship, and the dense mass of legionaries preparing to embark made the latest plans of General Plautius obvious for all to see. And so the handful of British cavalry scouts had hurried off to spread word of the impending river assault. The dispersed ranks of Caratacus' army quickly re-formed and made their way down towards the river bank opposite the Roman ships.

The assault had already been delayed by the need to unload the supplies carried by the transports, and the legionaries had fumed as they manhandled the unwieldy cargo onto the crude jetty and hauled it out of the way. While they laboured, more and more Britons arrived to reinforce the far bank. For those in the first wave the prospect of facing ever greater odds caused them to fret and swear at their comrades engaged in unloading the transports, urging them to finish the job more quickly.

The first transport was still some way from the bank when the Britons gave voice to their war cry, a note that rose to a crescendo and then dipped, then rose again. To Cato's unpractised eye the enemy seemed to number several thousand but any exact estimation of the seething mass was impossible. What was obvious was that the enemy greatly outnumbered the men in the first wave of the Second Legion and the rising volume of their challenge was unnerving. Turning his back to them, Cato forced himself to shake his head and smile.

'Musical lot, aren't they?' he said to the nearest men of his century and jerked a thumb over his shoulder. 'Be a different tune a little later.'

One or two men smiled back but most just looked resigned, or were struggling to conceal the fear that caused them to exhibit all manner of telltale nervous gestures. A few hours earlier these same men had seemed keen enough to avenge their centurion, but the aspirations produced by rage, Cato realised, tended to be greatly moderated by the imminent prospect of putting them into effect. As he stood above them, Cato could see that most of the men were looking at him, and the sudden sensation of being judged weighed heavily upon him. He knew that even now some of them still resented his appointment as their optio.

This was the moment when Macro would have offered them some last words of encouragement before they went into action. A number of quotable phrases rushed into his mind from all the histories he had read, but none seemed appropriate and, worse, none seemed to be the kind of thing that a young man could say without sounding hopelessly pretentious.

For a moment the legionaries and their acting centurion faced each other in a silence that grew steadily more awkward. Cato glanced over his shoulder and could clearly make out the features of individual Britons now. Whatever he said, he had to say it quickly. He cleared his voice.

'I-I know the centurion would have something good to say to you right now. Truth is, I wish he was here to say it. But Macro's gone, and I know I can't fill his boots. We've got this chance to make them pay for taking him from us, and I aim to see that plenty of them get to keep him company in Hell.'

A number of men cheered the sentiment, and Cato felt some sort of connection was being established between himself and these hardened veterans.

'That said, Charon doesn't give a discount for job lots, so save your money and stay alive!'

A poor joke, but for men in danger of losing their lives even the slightest light relief is prized.

Something splashed into the water close by the transport and Cato turned towards the sound just as a scattered volley of slingshot rattled off the prow and chopped up the smooth surface of the river.

'Helmets on!' Cato shouted and quickly fastened his chin strap, ducking down below the bulwark on the foredeck. Ahead, the trireme turned upriver and let the way pay off before dropping anchor. The first transport slipped under its stern and made for the river bank a hundred paces beyond. The slingshot continued to strike the vessel, but the boat crew and the legionaries crouched low enough to render the volley harmless.

'Easy on the oars!' the transport's captain bellowed and the men on the sweeps rested on their handles, waiting for the other transports to close up and form a line so that they would all reach the bank at the same time and not land their troops in a piecemeal fashion. Under fire from slingers and archers, the clumsy transports manoeuvred into position and waited for the trireme to commence bombarding the enemy massed on the river bank.

A sudden series of loud cracks split the air as the torsion arms of the bolt-throwers were released, and the heavy iron arrows shot towards the Britons on the bank. Swirls in their ranks marked the passage of the bolts, and the screams and shrieks of the wounded were added to the sound of their war cry. Moments later the auxiliary archers on the trireme began to add their volleys to the bombardment, and the scantily armoured among the Britons fell like leaves. As the support fire began to clear gaps on the bank, the captain of the lead transport gave the signal for the assault to begin and the crewmen bent themselves to their sweeps. The transports moved forward and the legionaries aboard raised their shields overhead against a hail of slingshot and arrows. The crew were afforded no protection, and as the lead transport neared the bank the port-side sweep dropped into the river as both of the crewmen went down; one hit by two arrows lay howling on the deck, while his comrade lay still, killed by a slingshot bursting through an eye into his brain. At once the drag on the port sweep began to pull the bows round. Seeing the danger, Cato dropped his shield and javelin and grabbed at the loose handle, dragging the oar blade from the river. Unused to the unwieldy sweep, he struggled to keep the prow of the transport in line with the bank, as slingshot rattled off the bow and arrows struck the deck with a splintering thwack.

He risked a look over the side and saw that the bank was close by; any moment the transport would ground and the assault would begin. A sudden dragging sensation indicated that the keel had made contact with the shallows of the river bed. The transport stopped moving forward and the captain ordered the crew to take cover. Cato dropped the handle and retrieved his shield and javelin, conscious that all eyes of the century were directed at him.

'Remember, lads,' he shouted, 'this one's for Macro . . . Ready javelins!'

The men rose to their feet and the first few moved up to the foredeck, ready to hurl their javelins.

'Release at will!'

The rest of the century fed their javelins forward to those on the foredeck and a steady fire brought down more of the enemy until the supply was exhausted. Cato looked round and saw that the trireme had ceased fire.

Now was the moment.

For an instant his mind began to weigh up the terrible risks and absurdity of what he was about to do, and he knew that if he delayed any longer his courage would fail him. He tensed and sprang over the transport's side, screaming for the others to follow him. The water was chest deep and his boots slipped into the soft silt of the river bottom. Around him the rest of the century splashed down and then they surged forward towards the bank.

'Come on! Come on!' Cato shouted above the din.

The Britons knew that this fight must be won before the Romans could secure a foothold on the bank, and plunged into the river to meet the attack. The two sides crashed headlong into each other, close to the transports. A huge man surged through the water making straight for Cato, spear raised high above his head, ready to strike. Cato threw his shield forward when the blow came, and knocked the spear to one side. The counterstrike was executed with a precision that would have made Centurion Bestia proud, and the dead centurion's ivory-handled sword plunged deep into the Briton's side. Cato ripped it free just in time to slash at the head of the next enemy. He fought his way to the shore foot by foot, teeth locked tight as an inhuman howl in his throat challenged all who stood in his way. The churned-up water flashed white and silver in the bright sunlight, and specks of crimson splashed up and sparkled like rubies before spattering down on the combatants.

The water about Cato's legs turned a muddy red as more Romans struggled through the shallows and attempted to link with legionaries who had landed moments before. Already the transports were being pushed back into the river and were making for the second assault wave as fast as the sweeps could be worked. Cato and the others were on their own until the next wave could join the battle, and the only thing that mattered was to live until that moment. He was only ankle-deep in the water now, and had to take care not to slip in the mud. He blocked with his shield and thrust with his sword in a steady rhythm, gritting his teeth against the pain from his burns. The rest of the century fought close by, forming a shield wall automatically as years of relentless training bore fruit. The initial mad scramble was over and the fight began to take a form more familiar to the Romans.

'Move left, with me!' Cato called out as he saw the nearest men from one of the other transports. Slowly, his century edged forward, onto the flattened grass of the river bank and began to sidestep towards their comrades. All the while the Britons hacked at their shields with sword, axe and spear. With a sharp cry the man next to Cato went down as the bloody tip of a wickedly barbed spear burst through his calf. With a vicious wrench the Briton at the end of the spear pulled it back and the legionary fell onto his back, screaming. The century closed up and moved on, their comrade's cries cut short as the Britons quickly butchered him. Little by little the small clusters of legionaries fell in with each other until they were able to form a solid line of four or five hundred men. And yet the Britons still swarmed around them in their thousands, desperately trying to push them back into the river.

'Steady, lads!' Cato shouted again and again as he cut and thrust at any faces and bodies that came within reach of his sword. The shield he presented to the enemy shuddered and thudded with the impact of their blows; a waste of effort and indicative of the poor training of these British levies who fought with unguided rage and simply attacked whatever part of the invader that fell before their weapons. But what the Britons lacked in quality they made up for in quantity, and although the ground was littered with their dead and dying, they came on as if they were possessed by demons. And maybe they were. A glance over their ranks revealed to Cato a scattered line of strangely garbed men with wild beards, urging the Britons on with arms raised imploringly to the heavens, and screaming savage curses. With a thrill of horror Cato realised these men must be Druids, tales of whose exploits were told to terrify Roman children.

But there was time for only the briefest of glances before he had to deal with the next crisis. A body of Britons, better armed and more determined than their comrades, suddenly confronted the Sixth Century and forced them back into the river. Several of Cato's men were down, some knocked over, others losing their balance in the slippery mud, and suddenly the shield wall was breaking apart. Before Cato could rally his men, he was aware of a presence at his side. He just had time to glance right and glimpse the snarling face of a black-haired Briton before the man slammed into his side and both men went tumbling into the shallows of the river.

A blinding flash of the sun. Then an instant of glittering spray and the world went dark before Cato's eyes. Water filled his mouth and lungs as he instinctively gasped for the next breath. The Briton was still on top of him, hands frantically fumbling for his throat. Cato had dropped his sword and shield as he fell; he grabbed at his attacker, trying to use the man to haul himself up out of the water, strangely devoid of the sounds of battle. But the Briton had a powerful physique, and firmly held him down. The agonised desire for air and the imminence of his death lent Cato a reserve of desperate strength. His hands groped for the man's face and his fingers thrust into the Briton's eyes. Abruptly the man released his grip on Cato's neck and Cato burst to the surface, spluttering water and gasping for breath. He kept his fingers clamped on the man's face and the Briton shrieked with pain, clawing at Cato's arms before some instinct made him smash a fist down at his opponent. The blow struck Cato's cheek and the world went white an instant before he was back under water with the weight of the man on top of him again.

This time Cato thought he must surely drown. His head felt as if it would burst, and his frantic writhing achieved nothing. He stared at the silvery surface of the water. The life-giving air, a scant foot away, might just as well have been a mile off, and as his world began to dim, Cato's last thought was of Macro: regret that he had failed to avenge the centurion. Then the water turned red and the sunlight was dimmed by thick blood. The Briton's hands still grasped him by the throat, but now another hand reached down through the water, grabbed his harness and yanked him up into the brilliant sunshine. Cato burst from the surface through a pool of red and filled his burning lungs with air. Then he saw the body of the Briton. The head was almost severed, only some gristle and sinew attaching it to the torso.

'All right?' asked the legionary holding his harness, and Cato managed to nod as he gulped down more breaths. A small band of men from the century stood guard about them and fended off blows from the nearest Britons.

'My sword?'

'Here you are, sir.' The legionary fished it out. 'Nice blade, that. You ought to look after it.'

Cato nodded. 'Thanks.'

'All right, sir. Century can't afford to lose more than one centurion a day.'

With a final shake to clear his head, Cato retrieved his shield and raised his sword. The pace of the fight had noticeably slackened as exhaustion took its toll. Neither Romans nor Britons seemed as keen for martyrdom as they had a while before, and in places small groups faced each other, each waiting for the other to make a move. Glancing back across the river, Cato saw that the second wave had almost finished embarking on the transports.

'Not long now, lads!' he called out, coughing with the effort of shouting with water still lodged in his lungs. 'The next wave's on its way!'

A series of thumping cracks from the trireme drew his attention, and as his eyes followed the arc of the bolts he saw a fresh column of British warriors approaching along the river bank. In the middle of the column was a chariot, ornate even by native standards, upon which stood a tall chief with long, flowing blond hair. He raised his spear and called out, and his men answered with a deep-throated roar. Something about their attire and the confident way they ignored the missiles from the ship was horribly familiar.

'Are those the bastards that jumped us last night?'

'Could be.' The legionary squinted. 'I didn't stay around long enough to memorise the details.'

The Druids had been working themselves up into a frenzy as they tried to drive their reluctant levies back onto the first wave of Romans. As they caught sight of the new column, they shrieked with delight and urged their men on with renewed ferocity.

'Heads up, lads! New enemy on the left flank!'

The word was quickly passed down the line and the centurion nearest the new threat swiftly organised his men into a flank guard, closing up on the remainder of the first wave – just in time, as the fresh arrivals didn't even attempt to deploy but just broke into a wild charge and hurled themselves at the Roman line. With a savage cry and sharp ringing of weapons the Britons hacked their way in among the Romans and it was clear to all that the fight was flowing in favour of the natives.

An anxious glance towards the river showed Cato that the first of the transports had set off, sweeps working furiously to gain the opposite bank. The war cry of the fresh troops and the exhortations of the Druids rekindled the fighting spirit of the levies who once more charged the Roman shields.

'Hold them back!' Cato cried. 'Just a little longer! Hold them!'

The remains of the Sixth Century closed up with a handful of other legionaries and grimly held on to the patch of ground they had won on the bank of the Tamesis. One by one they fell, and the shield wall closed up into an ever tighter knot of men until it seemed that their destruction was moments away. The left flank, if the battered groupings of defiant Romans could be said to constitute a line, slowly caved in under the ferocious attack from the elite British warriors. Since there was no chance of surrender or escape, the Romans fought until they died where they stood.

Of the thousand or so men who had made the first assault no more than half held on, and Cato was horrified to see that the transports were being carried downriver by the current. They grounded two hundred paces beyond the desperate struggle of their comrades and the second wave landed without opposition, so intent were the Britons on destroying the remnants of the first wave. Cato glimpsed the scarlet crest of the legate and beside him the eagle standard as the new arrivals hurriedly formed a battle line and marched swiftly upriver. The Britons saw the danger and turned to face them. Cato watched in desperation as Vespasian's advance slowed and then halted to deal with the fierce resistance fifty paces from the battered first wave.

From the left the Romans had been pushed back into a compact arc with its base on the river, and the Britons scented imminent victory. Their war cries now sounded with a new frenzied pitch as they hacked and slashed at the legionaries. In a moment it would all be over and they would crush the last men of the first wave and grind them into the mud.

But the end did not come. A British war horn sounded a series of notes above the cacophony of battle, and to Cato's astonishment the Britons began to disengage. With a last exchange of blows the warrior he was fighting stepped back carefully until he was well beyond the reach of Cato's weapon. Then he turned and trotted up the river bank, and on all sides the bright colours of the Britons flowed back from the Roman shields, back towards the Druids clustered about the chief mounted on his chariot. Then in good defensive order the enemy marched over the slight rise of the river bank and out of sight, under renewed fire from the trireme.

Cato stared out across the battlefield, strewn with the hacked bodies of the dead and the screams of the wounded, hardly able to believe that he was still alive. About him the remains of his century stared at each other in wonder.

'What the fuck are they up to?' someone muttered.

Cato just shook his head wearily, and sheathed his sword.

Vespasian's new arrivals altered the direction of their advance and formed a screen between the retreating Britons and the pitifully small number of survivors from the first wave.

'Did we beat them off? Couldn't they take it?'

'Use your brain!' Cato snapped. 'It must have been something else. Must have been.'

'Look there! To the left.'

Cato looked and saw tiny dark shapes rise up round the bend in the river: cavalry. 'Ours or theirs? I suppose it has to be ours.'

Sure enough a Roman cavalry pennant appeared near the front of the column. Plautius' deployment of forces upriver in search of a ford had not been in vain. Some of the Batavian cohorts had arrived on the British flank in time to save the vanguard of the Second Legion. But the new arrivals were not greeted with any cries of triumph. The men were simply relieved to have survived, and were too tired to do anything more than slump down on the river bank and rest their exhausted limbs. But Cato realised he could not do that just yet. His sense of duty would not permit it. First he must do a roll call of his century, check their fitness to continue fighting and then make his report to the legate. He knew he must do this, yet his mind was stupid with fatigue now that the immediate danger had passed. He yearned more than anything for a rest. Even the thought of it seemed to add vastly to the physical need to sleep. His eyelids slowly dropped; before he was aware of it, he started to slip forward and would have fallen to the ground had not a strong pair of arms caught him by the shoulders and held him in place.

'Cato!'

'What? What?' he managed to reply, eyes struggling to open.

The hands shook him, trying to break him out of his exhausted stupor. 'Cato! What the fuck have you done to my century?'

The question might have sounded bitter but beneath it was the familiar grudging tone he had grown used to over recent months. He forced himself to look up, to open his stinging eyes and face his questioner.

'Macro?'

Chapter Twenty-Seven

'Glad to see you still recognise me under all this crap!' Macro smiled and clapped his optio on the shoulder, carefully avoiding his injured side.

Cato silently beheld the spectacle standing before him. The centurion's head and chest were covered in dried blood and soiled with mud; he looked like a walking corpse. Indeed, for Cato, whose recent ferocity had been driven by grief at his centurion's death, the vision of Macro alive and grinning into his face was too shocking to accept. Stupid with exhaustion and disbelief, he just stared blankly, mouth open.

'Cato?' Macro's face creased with concern. The optio swayed, head drooping, sword arm hanging limply by his side. All around them stretched the twisted bodies of Romans and Britons. The bloodstained river lapped gently along the shore, its surface broken by the glistening hummocks of corpses. Overhead the sun beat down on the scene. There was an overwhelming sense of calm that was really a slow adjustment from the terrible din of conflict. Even the birdsong sounded strange to the ears of men just emerging from the intensity of battle. Cato was suddenly aware that he was covered in filth and the blood of other men, and a wave of nausea swept up from the pit of his stomach. He could not stop himself and threw up, splashing vomit down

Macro's front before the centurion could step back. Macro grimaced but quickly reached out to grab the lad's shoulders as Cato's legs buckled. He slowly lowered the optio onto his knees.

'Easy, boy,' he said gently. 'Easy there.'

Cato threw up again, and again, until there was nothing left inside him and then he retched, stomach, chest and throat in spasm, mouth agape, until at last it passed and he could gasp for air. A thin trail of drool curved down through the acid stench between his spread hands. All the weariness and strain of the previous days had found its release and his body could cope with no more. Macro patted his back and watched with awkward concern, wanting to comfort the boy, but too self-conscious to do so in front of the other soldiers. Eventually Cato sat back and rested his head between his hands, the grime on his face spattered with blood. His thin body trembled with the coldness of total exhaustion, and yet some final reserve of mental strength kept him awake.

Macro nodded with full understanding. All soldiers reached this moment at some point in their lives. He knew that the boy had finally passed the limit of physical and emotional endurance. He was past any exhortation to duty.

'Rest, boy. I'll take care of the lads. But you must rest now.'

For a brief moment it looked as if the optio would try to protest. In the end he nodded and slowly lowered himself onto the grassy river bank and closed his eyes, asleep almost at once. Macro watched him for a moment and then unclasped the cloak from a Briton's body and gently laid it over Cato.

'Centurion Macro!' Vespasian's voice boomed out. 'I'd heard you were dead.'

Macro rose to his feet and saluted. 'You were misinformed, sir.'

'Evidently. Explain yourself.'

'Nothing much to explain, sir. I was knocked to the ground, took one of them with me, and they left us both for dead. Soon as I could, I made my way back to the legion. Arrived just in time to hop on one of the boats in the second wave. Thought Cato and the lads might need some help, sir.'

Vespasian glanced down at the huddled form of the optio. 'Is the boy all right?'

Macro nodded. 'He's fine, sir. Just exhausted.'

Over the legate's shoulder the fresh-faced tribunes and other staff officers mingled with the weary legionaries who had survived the river assault. The legate's presence suddenly caused Macro to frown with concern.

'The lad's finished for the moment, sir. There's nothing more he can do until he has rested.'

'Easy there!' The legate chuckled. 'I wasn't looking to use him for another duty. I just wanted to make sure he was all right. The boy's done quite enough for his Emperor this morning.'

'Yes, sir. He has.'

'Make sure that he gets all the rest he needs. And see to your century. They've performed magnificently. Let 'em rest. The legion will just have to manage without them for the remainder of the day.' Vespasian exchanged a smile with his centurion. 'Carry on, Macro. It's good to have you back!'

'Yes, sir. Thank you, sir.'

Vespasian saluted and then turned and marched off to organise the defence of the hard-won bridgehead. The staff officers parted to let him through and then scrambled along behind.

With a final glance to check that his optio was still resting peacefully, Macro went off to see to the comforts of his surviving men. He carefully picked his way over the sprawled bodies and shouted out the order for the Sixth Century to assemble.

Cato woke with a start and sat up, bathed in a cold sweat. He had been dreaming about drowning, held down by an enemy warrior in a river of blood. The mental image slowly dissipated and was replaced with a velvet evening sky which dissolved into orange at the horizon. His ears filled with the crackle and clatter of campfire cooking. A pungent odour of stew filled his nostrils.

'Better now?' Macro leaned over him.

Macro alive.

Cato struggled up into a reclining position. It was dusk, the sun had just set and in the faint light he could see the legion camped along the river bank. The bodies had been removed and neat lines of tents stretched out on all sides. The silhouette of the distant rampart and palisade marked the fortifications that had been thrown up around the encampment.

'Want some food?'

Cato looked round and saw that he was lying close to a small fire over which a large bronze pot hung from a tripod. A faint sound of bubbling accompanied the steam gently wafting over the brim and the aroma instantly made him feel ravenous.

'What is it?'

'Hare,' replied Macro. He ladled some into Cato's mess tin. 'The place is thick with them. Never seen so many in my life. Lads have been taking pot shots at them all afternoon. Here you go.'

'Thank you, sir.' Cato put the mess tin down on the grass beside him. He took the spoon Macro handed him and began to stir the steaming food, impatient to begin eating. At the same time, there was a question he needed answering. 'Sir, how did you do it?'

Macro sat back and hugged his knees with a smile. The blood and filth that had made him such a grim spectacle earlier in the day had been washed away and the centurion sat barefoot in his tunic. 'I wondered when you'd ask. Luck, I guess. Fortuna must have taken a shine to me. I really thought it was all over. Just wanted to kill as many of the bastards as I could before I was taken down. We did manage to hold them for a while. Then some of them got between the shields and caught one of the lads. Once he went down, they were all over us in an instant. One of 'em leaped at me, knocked my sword to one side, and we went down into them bushes beside the path. I managed to get my dagger out and stuck him in the throat. Bugger's blood nearly drowned me!

'Anyway I lay still as the rest of them piled by. They must have thought I was done for, and they were keen as mustard to see to you and the rest of the lads. Once I was sure they were gone, I heaved the Briton off and slid into the marsh. I kept off the tracks and made for the river, and then headed downstream. Had to be careful, though, there were still plenty of them about. I finally hooked up with some of the lads from the Seventh Cohort, and we got back to the legion just in time to see you lot piling into the Britons on the far side of the river. You really have no respect for another man's century, do you? No sooner are you made acting centurion than you throw the lads back into the grinder.'

Cato stopped blowing on the spoonful of stew and looked up. 'The lads wanted to do it, sir.'

'So they say. But I think we've had enough heroics for now. One more fight like that and there won't be a century any more.'

'Did we lose many?' Cato asked guiltily.

'A few. The burial club funds are going to be badly hit,' the centurion added. 'Just hope we can make up the shortfall once the replacements arrive.'

'Replacements?'

'Yes. I had word from one of the clerks on the staff. A column is on its way over from Gaul. If we're lucky we'll get some men from the Eighth. But most of 'em are new recruits sent up from the legion training depots.' He shook his head. 'Bunch of bloody recruits to nursemaid in the middle of a campaign. Can you believe it?'

Cato said nothing. He looked down into his mess tin and continued eating. When he had joined the Second Legion the last thing he expected was that less than a year later he would be with the eagles fighting for his life in barbarian lands. Technically, he was still a recruit; his basic training was over but he had yet to reach the first anniversary of the date he had been signed into the Second Legion. His embarrassed silence did not go unnoticed.

'Oh, you're all right, Cato! You might not be much cop at drill, and you've still got to learn how to swim, but you're a good hand in a fight. You'll do.'

'Thanks,' he muttered, not quite certain how best to handle being damned by such faint praise. Not that he minded, being cursed with a temperament that was always suspicious of any praise aimed at him. Anyway, the stew was delicious and he had already polished off the mess tin and was scraping the bottom with his spoon.

'There's plenty more, lad.' Macro dipped the ladle back into the pot and scooped deep to make sure that Cato got plenty of meat. 'Fill up while you can. In the army the next meal's never guaranteed. By the way, how do the burns feel?'

Cato instinctively reached for the dressing on his side and discovered that it had been changed, and a clean roll of linen had been bound about his chest, tight enough not to slip and yet not too tight to be uncomfortable. A good job had been made of it and Cato looked up gratefully.

'Thank you, sir.'

'Don't thank me. That surgeon did it. Nisus. Seems our century's been assigned to his care, and you've seen to it that he's kept busy.'

'Well, I'll thank him for it sometime.'

'You can do it now.' Macro nodded over Cato's shoulder. 'Here he comes.'

Cato twisted his head and saw the huge hulk of the surgeon emerging from the dull shadows between the tents. He raised a hand in greeting.

'Cato! Awake at last. You were way down the Lethe last time I saw you. Hardly a murmur when I changed the dressing.'

'Thanks.'

Nisus slumped down by the fire between Cato and his centurion, and sniffed at the pot. 'Hare?'

'What else?' replied Macro.

'Any spare?'

'Help yourself.'

Nisus unhooked the mess tin and spoon from his belt and, ignoring the ladle, dipped the mess tin in and scooped it out almost filled to the brim. With a keen look of anticipation he moistened his lips.

'Please make yourself at home,' Macro muttered.

Nisus skimmed a spoonful off the surface, blew on it a moment and sipped cautiously. 'Lovely! Centurion, you're going to make someone a wonderful wife one day.'

'Fuck off.'

'So then, Cato, how are the burns today?'

The optio touched the dressing tenderly and winced immediately. 'Painful.'

'Not surprised. You've not given them a moment's rest. Some of the wounds are open and might've got infected if I hadn't cleaned them out when I changed the dressing. You're really going to have to take a bit more care of yourself. That's an order, by the way.'

'An order?' Macro protested. 'Just who the hell do you medics think you are?'

'We're qualified to look after the health of the Emperor's troops, that's who. Besides, it's an order from the top. The legate told me to make sure Cato rested. He's excused duties and is out of the line of battle until I say so.'

'He can't do that!' Cato protested. Macro looked at him sharply and Cato subsided, realising the foolishness of his protest.

'Might as well make the most of it, lad, since the order's come from the legate,' said Macro gruffly.

Nisus agreed with a vigorous nod, and then returned to his stew. Macro reached for one of the roughly hacked logs and placed it carefully in the flames. A small cloud of sparks swirled up and Cato's eyes followed them into the evening sky until their glow faded and they were lost against the dazzling pinpricks of the stars. Despite being asleep for most of the day, Cato still felt exhaustion weighing down every sinew of his body and would have been shaking with cold but for the fire.

Nisus finished his stew, set his mess tin down and lay down on his side, gazing at Cato. 'So then, Optio. You come from the palace.'

'Yes.'

'Is it true that Claudius is as cruel and incompetent as all his predecessors?'

Macro spluttered. 'What kind of a question is that for a Roman to ask?'

'A reasonable enough one,' Nisus replied. 'And anyway, by birth I'm not a Roman. African as it happens, though there's some Greek in there as well. Hence the occupation and my presence here. The only place the legions can get decent medical experience from is Greece and the eastern provinces.'

'Bloody foreigners!' Macro sniffed. 'Beat 'em in war and they profit from us in peace.'

'Thus it ever was, Centurion. The compensations of being conquered.'

Despite the levity of the comments, Cato sensed a bitterness behind the words and was curious. 'Where are you from then?'

'A small town on the African coast. Cartanova. Don't suppose you've ever heard of it.'

'I believe I have. Isn't it home to the library of Archelonides?'

'Why yes.' Nisus' face lit up with pleasure. 'You know it?'

'I know of it. The town's built over some of the foundations of a Carthaginian city, I think.'

'Yes.' Nisus nodded. 'That's right. Over the foundations. You can still see the lines of the old city wall, and some of the temple complexes and shipyards. But that's it. The city was razed pretty thoroughly at the end of the second patriotic war.'

'The Roman army doesn't do things by halves,' Macro said with a certain amount of pride.

'No, I suppose not.'

'And you trained in medicine there?' asked Cato, trying

to steer the discussion onto safer ground.

'Yes. For a few years. There's a limit to what can be learned in a small trading town. So I went east to Damascus and worked in a practice servicing the wide variety of ailments the rich merchants and their wives imagined that they suffered from. Lucrative enough, but dull. I got friendly with a centurion in the garrison. When he was transferred to the Second a few months back, I went with him. Can't say that it hasn't been exciting, but I do miss the Damascus lifestyle.'

'Is it as good as you hear?' Macro asked with the eagerness of all those who believe that paradise must exist somewhere in this life. 'I mean, the women have quite a reputation, don't they?'

'The women?' Nisus raised his eyebrows. 'Is that all that soldiers think about? There's more to Damascus than its women.'

'Sure there is.' Macro tried to be gracious for a moment. 'But is it true about the women?'

The surgeon sighed. 'The legions who garrisoned the town certainly seemed to think so. You'd think they had never seen a woman at all before. Bunches of slavering drunks staggering from one brothel to the next. Not so much in pursuance of the Roman peace as in pursuit of a piece for the Romans.'

Nisus gazed into the fire, and Cato saw his mouth fix into a tight, bitter line. Macro was also gazing into the fire, but the lazy flames showed a smile on his face as his mind dwelt upon the exotic pleasures of an eastern posting.

The difference between these two representatives of the ruling and conquered races troubled Cato. What was the value of a world ruled by uncouth womanisers who lorded it over their better educated subject races? Macro and Nisus were not typical examples of course, and the comparison was perhaps unfair, but was it always the case that strength would triumph over intellect? Certainly the Romans had triumphed over the Greeks, for all their science, art and philosophy. Cato had read enough to know how much the Romans had subsequently appropriated from the heritage of Greek civilization. In truth, the destiny of Rome depended upon her ability to ruthlessly overwhelm other civilisations and subsume them. The thought was very unsettling, and Cato turned to stare down towards the river.

There was no doubting that the Britons were barbarians. Aside from looking the part, the lack of neatly planned towns, metalled roads and regimented crops of agricultural estates spoke clearly of an inferior quality of existence. The Britons, Cato decided, lacked the refinements necessary to be called a civilisation. If the stories brought back from the misty isles by merchants and traders were to be believed, the natives were scratching a living on top of huge deposits of silver and gold. It seemed typical of the capricious nature of the gods that the most primitive of peoples were granted tenure of the most valuable of resources – resources they had little appreciation of, and which could be put to much better use by more advanced races, such as the Romans.

And there was the sinister issue of the Druids. Not much was known of them, and all that Cato had read depicted the cult in lurid and horrific terms. He shuddered at the memory of the grove he and Macro had discovered a few days earlier. The place had felt dark and cold, and filled with menace. If nothing else, the conquest of the misty islands would lead to the destruction of the dark cult of Druidism.

The disgust he suddenly felt for the British caused Cato to pause in this line of thinking. As arguments justifying the expansion of the empire, they seemed plausible and simple.

So much so, that Cato could not help being suspicious of them. In his experience, the things in life that were held up as eternal and simple truths were only so because of a deliberate limitation in thought. It occurred to him that everything he had ever read in Latin had presented Roman culture in the best possible terms, and infinitely superior to anything produced by any other race, whether 'civilised' like the Greeks, or 'barbaric' like these Britons. There had to be another side to things.

He looked at Nisus and took in the dark skin, dark features, thick curling hair and the strangely patterned amulets on his broad wrists. The Roman citizenship he had been awarded on joining the legions was less than skin deep. It was a mere legal label that conferred a certain status upon him. Beyond that, what kind of a man was he?

'Nisus?'

The surgeon looked up from the flames and smiled.

'Can I ask you something personal?'

The smile faded slightly and the surgeon's eyebrows twitched closer to each other. He nodded.

'What is it like not being Roman?' The question was awkward and blunt, and Cato felt ashamed for asking it but blundered on in an attempt to clarify himself. 'I mean, I know you are a Roman citizen now. But what was it like before? What do other people think of Rome?'

Nisus and Macro were staring at him. Nisus, frowning and suspicious, Macro simply astonished. Cato wished he had kept his mouth shut. But he was consumed with a desire to know more, to step outside the view of the world that had been fed to him since birth. Had it not been for the palace tutors, it was a view he would have accepted without question, without the slightest notion that it was partial.

'What do people think of Rome?' Nisus repeated. He considered the question for a moment, gently scratching the thick stubble on his chin. 'Interesting question. Not an easy one to answer. It mostly depends on who you are. If you happen to be one of those client kings who owes everything to Rome, and fears and hates his subjects, then Rome is your only friend. If you are a grain merchant in Egypt who can make a fortune out of the corn dole in Rome, or a gladiator and beast supplier providing the citizens with the means to idle away their lives, then Rome is the source of your wealth. The fineware manufacturers and the arms factories of Gaul, the traders in spices, silks and antiquities, all of them are sustained by Rome. Wherever there is money to be made from Rome's voracious appetite for resources, entertainment and luxury, there is a parasite feeding the demand. But for everyone else,' Nisus shrugged, 'I can't say.'

'Can't say, or won't say?' Macro chipped in angrily.

'Centurion, I am a guest at your fire, and only offer my opinion at your optio's request.'

'Fine! So give it then. Tell us what they bloody think.'

'*They?*' Nisus arched an eyebrow. 'I can't speak for them. I know little of the grain farmers along the Nile, forced to give up most of their crop each year, regardless of the yield. I've no idea what it means to be a slave taken in war and sold to a lead mine chain gang, never see my wife or children again. Or to be a Gaul whose land has been owned by the same family for generations, only to see it centurionated and handed over to a mob of discharged legionaries.'

'Cheap rhetoric!' Macro snapped. 'You don't really know at all.'

'No, but I can imagine how they might feel. And so can you – if you try.'

'Why should I try? We won, they lost, and that proves we're best. If they resent that then they're wasting their time. You can't resent the inevitable.'

'Nice aphorism, Centurion.' Nisus chuckled appreciatively. 'But there's nothing inevitable about the taxes the empire collects, or the grain, gold and slaves it squeezes out of its provinces. All to support the squalid masses living in Rome. Can you wonder if people are filled with bitterness and resentment when they look to Rome?'

For a fatalist like Macro this was fighting talk, and he ground his teeth. If they had been drinking he would simply have tired of the conversation and stuck his fist in the man's face. But he was sober, and in any case Nisus was his guest, so he had to endure the conversation.

'Why become a Roman then?' he challenged the surgeon. 'Why, if you hate us so much?'

'Who said I hated you? I am one of you now. I appreciate the fact that being a Roman grants me special status within the empire, but I have no feelings for Rome beyond that.'

'What about us?' Cato asked quietly. 'What about your comrades?'

'That's different. I live alongside you, and fight with you when necessary. That creates a special bond between us. But put the Roman citizenship and my Roman name to one side and I'm someone else. Someone who carries the memories of Carthage deep in his blood.'

'You have another name?' This was something Cato had not considered.

'Of course he has,' said Macro. 'All of them who join the eagles and take up citizenship have to take on a Roman name.'

'So what was it before you became Nisus?'

'My full name is Marcus Cassius Nisus.' He smiled at

Cato. 'That's how I'm known now in the army, and on every legal and professional document. But before that, before I became Roman, I was Gisgo, of the Barca line.'

Cato's eyebrows rose, and a cold sensation tickled the hairs at the nape of his neck. He stared at the surgeon a moment before he dared speak. 'Any relation?'

'A direct descendent.'

'I see,' muttered Cato, still trying to absorb the implications. He stared at the Carthaginian. 'Interesting.'

Macro threw another log on the fire and broke the spell. 'Would you mind telling me what's so bloody interesting? Just because he's got a funny name?'

Before Cato could explain, they were interrupted. Looming out of the dark came an officer, polished breastplate glittering with the reflection of the fire.

'Surgeon, are you the one called Nisus?'

Nisus and Macro jumped to their feet and stood stiffly to attention before Tribune Vitellius. Cato was slower, wincing with the painful effort to raise himself to his feet.

'Yes, sir.'

'Then come with me. I've an injury that needs seeing to.'

Without another word the tribune turned and strode off, leaving the surgeon with barely enough time to tip out the dregs of his stew, wipe his spoon on the grass, and re-attach them to his belt before trotting off to catch up with the tribune. Cato slumped back to the ground while Macro watched Nisus disappear between a line of tents.

'Strange one, that. Not quite sure what to make of him, except that I don't like him yet. Might see how we get on after a few drinks.'

'If he drinks,' added Cato.

'Eh?'

'There are some religions of the east that forbid it.'

'Why the fuck would they want to miss out on wine?'

Cato shrugged. He was too tired for theological speculation.

'And what was all that bollocks about his name?'

Cato propped himself up and gazed across the fire towards Macro. 'His family are descended from the Barcas.'

'Yes, I heard,' Macro said with heavy emphasis. 'So?'

'Does the name Hannibal Barca mean anything to you, sir?'

Macro was silent for a moment. '*The* Hannibal?'

'The same.'

Macro squatted down by the fire and whistled. 'Well, that might go some way towards explaining his attitude to Rome. Who'd have thought we'd have an heir of Hannibal fighting with the Roman army?' He laughed at the irony.

'Yes,' Cato said quietly. 'Who'd have thought it?'

Chapter Twenty-Eight

Work on the bridgehead fortifications continued at first light. A thin mist had risen from the Tamesis and wreathed the camp of the Second Legion in its clammy chill. In the pallid glow of the rising sun, a column of legionaries trudged out of the northern gate of the marching camp that had been hastily thrown up as soon as the main body of the legion was ferried across the river. The rest of the army would soon be joining the Second to continue the campaign, and the fortifications had to be extended to accommodate the other legions and auxiliary cohorts. Round the Second Legion's palisade the engineers had marked out a vast rectangle with surveying posts. A substantial stretch of earthworks had been raised the previous day, and the engineers set to work at once on extending the defences.

With weapons neatly stacked nearby, the legionaries continued excavating the surrounding ditch and piling the spoil to form an inner rampart. Once the spoil was packed down, a layer of logs was laid along the top to form a firm platform behind the palisade of sharpened stakes driven into the body of the rampart. A screen of men stood guard a hundred paces in front of their toiling comrades and far beyond them rode the distant figures of the legion's mounted scouts. Caesar's comments about the hit-and-run tactics of the British charioteers were fresh in the mind of the legion's commander, and he had made sure that any approaching enemy would be sighted in time to warn the engineering party.

With relentless effort the earthworks were extended from the river in sections of a hundred feet at a time. Years of drilling ensured that every man knew his duty, and the work was carried out with an efficiency that gratified Vespasian when he rode out to inspect their progress. But he was preoccupied and troubled. His thoughts turned yet again to the meeting of senior officers he had attended yesterday. All the legion commanders had been present, as well as his brother Sabinus, now acting as Plautius' chief of staff.

Aulus Plautius had commended their achievements, and announced that the army's scouts reported that there was no significant body of enemy soldiers for many miles to their front. The Britons had taken a beating and retreated far beyond the Tamesis. Vespasian had argued that the enemy should be pursued and destroyed, before Caratacus had a chance to regroup and reinforce his army from those tribes who were only just beginning to appreciate the danger posed to them by the legions in the far south of the island. Any delay in the Roman advance could only be to the benefit of the natives. Although the Romans had managed to harvest the crops they had marched through in the early weeks of the campaign, the Britons had quickly realised the need to deny the invader the fruits of the land. The vanguard of the Roman army was advancing over the smouldering remains of wheat fields and grain stores, and the legions were wholly dependent on the depot at Rutupiae, from which long supply trains of ox-drawn wagons dragged their loads forward to the legions. When conditions permitted, the supplies were shipped along the coast in the shallow-bottomed transports escorted by the warships of the

Channel fleet. If the Britons were to make use of their superior manoeuvrability and concentrate their attacks on these supply lines, the Roman advance inland would be seriously delayed. It made sense to strike at the Britons now, while they were still reeling from their defeats at the Mead Way and the Tamesis.

The general had nodded at Vespasian's arguments, but there was no shifting him from strict adherence to the instructions he had received from Narcissus, Emperor Claudius' chief secretary.

'I agree with everything you say, Vespasian. Everything. Believe me, if there were any ambiguity in the orders, I'd exploit the loopholes. But Narcissus was quite precise: the moment we secure a bridgehead on the far bank of the Tamesis we are to halt and wait for the Emperor to come and take personal command of the final phase of this campaign. Once we've taken Camulodunum, Claudius and his entourage will head home, we'll consolidate what we hold and prepare for next year's campaign. It'll be some years yet before this island is completely tamed. But we must make sure we are strong enough to deal with Caratacus. We've beaten him before, we can beat him again.'

'Only if we keep the upper hand,' replied Vespasian. 'Right now Caratacus has no army as such, just the scattered remnants of the forces we've defeated so far. If we push on we can wipe them out easily, and that'll be the end of any effective resistance before we reach Camulodunum.' Vespasian paused to choose his next words carefully. 'I know what the orders say, but what if we destroy the remainder of the enemy and then pull back to the bridgehead? Surely that would satisfy our strategic needs and the Emperor's political goals?'

Plautius clasped his hands together and leaned forward across his desk. 'The Emperor needs a military victory. He needs it for himself, and we are going to give it to him. If we do what you say and utterly crush the opposition, then who will he fight when he gets here?'

'And if we leave Caratacus alone until Claudius arrives, maybe we won't be able to beat the Britons at all. Maybe he'll arrive just in time to join the rout back to the ships. How will that look on his political record?'

'Vespasian!' Sabinus cut in, glancing sharply at his younger brother. 'I'm sure it won't come to that. Even if Caratacus does manage to field another army, we'll be reinforced by the men the Emperor brings with him. Most of the Eighth, some of the Praetorian Guard cohorts, and even elephants. Isn't that right?' Sabinus looked across the table to Plautius.

'Quite right. More than enough to crush anything the Britons can place in our way. Once those savages catch sight of the elephants, they'll bolt.'

'Elephants!' Vespasian laughed bitterly as he recalled a vivid account of the battle of Zama he had read as a boy. 'I rather think they pose more danger to our side than to the enemy. The Eighth are mostly a bunch of aged invalids and raw recruits, and the Praetorians are used to the soft life in Rome. We don't need them, any of them, if we strike now.'

'Which we cannot do under any circumstances,' Plautius said firmly. 'Those are the orders and we obey them. We don't attempt to interpret them, or skirt round them. That's an end to the issue.' The general stared fixedly at Vespasian, and the legate's final attempt at protest died in his throat. There was no point in pursuing the matter, even though all present must know it made good military sense. The effective deployment of military strategy had been overridden by a political agenda.

Sabinus sensed his brother's submission and quickly turned the discussion on to the next item on the agenda.

'Sir, we need to consider the allocation of replacements. It's most urgent.'

'Very well.' Plautius was eager to move on to a new subject. 'I've looked over your strength returns and decided on the allocations. The biggest share goes to the Second Legion.' He smiled placatingly at Vespasian. 'Your unit has taken the most casualties since we landed.'

Plautius completed his allocation of replacements, which left only the commander of the Twentieth unhappy with his lot. He was granted no extra men and, worse, his legion was relegated to the role of strategic reserve – a move guaranteed to diminish his share of the coming glory, assuming the campaign concluded successfully for the invaders.

'One final matter, gentlemen.' Plautius leaned back and made sure that he had the close attention of every officer. 'I've had reports that the enemy is using Roman army equipment: swords, slingshot and some scaled armour. If this was no more than one or two items, I might not be concerned. It is not unknown for a discharged veteran to sell his army issue to a passing trader. But the quantity recovered so far is too large to overlook. It would appear that someone has been running arms to the Britons. We'll deal with them after the campaign is over, but until then I want a record kept of every item you recover from the battlefield. When the trader is found we can round off the fighting with a nice little crucifixion.'

At once the fears Vespasian harboured about his wife's connections to the Liberators flowed to the forefront of his thoughts, accompanied by a chilling ripple up his spine.

'This trader has been rather busy, sir,' Hosidius Geta said quietly.

'Meaning?'

'Meaning that he must be running a sizeable export organisation if he's been shipping the quantity of equipment we've encountered so far. Not the kind of operation that goes easily unnoticed.'

'Do you have any objection to speaking your mind clearly?'

'None, sir.'

'Then please do so.'

'I think we're looking at something a little more sinister than some chancer hoping to turn a quick profit. The quantity of arms the Ninth has come across so far is too large. Whoever is backing this operation has access to money, some senior people in the arms factories, and a small fleet of trading vessels.'

'The Liberators emerging from the shadows again, no doubt,' Vitellius suggested with a mocking smile.

Geta turned on his stool towards him. 'You have a better explanation, Tribune?'

'Not me, sir. Just repeating a rumour that's doing the rounds.'

'Then kindly confine your remarks to ones that assist the deliberations of your betters. The rest you can save to impress the junior tribunes.'

A ripple of laughter swept through the senior officers, and Vitellius' face flushed with bitter humiliation. 'As you wish, sir.'

Geta nodded with satisfaction, and turned back to the general. 'Sir, we need to inform the palace at once. Whoever is responsible for supplying the Britons with our equipment will run for cover as soon as word gets out about what we've discovered.'

'A dispatch is already on its way to Narcissus,' Plautius replied smugly.

It occurred to Vespasian that the general wanted all those present to believe that he had already thought well ahead of his most seasoned commander. A message might well be en route to the chief secretary, but he doubted if it mentioned a word of Geta's conclusions. That message would hurriedly follow in the wake of the first, the moment the meeting closed. The speed with which Plautius moved on to the next item for discussion merely strengthened his suspicion.

At length Plautius pushed back his chair and ended the briefing. The legates and senior staff officers rose from their seats and filed outside to where their cavalry escorts waited to see them back to their legions. As Vespasian went to make his farewell to his brother, Plautius called him over.

'A quick word, if you'll excuse us, Sabinus?'

'Of course, sir.'

When they were alone, Plautius smiled. 'Some good news for you, Vespasian. You will have heard the Emperor is bringing a sizeable entourage with him.'

'Besides the elephants?'

The general chuckled politely. 'Don't mind them. They're strictly for show and won't be allowed within a mile of the battle line, if I have anything to do with it. All generals have to make a show of obeying orders in public; in private we try to do what we must in order to achieve victory. Generals must be seen to obey emperors, whatever their relative military merits may be. Wouldn't you agree?'

Vespasian felt the blood drain from his face as fear and anger spilled over his self-control. 'Is this another loyalty test, sir?'

'Not in this instance, but you're wise to be cautious. No, I was merely trying to reassure you that your commanding general is not quite the fool you seem to think he is.'

'Sir!' Vespasian protested. 'I never meant to—'

'Peace, Legate.' Plautius raised his hands. 'I know what you and the others must be thinking. In your place I would feel the same. But I am the Emperor's man, charged with doing his bidding. Should I fail to obey his orders I'll be damned as insubordinate, or worse. If I fail to beat the enemy I'm also damned, but at least I'll have the defence that I was only obeying orders.' Plautius paused. 'You must think me contemptibly weak. Maybe. But one day, if your star continues to rise, you will find yourself in my position, with a talented and impatient legate anxious to execute the necessary military strategy without once considering the political agenda from which it emanates. I hope you remember my words then.'

Vespasian made no reply, just stared coldly at the general, ashamed of his inability to confront the man's patronising comments. Homilies delivered by senior officers could only be listened to in frustrated silence.

'Now then,' Plautius continued, 'the good news I promised you. Your wife and child will be travelling with the Emperor.'

'Flavia will be in his entourage? But why?'

'Don't feel overly delighted at the honour. It's a large party, well over a hundred, according to Narcissus' dispatch. I imagine Claudius just wanted to be surrounded by colourful types to keep him entertained while he's away from Rome. Whatever the reason, you'll get the chance to see her again. Quite a looker, as I recall.'

The cheap comment soured Vespasian even further. He nodded, without any attempt to convey manly pride in the possession of a wife of such striking appearance. What was between them went far deeper than any superficial attraction. But that was personal, and he would break the confidence of such an intimacy with no man. The thrilling prospect that Flavia would soon be travelling towards him was quickly submerged by anxiety about her inclusion in the Emperor's entourage. People were requested to attend the Emperor on his travels for one of two reasons. Either they were great entertainers and flatterers, or they were people who posed a sufficient threat to the Emperor that he dare not leave them out of his sight.

In view of her recent plotting, Flavia could be in the greatest possible danger – if she was under suspicion. Within the pageantry of the imperial court's travelling party, she would be secretly watched. The faintest glimmer of treason would result in her falling into the sinister claws of Narcissus' interrogators.

'Will that be all, sir?'

'Yes, that's all. Make sure you and your men make the most of the time while we wait for Claudius to arrive.'

Chapter Twenty-Nine

Once the fortifications were completed, the Ninth and the Fourteenth legions were ferried across the Tamesis and moved into their allocated areas. The auxiliaries and the Twentieth legion remained behind to guard the army's draught animals which grazed over an enormous region on every available strip of pasture land. A string of small forts stretched out along the lines of communication all the way back to Rutupiae and occasional convoys of supplies trundled up to the front, returning empty apart from those bearing invalids destined for an early discharge and subsequent dependence on the corn dole in Rome. Most of the supplies were now being carried along the coast and thence upriver by the transports of the invasion fleet.

A huge supply depot had been established in the legions' encampment, and every day more rations, weapons and spare equipment were unloaded, carefully recorded by the quartermasters, and deposited within the meticulously marked-out grid laid down by the engineers. When the army next took to the field, it would be as well-provisioned and armed as it had been at the start of the campaign.

The legionaries rested while they waited for the Emperor and his coterie to arrive, although there were still many duties to perform. The fort's walls had to be manned, latrines dug and maintained, forage parties sent out to secure firewood and seize any supplies of grain or farm animals they might discover, and scores of other routine duties that comprised army life. Initially the forage parties had set out in full cohort strength, but as the cavalry scouts continued to report few signs of the enemy, smaller groups of legionaries were permitted to leave the camp during daylight hours.

Although Cato had been excused duties until he had fully recovered from his burns, he found that he needed to fill his days doing something useful. Macro had scoffed at his request to help him catch up with the administration. Most veterans placed a premium on snatching as much free time as possible and had learned all the tricks and scams to get out of duties. When Cato presented himself at the centurion's tent with an offer to help, Macro's first inclination was to question what the optio was really up to.

'I just want to do something useful, sir.'

'I see,' Macro replied with a contemplative scratch of his chin. 'Something useful, eh?'

'Yes, sir.'

'Why?'

'I'm bored, sir.'

'Bored?' Macro responded with genuine horror. The possibility of rejecting the chance to indulge in the panoply of off-duty activities of legionary life was something he had never considered. He pondered the matter for a while. Any normal optio might have discovered some new wheeze for screwing extra rations or pay out of the century's accounts. But Cato had demonstrated a quite deplorable integrity in his administration of the century's records. In his more charitable moments Macro assumed that Cato must be directing his powerful intelligence into some hitherto overlooked opportunity for personal enrichment at the army's expense. In his less charitable moments he put the lad's conscientiousness down to youthful ignorance of army ways, which experience would eventually put right. But here he was, abusing his excused-all-duties status, and actually requesting something to do.

'Well, let me think,' said Macro. 'The dead men's accounts need settling. How about that?'

'That's fine, sir. I'll get started right away.'

As the bemused centurion looked on, Cato heaved open the lid of the century's record chest and carefully extracted the financial accounts and wills of all the men marked down as 'discharged dead' on the most recent strength return. Before the wills could be validated, each dead man's accounts had to be brought up to date with every charge-able item of equipment offset against accumulated savings. The net value of the legionary's estate was apportioned according to the terms set out in the man's will. If no will existed, written or oral, then strictly speaking the estate should be conferred on the eldest male relative. But in practice most centurions claimed that the man had made an oral will bequeathing their worldly goods to the unit's funeral club. Such additional sources of revenue were needed on active service to fund the large number of memorial stones required. The increased demand pushed up prices, and the grief that the legion's masons felt at the deaths of their comrades was in some small measure assuaged by the tidy sums to be earned in preparing their tombstones.

In the shade of the awning at the front of the centurion's tent, Cato sat quietly, finger moving from item to item, mentally adding up the debts and subtracting the totals from the figures in the savings column. Many of the dead men had left behind more debts than savings, reflecting the fact that they were recent recruits, who were always less likely to survive than seasoned veterans. Most of the names meant little, but some leapt from the page and brought a wave of sadness: Pyrax, the easygoing veteran who had showed Cato the ropes when he had arrived in barracks; Harmon, the bovine brick shithouse who entertained his comrades with farmyard impersonations and ear-splitting farts on demand (perhaps that last was no great loss to civilisation, Cato decided on reflection). They were all men like himself, once living, breathing, laughing human beings with their complement of virtues and faults. Men he had marched alongside for the past months, men who knew each other better than most men know their own families. Now they were dead, their rich experiences of life reduced to a line of figures on a financial record scroll and the few personal belongings that made up their bequest.

Cato's stylus wavered above a waxed tablet, trembling in his uncertain fingers. He remembered that he had been told that death would be his constant companion throughout his career in the army. He had thought he understood the implications well enough, but now he knew that there was a wide gulf between fine concepts expressed in neat phrases, and the sordid reality of war.

In the days while he was recovering he had found that normal sleep did not come easily. He would be lying inside his section tent, eyes closed but mind working feverishly as terrible images of slaughter leapt unbidden before his mind's eye. Even when he was awake the same images forced themselves upon him relentlessly, until he began to doubt his sanity. As nervous exhaustion seeped in he began to hear sounds from the fringes of his waking world: a muffled clash of weapons, Pyrax shrieking out his name or Macro bellowing at him to run for his life.

Cato needed someone to talk to, but he could not unburden himself to Macro. The cheerful insensitivity and bluffness that made him so admirable both in everyday life and in the heat of battle was precisely what made it impossible for Cato to confide in him. He simply could not trust the centurion to understand the torment he was going through. Nor did he want to reveal what he considered to be his weaknesses. The very prospect of having Macro offer him pity or, worse, contempt, filled him with self-loathing.

The most nightmarish image from the grinding sequence of battles recurred when he eventually fell asleep. He would dream he was being held under water by the British warrior once again. Only this time the water was blood, and the thick salty redness of it filled his lungs and choked him. And the warrior did not die, but looked through the red river, face horribly mutilated by a savage wound yet fixed in a terrible grin as his hands held Cato down, far beneath the surface.

Cato would awake with a cry and find himself sitting bolt upright, skin bathed in cold, clammy sweat, the mumbled curses from the disturbed men in his tent shaming him. He would not be able to return to sleep again, and the long night would be spent fighting off the terrible images, until the grey of dawn diluted the thick darkness wrapped around him inside the tent.

This was why he had presented himself at his centurion's tent, desperate for some task that demanded fixed attention for long periods of time, long enough to chase away the demons that lurked at the fringes of his consciousness. Completing the dead men's accounts demanded enough of his attention to keep the worst excesses of memory and imagination at bay, but he applied himself to the task with such a single-mindedness that the job was completed more quickly than he wanted. So Cato went over the calculations once more, to ensure that they were correct, or so he told himself.

Eventually there was no further excuse for doubting his mathematical competence, and he neatly rolled up the scrolls and carefully placed them back into the records chest. He was just finishing when a shadow fell across the camp desk.

'Hello, Optio,' said Nisus. 'I see that slave-driver centurion of yours is keeping you at it.'

'No, my choice.'

Nisus tilted his head to one side, resting it against a long, thin trident. 'Your choice? Think I must have missed a touch of concussion when I examined you. That or some fever is getting a grip on you. Either way, you could do with a break. And, as it happens, so could I.'

'You?'

'Don't look so surprised. Some of our wounded survive my treatment for as much as several days. I just can't get them to die quickly enough. So what's needed is a little diversion. In my case that's fishing. And since we're camped by a river I don't want to waste the opportunity. Want to come along?'

'Fishing? I don't know. I've never tried it.'

'Never tried fishing?' Nisus recoiled in mock horror. 'What's wrong with you, man? The ancient practice of separating our scaly cousins from the water is a man's birthright. Where did you go wrong?'

'I've lived in Rome almost all my life. It didn't occur to me to go fishing.'

'Even with the mighty Tiber roaring through the heart of your city?'

'The only thing anyone ever caught from the Tiber was a nasty dose of Remus' Revenge.'

'Ha!' Nisus clapped his huge hands. 'No chance of that here, so come on, let's get going. They'll be feeding at dusk and we might actually catch something.'

After only a brief hesitation Cato nodded, closed the lid of the chest and slipped the bolt back in the catch. Then the pair of them made their way towards the gate in the east wall.

Macro lifted his tent flap back to watch them and smiled. He had been deeply worried about the lad's dark mood over the past few days. More than once he had looked in on Cato and seen the blank eyes and faintly shifting frown that spoke of a silent distress he had seen in all too many other legionaries after intense fighting. Most men coped with it soon enough but Cato was not yet a man, and Macro had enough sensitivity to realise that Cato did not have the soul of a soldier. An optio of the crack Second Legion he might be, but underneath the armour and army-issue tunic lived a person of quite a different quality. And that person was suffering and needed to talk about it to someone outside the close-knit world of the Sixth Century.

Much as he disliked the casual irreverence of Nisus, Macro was aware that the surgeon and Cato shared a similar sensibility, and that the lad might find some comfort in talking to him. He certainly hoped so.

Chapter Thirty

'Good,' mumbled Macro as he chewed the fish loaf. 'Bloody good!' He beamed happily at the Carthaginian beside him. They were sitting outside his tent. A dying fire glowed amid grey ashes and still cast its warmth out, while luring midges and mosquitoes to their doom. Any doubts Cato might have had about Nisus' recipe for the trout had been quelled, and now he helped himself to another fish loaf in the warm basket Nisus had brought along to the tent.

The fishing trip had been a new experience and Cato had enjoyed it more than he'd thought he might. It was strange to sit and watch the sunlight shimmer across the stream, to surrender to the pleasant music of nature. The rustle of the leaves in the soft breeze had mingled with the lapping of the water – and the strain of every moment spent on this campaign had begun to lift. Cato's admiration of Nisus had increased as the Carthaginian had combined skilful fishing with occasional bouts of softly spoken conversation.

'An African delicacy,' explained Nisus. 'I learned it from our cook when I was a child. Almost any fish will do. The secret is in the choice of herbs and spices.'

'And where would you keep those on campaign?' asked Macro.

'With the medical supplies. Most of the ingredients can be used in a variety of poultices.'

'How convenient.'

'Yes, isn't it?'

Cato watched the Carthaginian as he ate from his mess tin. There seemed a good deal of pride in his heritage, yet he served in the ranks of the army that had laid that heritage low. It was interesting, he reflected, how people adapted. He set his mess tin down beside him.

'Nisus,' he said, 'how does it feel to be a Carthaginian serving with the Roman army, given our mutual history.'

Nisus stopped chewing for a moment. 'Someone else asked me the same question just a few days ago. How does it feel? Most of the time I'm too busy to think about it. After all, it's far in the past. Doesn't seem to have a lot to do with me. Anyway, we're part of the empire now, and that's the world I live in. Take the Roman army. Not really a Roman army as such any more. Look how many races serve with the eagles now. Gauls, Spaniards, Illyrians, Syrians and even some Germans. Then there's the auxiliaries. Nearly every race in the empire is represented in their ranks. We've all got a vested interest in Rome. And yet there are times when I wonder . . .' Nisus' voice trailed off for a moment and he gazed into the glowing embers. 'I wonder whether we've surrendered rather too much of ourselves to Rome.'

'How do you mean?' asked Macro between munches.

'I'm not really sure. It's just that everywhere you travel in the empire, and even beyond it, there's Roman architecture, Roman soldiers and administrators, Roman plays in new Roman theatres, Roman histories and poetry in the libraries, Roman clothing in the streets, Roman words in the mouths of people who will never see Rome.'

'So what?' Macro shrugged. 'Is there anything better than Rome?'

'I don't know,' Nisus responded honestly. 'Not better perhaps, just different. And it's the differences that count in the long run.'

'It's differences that lead to war,' suggested Cato.

'Not usually. More often it's the similarities between our rulers. They're all after the same things: domestic political advantage, personal aggrandisement – in short, power, wealth and a niche in history. It's always the same whether you're talking about Julius Caesar, Hannibal, Alexander, Xerxes or any of them. It's men like that who make wars, not the rest of us. We're too busy worrying about the next crop, how to guarantee the town's water supplies, whether our wives are being faithful, whether our children will survive into adulthood. That's what concerns the small people all over the empire. War does not serve our ends. We're forced into it.'

'Bollocks!' Macro spat out. 'War serves my ends. I chose to join the army, no one made me. If it wasn't for the army I'd still be in a piss-poor little squat helping my father catch fish for a living. A few good campaigns under my belt and I'll have saved enough to retire in style. Same goes for Cato.' He glared at Nisus a moment; then, satisfied that he'd made his point, he went back to devouring his fish loaf.

Cato nodded once, with embarrassment, and tried to move the conversation on. 'But surely Rome's wars are justified in terms of what follows. Just think about how Gaul has been changed by being part of the empire. Where there were just loose confederations of warring tribes now we have order. That has to serve the Gauls' interests as much as ours. It's Rome's destiny to extend the bounds of civilisation.'

Nisus shook his head sadly. 'That's maybe what most Romans would like to think. But other nations might be brash enough to believe that they were already civilised, albeit by a different standard of civilisation.'

'Nisus, old lad.' Macro adopted his worldly-wise voice. 'I've seen a great deal of other so-called civilisations in my time, and take it from me, they've nothing to teach us. They better us in nothing. Rome is the best, root and branch, and the sooner they recognise that, as you have, the better.'

Nisus started, and his widened eyes reflected the glow of the embers for an instant before he cast them down. 'Centurion, I joined the army to gain the rights conferred by Roman citizenship. I did it for pragmatic reasons, not idealistic ones. I don't share your sense of your empire's destiny. In time it will pass, as all empires have passed, and all that will remain will be ruined statues half-buried in deserts that will merely evoke the curiosity of passing travellers.'

'Rome fall?' Macro scoffed. 'Do be serious! Rome is the greatest in every way. Rome is, well . . . you tell him, Cato. You have a better way with words than me.'

Cato glared at his centurion, angry at the awkward situation he had been thrust into. Much as he might believe in most of Macro's claims for Rome, he was well aware of the debt the empire owed to older cultures, and he had no wish to offend his new Carthaginian friend.

'I think what you're trying to say, sir, is that in a way the Roman empire marks an end to history, in that we represent an amalgam of the best qualities to be found in men, together with the blessings of the most powerful gods. Any war we fight is intended to protect those who enjoy the benefits of empire from the danger of the barbarians outside the empire.'

'That's right!' Macro said triumphantly. 'That's us! Well done, lad! Couldn't have phrased it better. What d'you say to that, Nisus?'

'I'd say that your optio is young.' Nisus was struggling to keep the bitterness out of his voice. 'He'll have his own wisdom in time, not second-hand. Maybe he'll learn something from the few Romans who possess real wisdom.'

'And who might they be?' asked Macro. 'Bloody philosophers, no doubt.'

'They might be. Then again they might be amongst the men around us. I've talked to some Roman soldiers who share my views.'

'Oh yes? Who?'

'Your tribune Vitellius for one.'

Macro and Cato exchanged a look of astonishment.

Nisus leaned forward. 'Now there's a man who thinks deeply about issues. He knows the limits of the empire. He knows what the expansion of the empire has cost its people, Roman and non-Roman alike. He knows . . .' Nisus paused, aware that he had said more than he should. 'All I meant to say is that he thinks these things through, that's all.'

'Oh, he thinks things through all right!' Macro replied bitterly. 'And stabs you in the back if you happen to get in his way. The bastard!'

'Sir,' Cato cut in, anxious to ease the awful tension between them, 'whatever we might think of the tribune, it's best we keep it to ourselves for now.'

If Nisus had befriended Vitellius, then they must take great care not to say anything that the tribune might be able to use against them, should Nisus repeat their conversation. The treachery over Caesar's pay chest still rankled, and the fact that Vitellius had not been called to account made him a dangerous enemy.

Macro checked his temper and sat in silence, chewing on a crust, frowning at the dark landscape of endless lines of tents and campfires.

Nisus waited a moment, then rose to his feet, brushing the crumbs from his tunic. 'I'll see you around, Cato.'

'Yes. And thanks for the fish loaves.'

The Carthaginian nodded, then turned and walked briskly away.

'If I were you,' Macro said quietly, 'I'd steer well clear of him. The fellow keeps unhealthy company. We shouldn't trust him.'

Cato looked from his centurion to Nisus' fast receding shadow and then back again. He felt bad about the way Macro had treated the surgeon and ashamed that he had felt compelled to go along with his centurion's facile line of argument. But what was the alternative? And in any case, Nisus was wrong. Especially in his appraisal of Tribune Vitellius.

Chapter Thirty-One

As soon as the ramparts had been completed, General Plautius ordered the men to construct a string of forts to guard the approaches to the main camp. At the same time, the engineers started on the pontoon bridge. They drove piles into the river and secured the vessels in position by day, and laid the roadway by night. Working from each bank, the engineers were steadily closing the gap and soon men and supplies would be able to pass freely across the Tamesis. Nisus watched them from a tree stump above the river, his eyes on the shimmering reflection of torches in the dark water. He was frowning as he gazed down on the river, and was so deeply immersed in his thoughts that he did not notice his visitor until the man sat down on a log close by.

'Well, my Carthaginian friend, you do look gloomy!' Vitellius gave a small laugh. 'What's up?'

Nisus thrust his dark thoughts aside and forced a smile. 'Nothing, sir.'

'Come now, I can read a man's body like a book. What's the matter?'

'Just needed some time alone.'

'I see,' replied Vitellius and rose from the log. 'Then please excuse me. I thought we might talk, but I can see that you don't want to . . .'

Nisus shook his head. 'No need to go. I was just thinking, that's all.'

'What about?' Vitellius smoothly seated himself again. 'Whatever it was, it seems to have upset you.'

'Yes.' Nisus said no more and simply stared out across the river once again, leaving the tribune to sit silently at his side.

Vitellius was shrewd enough to know that the men he wished to manipulate needed to trust him first. And more, he must seem considerate and empathetic to a degree that indicated compassion rather than comradeship. So he waited patiently for Nisus to speak. For a while the surgeon continued to stare at the river in silence. Then he shifted his position and turned his head to the tribune, not quite able to shift the despair from his expression.

'It's strange, but no matter how many years I've served Rome I still feel, and am made to feel, like an outsider. I can mend the men's wounds, I speak to them in their tongue and I share their suffering in long campaigns. Yet the moment I mention my race or origins, it's as if a sour smell has come between us. I can see them almost recoil physically. You'd think that I was Hannibal himself from the way some of them react. The moment I mention Carthage it seems that nothing has changed in the last three hundred years. But what have I done to cause them to react this way?'

'Nothing,' replied Vitellius gently. 'Nothing at all. It's just the way we're raised. Hannibal is a name that has passed into our folklore. And now everything Carthaginian is associated with the terrible monster who once came within a whisker of wiping out Rome.'

'And is that how it will always be?' The aching bitterness in Nisus' voice was clear. 'Isn't it time your people moved on?'

'Of course it is. But not while there's still some political advantage to be wrung out of old fears. People need someone to hate, to be suspicious of, to blame for the unfairness in their lives. That's where you come in. And by "you" I mean all non-Romans who live cheek by jowl with the citizens. Take Rome. At first it was threatened by Etruscans, then the Celts, then the Carthaginians. All very real threats to our survival which made us stick together. But once we became the most powerful nation on the earth and there were no longer any enemies to make Rome tremble, we found it was still expedient to have someone to fear and hate. Being Roman means thinking you're the best. And being the best only has meaning if there is something less worthy to compare yourself to and pit yourself against.'

'And you Romans seriously think you are the most superior race in the whole world, I suppose.'

'Most do, and the truth of that, as they would see it, is more evident with every victory over an enemy, with every piece of land that is added to the empire. It encourages the mob in Rome, and it gives them something to be proud of as they eke out their lives in appalling squalor.'

'And you, Tribune?' Nisus fixed his dark eyes on the tribune. 'What do you believe?'

'Me?' Vitellius looked down at the dark shape of his boots. 'I believe that Romans are no better or worse than other people. I believe that some of our leaders are cynical enough to realise that there's no political capital to be made out of such a notion. Indeed, they realise that as long as they can focus people's discontent away from their real conditions of existence then the plebs will bump along nicely and cause few problems to their rulers. That's one of the reasons why Rome has so many public holidays and spectacles. Bread, circuses and prejudices: the three legs upon which Rome stands.'

Nisus regarded him silently for a moment. 'You still haven't told me what you believe in, Tribune.'

'Haven't I?' Vitellius shrugged. 'Maybe that's because one has to be very discreet about what one believes in these days.' He reached to his side and slipped a small wineskin off his belt, pulled out the stopper and squeezed a jet of liquid into his mouth. 'Ah! Now that's good stuff! Want some?'

'Thanks.' Nisus reached for the wineskin and tipped his head back and drank. He swallowed, and smacked his lips. 'What is it?'

'A family wine. From a vineyard my father owns in Campania. I've been drinking it since I was a kid. Nice.'

'Nice? Lovely!'

'Maybe. Anyway, I find it helps clarify life's little problems if taken in sufficient quantities. It's strong and a small amount goes a long way. More?'

'Yes, sir.'

They drank in turn, and soon the warm wine worked its way with them, and Nisus slipped into a more content and receptive frame of mind. The wine seemed to have affected the tribune equally. He lifted a knee and cupped it with his hands.

'We live in a strange age, Nisus.' Vitellius carefully slurred his words. 'We have to be careful about what we say and who we say it to. You asked me what I believe.'

'Yes.'

'Can I trust you?' Vitellius turned and smiled at him. 'Can I afford to trust you, my Carthaginian friend? Can I assume you are what you purport to be, and not some cunning spy of the Emperor?'

Nisus was hurt by the accusation, as Vitellius had hoped he would be.

'Sir, we haven't known each other long,' the wine caused him to stumble over the words, 'but I think, I'm sure, we can trust each other. At least, I trust you.'

Vitellius smiled faintly and clapped the Carthaginian on the shoulder.

'And I trust you. Really I do. And I'll tell you what I believe.' He paused to look round carefully. Aside from the restless toil of the engineers, only a handful of men moved among the ranked tents. Satisfied that they would not be overheard, Vitellius leaned closer.

'What I believe is this. That the rightful destiny of Rome has been perverted by the Caesars and their cronies. The Emperor's only concern has been to keep the mob happy. Nothing else matters. Remove Claudius and the mob won't need to be quite so spoiled all the time. And that means the burden can be lifted from the rest of the empire. Then maybe we can look forward to an empire based on partnership between civilised nations rather than one based on fear and oppression. Who knows, even Carthage might return to her rightful position in such an empire . . .'

Vitellius saw the effect his words were having on Nisus. His face was now fixed with an expression of idealistic zeal. Vitellius had to stop himself smiling. It amused him immensely that men were so easily suborned to idealistic causes. Provide them with a sufficiently attractive set of ideals to flatter themselves with, and you could command them to do anything for the sake of the cause. Find a man who craved significance and the admiration of others, and you found a fanatic. Such men were fools, Vitellius told himself. Worse than fools. They were dangerous to other people, but more importantly, they were dangerous to themselves. Ideals were figments of deluded imaginations. Vitellius believed he saw the Roman world as it truly was – the means by which those with sufficient guile to bend it to their will could achieve their ends, nothing more. People too stupid to see this were merely tools waiting to be used by better men.

Or women, he reflected, as he recalled the skill with which Flavia had made her play against the Emperor, behind the back of her husband. She and her friends might have succeeded, but for the brutal methods of Narcissus and his imperial agents, like Vitellius himself. Vitellius recalled the man who had had to be virtually beaten to death before he yielded her name. He had been executed immediately afterwards, and now the only person other than himself who knew of Flavia's complicity was Vespasian.

'Carthage reborn,' Nisus mused softly. 'I've only dared dream of that.'

'But first we must remove Claudius,' Vitellius said quietly.

'Yes,' Nisus whispered. 'But how?'

Vitellius stared at him, as if considering how far he would go down this line. He took another mouthful of wine before continuing in a voice scarcely louder than the surgeon's, 'There is a way. And you can help me. I need to get a message through to Caratacus. Will you do it?'

The moment of decision had arrived and Nisus lowered his head into his hands and tried to think. The wine helped to simplify the process, if only because it stopped any cold, logical thinking interfering with his emotions and dreams. With very little effort it was clear to him that Rome would never accept him into her bosom. That Carthage would always be treated with harsh contempt. That the iniquities of the empire would last for ever – unless Claudius was removed. The truth was clear and uncomfortable. Drunk as he was, the prospect of what he must do filled his heart with cold terror.

'Yes, Tribune. I'll do it.'

Chapter Thirty-Two

'Where's your Carthaginian friend?' asked Macro. He was sitting with his feet up on his desk, admiring the view from his tent down to the river. The evening meal was finished and tiny insects swirled in the glimmering light. Macro slapped at his thigh and smiled as his lifted hand revealed a tiny red stain and the mangled smear of mosquito. 'Ha!'

'Nisus?' Cato looked up from the letter he was writing at his camp desk, pen poised above a pot of ink. 'Haven't seen him for days, sir.'

'Good riddance, I say. Trust me, lad. His kind are best avoided.'

'His kind?'

'You know, Carthaginians, Phoenicians and all those other shifty trading nations. Can't be trusted. Always looking for an angle.'

'Nisus seemed honest enough, sir.'

'Rubbish. He was after something. They all are. When he realised you had nothing he wanted, off he went.'

'I rather think he went off, as you put it, due to the nature of the conversation we had that night he cooked us a meal, sir.'

'Please yourself.' Macro shrugged, hand poised over another irritating insect weaving dangerously close to his arm. He slapped, missed, and the mosquito whirled away with a high-pitched whine. 'Bastard!'

'That's a bit strong, sir.'

'I was talking to a bug, not about your mate,' Macro replied testily, 'though one's as much of a nuisance as the other.'

'If you say so, sir.'

'I do, and now I think I need a little refreshment!' He rose to his feet and arched his back, hands on hips. 'We all sorted for the night?'

It was the century's turn for watch duty on the east wall; the recent battle losses meant that each watch had to stand for nearly twice the normal length of time. It was unfair but, as Cato had come to learn, fairness was not at the forefront of the military mind.

'Yes, sir, I've sent the rota up to headquarters and I'll make the rounds myself just to make sure.'

'Good, I don't want any of our lads trying to sneak a quick kip. We're low enough on numbers already, thanks to the locals. Can't afford to make matters worse by having any of them stoned to death.'

Cato nodded. Sleeping on sentry duty, like so many other active-service offences, carried the death penalty. The execution had to be performed by the comrades of the guilty man.

'Right then, if anyone needs me I'll be in the centurion's mess tent.'

Cato watched him disappear into the gloom with a sprightly step. The centurions had managed to wangle a number of wine jars out of one of the transport ship captains. The consignment had been intended for a tribune of the Fourteenth, but the man had drowned one night when he had decided to go for a swim after far too much drinking, and his new supply was snapped up before the slow-witted captain thought to return the cargo to its sender. Long before the Gaulish wine merchant received word that his customer was well past paying the bill, the wine would have been guzzled.

Left on his own, Cato hurried through the day's administration without any interruption and tidied the scrolls away. This was his chance for some peace and quiet. Much as he admired and liked his centurion, Macro was annoyingly sociable and insisted on conversation at the most inconvenient moments. So much so that Cato often found himself grinding his teeth in frustration while Macro prattled on in his soldierly manner.

Cato was painfully aware of how difficult it was for him to make small talk with his military comrades, even now after several months in the army. The easy masculine jocularity of the legionaries irritated him terribly. Crude, obvious and embarrassing, it was second nature to them, but he found it difficult to join in, not least because he feared that any attempt he made at the appropriate argot would be seen through in an instant. There was nothing worse, he reflected, than being caught out in a patronising attempt at slumming it with the common soldiery.

Cato occasionally tried to steer his conversation with Macro round to more stimulating matters. But the blank and sometimes annoyed expression that greeted his efforts quickly stilled his tongue. What Macro might lack in sophistication he made up for with generosity of spirit, courage, honesty and moral integrity, but right now Cato just wanted someone to talk to – someone like Nisus. He had enjoyed their fishing expedition, and had hoped to cultivate a real friendship with the Carthaginian. The surgeon's quiet sensitivity was a balm to the raw emotions grating inside him. But Nisus had been driven away by the blunt hostility of Macro. Worse, he seemed to be falling under the spell of Tribune Vitellius. So who could he unburden his feelings to now?

Cato wondered if the answer was to keep a diary and commit his troubles to paper. Better still, he would write to Lavinia and make the most of the tortured poet-philosopher role he had been using to impress her. As real as the traumatic experiences of battle had been for him, he was also analytical and intelligent enough to see them as being in some way instructive. They would confer on him a sense of enigmatic world-weariness that was sure to impress Lavinia.

Carefully spreading out a blank scroll with his forearm, Cato dipped his pen into the inkpot, wiped off the excess ink and placed the tip on the plain surface of the scroll. There was light enough to write by for a while yet before he would have to resort to the dull glow of the oil lamp, and he took time to order his thoughts carefully. The pen made contact with the scroll, and neatly scratched out the formal greeting:

From Quintus Licinius Cato to Flavia Lavinia greetings.

The pen paused interminably as Cato faced the familiar challenge of the first sentence. He frowned with the effort of producing an opening line that would be impressive without being unnecessarily florid. A flip sentence would put Lavinia in the wrong frame of mind for what would follow. Conversely, an overly serious tone at the outset might be off-putting. He slapped the side of his head.

'Come on! Think!'

He glanced up to make sure he hadn't been overheard, and coloured as he met the twinkling eye of a passing legionary. Cato nodded back and smiled self-consciously before he charged the pen with ink and wrote the first sentence.

> My darling, scarcely a spare moment goes by when I do not think of you.

Not bad, he reflected, and true in word, if not wholly in spirit. In the few moments when his life was not busy with some duty or other, he did indeed think of Lavinia. Especially that one time they had made love in Gesoriacum shortly before she had left for Rome with her mistress, Flavia.

He bent his head and continued. This time inspiration came easily, and his pen hurriedly scratched out the words that poured from his heart, flying back and forth between the inkpot and the scroll. He told Lavinia of the very personal way in which he loved her, of the passion that burned in his loins at the very thought of her, and of how every day marked one less before the next time they would be in each other's arms.

Cato paused to read over his work, grimacing here and there as his eyes froze on the odd glib phrase, cliché or clumsy expression. But overall he was pleased with the effect. Now he wanted to tell her his news. What he had been doing since they had parted. He wanted to unburden himself of all the terrible things he felt compelled to remember but could never make sense of. The guilt at the recall of a killing thrust, the stench of a battlefield two days later, the foul oily smoke of the funeral pyres blotting out the sun and choking the lungs of those caught downwind. The way blood and intestines glistened as they were spilled on a bright summer day.

Most of all he wanted to confess to the bowel-clenching terror he had felt as the transport had approached the screaming ranks of the Britons on the far side of the Tamesis. He wanted to tell someone how close he had come to cowering down in the scuppers and screaming out his refusal to take any more.

But just as he feared that his comrades would react with disgust and pity at his weakness, so he feared that Lavinia, too, would consider him less than a man. And conscious of his youth and lack of worldliness compared to the other men of the legion, he feared that she would despise him as a frightened little boy.

Dusk dimmed into night, lit only by the thin crescent of a waning moon, and finally Cato decided that he could not tell Lavinia any more than a bald outline of the battles he had fought in. He lit the lamp, and by its guttering glow he leaned over the scroll and briskly and simply described the progress of the campaign so far. He had nearly finished by the time Macro rolled in from the centurions' mess, swearing loudly as he stubbed his toe against a tent peg.

'Who the fuck put that there?' His anger only made his speech more slurred. He stumbled past Cato into the tent and collapsed heavily onto his camp bed, which in turn collapsed with a splintering crack. Cato raised his eyes and shook his head before wiping his pen and clearing his writing materials away.

'You all right, sir?'

'I'm far from all right! Bloody crap bed's croaked on me,' the centurion mumbled bitterly. 'Now fuck off and leave me alone.'

'Right you are, sir. Fuck off it is.' Cato smiled as he rose and ducked his head under the fringe of the awning. 'See you in the morning, sir.'

'In the morning, why not?' Macro replied absently as he struggled with his tunic, and then decided to give up, slumping down on the ruins of his camp bed. Then he lurched up on an elbow.

'Cato!'

'Sir?'

'We've orders to see the legate first thing tomorrow. Don't you go and forget, lad!'

'The legate?'

'Yes, the bloody legate. Now piss off and let me get some sleep.'

Chapter Thirty-Three

The first hour watch sounded from the general's headquarters, followed at once by the calls from the other three legions camped on the north bank of the Tamesis, and an instant later from the legion still on the south bank. Although General Plautius was with the larger force, co-ordinating the preparations for the next phase of the advance, the eagles of all four legions were still housed in a headquarters area constructed on the other side of the river, so officially the army had not yet crossed the Tamesis. That triumph would be accorded to Claudius. Emperor and eagles would cross the Tamesis together. It would be a magnificent spectacle, Vespasian had no doubt of that. The greatest possible political advantage would be wrung out of the advance to the enemy capital at Camulodunum. The Emperor and his entourage, dressed in dazzling ceremonial armour, would lead the procession, and somewhere in the long train of his followers would be Flavia.

Flavia, like all those close to the Emperor, would be carefully watched by the imperial agents; all those she spoke to and every overheard conversation would be dutifully noted and forwarded to Narcissus. Vespasian wondered whether the Emperor's most trusted freedman would be accompanying his master on the campaign. It depended on how much faith Claudius had in his wife and in the prefect of the Praetorian Guard commanding the cohorts left in Rome. Vespasian had met Messalina only once, at a palace banquet. But once was enough to know that a needle-sharp mind contemplated the world from behind the dazzling mask of her beauty. Her eyes, heavily made up in the Egyptian style, had burned right through him, and Vespasian had only just managed to prevent himself from shifting his gaze. Messalina had smiled her approval at his temerity as she held out her hand to be kissed. 'You ought to watch this one, Flavia,' she had said. 'Any man who so easily withstands the gaze of the Emperor's wife is a man who would be capable of anything.' Flavia had forced a thin-lipped smile, and quickly led her husband away.

It was ironic, thought Vespasian as he recalled the event, that it was him rather than Flavia who had been singled out as the potential conspirator, however lightly. Flavia had seemed to be the loyal wife and model citizen in every respect, and had never given him cause to fear that she might become involved in anything more perilous than a trip to the public baths.

Looking back, the small social lunches she had given or been invited to without his presence now looked positively sinister, especially as a number of those with whom she had dined had subsequently been condemned following investigation by Narcissus' network of spies. Vespasian still did not know how deep her involvement was with those who were plotting against Claudius. Until he confronted her, he could not be sure. Even then, supposing she was half the cold-blooded traitor that Vitellius claimed, how would he know if her version of events was truthful? The possibility that Flavia would lie, and he would not be able to recognise the lie, filled him with a terrible sense of self-doubt.

The tramp of feet on the boards outside his office tent caught his ear and he quickly grabbed the nearest scroll and concentrated his gaze on it: a request for extra hospital capacity from the legion's senior surgeon.

A hushed exchange of words took place before the sentry barked out: 'Wait here!'

The flap parted and a shaft of daylight slanted across the desktop, causing Vespasian to squint as he looked up. 'What is it?'

'Excuse me, sir, Centurion Macro and his optio to see you. Says he was ordered to be here by the first hour signal.'

'Well, then he's late,' Vespasian grumbled. 'Get them in here.'

The sentry ducked out and stepped to one side, holding back the tent flap. 'All right, sir. The legate'll see you now.'

Two shapes stepped into the shaft of light and marched up to his desk, then stamped their feet down and stood to attention.

'Centurion Macro and Optio Cato reporting as ordered, sir.'

'You're late.'

'Yes, sir.' Macro briefly thought about apologising, but kept his silence. No apology was acceptable in the army. One either did as one was ordered or one didn't and there were no excuses.

'Why?'

'Sir?'

'Why are you late, Centurion? The first hour was sounded a short while ago.'

'Yes, sir.'

Vespasian knew when he was being stonewalled. As his vision readjusted to the dim light of the tent's interior he saw that the centurion was heavy-eyed and looked tired. In view of the man's record, he decided an unofficial warning would suffice. 'Very well, Centurion, but if you let it happen again there will be consequences.'

'Yes, sir.'

'And if I ever hear that you've been letting drink get in the way of duty I swear I will have you returned to the ranks. Got that?'

'Yes, sir,' Macro replied with an emphatic nod.

'Right then, gentlemen, I've got some work for you. Nothing too dangerous but important nonetheless, and it won't get in the way of the optio's recuperation.' Vespasian searched through some documents on one side of the desk and carefully extracted a small sheet with a seal in one corner. 'Here's your warrant. You will take your century back to Rutupiae. There you'll meet the replacements from the Eighth. I want you to take the pick of the crop for the Second. Get 'em signed on to our strength right away and the other legions can have the rest. Understood?'

'Yes, sir.'

'And if you're quick, you can load your men onto one of the transports taking the wounded down the coast. Dismissed.'

Alone in his tent once more, Vespasian's mind switched to another matter that had been causing him anxiety. Earlier in the day he and the other legion commanders had been summoned by General Plautius to be briefed on the latest attempts to negotiate with the British tribes. The news from Adminius was not good. The failure of the Roman army to advance any further towards Caratacus' capital had alarmed the tribes who had promised themselves to Rome. They had been led to understand that the confederation headed by the Catuvellauni would be knocked out of the war in a matter of weeks. Instead, the Romans were hiding within the ramparts of their fortifications while Caratacus quickly rebuilt his army. Dire threats had been issued by the Catuvellauni against tribes who were slow to join those already resisting Rome. Plautius had countered by issuing his own threats, via Adminius, about the consequences of reneging on the putative deals these tribes had struck with Rome.

Adminius reported that the tribes had now come up with a compromise. If Camulodunum fell to the legions before the end of the campaigning season they would honour their earlier promise to make peace with Rome. But if Caratacus was still in control of his capital they would feel obliged to join the confederation of tribes sworn to destroy Plautius and his army. Thus reinforced, Caratacus' army would vastly outnumber Plautius'. Retreat, if not defeat, would be inevitable, and the eagles would be hurled back from British shores.

Once more Vespasian cursed the enforced delay while the army waited for Claudius and his court to appear. Four weeks had already passed and Plautius said that it could be another month before they advanced on Camulodunum. It would be September at the earliest when the eagles arrived before the capital – assuming that Caratacus and his new army could be brushed aside easily. All because the Emperor insisted on being there for the advance.

The vanity of Claudius might yet kill them all.

Down at the river, the remains of the Sixth Century waited patiently for the loading of the injured to be completed. The legion's medical orderlies were carefully carrying the severely injured up the boarding ramps of the transports and laying the stretchers down under the awnings stretched across the decks. It was a depressing business to watch. These were the men who would be given medical discharges from the army and sent back to their homes with missing limbs or shattered bones that would never fully mend. These men were comrades, and some were good friends, but the men of Macro's century kept their silence, uncomfortable with their knowledge of the dismal future awaiting the invalids. Many were still in pain and cried out at any jarring movement.

Cato walked down the makeshift jetty looking for Nisus, hoping that it might be possible to renew their friendship in some way. The Carthaginian was easy enough to find. He was standing on top of a pile of grain sacks, bellowing out instructions and curses to his orderlies as they struggled to load the stretchers aboard the transports. As Cato approached, Nisus nodded curtly.

'Good morning, Optio. What can I do for you?'

Cato had been about to clamber up and join him, but his cold tone warned him off.

'Well, Optio?'

'Nisus, I . . . I just wanted to say hello.'

'Well, you've said it. Now, is there anything else?'

Cato stared at him, frowning, and then shook his head.

'Then if you don't mind, I've got work to do . . . You do that again and I'll kick your bloody Roman arses into the river!' he bellowed at a pair of orderlies whose struggles with an overweight casualty had caused the raw stump of his leg to knock against the side of the transport. The man was screaming.

Cato waited a moment longer, hoping for some glimmer of change in the Carthaginian's mood, but Nisus was making it quite clear that he had nothing more to say to him. Cato turned sadly away and returned to the century. He sat down some distance from Macro and just stared at the river.

Eventually the last of the wounded were loaded and the transport's captain beckoned to Macro.

'Time to move, lads! Let's be having you!'

The century filed across the boarding plank and dropped heavily onto the deck where they were guided forward. Macro gave the men permission to down packs and remove their armour. The sailors fended the transport away from the river bank, idly watched by some of the legionaries. Most of the century stretched out on the deck and dozed in the warm sun.

As Cato looked across the slowly widening gap between the transport and the shore, he saw Nisus leading his orderlies back up the slope towards the hospital tents. Casually striding down in the opposite direction came Tribune Vitellius. He caught sight of Nisus and with a broad smile raised his hand in greeting.

Chapter Thirty-Four

Although only two months had passed since the Second Legion had landed at Rutupiae, the hurriedly constructed fort guarding the landing beach had been transformed into a vast supply depot. Scores of ships were anchored in the Channel waiting for their turn at the jetty to unload their cargoes. Over a dozen vessels were tied up alongside, and hundreds of auxiliary troops were carrying sacks and amphorae from the deep holds of the broad-beamed cargo ships to stack them on carts for bulk transport into the depot.

Up the short rise from the shore stood a heavily fortified gate, and beyond that the earth ramp and palisade stretched across the landscape. Granary sheds built on low brick piles stretched out in long ranks to one side of the depot. Next to them stood neatly demarcated stacks of stoppered amphorae filled with oils, wine and beer. There were other areas set aside for military stores of javelins, swords, boots, tunics and shields.

A small stockade held a dense mass of British prisoners who had been squatting in the glare of the sun for days. In due course they would be herded into the hold of a ship returning to Gaul, and after a long journey they would end up at the great slave market in Rome.

A short distance beyond the walls of the great depot stood the field abattoir, where skilled butchers slaughtered pigs and oxen. To one side of the facility stood a vast mound of intestines, organs and other unusable parts of the butchered animals. The mound glistened in the bright sunlight, and a swarm of seagulls and other carrion gorged themselves amid a frenzy of flapping wings and shrill cries. The sound carried clearly across the Channel, borne on a light breeze that unfortunately carried the stench of the mound with it.

The foul odour strengthened as the transport approached the jetty, and more than one of Macro's men felt their stomachs turn. But a hundred feet or so from the jetty the ship was no longer directly downwind of the offal mound and the air became more breathable. Cato gripped the wooden rail and gulped down some deep breaths to flush his lungs. With a well-practised hand the steersman twisted the broad steering paddle suspended over the quarter, and the transport glided round to present its beam to the jetty.

'Ship oars!' the captain roared through cupped hands and the crewmen quickly pulled the sweeps in hand over hand and stowed them on the deck. Fore and aft stood men with coils of mooring ropes, and as the transport slowly approached the jetty, they cast the lines to men waiting by the mooring posts. They heaved and drew the transport up against the timber piles with a gentle bump before tying the mooring lines off.

Immediately a hinged gangway was placed over the side and a junior tribune ran across from the slope beyond the jetty where scores of men were lying on litters and stretchers. Some Spanish auxiliaries squatted nearby. The tribune looked around the deck, caught sight of Macro and hurried over.

'Centurion! What cargo do you have?'

'My century and some medical discharges, sir.' Macro saluted and took out a folded wax board from the forage bag hanging on his belt. 'There's my orders, sir. We're to pick up replacements for the Second Legion and march them up to the Tamesis.'

The tribune glanced over the tablet and nodded at the imprint of the Second Legion's seal in the wax.

'Very well, get your men landed and go up to headquarters. They'll sort you out with some tents and rations for the night. Right, off you go.' He waved impatiently and stood at the side of the gangway, drumming his fingers on the rail, until the last of Macro's century had tramped ashore. Cato watched as the tribune shouted out an order, and the auxiliaries began carrying the long line of stretchers aboard the transport. Many had bandaged stumps where arms and legs should have been, while one man, his head wrapped in stained cloth, ranted at the top of his voice, meaningless words hurled at all those around him. Cato stared at the man and shuddered.

'There'll be more like him before this campaign's over,' said Macro quietly.

'I think I'd rather die.'

Macro watched as the man suddenly thrashed about violently, threatening to topple himself and his stretcher bearers off the gangway and into the water between the transport and the jetty. 'Me too, lad.'

Picking up his yoke, Macro shouted out the order to raise packs, and the men marched up the hill and through the main gate of the depot. At the headquarters a smarmy civilian clerk grudgingly accepted the requests for replacement equipment Macro had been given by the Second's quartermaster. The clerk did a quick head count of the century and assigned them some tents in the furthest corner of the depot.

'And our rations?'

'You can draw some hard tack from the Eighth's stores.'

'Hard tack! I don't want hard tack. My men and I want some fresh meat and bread. You see to it.'

The clerk laid down his pen, leaned back and crossed his arms. 'Fresh meat and bread aren't available. They're for the men at the front. Now then, Centurion, if you don't mind I've got some real work to be getting on with.'

'That fucking does it!' Macro exploded, dropping his yoke and reaching across to grab the clerk's tunic. With one powerful tug he jerked the clerk across his table, scattering his paperwork and knocking his inkpot over.

'Now listen, you little shit,' Macro hissed through clenched teeth. 'See these men? They're all that's left of my century. The rest died at the front. You got that? And where the fuck were you when they were killed?' He breathed heavily, then slowly untwisted his fists from the clerk's tunic. 'Now, I'll only say this once. I want fresh meat and bread for my men. I want it taken to our tents. If it's not there by the time the evening watch is called, I'll come back here and gut you personally. Got that?'

The clerk nodded his head, eyes wide with terror.

'Can't hear you. Speak up, and make it loud.'

'Yes, Centurion.'

'Yes what?'

'Yes, I'll see to your men's food and would you like some wine?'

Behind Macro, the men shouted their approval. Macro allowed himself a thin-lipped smile and nodded. 'That's very thoughtful of you. I think we might just get along after all.'

He turned back to his men and they gave a ragged cheer before he led them off to the tents. Cato laughed at the clerk then turned and joined his centurion.

While he took some pleasure in the cheers of his men, Macro knew he should watch his temper. Assaulting a mere clerk in no way enhanced his authority. Weariness and the remains of his hangover were responsible, and he made a mental note to be careful how much wine he drank that evening. Then he recalled that the wine was free; it would be both churlish and foolish to pass by such an opportunity. He'd compensate by drinking less wine another night, he decided.

It was not long before Macro was chewing contentedly on a tender piece of beef, grilled rare over the glowing embers of a fire. Opposite him sat Cato. He carefully dabbed away meat juices from around his lips and tucked the rag back into his belt.

'These replacements we're going to get tomorrow, sir.'

'What about 'em?'

'How do we go about it?'

'Old army custom.' Macro swallowed before he continued. 'We get first pick. The very best we keep for our century. Once we're up to strength, the next best go to the other centuries of the cohort, then the other cohorts, and what's left we give to the other legions.'

'That's not very fair, sir.'

'No it isn't,' agreed Macro. 'Not fair at all, but right now that's bloody wonderful. About time our century got a break, and this is it. So let's just cheer up and make the most of it, eh?'

'Yes, sir.'

The thought of making good the losses of his sadly depleted century was most gratifying, and Macro downed the dregs of wine in his battered cup, poured himself another and downed that. Then he paused to let out a gut-wrenching belch that turned heads from the men nearby, and lay back on the ground, arms crossed under his head. He smiled, yawned and closed his eyes.

Moments later, familiar deep snores rumbled from the shadows beyond the glow of the cooking fire, and Cato cursed his fate at not being able to get to sleep first. The rest of the century had also eaten their fill, and drunk more wine than was good for them since there would be no sentry duties for them tonight at least. Nearly all were asleep, and for a while Cato sat hugging his knees, close to the fire. In its wavering heart the orange glow curled and flowed in a hypnotic fashion and he found his wine-befuddled mind drifting off to Elysian reveries. A vision of Lavinia effortlessly interposed itself before the flames, and he allowed himself to contemplate the loveliness of the image before he laid his head down on his folded cape and drifted off to sleep.

Chapter Thirty-Five

'Name?' Macro barked at the legionary standing in front of the desk.

'Gaius Valerius Maximus, sir.'

'Tribe?'

'Velina.'

'How long have you served with the eagles?'

'Eight years, sir. Seven with the Twenty-Third Martia, before it was disbanded and I was sent to the Eighth.'

'I see.' Macro nodded gravely. The Twenty-Third had been heavily implicated in the Scribonianus mutiny and had paid the ultimate price for their tardy loyalty to the new Emperor. Be that as it may, the man standing before him was a veteran and looked tough enough. More tellingly, his kit was in perfect condition; belts and buckles gleamed in the sunlight, and he had invested in a set of the new segmented armour that was becoming popular in the army.

'Let's see your sword, Maximus,' Macro growled.

The legionary reached to his side and smartly withdrew the sword from its sheath, turned it round and held the handle towards the centurion. Macro respectfully closed his fist round the handle and lifted the blade up for close inspection. The standard of care with which it had been maintained was immediately evident, and a light touch to the edge revealed a pleasing sharpness.

'Good! Very good.' Macro handed the weapon back. 'You'll get your unit assignment by the end of the day. Dismissed!'

The legionary saluted, turned and marched away, a little too stiffly for Macro's liking.

'Shall I put him down for the Second, sir?' asked Cato, sitting at Macro's side, four scrolls unrolled in front of him. He dabbed his pen in the ink and held it poised above the Second's scroll.

Macro shook his head. 'No. Can't use him. Look at the left leg.'

Cato saw a vivid white line running down from thigh to calf, the tightness of the scar tissue causing the man to drag his leg slightly.

'He'd be a liability to himself, and more importantly to us, on a forced march. Put him down for the Twentieth. He's only fit for reserve duties.'

Macro raised his eyes to the line of legionaries waiting to be assigned. 'Next man!'

As the day wore on, the long line of replacements was slowly whittled down, and the lists of names on Cato's scrolls grew longer. The process was not completed until late in the evening, when Cato checked his lists by lamplight against the tally sent from the Eighth Legion's headquarters to ensure that no names had been missed out. To his credit, Macro had balanced out the numbers so that each legion got replacements in proportion to their losses. But the best men went to the Second Legion.

The next morning Cato rose at first light and had four men from his century round up each legion's replacements and quarter them according to their allocated units so that they got used to their new identity as soon as possible. Macro busied himself at headquarters chasing up the

Second's replacement equipment. Somehow the requests had been misplaced, and a clerk had gone off to look for them, leaving the centurion sitting on one of the benches lined up outside the headquarters entrance. As he sat waiting, Macro began to feel like some lowly client awaiting his patron back in Rome, and shifted about angrily on the bench until finally he could stomach it no more. Storming into the tent he found the clerk back at his desk with the requests lying on one side of the desk.

'Found 'em then? Good. Now I'll come with you while we get things sorted.'

'I'm busy. You'll have to wait.'

'No. I won't. On your feet, laddie.'

'You can't order me around,' the clerk responded sniffily. 'I'm not army. I'm part of the imperial service.'

'Oh really? Must be a cushy number. Now let's go, before you delay the war effort any longer.'

'How dare you? If we were in Rome I'd report you to the prefect of the Praetorian Guard.'

'But we're not in Rome,' Macro growled, leaning across the desk. 'Are we?'

The clerk saw the prospect of imminent violence in the centurion's glowering expression.

'Very well then, *sir*,' he conceded. 'But let's make this quick.'

'Quick as you like. I'm not being paid by the hour.'

With Macro in tow, the clerk scurried round the depot and authorised the provision of all the requested weapons and equipment, as well as carts to carry them on the march back to the Tamesis.

'I can't believe you don't have any transports available,' Macro challenged him.

'Afraid not, sir. All available shipping has been sent to

Gesoriacum for the Emperor and his reinforcements. That's why we've been sent ahead. To help out with the admin.'

'I wondered what your lot was doing at headquarters.'

'When something needs organising properly,' the clerk puffed out his chest, 'the experts have to be called in.'

'Oh, really?' Macro sniffed. 'How reassuring.'

After the midday meal Macro assembled the new recruits for his century and had them parade in front of his tent. They were all good men; fit, experienced and with exemplary records. When he led the Sixth Century against the Britons again, they would cleave a path right through the heart of the enemy ranks. Satisfied with his selection, he turned to smile at Cato.

'Right then, Optio. You'd better introduce this lot to the Second Legion.'

'Me, sir?'

'Yes, you. Good practice for command.'

'But, sir!'

'And make it inspiring.' Macro nudged him. 'Get on with it.' He stepped back into his tent and, sitting on a stool, calmly began to sharpen the blade of his dagger.

Cato was left standing alone in front of two ranks of the hardest looking men he had ever seen. He cleared his throat nervously and then stiffened his spine and stood as tall as he could, hands clasped behind his back as his mind raced for suitable words.

'Well then, I'd just like to welcome you to the Second Legion. We've had a pretty successful campaign so far and I'm sure that soon you will all be as proud of your new legion as you were of the Eighth.' He glanced along the lines of expressionless faces and his self-confidence withered.

'I–I think you'll find that the lads of the Sixth Century will make you feel welcome enough; in a way, we're like one big family.' Cato gritted his teeth, aware that he was wallowing in a mire of clichés. 'If you have any problems you ever want to talk over with anyone then the flap of my tent is always open.'

Someone snorted derisively.

'My name's Cato, and I'm sure I'll get to know all your names quickly enough as we make our way back to the legion . . . Erm. Anybody want to raise any questions at this stage?'

'Optio!' A man at the end of the line raised a hand. His features were strikingly rugged and fortunately Cato managed to recall his name.

'Cicero, isn't it? What can I do for you?'

'Just wondered if the centurion's having us on. Are you really our optio?'

'Yes. Of course I am!' Cato coloured.

'How long have you been in the army, Optio?'

A series of chuckles rolled lightly down the line of men.

'Long enough. Now then, anything else? No? Right then, roll call at first light in full marching order. Dismissed!'

As the replacements ambled off, Cato clenched his fists angrily behind his back, ashamed of his performance. Behind him in the tent he could hear the regular rasp of Macro's blade on the whetstone. He could not face the inevitable ridicule of his centurion. At length the noise stopped.

'Cato, old son.'

'Sir?'

'You might well be one of the brightest and bravest lads I've served with.'

Cato blushed. 'Well, thank you, sir.'

'But that was about the most dismal welcome address I've ever witnessed. I've heard more inspiring speeches at accounts clerks' retirement bashes. I thought you knew all about inspiring rhetoric and all that sort of thing.'

'I've *read* about it, sir.'

'I see. Then you'd better supplement the theory with a bit more practice.' This sounded rather good to Macro, and he smiled at the happy turn of phrase. He felt more than a little gratified by his subordinate's failure to do the job properly, in spite of his privileged palace education. As was so often the case, evidence of a weak chink in another man's accomplishments produced a warm, affectionate feeling in him and he grinned at his optio.

'Never mind, lad. You've proved yourself often enough up to now.'

As Cato struggled to find a face-saving response, he became aware of a ripple of excitement sweeping across the depot. Over in the direction of the jetty, men were scrambling up the reverse slope to the palisade where they crowded along the sentry walk.

'Hello. What's going on?' Macro came out of the tent and stood at his optio's side.

'Must be something coming in from the sea,' suggested Cato.

As they watched, more men crowded the palisade, and still more men flowed between the tent lines to join them. There were shouts now, just audible above a swelling din of excited chatter. 'The Emperor! The Emperor!'

'Come on!' said Macro and he trotted towards the far side of the depot, with Cato close behind him. Soon they merged with the others hurrying towards the channel. After much jostling and panting they squeezed their way up onto the sentry walk and pushed through to the palisade.

'Make way there!' Macro bellowed. 'Make way! Centurion coming through!'

The men grudgingly deferred to his rank, and moments later Macro was hard up against the wooden stakes, with Cato by his side, both staring out across the channel at the spectacle serenely making its way in from the sea. A few miles off, caught in the full glare of the afternoon sun, the imperial squadron was making its way towards them. Flanked by four triremes, which it utterly dwarfed, was the Emperor's flagship. It was a massive vessel of great length and breadth, with two towering masts mounted between the elaborately crenellated bow and stern. Two huge purple sails hung from their spars, tightly sheeted home to ensure that the gold eagles emblazoned on them were displayed to best effect. Cato had seen the vessel once before, at Ostia, and had marvelled at its huge dimensions. Great oars rose from the water, swept forward in shimmering unison, and sank back smoothly into the sea. Behind the flagship a line of warships entered the channel, followed by transports, and then by the navy afterguard, by which time the flagship was drawing close to the shore with all the stately grace that its highly trained crew could muster. The draught of the flagship was such that it would have run aground had it attempted to make for the jetty. Instead, the vessel heaved to a quarter of a mile from the shore, and anchors were run out fore and aft. The triremes swept past and headed for the jetty, decks crowded with the white uniforms of the Praetorian Guard. Once the warships had moored, the Praetorians filed ashore and formed up along the slope outside the depot.

'Can you see the Emperor?' Macro asked. 'Your eyes are younger than mine.'

Cato scanned the deck of the flagship, running his eyes over the milling ranks of the Emperor's entourage. But there was no sign of any obvious deference, and Cato shook his head.

The legionaries waited excitedly for a sign of Claudius. Someone started a chant of 'We want the Emperor! We want Claudius!' that quickly caught on. It rippled along the palisade and echoed out across the channel to the flagship. But there was still no sign of the Emperor, despite a number of false alarms, and slowly the mood changed from excitement to frustration, and then apathy as the Praetorian cohorts were marched off to the side of the depot furthest from the field abattoir and began making camp for the night.

'Why's the Emperor not landing?' asked Macro.

From his childhood in the imperial palace Cato recalled the lengthy protocols that accompanied the official movements of the Emperor, and could guess at the reason for the delay easily enough. 'I expect he'll land tomorrow, when the full ceremony for welcoming an emperor can be laid on.'

'Oh.' Macro was disappointed. 'Nothing worth seeing tonight then?'

'I doubt it, sir.'

'Right, well, I expect there's some work we can be getting on with. And there's some of that wine that still needs drinking. Coming?'

Cato knew Macro well enough by now to recognise the difference between a genuine choice and a politely worded order.

'No thank you, sir. I'd like to stay and watch for a while.'

'Suit yourself.'

As dusk gathered, the other men on the wall slowly drifted away. Cato leaned forward, resting his elbow in the notch between two stakes and cupping his chin on one palm as he gazed at the array of shipping now filling the channel around the flagship. Some vessels carried soldiers, some carried the servants of the imperial household, and a few others the expensively dressed members of the Emperor's entourage. Further out some large transports were anchored with curious grey humps showing above the coping of their holds. Once the triremes that had unloaded the Praetorians moved away from the jetty, the large transports were eased alongside the jetty and Cato had a clearer view of their cargo.

'Elephants!' he exclaimed.

His surprise was shared by the few men remaining along the palisade. Elephants had not been used in battle for over a hundred years. Though they presented a terrifying spectacle to those facing them on the battlefield, well-trained soldiers could neutralise them very quickly. And, if badly handled, elephants could be as much of a danger to their own side as the enemy. Modern armies had little use for them and the only elephants Cato had ever seen were those in the beast pens behind the Circus Maximus. Quite what they were doing here in Britain was anybody's guess. Surely, he thought, the Emperor can't be intending to use them in battle. They must be here for some ceremonial purpose, or to put the fear of the gods into the hearts of the Britons.

As he watched one of the elephant transports, a section of the vessel's side was removed and a broad gangway was manhandled onto the jetty. Sailors lowered a heavy ramp into the hold and spread a mix of straw and earth up the ramp and across the gangway. These familiar smells would be a badly needed comfort to the animals after the uncertain motion of the sea journey from Gesoriacum. Satisfied that all was in place, the captain gave the order to unload the elephants. A moment later, amid anxious trumpeting, an elephant driver urged an elephant up the ramp and onto the deck. Even though Cato had seen them before, the sudden emergence of the vast grey bulk of the beast with its wicked tusks still awed him and he caught his breath before reassuring himself that he was safe enough where he was. The elephant driver tapped his stick against the back of the animal's head and it tentatively lumbered onto the gangway, causing the transport to tip slightly at the shift in weight. The elephant paused and raised its trunk, but the driver whacked the stick down and with clearly visible expressions of relief from the crew, the elephant crossed to the jetty.

The last elephant came ashore as the daylight faded, and the ponderous beasts were led away to an enclosure some distance from those of other animals who were afraid of the elephants. As Cato and the remaining legionaries watched them move off with their curious slow, swaying gait, the transports made way for yet more shipping – this time the smartly painted warships carrying the Emperor's household and entourage. Across the gangways spilled the social elite of Rome: patricians in purple striped togas, their wives in exotic silks and coiffured hair. After them came the lesser nobility, the men in expensive tunics, their wives in respectable stolae. Finally came the baggage, portered across the gangways by scores of slaves carefully supervised by each household's major domo to ensure nothing was broken.

As each household gathered in clusters along the jetty, clerks from the depot's headquarters scurried around searching for names on their lists and escorting their guests to the tented area prepared for them in a fortified enclosure appended to the depot. Few of the new arrivals deigned to look up at the legionaries lining the palisade. For their part the legionaries stared silently, marvelling at the flamboyant wealth of the aristocracy of Rome whose lifestyle depended upon the blood and sweat shed by the men of the legions.

As Cato's eyes drifted over the colourful throng on the jetty, a face in the crowd abruptly turned towards him in a way that instantly drew his attention. He felt his heart thrill inside his chest and was conscious of a rapid quickening of his pulse. His breath stilled as he drank in the long dark hair, held back by combs, the fine dark line of the eyebrows and the heart-shaped face coming to a gentle point at the chin. She was wearing a bright yellow stola that emphasised the slender curves of her body. There was no mistaking her, and he stared dumbstruck, wanting to call out her name but not quite daring to. She turned back to her mistress and continued their conversation.

Thrusting himself away from the palisade, Cato ran down the reverse slope in the direction of the depot's main gate, all the weariness of the past weeks swept from his body at the prospect of holding Lavinia in his arms again.

Chapter Thirty-Six

'Lavinia!' Cato called out as he pushed through the milling bodies of the Emperor's entourage, heedless of the astonished expressions and sharp curses that followed him. Ahead, a short distance off, he saw her yellow stola flash between a gap in the crowd, and Cato pushed on towards it, calling out again, 'Lavinia!'

She caught the sound of her name and turned her head, searching for its source, and her gaze came to rest on Cato as he brushed between a senator and his wife twenty feet away.

'Cato?'

At Lavinia's side her mistress, the lady Flavia, turned to follow her gaze. Flavia's face broke into a smile as she, too, caught sight of the young man she had first met at the imperial palace ten years earlier. While she had been a minor figure at court, Flavia had taken an interest in the shy boy, and seen to it that he was given access to the palace library, and protected as far as possible from the endemic bullying amongst the imperial slaves. In return Cato had been utterly loyal to her ever since.

'I say!' the senator protested. 'Bloody watch where you're going, young man!'

Cato ignored him and ran the last few paces, arms outstretched as Lavinia's expression broke into a wide-eyed

274

grin of delight. She squealed out a greeting and raised her arms, and an instant later was crushed in his embrace. It lasted only a moment before Cato pulled back, raising his hands to her cheeks, cupping her smooth skin and wondering once more at the dark, piercing beauty of her eyes. She smiled, and then couldn't help laughing at the pure joy of the moment, and he laughed with her.

'Oh Cato! I'd so hoped to see you here.'

'Well, here I am!' He leaned forward and kissed her on the mouth, before his cursed self-consciousness returned and made him aware of the surrounding crowd. He pulled back from her and glanced about. A number of people were staring at them, some in amused surprise, some frowning at the unseemliness of such behaviour in public. The senator was still looking angry. Cato flashed him an apologetic smile, and returned his eyes to Lavinia.

'What-what are you doing here? I thought you were on the way to Rome.'

'We were,' said Flavia, stepping round to one side of the couple. 'We'd just reached Lutetia when I received instructions from Narcissus to return to Gesoriacum and wait for the Emperor.'

'And here we are!' Lavinia concluded happily. Then she looked down and caught sight of the livid scar on his arm. 'Oh no! What happened to you? Are you all right?'

'Of course I'm all right. Just a burn.'

'My poor baby,' Lavinia cooed, and kissed his hand.

'Have you had it treated properly?' asked Flavia as she examined the scar. 'I know what these army quacks are like. I wouldn't trust them to treat a cold.'

The attention was making Cato feel embarrassed and he quickly insisted that all was well – yes, it looked bad, but it was healing; no, there weren't any other injuries; yes, he'd make sure he was more careful in future; no, it wasn't Macro's fault.

'And did you really miss me?' Lavinia concluded quietly, intently watching his expression.

'Do fish live in the sea?' Cato replied, smiling.

'Oh you!' Lavinia punched his chest. 'You could just say yes.'

'Well, yes then. I did. Very much.' Cato kissed her again, automatically running one hand down the small of her back to the swell of her buttocks. Lavinia chuckled. 'Jupiter! You just can't wait for it, can you?'

Cato shook his head.

'Well then,' Lavinia leaned forward and whispered in his ear, 'we'll have to sort something out a little bit later . . .'

'Look here,' Flavia intruded. 'I hate to interrupt this distastefully amorous reunion, but a more secluded venue would be appropriate, don't you think?'

The tents provided for the imperial entourage were luxuriously appointed, and for Cato, starved of such a lifestyle for almost a year now, a welcoming reprieve from the rough and ready accommodation of the legions. Lady Flavia, Lavinia and he were sitting on heavy bronze chairs arranged around a low table on which sweet pastries and savouries were artfully arranged on gold platters. Cato sat beside Lavinia, while her mistress sat on the opposite side of the table where the light cast by the oil lamps was dim.

'Nice.' Cato nodded at the ornately decorated snacks, mindful of the battered mess tin waiting for him back in his tent.

'Not mine,' said Flavia. 'My husband disapproves of fripperies. It's part of the service Narcissus has laid on for the Emperor's companions. In case we should get homesick.'

'Rather pretty, aren't they?' Lavinia smiled, flashing her perfect white teeth at Cato. She helped herself to a small filled pastry and bit into it. Flakes and crumbs fell down her front and Cato's eyes followed them as far as her breasts. And then flickered back to her face as he blushed.

'Pretty enough, my dear.' Flavia reached over and deftly flicked the crumbs from her handmaid's stola. 'But they're only snacks when all is said and done. One shouldn't be too concerned with appearances. It's the essence of a thing that matters. Isn't that right, Cato?'

'Yes, my lady.' Cato nodded, wondering why Flavia was attempting to warn him off Lavinia. 'But since the essence of a thing is a matter of conjecture, might we not be better off simply judging by appearances, my lady?'

'Think that if you will.' Flavia shrugged, unimpressed by his glib sophistry. 'But life will be a harsh teacher if you persist in such a view.'

Cato nodded. He disagreed with her but was keen not to risk disturbing the happy ambience of their reunion. 'Might I have some more wine, my lady?'

Flavia gestured towards his cup and a slave with a decanter hurried from the shadows at the rear of the tent. Cato held out his cup and the slave quickly refilled it and stepped back discreetly, as still and silent as before.

'I wouldn't drink too much of that,' Lavinia said with a cheeky smile, and nudged Cato gently in the ribs.

'To you, my lady.' Cato raised his cup. 'To you, and your husband.'

Flavia nodded graciously, and then leaned back in her chair, eyes fixed on the young optio. 'And is the legate enjoying a successful campaign?'

Cato paused before he replied. The campaign was undoubtedly a success as things stood, but he was still too close to the experience of how it had been won by the rank and file of the legions to feel much sense of triumph. Any success that future historians might lightly allude to when writing about the invasion of this island would never acknowledge the pain, blood, filth and soul-numbing exhaustion it had cost. A vivid image of Pyrax being cut down as he struggled to free himself from the mud flashed into Cato's mind. He knew that historians would regard the death of Pyrax as a pitifully insignificant detail unworthy of a place in history.

'Yes, my lady,' Cato said carefully. 'The legate has won his share of the glory. The Second has acquitted itself well enough.'

'Maybe. But I'm afraid the plebs want heroism, not competency.'

Cato smiled bitterly. His newly acquired status as a Roman citizen technically ranked him as one of the plebeians that Flavia spoke of with such contempt. Yet the accusation was valid enough.

'The Second has proved itself in every battle it has fought in. You can be proud of your husband. And it's not as if the Britons aren't being helped.'

'No?'

'No, my lady. Time and again we've found that the Britons are using Roman slingshot and swords.'

'Did they capture them from our men?'

'Hardly. We've won every fight so far, they've not had any pickings from the battlefield. Someone must be supplying them.'

'Someone? Who do you mean?'

'I have no idea, my lady. All I know is that the legate is investigating the matter and said he'd report it to the general.'

'I see.' Flavia nodded thoughtfully, and twitched the hem of her gown. Without looking up she continued, 'Now then, I expect you two might want to catch up on a few matters. It's a lovely night for a walk. A long walk, I should think.'

Lavinia grasped his hand as she quickly stood up, and gave him a sharp tug. Cato rose, and dipped his head in a bow to Flavia. 'It's good to see you again, my lady.'

'And you, Cato.'

Lavinia led the way to the tent flap. Just before they disappeared outside, Flavia called out after them, 'Enjoy yourselves, while you can.'

Chapter Thirty-Seven

It was just before dawn and a milky grey mist had risen from the channel. It hung about the depot gate like a clammy shroud, illuminated by the close glow of dying torches on the sentry walk. The men were quiet, shuffling in their assigned unit columns, their subdued conversation punctuated by occasional coughs in lungs unaccustomed to the damp air of the island. A long day's march lay ahead of them. They had been fed on quickly heated porridge that felt like a stone inside them now.

For nearly all of them a new life awaited in a legion they might have only heard of before, whose men would regard them with no more than grudging acceptance for the next few months, until they had proved themselves better than their reserve legion status implied. For some the transition to a combat unit would be smooth enough, having been sent to the Eighth from one of the frontier legions. In preparation for the invasion of Britain, the imperial general staff had pulled veteran cohorts out of those legions facing quiescent barbarians, and marched them to Gaul for temporary attachment to the Eighth.

The older men who had hoped for a peaceful end to their career under the eagle were naturally resentful to find themselves drawn into the decisive phase of this year's campaign. They were no longer as fit and quick as they had once been, and so the odds of surviving the coming battles were not encouraging.

Then there were the young men, recent recruits, fresh out of training and more afraid of their officers than any enemy. In brightly polished segmented armour, the cost of which would be subtracted from their meagre pay for many years yet, wearing tunics whose red dye had not yet begun to fade, and with sword grips not yet worn smooth from frequent handling, they were keen to get stuck in, and develop the easy-going swagger of the veterans.

'All present?' asked Macro as he strode up to Cato, fastening the strap of his helmet.

'Yes, sir.'

'Then let's get going.' Macro turned to the head of the dimly visible column and shouted, 'Fall in!'

The ranks quickly formed up into marching order, four abreast.

'Column ready! . . . Forward march!'

Even the rawest recruit amongst them had undergone enough drilling to respond instantly to the word of command and the column moved as one into the standard marching step. The noise of boots crunching on the chalky soil was softened by the damp air. With Cato at his side, Macro waited for the advance guard to pass before taking his place at the head of the main body. As they passed out of the depot gate, Cato twisted his head round and gazed up at the sentry walk, running his eyes along the dark outline of the palisade until he saw Lavinia. He quickly raised a hand so that she could pick him out, and his heart lifted when her arm rose in reply.

'I take it you didn't get much sleep then?'

'No, sir.' Cato turned back. 'None at all.'

'Good for you, lad!' Macro nudged him, but Cato was

past being offended by his centurion's bluntness. 'Feel better for it? I find a quick roll in the hay leaves me feeling fresh as a daisy.'

'It wasn't that quick, sir.' Cato yawned before he could stop himself.

'I see. Well, you'd better not drop off on the march. Do that and I'll leave you to the tender mercies of the Britons.'

The march back to the legion took them along the route by which the army had advanced only a few weeks before. The engineers had been very busy in the meantime. The land on each side of the track had been cleared of undergrowth and any possible concealment for enemy forces, and the brow of every hill and every ford was now protected by a small fort manned by auxiliaries. The column of replacements overtook heavy supply wagons hauling food and equipment up to the legions. In the opposite direction trundled empty wagons returning from the front, heading for the depot to load up for the next round trip. It was part of the relentless Roman efficiency that would ensure that the advance on Camulodunum would take place with its legions properly armed and well-fed.

When they next took to the field, the legions would be led by the Emperor in person, accompanied by his elite Praetorian cohorts and the vast lumbering elephants that would be driven into the enemy ranks and trample huge swathes through their lines. Cato could almost bring himself to feel sorry for the natives. But not quite. Not after the dread and despair of the recent battles. What he wanted now was a swift end to the campaign. A single crushing blow that would utterly break the will of the Britons to resist the inevitable. If Caratacus and his army could be comprehensively crushed, surely the other tribes would realise there was no point in any further resistance. The island would become a province one day, there was no doubt of that. Not now the Emperor was here. No matter how many legions, or elephants, it took, the Britons would be forced to their knees. Cato promised himself, when it was all over, he would find a way to be with Lavinia again.

Each evening, when the last light of day had all but gone, Macro halted his column in the temporary marching camps attached to the forts. Before first light he roused his men and the column marched on well before the sun had raised its head above the distant horizon. The hard pace was as much a test of his new men as it was a result of his desire to get back to his legion. It was gratifying to him that not one of the men he had chosen for his century fell out of line and joined the ragged column of stragglers destined for the other legions. Only a handful of those picked for the Second failed to keep the pace he set. Vespasian would be pleased with his replacements. With such men in his legion the Second would win a fine reputation in the rest of the campaign. And Vespasian, Macro knew, was not a man who forgot those who served him well.

It felt strange to retrace a route so recently taken at such a cost in lives. Here was the forest track where the Second had been ambushed by Togodumnus and would have been crushed, had it not been for the timely intervention of the Fourteenth Legion. Macro could even see the oak tree on the distant hill where he had killed Togodumnus in single combat as the British chieftain fled towards the marshes with his men.

The following day they marched across a pontoon bridge over the Mead Way where, only weeks before, their comrades had withered under such a hail of arrow and slingshot that the smooth flowing water was stained red. The route then turned north and passed over a gentle ridge and down towards the Tamesis, through the gorse-choked marsh to the fortress on the south bank, where they waited for transports to ferry them across to the main body of the army. The bridge was nearly finished and the engineers were being driven hard to complete it in time for the Emperor to lead the eagle standards and his reinforcements over into enemy territory.

The column of replacements waited wearily while the transports shuttled back and forth across the Tamesis. At last it was the turn of the Second's replacements to cross. On landing, Macro dismissed his century and led the rest of his column up to the Second's headquarters to parade them on the wide avenue opposite the main entrance. Inside the clerical tent he handed over the roster, after having marked off the names of those men he had chosen for his century.

'Looks like you've picked only the best for us, Centurion.'

Macro turned and quickly stood to attention at the sight of his legate.

'Yes, sir. The best.'

'Well done.' Vespasian pulled on his helmet with its bright red crest. 'Now I'll introduce myself to them officially.'

Cato, meanwhile, took his kit to the section tent and then went in search of Nisus, determined to get to the bottom of the surgeon's cold formality towards him. Cato had not yet reached the age where the opinion of others was no longer the critical issue of his social relations. More than anything he strove to be worthy of respect, and at the least he wanted an explanation from Nisus for the sudden withdrawal of his friendship.

But Nisus was not in the field hospital, not in his tent, not sitting down by the jetty. Eventually Cato went back to the field hospital and asked one of the orderlies where Nisus might be found.

'Nisus?' The orderly's eyebrows rose.

Cato nodded and a flash of recognition lightened the orderly's face.

'You're that mate of his, aren't you? I'm surprised you don't know.'

'Don't know?' Cato felt his blood run cold. 'I've been out of the camp. What's happened?'

'Nisus has gone.'

'Gone?'

'Disappeared. Two days ago. Just walked out of the camp to go fishing, and never came back.'

'Who saw him last?'

'Don't know.' The orderly shrugged. 'He was supposed to meet someone by the river and never showed up. That's how it got reported.'

'Who was he supposed to meet?'

'A tribune. The resident broad-striper.'

Vitellius. Cato nodded slowly.

Chapter Thirty-Eight

It was noon before Vespasian reached the last of the fortified outposts ringing the main camp. He had not given any warning of the inspection, wanting to catch each garrison at its habitual level of operational readiness rather than presenting a show for the visit of a high-ranking officer. Vespasian was gratified to see that he was challenged as he rode up towards each fort, and that admission was steadfastly refused unless the correct password was given. Beyond the gates most of the fortlets were well ordered, with infantry weapons close to hand and an adequate supply of ammunition on the bolt-thrower platforms.

The last fort was no exception, and as Vespasian and his mounted escort trotted through the gate he was immediately confronted with a line of legionaries standing across the entrance. Their optio gave the order for the gate to be closed the moment the last of the legate's escorts had passed inside.

'What's this, Cato?' Vespasian waved his hand at the legionaries as he dismounted. 'An honour guard?'

'A precaution, sir.' Cato saluted. 'The gate is always the weakest point of a defence.'

'Archimedes?'

'Yes, sir. From his treatise on siege warfare.'

'Well, he's right, and you do well to pay heed to him. What's your strength?'

'Forty men, sir. And forty in the other half of the century in the next outpost with Centurion Macro.'

'So, you're up to full strength once again, with the cream of the crop. I'll be expecting nothing but the best from the Sixth Century of the Fourth Cohort from now on. See to it that I'm not disappointed.'

'Yes, sir.'

'Right then, let's have a look round.'

Vespasian strode off to begin his inspection, with the anxious optio following in his wake. The tents were scrutinised for any signs of slack guy ropes, leaking seams and untidy stowage of bedding. The latrine was examined to ensure that it had not reached the level where it must be filled in and a new one dug. Then Vespasian climbed up onto the turf ramp and began a tour of the palisade. At the artillery platform he carefully examined the winding mechanisms to ensure that they were adequately greased, and nodded approvingly at the scent of linseed oil on the torsion springs. He was experimenting with the elevating gear when there was a shout from the watchtower.

'Enemy in sight!'

The legate and the optio quickly glanced up at the stark silhouette of the sentry on the trestle platform high above them.

'What direction and what force?' Cato snapped.

'To the west, sir! Maybe two miles away.' The sentry pointed with his javelin. 'Small group of horsemen, maybe fifteen or twenty. Heading this way.'

'Come on!' Vespasian led the way up the rough wooden ladder of the watchtower. He emerged through the opening on the platform and stepped over to the side of the sentry as Cato scrambled up behind him.

'Over there, sir.' The sentry pointed again and beyond

the tip of the javelin lay a distant hill. Vespasian could make out the tiny shapes of horses galloping ahead of a thin smudge of brown from the dust kicked up by their hooves. The land stretching out from the fortlet was mostly grass, mixed with random copses of oak, but the horsemen made no attempt to conceal their approach and pounded directly towards the fortlet.

'I hardly think they mean to attack us,' muttered Vespasian.

'Nevertheless, sir, I think we should stand the men to,' said Cato.

'Very well.'

Cato bellowed the order and the half-century snatched up their weapons and manned the wall. The legate continued to watch the approaching horsemen. They were closing rapidly and he could see now that there were two groups. A cluster of three was leading the way, and from the frequent glances back over their shoulders it was evident that they were being pursued by the others. The shrill cries of the pursuers were faintly audible now.

'Load the bolt-thrower!' Cato called down to the palisade. The artillery crew strained on the winch sheers, and the clank of the ratchet competed with the excited hubbub of the soldiers watching the chase. The men's mood was understandable, but not tolerable and Vespasian raised an eyebrow at the optio. Cato leaned over the rail.

'Silence there! Next man who opens his mouth is on a charge!'

The horsemen were barely a quarter of a mile away now and Vespasian could make out the purple cloaks and long hair whipping out behind the three being pursued. The gap between the two groups had narrowed to a few score yards and the men behind howled their triumph as they chased down their prey, swooping for the kill with their narrow-bladed cavalry spears. The man nearest the fortlet suddenly looked up and waved at the Romans.

Vespasian started. 'It's Adminius! Open the gate, Optio! Quickly, man!'

The section on the gate removed the bar and pulled the gate inwards. Cato ordered the bolt-thrower crew to make ready to fire.

'Aim for the second group. Fire the instant the first lot are clear!'

As the horsemen galloped up towards the fortlet, barely fifty feet separated the two groups. Adminius and his bodyguards slewed round in an arc and approached the open gate from the side, clearing the way for the artillery crew. A legionary flipped the firing lever and the bolt-thrower discharged its missile with a loud crack. There was a sharp thwack as the bolt struck one of the British cavalrymen just below the throat, passed clean through him, and buried itself in the shaggy forehead of the horse immediately behind. Beast and rider fell in a sprawling, kicking mass, right in the path of the horsemen behind. Only a handful managed to ride on and keep up with their quarry. As they caught sight of the gateway, the leading Briton realised he had lost the race, and hurled his spear after Adminius and his men. The dark shape curved through the air and struck the rearmost man squarely between the shoulders and he toppled to one side as Adminius spurred his beast inside the fortlet.

The section on the gate ran into the opening and presented their shields and javelins to the Britons chasing Adminius. At sight of the legionaries, the horsemen drew up, savage expressions of rage and frustration etched on their features.

'Get 'em!' Cato shouted from the watchtower. 'Use your javelins!'

The section responded at once and moments later two more men and their horses were down, thrashing about in the dirt track in front of the gate. The others turned and galloped off, leaning low across the necks of their beasts in case any more javelins came after them.

Cato followed the legate down the ladder and the two of them ran over to the gate where Adminius had dropped from his mount and lay on his back, gasping for breath, eyes clenched shut in pain. There was a large tear in the side of his tunic, which was drenched with blood.

'He's wounded.' Vespasian turned towards his escort to shout an order for a surgeon to be brought up from the main camp immediately. Adminius' eyes snapped open at the sound of the legate's voice and he struggled to raise himself up on one elbow.

'Easy there! Rest yourself. I've sent for a surgeon.' Vespasian knelt down beside Adminius. 'I see the negotiations with the tribes didn't go so well this time.'

Adminius grinned weakly, his face white from loss of blood. He reached up and clenched his fist on the clasp holding the legate's cloak. Cato started forward but was waved back.

'S-something I have to tell you!' Adminius whispered anxiously. 'A warning.'

'Warning?'

'There's a plot to kill your Emperor.'

'What?'

'I don't know the full details . . . Only heard a rumour at the last gathering of tribal representatives.'

'What rumour? Tell me.'

'I was in disguise . . . because Caratacus was there, trying to get the others to join his fight against Rome . . . One of his advisers was drunk . . . started to brag that the invaders

290

would soon leave the island . . . that a war amongst the Romans would start the moment the Emperor was killed. The man told me that it would be a Briton who would strike the blow . . . and that the assassin will be provided with the means by a Roman.'

'A Roman?' Vespasian could not hide his shock. 'Did this adviser of Caratacus give any names?'

Adminius shook his head. 'He was stopped before he could. Caratacus called him away.'

'Does Caratacus know what the man revealed?'

Adminius shrugged. 'Don't know.'

'Those men chasing you – might they have been sent after you?'

'No. We ran into them. They weren't following us.'

'I see.' Vespasian thought for a moment, then turned to Cato. 'You heard all that?'

'Yes, sir.'

'You will not reveal one word of what Adminius has said. Not one word unless I give you express permission. Not to anyone. Understand?'

Vespasian and his escort returned to the main camp late in the afternoon. The legate dismissed his men and made straight for General Plautius' headquarters. Vespasian's creased brow was eloquent expression of his unease as he strode down the lines of tents. The rumour Adminius had spoken of might be no more than drunken bravado by one of Caratacus' followers anxious to be thought of as a man in the know, but the threat could not be ignored given the large quantity of Roman arms being found in the hands of the natives. The whole thing smacked of a grand conspiracy. Was it possible that the Liberators' network reached as far as Britain? If so, then they were truly a force to be reckoned with. If Adminius' information was well-founded, then there was a traitor in the army.

Vespasian's first thought was Vitellius. But would the tribune take such a terrible risk with his life? Vespasian wished he knew the man well enough to make that judgement. Was Vitellius so arrogant and imprudent as to make yet another direct attempt to further his lofty political ambitions? Surely he had more sense than that.

On the other hand the assassin's Roman contact might not be in the army at all. There was already a large number of civilians following in the wake of the army; slave agents from Rome looking for bargains, wine merchants anxious to supply the legions, land agents mapping the best of the farmland for quick purchase from the Emperor, and all manner of camp followers and traders now that the army had firmly established itself as far as the Tamesis. Perhaps the traitor was among the imperial entourage itself. Certainly such a person would be well-placed to assist an assassin. This possibility made Vespasian's heart sink like a rock, and he suddenly felt very weary and utterly depressed.

Flavia was in the imperial entourage.

All the dreadful uncertainty about the woman he wanted to love unreservedly tortured him anew. How could she? How could she risk so much? Not just for herself, but for him and their son, Titus. How could she put them all in such danger? But, he told himself, Flavia might be innocent. It might be an altogether different person who was the traitor. In all likelihood it was.

Whatever the truth, if indeed there was a plot to kill the Emperor, then General Plautius must be informed at once. Regardless of the risk to Flavia.

Chapter Thirty-Nine

The general was just leaving his headquarters tent when Vespasian arrived. Aulus Plautius was wearing his full ceremonial armour and the afternoon sun was brilliantly reflected in the fine cuirass and gilded helmet. Around him his senior officers gathered in equally gaudy attire. A string of neatly groomed horses was being led up the slope to where they waited outside the general's headquarters.

'Ah! There you are, Vespasian. I trust your day went well?'

'Sir, I have to tell you something. In private.'

'In private?' Plautius looked irritated. 'Then it'll have to wait.'

'But, sir, it's vital I tell you what I know straight away.'

'Look, we can't delay any longer. The Emperor and the reinforcements are just beyond that ridge on the far side of the river. He has to be met with the full formalities as he enters the southern camp. Now go and get your ceremonials on. Then join me as fast as you can on the other side of the river.'

'Sir—'

'Vespasian, you have your orders. Kindly carry them out.'

The horses had reached the headquarters tent and without another word or glance at Vespasian, Aulus Plautius hoisted himself onto a glossy black mare and pulled the

293

reins to turn the horse in the direction of the newly completed bridge. After a sharp kick of his booted heels the beast lurched forward into a canter and the rest of the staff scrambled onto their mounts and hurried to catch up. Vespasian watched them go, arm raised to protect his mouth from the dust churning through the air. Then he slapped his thigh angrily and marched back towards his legion.

Claudius and his reinforcements would have arrived in the camp on the south bank just before dusk, but for Narcissus. In the event, the column was halted on the far side of the ridge while the freedman went on ahead in his litter to make the appropriate arrangements for a dramatic entry. The litter drew up in front of the assembled ranks of officers and they waited in hushed anticipation for the occupant to emerge. With painstaking exactness the bearers lowered the litter to the ground, and a pair of footmen hurried to the silk curtains and drew them back. The plumes of the officers' helmets tilted as they craned their necks to get a good view of the litter, fully expecting the Emperor to emerge in some strange twist of protocol. There was an audible sigh of disappointment as Narcissus stepped out of the litter, rose to his feet and greeted the general.

'Aulus Plautius! Nice little camp site you've got here.' Narcissus paused to examine the scarlet cloaks and polished breastplates massed before him. 'Hello, gentlemen, I'm most touched by this welcome. You really shouldn't have.'

Aulus Plautius ground his teeth in an effort to control his temper. He stood silently as the freedman stepped up to him with a broad smile and pumped his hand.

'Now then, let's not hang about any longer. We need to get on and make preparations for the arrival of the Emperor. Have your staff officers stay to help with the organisation.

The rest of these chaps can go and wait wherever it is you soldiers go between battles.'

While the officers milled about impatiently in the over-crowded officers' mess tent, Narcissus quickly issued instructions that sent legionaries scurrying around the camp to assemble the materials necessary to achieve the theatrical effect that the Emperor's chief secretary wanted. Vespasian, bathed, scented and clad in ceremonial finery, managed to join the officers reassembled outside the headquarters just as proceedings began.

Long after the last rays of the sun had been blotted out by night, a strident blaring of trumpets at the main gate announced the arrival of Claudius. The avenue from the gate to the wooden praetorium was lined with legionaries holding blazing torches aloft. By the light of the orange and gold flames the senior cohort of the Praetorian Guard marched into the camp. The spotless white of their uniforms and shields engendered a certain amount of quiet resent-ment in the men who had had to fight their way to the Tamesis. More cohorts followed and formed up on the parade ground in front of the Praetorium. Next came a score of young boys in purple tunics, carrying gilded wicker baskets, who showered flower petals along the route. Finally, another blast from the trumpets split the night air, this time accompanied by a different kind of trumpeting, which few men in the invading army had ever heard before.

Lumbering into view down the avenue of flickering torches came the elephants, with the Emperor himself riding the first in the line. Right on cue the legionaries along the route began to shout out 'Imperator! Imperator! Imperator!' the traditional acclamation for a beloved and respected commander. Claudius sat behind an elephant driver on an elaborate throne specially made to be carried on the back of an elephant. Without inclining or turning his head, the Emperor waved one hand in acknowledgement. He wore a magnificent silver cuirass studded with jewels that gleamed like eyes of red and green in the torchlight. Flowing around him was a cloak of imperial purple. On his brow he wore a golden wreath whose lustre reflected the flickering glow.

Magnificent as the spectacle was, the principal member of the cast would have benefited from a dress rehearsal. The unusual rolling motion of riding an elephant is uneasy on the stomach of someone new to elephants and the motion necessitated frequent adjustments to the wreath to keep it at an aesthetically pleasing angle. Otherwise, judged Vespasian, Claudius was making a decent enough fist of it.

The elephant driver halted the Emperor's beast and urged it down with a set sequence of kicks and orders. The front knees gracefully buckled and the Emperor, still waving nonchalantly to his cheering troops, was almost pitched out of his throne and only avoided this indignity by throwing himself backward and grabbing the arms. Even so the imperial wreath was dislodged. It bounced down the flank of the elephant and would have landed on the ground had not Narcissus leaped forward and fielded it with a neat one-handed catch. The beast lowered its rear and the Emperor pulled a hidden lever to release the side of the throne, which folded out to provide a nicely angled series of steps down to the ground.

'Ohh! Very neat!' Vitellius marvelled, standing in his place next to Vespasian.

The Emperor descended, replaced the wreath discreetly returned to him by Narcissus, and limped forward to greet the general of his army.

'My dear Aulus Plautius. It d-d-does my heart good to s-see you again!'

'The pleasure and honour is all mine, Caesar,' uttered Plautius and bowed his head.

'Yes, m-most kind of you, I m-m-must say.'

'I trust Caesar's journey was comfortable?'

'No. N-not really. Bit of a s-storm after we left Ostia and the roads in Gaul n-need upgrading. But the chaps on the British f-f-fleet were very accommodating. And do you know, P-Plautius, every fort I've passed th-th-through since I landed at Rutupiae has hailed me as Imperator! What about that then?' The eyes gleamed proudly, and the nervous tic he had never quite managed to master emphasised his pride with a sudden sideways twitch of the head that nearly shook the wreath off again. It now hung at a slight angle above his left eye and behind him Narcissus had to still his hand as it instinctively started to reach out to straighten his master's symbol of office. Abruptly Claudius swung round towards his chief secretary.

'Narcissus!'

'Caesar?'

'How many times did they call me Imperator?'

'Eighteen times, including tonight, Caesar.'

'Th-there! What about that? More than either Augustus or Tiberius ever got!'

Narcissus inclined his head and smiled modestly at the achievement.

'No more than you deserve, Caesar,' Plautius said respectfully. He stood to one side and indicated his senior officers with a wave of his hand. 'May I present my legates and tribunes to you, Caesar?'

'What did you say?' Claudius craned an ear towards him. In the background the troops had got a little too enthusiastic in their cheering and it was becoming hard to conduct a conversation at the prescribed distance between Emperor and subordinate. A quite different arrangement existed between Emperor and freedman since the latter was so far down the social order that no protocol existed. Claudius waved Narcissus over and shouted into one ear.

'Look, it's terribly n-nice of them and all that, b-b-but would you have someone tell them to shut up. Can't hear a th-th-thing.'

'At once, Caesar!' Narcissus bowed, backed away and pointed to the assembled senior centurions of the Praetorian Guard and then pointed to the ground before his feet. Vespasian watched in astonishment as the centurions immediately trotted over in response to the freedman's summons. Clearly, Narcissus was so firmly positioned at the Emperor's side that he could command instant obedience from these free-born citizens of Rome, who were nominally his social superiors. The instructions were quickly issued and the centurions hurried off waving their arms at the men lining the route, and quickly the shouting began to subside.

'Ah! Much b-better! Now then, Plautius, you were s-s-saying?'

'My officers, Caesar. I would like to present them to you.'

'Of course you would! Jolly g-good idea.'

The Emperor went down the line of legates and tribunes, arranged by legion, repeating a series of stock phrases as he passed along.

'Having a good campaign? Wished I could have j-joined you earlier. Maybe n-n-next time, eh?

'Had some good b-b-battles, I hear. Hope you sh-sh-showed them how tough we Romans are!

'Hope you've left me enough b-barbarians for a decent fight! I've got a deal of f-f-fighting to catch up on!'

Until he approached Vespasian.

He limped along from the last tribune of the Ninth Legion and stood before the legate of the Second.

'Having a . . . Why, it's Flavius Vespasian. How are you, my lad?'

'I'm well, Caesar.'

'Well, that's good. Jolly g-good. Been hearing excellent things about your brother. Must be proud of him.'

'Yes, Caesar,' Vespasian replied icily before he could stop himself.

'Still, keep up the g-good work and maybe one day you can have a legion of your own to c-command.'

'Caesar.' Narcissus stepped up smoothly. 'This *is* the Flavian brother who commands the Second.'

'Then who's the other fellow?'

'Flavius Sabinus. Attached to the staff.'

The light of realisation dimly dawned in the Emperor's countenance. 'Aha! Then this is the one with that w-w-wife. What's her name?'

'Flavia, Caesar,' Vespasian answered.

'You're right! That's her name. She's got that gorgeous little slave g-girl, hasn't she? Wouldn't mind having a close look at her myself sometime. The slave girl, that is,' Claudius hastily added as Vespasian tried to hide his outraged expression. 'But your Flavia's a n-n-nice looking filly as well. B-bit cheeky too, eh, Narcissus?' The Emperor made to wink at his freedman but his tic got the better of him and his face convulsed. Narcissus coloured slightly and turned to Plautius.

'Introduce the next officer, please.'

'Vitellius, senior tribune of the Second, Caesar.'

'Vitellius, my boy, doing well?'

'As ever, Caesar,' Vitellius said with a smirk.

'Your father sends his g-greetings, and hopes . . . and

hopes . . .' Claudius' face crinkled with concentration before the memory drifted back. 'Ah! I have it now! Hopes you're keeping the f-family end up! There! Are you joining us for the f-f-feasting tonight?'

'Sorry, Caesar, but due to the onerous nature of the duties my legate heaps upon me I need an early night.'

Claudius laughed. 'Your loss, my boy. T-take care, young Vitellius, and you'll go a l-long way.'

'I fully intend to, Caesar.'

Claudius continued down the line of officers and Vitellius risked a quick wink at his fuming legate. Once the last of the senior officers had been dealt with, Claudius formally saluted the standards and made the requisite libation at the army altar. Then Narcissus led the Emperor to the elaborate quarters that had been erected for him within the walls of the Praetorium. As soon as Claudius was out of sight, General Plautius dismissed the officers and gave the signal for the Praetorian units and elephants to stand down. They were being quartered in tents already prepared next to the parade ground, the closest possible position to the Emperor they were sworn to protect with their lives.

Vespasian hurried up to his commander and set himself foursquare in front of him, determined to deliver his warning without any further delay. Plautius eyed him warily and pursed his lips. 'Can't it wait until after you've caught up with your wife?'

'No, sir.'

'All right then, a moment only.' The other tasks on his schedule before turning in were obviously going to have to be put back.

'In private, sir.' Over the shoulder of the general Vespasian could see Vitellius lingering within earshot. 'What I have to say is for your ears only.'

'Damn it! I haven't time for this.'

'Yes you have, sir. Believe me.'

That the legate had risked being so insubordinate was not lost on Plautius. He nodded quickly, led the way into the headquarters lobby, and took a turn into the first office. A number of clerks looked up from their paperwork in surprise.

'Leave,' Plautius ordered, and the clerks instantly laid down their pens and scurried from the room. Plautius closed the flap and turned round angrily.

'Now, would you mind telling me what's so bloody important that I have to hear it in person and in private.'

Vespasian told him.

Chapter Forty

The camp on the south bank had long since settled down for the night when the flap to Flavia's chamber was lifted. A dark shadow crept in and quietly stole up to the travel bed. Vespasian trod softly into the weak glow of the single oil lamp, still burning on a nearby stand, and looked down on the sleeping form of his wife, marvelling at her perfection in repose. Flavia's face was smooth in the gentle orange glow and with lips slightly apart she breathed deeply in an even rhythm that sounded like the far-off sea. Dark strands of her hair lay across the silk bolster and he leaned forward to sniff them, smiling at the familiar scent. Straightening up, Vespasian let his eyes travel down to her breast, softly rising and falling with each breath, and then his gaze took in the ripples of silk that clung in fuller curves to the outline of her body.

For a moment he surrendered to the raw love he felt for her. She was so close that she was almost flesh of his flesh, so guileless in her slumber that she appeared to him as she had in the first hot heady days of their passion. The fruit of that passion, he knew, lay in the very next chamber.

He had looked in on young Titus before coming to his wife. The boy had been lying on his back, one arm raised across the top of his head, mouth gaping open, the shock of dark hair soft to the touch. So many of his mother's features were reproduced in him in cherubic miniature, and yet Vespasian had felt a twinge of rage at his wife for spoiling the moment.

For a while he stood gazing at his wife, then he slowly lowered himself onto the soft mattress. There was a light rustle of silk against the coarser wool of his military tunic and a displacement of the comfortable position her body had settled into while asleep. Flavia rolled onto her side, disturbing the rhythm of her breathing and a loud click at the back of her throat turned into a snort. Her eyes flickered open, closed a moment and split open again, much wider this time. She smiled.

'Thought you'd never come.'

'I'm here now.'

'I can see that. Just wondered where you'd got to.'

'I had work to do.'

Flavia propped her head up on her hand. 'So important you couldn't see me first?'

Vespasian nodded. 'Yes, that important, I'm afraid.'

She stared at him a moment and then suddenly wrapped her arm round his neck and drew his head down towards her. Their lips met. Soft and tentative at first, and then with the comforting firmness of a long and loving relationship. Vespasian drew back and looked down at her closed eyes.

'I needed that,' she whispered. 'Any more where that came from?'

'Later.'

'Later?'

'We must talk. It can't wait.'

'Talk?' Flavia smiled. 'Surely not.'

Sliding her hand to the hem of the silk sheet, she drew it down her naked body – like a sinuous serpent sloughing off its skin, thought Vespasian. The disturbing simile drew his mind back to what he must do. Now. Without further delay. He gently grasped her hand and drew the sheet back up over her breasts. His deliberate movements astonished Flavia. She was offended and her brows drew together in a frown.

'What's the matter? Darling, tell me.'

Vespasian stared down at her with cold eyes, not trusting himself to speak before he was in full control of his emotions.

Flavia was alarmed now and quickly eased herself up so that she was sitting facing her husband. 'You don't love me. That's it. Isn't it?' Her almond-shaped eyes widened in panic and her lips trembled. She clenched her jaw to still them.

This was not what Vespasian had anticipated; that he would have to convince her of his love first before accusing her of treason. He shook his head.

'Then what? Why are you so cold to me, husband?'

There was fear in her face now, and a look that he was reluctant to interpret as dawning suspicion that her intrigues had been discovered. Fortunately, it wasn't.

'You bastard!' She slapped him hard. 'Who is she? What's the name of the little tart?'

'What are you talking about?' Vespasian grabbed her wrist as her hand came sweeping in to deliver another blow. 'There is no other woman! This is about you!'

'Me?' Flavia froze. 'What about me?'

'I have to know about you . . . and your relationship to the Liberators.'

'I don't know what you're talking about.' She dropped her hands to her chest and stared at him, returning his searching gaze with what seemed to be frankness.

'You've heard of the Liberators, Flavia?'

'Of course. There've been wild rumours circulating about them for months. But what has it got to do with me?'

Vespasian looked down into his lap and his voice had a hard quality to it when he continued. 'Flavia, I know about your involvement in the plot against the Emperor. I know that you were working with those who were trying to get the army to mutiny before the invasion began. You tried to keep it all from me, but I know everything now. To conspire with these so-called Liberators was bad enough, but how could you have involved Titus in your treachery? How could you? Your own son? I also know you tried to have Narcissus killed. And what are you and your Liberator friends up to now? Supplying our enemies with weapons! Conspiring to kill the Em—'

'This is preposterous!' Flavia spat at him. 'From what madness does all this poison come?'

'From you, my wife.'

'You're mad.'

'No, only blind,' Vespasian said softly. 'Until recently.'

Flavia sat bolt upright ready to renew her protests, but Vespasian stabbed a finger at her.

'No! Let me finish. I would never have suspected you, never. I'd thought we were as one mind, one purpose in life. I trusted you in every detail. Then, when your schemes were unveiled to me, I thought the accusations were laughable. But the moment I forced myself to piece the details together, your guilt was inescapable. Oh Flavia! If only you could know how hurt I feel.'

'Who told you this? Who accuses me?'

'It doesn't matter.'

'Of course it does. Are you so naïve as to take one person's word for it? And would you believe another before your own wife?'

'I believe my own mind. I've had to think most of it through for myself.'

'Husband, did it not occur to you to question the motives of the person who caused you to question mine? Why would they want to plant such seeds of doubt in your mind? If you tell me the source of these false accusations, I might be able to explain their true purpose.'

The sincerity in her expression and voice caused Vespasian to pause. Was this the sign of guiltlessness he sought? Could she truly be innocent? Might his deliberations on her treachery be so very misdirected after all?

'The name?' she insisted.

Why was she so determined to have the name? Vespasian wondered. Surely if she was innocent, then the name mattered far less than the content of the accusations. Then it occurred to him that the real purpose of knowing the name might be revenge, or the intention to remove the source of the accusations to protect those it accused.

'There's no need for you to know the name.'

'There is, husband. I told you why.'

'I'd have thought you'd be more concerned to convince me of your innocence, rather than another person's guilt. It would seem more natural.'

'I see.' Flavia leaned back, away from him, regarding her husband coldly as she considered her next move. 'You think I'm unnatural, some kind of monster? The same monster that gave life to your son!'

'That's enough, Flavia!' Vespasian was too weary to pursue such an argument. It was getting too far outside the range of the discussion he had intended. He had hoped that he knew his wife well enough to detect any falsehood. He had made his accusations and she had refuted them and still he was no clearer about whether or not she was involved with the Liberators.

'Look, I have to ask. I have to know what you are up to.

If you are working with the enemies of the Emperor, however distantly, you must tell me. I will do my best to protect you from the consequences. I'm no fool, Flavia. If there's any way that we can keep this matter from Narcissus' agents then I'll do it. Better a guilty secret than a dangerous exposure. But you must swear to me to cut all connections with these traitors and never have any dealings with them again. Tell me everything, swear to tell me the truth and all of this can remain hidden in the past.' He stared at her fixedly to gauge the effect of his words, and waited for her response.

Flavia reached for his hand and pulled it to her breast. 'Husband, I swear on my life that I am not involved with the Liberators. I swear it.'

Vespasian wanted to believe her. Wanted it so desperately, and yet despite her promise some small reserve of doubt brooded darkly at the back of his mind and would not be satisfied.

'Very well. I will accept your word. And I'll do it gladly. But Flavia, if you are playing me for a fool and I ever discover it . . .'

No threats were necessary. He could see that she knew what the consequences of such a discovery would be. Flavia returned his probing stare for a moment before she nodded solemnly.

'We understand one another then.' Vespasian squeezed her hand in order to reassure her of his feelings, whatever else passed between them. 'Now, I'm tired, very tired. Is there room for two on that bed?'

'Of course, husband.'

'Good. I can't tell you how much I have missed sleeping in your arms.'

'I know,' Flavia whispered.

Vespasian slipped the tunic over his head and leaned down to undo the laces of his boots. While he undressed, Flavia tentatively placed her fingers on his back and traced them lightly across his skin in the way that she knew he liked. But there would be no passion tonight. Too much uncertainty and hurt had passed between them for that. Vespasian climbed under the sheet and kissed his wife gently on the forehead. She waited in case there was more but his eyes closed and very quickly his breathing fell into a deep, even rhythm.

She stared at him awhile, then turned over and gently arched her body into the curve of his, felt the rough hair of his genitals against the soft skin of her buttocks. But there was little pleasure in this reunion with her husband, and long after he had fallen asleep she lay awake, deeply troubled.

It pained her to have misled her husband, but she had taken an earlier oath – on the life of her son – that must take precedence. The Liberators demanded absolute secrecy and threatened the most terrible revenge on those who failed to honour that secrecy. Although she had served them loyally for nearly two years, the daily dread of discovery had finally become too much to bear. She was no longer working for the Liberators, and to that extent she had been honest with her husband. Still, she had learned enough to know that the supply of weapons to the Britons had been arranged by the Liberators when the previous Emperor – the mad Caligula – had resolved to conquer Britain. The plan had always been to undermine any campaign that sought to boost imperial prestige. With every military defeat, and every whispering campaign launched on the streets of Rome, the credibility of the imperial family would be steadily whittled away. In the end, the mob would be begging the aristocracy to seize control of the empire. That would be the Liberators' crowning achievement.

That day was still distant, Flavia had come to realise. The few people she had known who had been linked to the secret organisation were now dead, and Flavia did not want to share their fate. She had sent a message in code to the usual drop in Rome: a numbered box in the office of a correspondence agent on the Aventine. Flavia had simply stated that she would no longer work to further their cause. She knew that the Liberators would be unlikely to accept her withdrawal as readily as she had tendered it. She would have to be on her guard.

Flavia was deeply shocked that her involvement with the Liberators had been uncovered by Vespasian. And if by him, then by who else? Narcissus? But if the chief secretary was aware then surely she would be dead by now. Unless he was playing some deeper game – using her as bait to lure out other members of the conspiracy.

Chapter Forty-One

Far from the pageant of the Emperor's arrival Cato was doing the rounds of the fort assigned to his half of the century. Five hundred paces further along the ridge was the fort manned by Macro and the other forty men. The line of outposts formed a perimeter to the main army camp, a mile away down by the river and the ridge gave good views over the countryside north of the Tamesis. In daylight no British force would be able to approach undetected and the small garrisons would have ample time to fall back on the main army, if necessary.

At night, however, the situation was very different and the sentries' eyes and ears strained to identify every suspicious noise and shift of shadow beyond the turf walls. With the arrival of the Emperor the sentries were more jumpy than usual and Cato had ordered the night watches to be relived every time the signal trumpets down in the main camp sounded the hour. Better that than have the men exhausted the next day, or making sightings of the enemy based on an overheated imagination.

Cato climbed the rough wooden steps to the sentry walk and made his way along the fort's straight sides, ensuring that every man was alert and had not forgotten the challenge and password. Words were quietly exchanged as each man made his report and as usual there were no signs of enemy activity. Finally Cato ascended the watchtower with its wicker side and front guards. Forty feet above the ground he pulled himself through the opening at the back and saluted the man watching the northern approaches.

'All quiet?'

'Nothing to report, Optio.'

Cato nodded, and leaned against the broad timber post at the rear of the tower, looking back down the slope to the main camp delineated by a mass of brilliant orange flares from torches and fires. Beyond lay the narrow lines of torches that marked out the bridge stretching across the silver-grey loom of the Tamesis, tailing off into the night in a broad sweep. On the far bank glittered the outline of the camp where the Emperor, his followers and reinforcements now slept. And somewhere amongst them slept Lavinia. His heart lifted at the thought of her.

'Bet those bastards over there are living it up.'

'I suppose so,' Cato replied, sharing every sentry's innate suspicion that the fun only ever began once they were on watch. The thought of Lavinia enjoying the high life of the imperial court a scant two miles away filled him with anxiety and jealousy. While his duty kept him from her in this benighted little outpost, others could be wooing her. An image of the flashy young aristocrats of the imperial court filled him with dread, and with an impulsive thump of the wicker side guard he tore his mind away from Lavinia and forced himself to think about more immediate concerns. Some hours had passed since he had last left the fort to check on the picket line. That would keep him occupied, and keep Lavinia from preying on his thoughts.

'Carry on,' he muttered at the sentry and swung himself back onto the ladder to descend into the gloom of the fort. No time had been wasted on constructing permanent shelters, and the off-duty men slumbered and snored on the ground, preferring to risk the irritation of insect bites rather than suffer the stifling air inside their leather tents. Cato picked his way along the inside of the turf wall until he reached the fort's only gate. A quick order to the section leader responsible for the eight men on standby had the bar removed and one of the panels swung inwards. He headed off into the night, keeping in line with the dark mass of Macro's fort. Behind him the gate grated back into place.

Outside the reassuring turf walls, the night was alive with a sense of imminent danger and Cato felt a cold thrill of tension tickle its way up his spine. Looking back he could see the dim outline of the palisade already too far off for comfort and his hand slid down to the pommel of his sword as he strode quietly through the tall grass. A hundred paces on, Cato slowed down in anticipation of the first challenge and sure enough a voice hissed out of the darkness from close at hand. A dark shape rose from the grass.

'Stand and be recognised!'

'Blues triumphant,' Cato replied quietly. Using his favourite chariot team for a password was not perhaps very original, but it was easy to recall.

'Pass, friend,' the sentry responded sourly, slinking back into cover. Clearly a devotee of a rival team, Cato realised as he crept on. At least the man was alert. This post was the most dangerous on the sentry roster and any man who fell asleep out here was asking to have his throat cut by a British scout. And the scouts were out there all right. Caratacus may have pulled his main force back, but the British commander knew the value of good intelligence and kept probing the Roman lines under the cover of darkness. There had been more than one vicious skirmish fought in the dead of night over recent weeks.

A hundred paces further on Cato began looking for the next sentry. Crouching low he slowed to a creeping step and picked his way forward to where the man should be. No challenge greeted him and Cato quickly looked up to check that he was still in line with the rampart of his fort and that of Macro. He was, near enough, and there was the crushed grass where the sentry had been squatting. But no sign of the man. Cato wondered if he should call out. Just as he was about to, the terrible thought that something had happened to the sentry jumped into his mind. Supposing the man had been discovered by a British scout and killed? Supposing the scout was still close by? Cato went for the handle of his sword and slowly drew it from its scabbard, wincing at the metallic rasp of its passage.

'Keep still, Optio,' a voice whispered so softly he might have mistaken it for a breeze rustling the grass, had the air not been so still. Cato's blood froze at the sound and then he felt anger rising up inside him. This wasn't a proper challenge. What the bloody hell was the man playing at?

'Over here, Optio. Stay low.'

'What's going on?' Cato whispered back.

'We've got company.'

Cato slipped down onto his hands and knees and eased his way through the grass in the direction of the sentry's voice. The sentry, Scaurus, was one of the replacements, a man with a good record, Cato recalled. There he was, dark form squatting on his haunches, javelin held down out of sight. No shield to burden him if he needed to sprint back to the fort. Cato crept to his side.

'What is it?'

Scaurus didn't reply for a moment, and remained quite still, head fixed in one direction, down the slope towards enemy territory. He raised his arm and pointed into the shadows of some tall shrubs growing halfway up the slope. 'There!'

Cato followed his direction but saw only stillness. He shook his head. 'Can't see anything.'

'Don't look, listen.'

The optio tilted an ear towards the shrubs and tried to distinguish any noise that ought not to be there. A single bird whose call he could not recognise sang a melancholy refrain over and over again, and a hunting owl briefly added its mellow hooting before it abruptly fell silent. Cato gave up. Whatever was out there had either gone or more likely, had simply been the product of Scaurus' imagination. He made a mental note to ensure that Scaurus was given only tower duties from now on. At that moment something snorted down in the shrubs. A horse.

'Hear that?' said Scaurus.

'Yes.'

'Want me to go down and look?'

'No. We wait here. See who it is.'

It might be a Roman scout, lost on patrol and unaware how near he had wandered to his own lines. So they waited, stiffly poised, heightened senses straining for further sign of the intruder. The owl called out again, louder this time, and Cato was about to curse it when there was a disturbance down the slope, and a dark shape detached itself from the shrubs: a man leading a horse. He drew the animal up the slope, almost in line with Cato and Scaurus, so that he must pass within ten feet of them. The horseman came on, carefully picking his way in case the ground contained any obstacles that might trip him up and attract unwanted attention. The footfall of the horse was much more obvious, a dull scuffing clomp as it followed its rider, oblivious of the need for secrecy. When the rider was no more than twenty feet away, Cato nudged Scaurus and whispered, 'Now.'

The sentry leaped to his feet, javelin arm raised and moving smoothly back into the throwing position as he called out his challenge. Cato moved out to one side, sword drawn, ready to fight.

'Stand still and be recognised!'

The rider jumped back with a cry of alarm, causing the horse to shy off to one side with a frightened whinny. The moment of shock passed in an instant and before either Cato or Scaurus could react, the rider had thrown himself onto his mount and was kicking it with his heels.

'Don't let him get away!' Cato screamed.

There was a blur of movement and a sickening thunk. The rider cried out and for a moment reeled in his saddle. Then he folded to one side and, head first, rolled off his horse. The beast reared up, nearly toppling back onto its rider, before twisting to one side at the last moment and galloping back down the slope and into the night. The grass rustled briefly as Cato and Scaurus sprinted over to the rider. He lay on his back gasping for breath, the shaft of the javelin embedded in his stomach. He cried out a few words in a strange tongue before he passed out.

'Want me to finish him off, Optio?' asked Scaurus as he braced his foot on the man's chest and pulled out the javelin with a wet sucking noise.

'No.' Cato was puzzled by the language the man had used. It sounded like no Celtic he had ever heard. 'Give me a hand, let's get him into some light.'

Scaurus hooked his arms under the man's shoulders and Cato took his feet. He gauged the relative distances between his fort and the centurion's.

'Come on. Macro's going to want to see this!'

The rider was a big man and the two of them struggled to carry the awkward burden along the ridge towards the fort. As they approached the gate, Cato had time to be gratified by the early challenge – clearly Macro's men were alert and watching keenly.

'Blues triumphant!' Cato called out.

'That'll be the day,' he heard someone mutter.

'Open the gate!'

'Who's there?'

'The optio! Now open the bloody gate!'

A moment later the gate swung in and Cato and Scaurus heaved the body inside and let it drop to the ground while they bent over to catch their breath.

'What's all this?' Macro's voice bellowed. 'Which of you stupid sods gave the order for the gate to be opened? Trying to get us all killed?'

'It's me, sir,' Cato panted. 'Caught someone trying to get through the picket line. Horseman.'

'Get a light there!' Macro ordered and a sentry ran off to fetch a torch. 'You unharmed, lad?'

'Yes, sir . . . Scaurus pegged him with a javelin . . . before he could do a thing.'

The sentry returned, the torch crackling brightly in his hand.

'Now then, let's see what you've caught.' Macro took the torch and held it over the body on the ground. By the flickering glare they could make out neat leather boots, a bandage wound round the man's left knee and thigh, a neat blue tunic. Cato looked at the rider's face and gasped in astonishment.

'Nisus!'

Chapter Forty-Two

Vitellius was about to make another owl call when he heard the sentry's challenge. Instantly he flattened himself into the grass, heart pounding as he tried to hear what was going on.

'Don't let him get away!'

A sharp cry of pain splintered through the dark night, then came the sound of hooves pounding swiftly into the distance, until only low voices and moaning could be heard. More heartbeats passed before he risked raising his head above the grass for a quick glance. Swiftly scanning left and right he caught sight of the dark mass of two men bent over something they were carrying towards the nearest fort.

There was no doubt about it then: Nisus had been caught trying to cross back over the Roman lines. Vitellius bit back on the oath that nearly sprang to his lips and thumped the ground angrily. Bloody fool! He cursed himself. Bloody stupid fool. He should never have used the Carthaginian; the man was a surgeon, not trained in the arts of espionage. But there had been no one else he could use, he reflected. He had had to make do with an amateur and tonight's catastrophe was the result. It seemed that Nisus had fallen into Roman hands alive. What if the man could be interrogated before he died? And die he would, if not from his injuries then from the stoning he would receive for deserting his unit in the face of the enemy. If Nisus was made to talk then he, Vitellius, would surely be implicated.

The situation was extremely dangerous. Best get back to the camp before he was missed. He desperately needed time to think, time to find a strategy to deal with this predicament.

Crouching low, Vitellius turned down the slope towards the twinkling fires of the army. He had told that dull-witted optio of the Ninth on the gate that he was making an external inspection of the rampart. That would have taken plenty of time, more than enough for him to make his way to the ridge and meet Nisus at the point they had arranged several days earlier.

Now there was no knowing how Caratacus had responded to his plan. No way of knowing at all, unless he could get to Nisus and speak to him before he died. It was rotten luck. No, he corrected himself, it was rotten planning. He had to blame himself. He should never have used Nisus, and he should never have picked this meeting point. Most officers didn't place pickets between the forts during the night. Trust him to pick the section of the front line guarded by a thorough officer.

Having given the password, Vitellius was re-admitted through the gate. He nodded his thanks to the watch optio and reassured him that the perimeter defences were in excellent order. Striding back through the lines of tents, Vitellius made his way to his quarters and collapsed on his camp bed fully dressed. He might sleep later, but now he must give thought to the grim situation Nisus' capture had placed him in. That the surgeon would have to be silenced was in no doubt. If the sentry hadn't seen to it already, he himself would. Then he must recover Caratacus' reply from Nisus before the body was searched too thoroughly. Even the best codes could be broken in a matter of days, and the simplicity of the code they had agreed on would be deciphered the moment anyone recognised what they were looking at. If that happened, he could only hope that the message did not include any detail that implicated him directly. If one whiff of his complicity reached Narcissus, he would be quietly, and painfully, executed.

It was a dangerous game that he played. Roman politics had always been dangerous, and the higher one rose, the greater the risks one had to take. That excited Vitellius. Not to the point where he might be careless. He had far too much respect for the intelligence of the other players to ever underestimate them. Fortunately many of his rivals did not return the compliment; they were the kind of people whose intelligence was fatally blighted by their arrogance. Like Cicero, they required regular acknowledgement of their powerful intellects, and it was in those incremental moments of weakness that their ultimate fall was assured. Vitellius had broken this rule just once and then only to persuade Vespasian that the consequences of exposing him would be far more calamitous for the legate than for him. Even so, he still felt he had said too much and vowed never again to say one word more than was necessary.

Vitellius took pride in the fact that he had quickly learned never to subscribe to someone else's cause. The very notion of a 'secret organisation' was an oxymoron; there was an almost exponential increase in the possibility of betrayal or exposure every time such an organisation recruited a new member. No, it was far safer to work alone; towards a specific end, with no obligations to causes or comrades. Isolation from such groups was his strength and their weakness, as his present scheme proved.

It was now a common assumption amongst the senior

officers that the Roman weapons they had discovered in the hands of the Britons must have been supplied by the Liberators. Clearly these traitors had assumed that the Britons would hurl the invaders back into the sea and that such a military catastrophe must lead to the fall of Claudius. In the ensuing chaos the Liberators saw themselves emerging as the champions of a new republic. Had the invasion failed, no one would have been more delighted than Vitellius. If the political system could be kept unstable for long enough, he would have time to develop his political position. One day, when he was quite sure the moment was ripe, he would seize power for himself.

Now the Liberators' latest perceived treachery meant that their name would be blackened back in Rome. From the lowliest squat in the slums of the Subura to the wealthiest dinner tables of the Janiculan, the Liberators would be cursed in the harshest possible terms. Vitellius was working to add to their damnation with the plot to kill Claudius. It would have been impossible to carry it through alone, but the careful cultivation of Nisus' deep-rooted resentment of Rome had borne fruit. Caratacus had proved to be an enthusiastic ally when the possibility was broached via the message carried by the prisoner Vitellius had helped to escape. Any political disorder in Rome that caused the invaders to withdraw from Britain was worth the stigma of being involved in an assassination.

Vitellius found himself warming to Caratacus. He had never met the British leader in person, but the quality of the man's mind was evident in his arrangements for the plot. Despite having the terrible disadvantage of coming from a warrior culture which valued a man's honour above all else, Caratacus was admirably pragmatic. He would be making a stand against Claudius before Camulodunum. That was a certainty. To allow the capital to fall without a single sword being raised in its defence would demoralise any will to resist in the other tribes of the island. The defiant posture would have to be maintained, even at the cost of yet another defeat. There was always the possibility, however unlikely, that the battle could be won, or at least a Roman victory could be made so Pyrrhic that it held up the conquest of the island.

If the coming battle ended in another defeat for the Britons, then the assassination could be attempted at the subsequent surrender of the tribes taken by the Emperor in person. Caratacus had managed to persuade one of his followers to accept the suicidal duty of wielding the blade. It only remained for Vitellius to see to it that the man was provided with a knife after being searched prior to his presentation to the Emperor. But without the message Nisus had been carrying, Vitellius would not know the identity of the assassin. Without that knowledge, there could be no attempt on the Emperor's life.

Whether the assassination of Claudius succeeded or not, the blame would be attached to the Liberators. It might well be a British knife that plunged into the Emperor's heart but those investigating the plot would be sure to find some way of implicating the Liberators, particularly if they were encouraged to do so.

Vitellius suddenly sat upright on his camp bed, angry with himself. There was no point in thinking about the pleasures the future had to offer when at any moment his complicity in the plot could be revealed by Nisus. Equally, there was little he could do about it until Nisus, or news of Nisus, was brought into the main camp. Then he could justify his attendance on the man by acting the concerned friend. In the meantime, he admonished himself, he must be calm. He must not give the appearance of being fretful lest anyone who saw him remember it when giving evidence to any investigation that might take place if the worst happened. Better to think about something more pleasing.

It was then that he recalled having seen Flavia amongst the imperial entourage. Behind Vespasian's wife had stood that terribly attractive slave girl he had once had a fling with when the Second had been stationed in Germania. Even that lecherous old dotard Claudius had noticed her. As he recalled her features, Vitellius smiled at the prospect of renewing their relationship.

Chapter Forty-Three

'Get him under the lamps!' the senior surgeon shouted as two legionaries carried the stretcher into the treatment tent. 'Take care, you fools!'

Cato walked beside them, pressing a blood-drenched rag to the wound. The senior surgeon, dark skinned like Nisus, helped them ease the stretcher up onto the wooden top of the examination table and then slackened off the cord that lowered the pulley lamps. By their dim light he removed the compress to inspect the javelin's entry point, but the entire front and sides of the torso were covered in a sticky red slick. The surgeon grabbed a sponge from a highly polished copper bowl and swabbed the blood away. He uncovered a dark hole the diameter of a man's thumb which instantly welled up with blood. He clapped the compress back on.

'Where did you find him?'

'He was trying to get through our picket lines,' Cato replied. 'One of my men stopped him.'

'I'll say.' The senior surgeon lifted the compress again to examine the wound, and grimaced at the unstaunched flow of blood.

Nisus' head came up as he suddenly screamed, then he dropped back with a jarring thud on the examination table, muttering and moaning.

'We must stop the bleeding. It looks like he's lost too much already.' The senior surgeon looked up. 'How long ago did you say you found him?'

Cato calculated from the watch signals. 'Half an hour.'

'And he's been bleeding like this all the time?'

'Yes, sir.'

'Then he's had it. Nothing I can do.'

'There must be something, sir,' Cato said desperately.

'Friend of yours?'

Cato paused a moment before he nodded.

'Well, Optio, I'm really sorry about your friend, but there really is nothing we can do for him. This kind of injury is always fatal.'

Nisus was trembling now, and his moaning had a keening note. His eyes flickered and were suddenly wide open, glancing around in a dazed panic before they rested on Cato.

'Cato . . .' Nisus reached out a hand.

'Lie still, Nisus,' Cato ordered. 'You need to rest. Lie back.'

'No.' Nisus smiled weakly, then his lips twisted as an agonising spasm gripped him. 'I'm dying. I'm dying, Cato.'

'Nonsense! You won't die!'

'I'm the bloody surgeon! I know what's happening to me!' His eyes blazed fiercely, then clamped tightly shut as the next spasm shot through him. 'Ahhh! It hurts!'

'All right, Nisus.' The senior surgeon patted his shoulder. 'It'll be over quite soon. Want me to make it easier for you?'

'No! No triage.' He was panting now, in shallow rasping breaths. His hand still grasped Cato's and the powerful grip was almost painful as he struggled to keep a hold on the living world even as death gradually drew him away. With a supreme effort, and driven by what spark of consciousness

324

remained, he seized Cato with his other hand and pulled the optio close to his mouth.

'Tell the tribune, tell him . . .' The voice tailed off into a whisper and Cato was not even sure whether he was hearing words or the last wheezing breaths of a dying man. Slowly the Carthaginian's grip slackened, his breathing faded into silence. Nisus' head lolled back and his lifeless eyes glazed over, mouth hanging slightly open.

For a moment there was silence, then the senior surgeon felt for a pulse. He found nothing.

'That's it. He's gone.'

Cato was still holding Nisus' hand, conscious that it was only lumpen flesh and no spark of life moved within it any more. He felt rage at his powerlessness to save the man's life. There had been so much blood; he had tried to stem the flow but it just kept pumping out.

'Where the hell has he been the last few days?' asked the senior surgeon.

'I've no idea.'

'What did he say to you at the end?'

Cato shook his head. 'I don't know.'

'Did he say anything?' the senior surgeon pressed him. 'Did he say his death rites?'

'Death rites?'

'He's Carthaginian, like me. What did he say, just before he died? He whispered something to you.'

'Yes. But I couldn't make it out . . . Something about a bell, I think.'

'Then I'll have to do the death rites for him.'

The senior surgeon prised Cato's hand free and gently pushed him away from the body. 'Won't be a moment, but it has to be said, otherwise he'll be forced to linger on the earth, like your Roman lemures.'

The thought of the uneasy spirit of Nisus walking the shadows of the earth filled Cato with horror, and he backed away from the examination table. The senior surgeon pressed his right hand down over the dead man's heart and began quietly chanting an ancient Punic ritual. It was over quickly, and he turned back to Cato. 'You want to give him Roman rites as well?'

Cato shook his head.

'Want to stay with him a moment?'

'Yes.'

The senior surgeon ushered the legionaries out and Cato was alone with Nisus' body. He was not sure how he felt. There was grief at having lost a friend, and bitterness that he should die so wastefully on the point of a Roman javelin. There was anger too. Nisus had betrayed his friendship, firstly by forsaking him in favour of Tribune Vitellius and secondly by deserting – or whatever it was he had been involved with when he had disappeared from the camp. The very last words Nisus had uttered had been for Vitellius, and that galled Cato more than anything else. Whatever had caused Nisus to disappear, Cato suspected it had something to do with Vitellius. The contrasting emotions turned over and over inside him as he stared at the body.

'You've made your peace, Optio,' the senior surgeon said quietly as he re-entered the tent a while later. 'Now I'm afraid we must take over. In this heat we have to see that bodies are dealt with as quickly as possible.'

Cato nodded and moved off to one side of the tent as the senior surgeon waved in a pair of medical orderlies. With an efficiency born of regular grim practice, the medics straightened the body out and began removing all the clothes and personal effects.

'You don't have to stay and watch if you don't want to,' said the senior surgeon.

'I'm all right, sir. Really.'

'As you wish. I'm afraid I have to go. I've other duties to see to. I'm sorry I couldn't save your friend,' the senior surgeon added gently.

'You did your best, sir.'

The orderlies were busy stripping away the clothes, separating out those that were free of blood and could be re-used. The rest were placed aside for disposal. The wound had stopped bleeding now that the heart beat no more. The smear of blood on the surrounding skin was quickly sluiced away with a bucket of water. One of the orderlies began to unravel the bandage wound round Nisus' left knee. Suddenly he stopped, craning his head forward to look more closely.

'Hello. That's odd,' he muttered.

'What's odd?' replied his companion as he removed the boots.

'There's nothing under this bandage. No injury, not even a scratch.'

'Course there is, people don't just wear bandages for fun.'

'No, I'm telling you there's nothing here. Only these strange marks.'

Curiosity got the better of Cato's grief and he came over to see what was causing the mild commotion.

'What's the problem?'

'Here, Optio. Look at this.' The orderly handed him the bandage. 'Not a scratch on his leg. Just some marks on this lot.'

Cato went over to the side of the tent where a rough bench had been erected and slowly sat down, gazing at the curious lines and curves on one side of the cloth. He could make no sense of them. He tucked the bandage inside his tunic, deciding that it needed closer inspection by daylight.

He looked up at the body on the table. Nisus' face was serene and restful now that the strain of dying was over. What had he been up to these last few days?

Cato became aware of a new presence in the tent. Tribune Vitellius had entered so quietly that no one had noticed. He stood in the shadows by the tent flap and gazed at the body. For a moment he did not notice Cato and the optio could see anxiety and frustration playing across the tribune's face. Anxiety and frustration – but not grief. Then Vitellius saw him and frowned.

'What are you doing here? You're supposed to be on duty.'

'I brought Nisus in, sir.'

'What happened to him?'

'One of my sentries caught him trying to cross our lines. He didn't answer the challenge, and when he made a run for it the sentry took him down with a javelin.'

'That's bad luck,' Vitellius muttered, and then more loudly, 'Very bad luck. We didn't get a chance to interrogate him and find out what he's been playing at since he disappeared from the camp. Did he have a chance to say anything before the end?'

'Nothing that made any sense, sir.'

'I see,' the tribune said quietly. He sounded almost relieved. 'Well, you'd best get back to your unit, straight away.'

'Yes, sir.' Cato stood up and exchanged salutes with the tribune. Outside the sweltering heat of the tent, the air felt cool and moist; dawn was not far off. Cato marched towards the gate, keen to get away from Vitellius as quickly as possible.

Inside the tent, Vitellius made his way over to the body, now being rubbed down with scented oils by the two orderlies, ready for cremation. The tribune ran his eyes over Nisus before turning to his clothes and carefully sifting through them.

'Looking for something, sir?'

'No, just wondering if you'd found anything . . . unusual on him.'

'No, sir, nothing out of the ordinary.'

'I see.' Vitellius scratched his chin and scrutinised the orderly's expression. 'Well, if you do find anything unusual, anything at all, bring it to me immediately.'

After the tribune had left, the other orderly turned to his mate. 'Why didn't you tell him about the bandage?'

'What bandage?'

'The one that we found on him.'

'Well, it ain't here now. Besides,' the orderly paused to spit into the corner of the tent, 'I don't get involved in anything that involves officers. I tell him about the bandage and immediately I'm involved in something. Get it?'

'Too right.'

Chapter Forty-Four

At dawn the watches at the forts changed and Cato led his half-century back down the slope to the camp. The strain of the night watch was over, and the men were looking forward to spending the day resting, especially as the army would soon be on the move. All the rigours of marching with fully loaded yokes and packs, constructing marching camps and eating endless meals of millet porridge would begin again.

Although the clear sky promised another perfect day, Cato could not share their light mood this morning. Nisus was dead. Warfare was wasteful enough of human life without adding to its toll by accident. What made the death of Nisus even harder to bear were the mysterious circumstances of his earlier disappearance. If he had been killed in battle then that would have been sad but not unexpected. But something was very wrong about this death, and his recent actions made Cato suspicious. He needed to know more, and right now the only clue he had was the strangely marked bandage tucked inside his tunic. He firmly believed that the solution to the mystery somehow lay with Vitellius. The tribune had worked on Nisus, changed him and made him complicit in whatever treachery Vitellius might be planning.

Cato had to speak to someone. Someone he could trust, who would take his suspicions seriously. Macro might ridicule his fears, or just as easily charge in with some formal complaint against the tribune. It had to be someone else . . . Lavinia. Of course. He would find her, take her to some peaceful place away from the camp, and open his heart to her.

He stripped off his armour and weapons, scrubbed the dried splashes of blood from his face and hands, and put on his spare tunic.

As he crossed the bridge, he noted the frantic activity of the camp on the south bank; the army was preparing to move on to the offensive. Cato had to pick his way through the massed baggage of the imperial entourage and the Praetorian Guard. Unlike the camp on the other bank, this one was filled with a sense of eager anticipation, as if the army was about to lay on a spectacular military display rather than go out and fight a determined and dangerous enemy. The wagons of the imperial court were heaped with expensive furniture that had never been designed to leave the luxurious boudoirs of Rome and had suffered a battering as a result. There were huge chests of clothes, musical instruments, ornamental dinner services, and a plethora of other luxuries all attended by expensive household slaves who travelled badly. The wagons of the Praetorian Guard cohorts were piled high with ceremonial uniforms and equipment, in readiness for the Emperor's spectacular victory celebration at Camulodunum.

Cato threaded his way out of the wagon park and headed for the enclosure used by the Emperor's entourage. A large gate connected it to the main camp, although only one of the large timber doors was open. The gate was manned by a dozen Praetorians in campaign whites and full armour. As Cato approached the open door, the guards on either side crossed their spears.

'Purpose of your visit?'

'To see a friend. Handmaid to the Lady Flavia Domitilla.'

'Do you have a pass signed by the chief secretary?'

'No.'

'No entry then.'

'Why?'

'Orders.'

Cato glared at the guards, who stood at attention staring casually back, quite unfazed. Cato knew that there would be no talking his way through. The men of the Praetorian Guard were experts at gate-keeping and obeyed orders to the letter. Shouting abuse would be a waste of breath, Cato decided. Added to which, the guard who had addressed him had the physique of a gladiator; he was not the kind of man he wished to be confronted by if ever they met off duty.

Cato turned and strolled into the wagon park. Amid the confusion of soldiers, clerks and household slaves, he ran his eyes over the outside of the enclosure surrounding the imperial entourage. A number of the wagons had already been packed and dragged to one side, close to the palisade. One wagon in particular caught his attention: a heavy four-wheeled affair piled high with brightly decorated leather tents, folded and tied down. The load was so high that it stood level with the top of the palisade. Cato made his way round the wagon park so that he could approach the wagons out of sight of the guards. After quickly checking to make sure that no one was watching him, he slipped between the packed wagons and worked his way over to the one carrying the tents. He clambered up and lay flat on the top, only raising his head to peer over the palisade and into the enclosure of the Emperor's travelling companions.

Out of sight of the army, the social elite of Rome made

camp with the smallest of concessions to the hardships of campaigning. Huge tents sprawled across the enclosure, and through the openings of those tents facing him Cato could see ornately tiled flooring and expensive furniture within. Some members of the imperial court had awnings erected outside their tents and they reclined on upholstered benches, waited upon by the slaves they had brought with them from the city. The centre of the enclosure had been left open to serve as a social space, but the intensity of the previous night's partying meant it was almost empty. Cato looked carefully at the few figures visible but none of them was Lavinia. So he lay on top of the wagon and waited, sometimes nearly dozing off in the sun's warm glow. Every time a female figure emerged from a tent, Cato raised his head and strained his eyes to see if it was Lavinia.

Then at last, not far from where he lay, a tent flap was flicked open and a slender woman in a diaphanous green gown stepped stiffly into the shadow of the awning. She stretched out her arms and yawned, before moving into the sunlight where Cato could see the jet-black tresses of her hair. He was filled with a heady sense of lightness. For a moment he watched Lavinia, drinking in her every movement as she leaned back against the post supporting the front of the awning, and tipped her face up towards the sun.

Then she scratched her backside and turned to go back into the tent. Cato began to rise, desperate that she should see him and not disappear after such a tantalisingly brief appearance. If she caught sight of him, he might be able to indicate that they could meet outside the enclosure. Cato raised his hand, and was about to wave when a movement at the periphery of his vision attracted his attention.

Through the gate of the enclosure strode Tribune Vitellius. The chill that Cato always experienced at the sight of the man returned to him instantly, as with sickening inevitability the tribune walked straight towards Lavinia, who had her back to him and was unaware of his approach. Vitellius stalked up to her and laid his hands on her shoulders. She spun round with a start. Cato rose to his knees, ready to rush to her rescue without regard to the impossibility of reaching her in the heavily guarded enclosure. He raised his hands to call out but before he could utter a sound he was suddenly pulled by his feet with great force off the top of the wagon. He tumbled down the side and landed heavily on the ground, the breath driven out of him. A pair of boots thudded down by his face, and an instant later Cato was hauled up, gasping for air like a stranded fish.

'And what the fuck d'you think you're up to, my lad?'

Cato recognised the face of the Praetorian Guardsman from the enclosure gate. He tried to reply, but the lack of breath in his lungs caused him to wheeze instead.

'Refusing to answer, eh? Well then, let's see if my centurion can loosen your tongue, and maybe a few teeth while he's at it.'

The guard twisted his fist into Cato's hair and half pulled, half dragged him across the wagon park towards the headquarters tent. The slaves and legionaries packing the remaining wagons paused to watch the unedifying spectacle. Some laughed and Cato felt himself colour at the shame of being seen to be treated like some naughty schoolboy.

Chapter Forty-Five

'All ready?' General Plautius glanced round. The last officers were forming up on one side of the route leading from the bridge into the main camp. 'Right then, give the signal.'

Sabinus nodded to the staff tribune in charge of communications, who shouted a quick order to the assembled bucinas and cornicens to ready their brass instruments. A short pause as air was sucked in and lips pursed, then on the mental count of three an ear-splitting note blared out across the river. Despite being battle-trained, the staff horses shied uneasily at the noise and the carefully ordered ranks of senior officers were momentarily disrupted. On the far side of the bridge the brass instruments of the Praetorian Guard cohorts acknowledged the signal.

'Here we go,' Plautius muttered.

The white figures of the front ranks of Praetorians emerged from the other camp and with perfect parade-ground precision they marched out onto the bridge in military step. Highly polished bronze helmets glittered in the bright morning sunshine, in vivid contrast to the dark clouds creeping up from the south. The air was still and humid before the coming storm.

'I do wish they wouldn't march in step,' grumbled the prefect of engineers. 'It's not good for my bridge. Any fool knows that troops should break step when crossing a bridge.'

'And destroy the aesthetic effect?' Vespasian replied. 'Narcissus wouldn't stand for it. Just pray that he doesn't require the elephants to march in step.'

The engineer started in alarm at the prospect, then relaxed as he realised the legate was joshing him.

'Last thing we need is a truncated campaign,' quipped Vitellius and the senior officers winced.

The long white column extended along the bridge like a huge caterpillar, until at length its head reached the north bank and began marching up the slope towards the main gate.

'Eyes . . . right!' barked out the senior centurion as he led his men past the general and his staff. With neat timing the Praetorians snapped their heads round, while the right-hand markers kept looking ahead to ensure the line stayed properly dressed. General Plautius solemnly saluted as each century marched smartly by.

On the far side of the main gate the rest of the army was formed up ready to advance on the enemy. The Praetorian cohorts would lead the thrust into enemy territory. Their privileged position at the head of the line of march meant that the dust kicked up by the passage of thousands of nailed boots would not choke their throats or soil their brilliant white tunics and shields. At the far end of the bridge a small gap appeared in the column, and then a rippling hedge of scarlet and gold appeared as the army's standards marched out. Behind and towering above them came the first of the elephants, richly adorned and carrying the Emperor.

'Now we'll see how good an engineer you really are,' said Plautius, keenly watching the bridge for the first signs of collapse. To his side the prefect of engineers looked distraught at the possibility of an imperial drenching finding its way onto his curriculum vitae.

The elephants' swaying progress looked peculiar after the stiff regularity of the Praetorian cohorts, and to the prefect's relief the line of huge beasts was totally unsynchronised and the bridge remained stable. Behind the last elephant a gap opened up. The imperial entourage and their wagons would be travelling with the rest of the baggage train at the rear of the army and would not be setting out for some hours yet.

The last of the standards passed by, and then the Emperor lurched up from the bridge and his elephant driver tapped the elephant on the side of the head to make it stop in front of Plautius and his officers.

'Good morning, Caesar.'

'General.' Claudius nodded. 'No p-problems with the advance, I trust.'

'None, Caesar. Your army is formed up and ready to follow you to a glorious victory.' It was a trite phrase, and Vespasian struggled to keep a mocking expression at bay, but the Emperor seemed to take it at face value.

'Wonderful! Quite w-wonderful! Can't wait to get stuck into those B-B-Britons. Let's give them a stiff dose of R-Roman steel, eh, Plautius!'

'Well, yes, quite, Caesar.'

The last of the elephants halted, and Narcissus rode up. He was perched on the back of a small pony that flinched nervously as one of the elephants lifted its tail and deposited a small mound directly in its path. The chief secretary quickly negotiated the distasteful obstacle and trotted up to the side of his master's beast.

'Ah! There you are, Narcissus. About t-time too! I think I'll transfer to my litter now.'

'Are you sure, Caesar? Think of the heroic image you cast up there on such a magnificent beast. A veritable god leading his soldiers into war! How inspiring it'll look to the men!'

'Not when this st-st-stupid animal makes me throw up, it won't. Driver! Get this animal down, right now.'

After his last experience of disembarking from an elephant, Claudius gripped the sides of his throne tightly and leaned back as far as he could when the elephant's front legs folded. Safely back on terra firma, the Emperor gazed at the elephant with disapproval.

'Quite how that scoundrel H-Hannibal coped, I don't know. Now then, Narcissus. Have my litter fetched at once.'

'Yes, Caesar. I'll have it fetched from the baggage train.'

'What is it doing back there?'

'You ordered it, Caesar. You may recall that you had intended to lead the advance on the back of an elephant.'

'Oh?'

'You wanted to "out-Hannibal Hannibal". Remember, Caesar?'

'Hmmm. Yes. Well, that was yesterday. Besides,' Claudius waved a hand to the south, 'I don't fancy being stuck on an e-e-elephant when that lot breaks.'

Narcissus turned to look at the black clouds rolling in towards the Tamesis. A flicker of white light illuminated them from within and moments later a deep rumble echoed towards the Roman camp.

'The litter please, Narcissus. Quick as you can.'

'At once, Caesar.'

While the chief secretary hurriedly passed the instruction on, the Emperor stood and watched the approaching storm with a frown, as if his displeasure might ward it off. A jagged white line stabbed down in the marshland a short distance upriver and the air was split by a terrible sound like tearing metal.

Sabinus manoeuvred his horse alongside his brother.

'Bloody typical,' he said quietly. 'We sit on our arses for the best part of two months waiting for the Emperor in glorious sunshine, and the moment we get back on the offensive we're hit by a storm.'

Vespasian let out a low, bitter chuckle and nodded. 'And no hope of us sitting the storm out, I suppose.'

'None, brother. There's too much riding on this campaign, and Claudius dare not be absent from Rome any longer than absolutely necessary. The advance goes ahead whatever the weather.'

'Oh shit.' Vespasian felt a splash on his hand. Then came a soft pattering of heavy raindrops on helmets and shields. Across the wide surface of the Tamesis a belt of grey swept towards the north bank. Suddenly the downpour began in earnest, hissing through the air and drumming down on every surface. A light breeze picked up with the rain, tossing the branches in nearby copses and stirring the heavy military cloaks of the officers as they hurriedly pulled them round their bodies. Claudius looked up at the sky just as lightning burst upon the world in a dazzling sheet of white light and froze the angry expression on his face for the briefest of moments.

'Do you think this might be an omen?' Sabinus asked half seriously.

'What kind of an omen?'

'A warning from the gods. A warning about the outcome of this campaign perhaps.'

'Or a warning to Claudius?' Vespasian turned to exchange a knowing look with his older brother.

'Do you really think it is?'

'Maybe. Or it might just be a sign from the gods that it's going to piss down for a few days.'

Sabinus' disapproval of this casual mocking of superstition was evident in his frown. Vespasian shrugged and turned back to watch the Emperor who was shouting something at the heavens. His words were drowned out by the crash of thunder and the slashing of rain. The elephants were jostling against each other nervously despite the best efforts of their drivers and the agitation of these vast animals was beginning to affect the horses.

'Get them out of here!' Plautius shouted out to the drivers. 'Get them away from the road! Quick! Before you lose control of them!'

The elephant drivers saw the danger and frantically kicked their heels and beat at the grey wrinkled domes of their elephants' heads until the beasts lumbered off the track and made for the edge of the river, huddling together away from the bridge.

Claudius gave up berating the gods and made his way across the track towards the mounted officers.

'Where's my b-bloody litter?'

'Coming, Caesar,' replied Narcissus, pointing back down the bridge to where a dozen slaves were jogging across with a large gilded two-seater. By the time the litter reached the near bank, the track was running with rivulets and the dry, hard surface of moments before had become slippery underfoot. The litter-bearers struggled to keep their footing as they made their way towards the Emperor who was waiting with furious impatience. Once on level ground, they increased their pace and quickly lowered the litter by the Emperor's side.

'About time!' Claudius was drenched, his thinning white hair lay plastered to his head in messy strands and his once bright purple cloak was dark and hung in wet folds about his shoulders. With a last angry look at the skies he dived inside the litter. Through the curtains he called out to General Plautius.

'Yes, Caesar?'

'Get things moving! This army's g-going on the offensive, come rain or sunshine. S-s-see to it!'

'Caesar!'

With a quick wave Plautius signalled to his assembled officers, who turned their horses and in a rough column headed back to their units to prepare for the advance. Sabinus continued to ride alongside his younger brother, head tucked down into the folds of his cloak. The ceremonial crest of his helmet was soaked and drooped sadly from its holding bracket. Around them the rain thrashed down, accompanied by frequent brilliant flashes followed by darkness and ear-splitting thunder that made the very earth tremble. It was hard not to see the fact that the storm had broken just as the army was breaking camp as a sign from the gods that they disapproved of the advance on Camulodunum. However, the army's priests had read the entrails at first light, and the ground had freely yielded the standards when the legion's colour parties had collected them from the standards' sanctuary. Despite these conflicting signs of divine favour, Claudius had nevertheless ordered the army to advance according to the strategy he had outlined to his senior officers. Sabinus was apprehensive.

'I mean, even I know that we should be scouting ahead of the line of advance. It's enemy territory and who knows what traps Caratacus has set for us. The Emperor is no soldier. All he knows about war is what he's learned from books, not from being in the field. If we just plough blindly into the enemy we're asking for trouble.'

'Yes.'

'Someone has to try and reason with him, set him right. Plautius is too weak to object and the Emperor thinks Hosidius Geta is a fool. It has to be someone else.'

'Like me, I suppose.'

'Why not? He seems to like you well enough, and you've got Narcissus' respect. You could try and get him to adopt a safer strategy.'

'No,' Vespasian replied firmly. 'I won't do it.'

'Why, brother?'

'If the Emperor isn't going to listen to Plautius, then he's hardly going to listen to me. Plautius commands the army. It's up to him to approach the Emperor. Let's talk no more about it.'

Sabinus opened his mouth to make another attempt to persuade his brother but the fixed expression on Vespasian's face, familiar from childhood, stopped him. Once Vespasian decided a subject was closed, there was no shifting him; it would be a waste of time to try. Over the years Sabinus had grown used to being frustrated by his younger brother; moreover, he had come to realise that Vespasian was a more able man than he was. Not that Sabinus would ever admit it, and he continued to act the part of the older, wiser brother as best as he could. Those who came to know the brothers well could not help but draw a telling comparison between the quiet competence and steely determination of the younger Flavian, and the nervous, edgy, too-willing-to-please superficiality of Sabinus.

Vespasian directed his horse to follow the other officers up the slope towards the main gate. He was glad his brother had fallen silent. It was true that Plautius and his legates had been deeply concerned by the over-bold strategy outlined to them by an excited Emperor. Claudius had run on and on, his stammer worsening as he delivered a long rambling lecture on military history and the genius of the bold, direct offensive. After a while Vespasian had ceased to listen, and brooded on more personal matters instead. As he continued to do now.

Despite Flavia's protestations, he still could not shake himself free of the suspicion that she was involved with the Liberators. There had been too many coincidences and opportunities for conspiracy in recent months for him simply to dismiss them on the word of his wife. And that made him feel even worse about the whole matter. They had exchanged a private vow of fidelity in all things when they had married, and her word should be good enough. Trust was the root of any relationship and it must thrive for a relationship to grow and mature. But his doubts ate away at this root, insidiously gnawing their way through the bond between man and wife. Before long he knew he must confront her over the threat to the Emperor that Adminius had stumbled upon. Thus it would be again and again between himself and Flavia, until he had driven out every shred of his doubt and uncertainty – or discovered proof of her guilt.

'I must get back to my legion,' Vespasian announced. 'Take care.'

'May the gods preserve us, brother.'

'I'd rather we didn't have to count on them,' said Vespasian, and gave a thin smile. 'We're in the hands of mortals now, Sabinus. Fate is just an onlooker.'

He kicked his heels into his mount and urged it to a trot, passing along the huddled lines of legionaries squelching towards Camulodunum. Somewhere ahead of them Caratacus would be waiting with a fresh army he had amassed in the month and a half of grace that Claudius had given him. This time the British warrior chief would be fighting in front of his tribal capital, and both armies would be locked in the most bitter and terrible battle of the campaign.

Chapter Forty-Six

The storm continued for the rest of the day. The tracks and trails along which the army advanced quickly turned into greasy morasses of mud that sucked at the boots of the legionaries as they struggled forward under back-breaking loads. Further back the baggage train quickly bogged down and was left behind under the guard of an auxiliary cohort. By the evening the army had covered no more than ten miles and defensive earthworks were still being dug as the exhausted rearguard trudged into their tent lines.

Just before the sun set, the storm abated, and through a gap in the clouds a brilliant shaft of orange light lit up the sodden army, gleaming on its wet equipment and glistening on the churned-up mud and puddles. The hot tension in the stormy air had gone, and it now felt cool and fresh. The legionaries quickly set up their tents and removed all their wet clothing. Cloaks and tunics were slung over each section's tent ridge and the men began to prepare their evening meal, grouching at the lack of any dry firewood. From their packs the soldiers ate their issue of biscuit and strips of dried beef, cursing as they worked sinewy shreds loose and chewed them over and over before they could be swallowed.

The sun went down with a final glittering display of light along the horizon and then the clouds closed in again, thicker and more gloomy, sweeping along as the breeze returned and steadily strengthened. As night drew on, the wind whined shrilly through the guy ropes and the tent canvas boomed and flapped with the strongest gusts. Inside the tents, the legionaries shivered in wet cloaks wound tightly about them, trying to get warm enough to sleep.

Under the mood of sullen depression hanging over the tents of the Sixth Century, Cato was even more miserable than most. His ribs still throbbed from the kicking he had received from the Praetorian Guard centurion after being caught spying on the imperial entourage's encampment. His eyes were puffed up and purple with bruises. It could have been a lot worse, but there was a limit to the summary punishment that could be meted out before questions were asked.

Now, a night later, sleep was denied to him. He sat hunched up, staring blankly out through the slit between the tent flaps. His thoughts were not filled with nervous apprehension about the coming battle. He was not even considering the ultimate prospects of glorious victory or ignoble defeat, or even death. He was consumed with bitter thoughts of jealousy, and fear that Lavinia, in whose arms he had rested only a few days before, might even now be lying with Vitellius.

Eventually the bitter poison of his despair became too much for him. He just wanted to blot it out, to cease enduring this relentless misery. His hand groped for his dagger belt and his fingers closed round the polished wooden handle, tensing as he prepared to draw the blade.

Then he relaxed his grip and took a deep breath. This was absurd. He must force himself to think of something else, anything that might distract him from thoughts of Lavinia.

Still tucked against his breast was the bloodless bandage that Nisus had worn round his knee. Cato pressed a hand to it and made himself think about the strange markings on the inside of the bandage. They must be significant, he reasoned, if only because of the suspicious circumstances under which the bandage had been obtained. And if the markings were some kind of coded message, who was it from and to whom had Nisus been trying to deliver it?

In answer to the latter question Cato already suspected Tribune Vitellius. And since the only people beyond the Roman lines were the natives then it followed that the message was from them. It stank of treason, but Cato dared not move against the tribune without incontestable evidence. As yet, all he had was his own bad opinion of Vitellius and strange black lines on a bandage, hardly enough to build a case on. It was too vexing, and as Cato tried to think his way round the problem, his tired mind embraced the subtle coming of sleep. Heavy eyelids drooped and slowly shut and before long Cato was snoring along with the rest of the century's veterans.

The next morning the legionaries were rousted into activity by a rumour that swept through the camp like a brush fire: the enemy army had been sighted. A day's march to the east an advance guard of auxiliary cavalry had come up against a series of defensive fortifications and redoubts. The auxiliaries had been showered with arrows and light spears and had backed away as quickly as possible, leaving several of their number wounded or dead before the British lines. Even as the auxiliaries made their report to the Emperor, word of their encounter spread through the army. The prospect of battle excited the legionaries, and they were relieved that the enemy had decided to fight a set-piece battle rather than a prolonged guerrilla war that could drag on for years.

The discomfort of the day before was forgotten as the men dressed and armed hurriedly. The cold morning meal was eaten under leaden skies, across which dark clouds scudded in the strong breeze. Macro looked up anxiously.

'Wonder if it'll rain.'

'Looks like it might, sir. But if Claudius moves quickly then we might beat the rain and reach the Britons before nightfall.'

'And if we don't then it's another day of marching in wet clothes,' grumbled Macro. 'Wet clothes, shitty mud and cold food. Anyway, who's to say those bloody natives won't just do a runner?'

Cato shrugged.

'Better get the lads fallen in, Optio. It'll be a long day one way or another.'

The centurion's fears about the weather proved to be groundless. As the morning wore on, the clouds cleared, the wind died away completely and by noon the sun blazed down upon the army. A thin haze of vapour wafted up from the drying clothes, of the legionaries as they trudged along in the muddy wake of the Praetorian vanguard.

Late in the afternoon the Second Legion rounded a small hill and came in sight of the enemy lines. Ahead, some two miles distant, lay a low ridge, bristling with defences. In front lay an extensive system of ramps and ditches designed to deflect a direct assault and expose the attackers to missile fire for as long as possible before they reached the defenders. To the right of the enemy line the ridge tumbled down into a vast expanse of marsh through which a wide river curved behind the ridge in a long, grey sweep. To the left of the enemy line the ridge disappeared into a dense forest that covered the undulating ground as far as Cato could see. The position was well chosen; any attacker would be forced to make a frontal assault up the slope between the forest and the marsh.

The Fourteenth Legion had arrived ahead of the Second and was well advanced in preparing the army's fortifications for the night. A screen of auxiliaries stood at the bottom of the slope and beyond them small groups of cavalry scouts were making a close inspection of the enemy's defences. A staff officer directed Macro's century to the row of pegs that marked their tent line and the centurion barked out the order to down packs. There was no suppressing the excitement of the men as they hastily erected their tents and then sat down on the slope to gaze across the shallow vale at the enemy fortifications opposite. The setting sun twinkled on the helmets and weapons of the Britons massing behind their defences. The tension in the still air was heightened by the growing humidity as clouds thickened along the southern horizon once again. But this time there was not a breath of wind, and the myriad sounds of an army preparing to bed down for the night hung strangely in the still air.

At dusk, fires were lit and in the gathering gloom twin carpets of sparkling orange confronted each other across the vale, and smoke from the flames smudged the air above each army. Vespasian had given orders that his men be given an extra issue of meat to fill their bellies for the coming battle, and the legionaries gratefully settled to eat the salt beef and barley stew as night fell. Cato was mopping up the dregs of his stew with a biscuit when he became aware of a strange sound carrying faintly on the air. It was a rising chant that ended in a roar, accompanied by a muffled clatter. He turned to Macro who had already finished his meal with voracious efficiency, and now lay on his back picking shreds of meat from between his teeth with a small twig.

'What's happening over there, sir?'

'Well, sounds to me like they're trying to whip up a bit of battle fever.'

'Battle fever?'

'Of course. They know the odds are against them. We've given them a good kicking in every fight so far. Morale won't be high so Caratacus will be doing everything he can to make them fight hard.'

A fresh roar burst out from the enemy camp, and another rhythmic clatter.

'What's that noise, sir?'

'That? It's the same trick we use. A sword beating on a shield. You get everyone to beat to the same rhythm and that's the sound you get. Supposed to scare the shit out of the enemy. That's the idea, at least. Personally, I find it just gives me a headache.'

Cato finished his stew and set the mess tin down beside him. The contrast between the two camps disturbed him. While the enemy seemed to be having some kind of wild celebration, the legions were settling down for a night's sleep, as if tomorrow was merely another day.

'Shouldn't we be doing something about that lot?'

'Like what?'

'I don't know. Just something to break up their party. Something to unsettle them.'

'Why bother?' Macro yawned. 'Let them have their fun. It won't make any difference when our lads get stuck into them tomorrow. They'll just be more tired than us.'

'I suppose so.' Cato licked the last drips of stew from his fingers. He tore up some grass and wiped his mess tin clean. 'Sir?'

'What is it?' Macro replied sleepily.

'Do you think the baggage train would have been able to catch up with us today?'

'Don't see why not. No rain today. Why do you ask?'

'Er, just wondered if we'd be getting artillery support tomorrow.'

'If Claudius is sensible, we'll be getting all the fire support we can manage against those fortifications.'

Cato rose to his feet.

'Going somewhere?'

'Latrine. And maybe a quick stroll before I turn in, sir.'

'Quick stroll?' Macro rolled his head to one side and looked at Cato. 'Haven't you had enough walking over the last two days?'

'Just need to clear my head, sir.'

'All right then. But you'll need a good night's sleep for tomorrow.'

'Yes, sir.'

Cato strolled off towards the centre of the camp. If the baggage train had caught up with the army then he might see Lavinia. This time there would be no enclosure to keep him out. A few guards maybe, but they could easily be avoided in the dark. And then he would hold Lavinia in his arms again and smell the scent of her hair. The prospect filled him with a keen sense of anticipation and he quickened his pace as he walked up the via Praetoria in the direction of the legate's tents. The jaunty spring in his stride carried him forward with such momentum that he nearly floored a figure who suddenly emerged from a tent flap and stepped directly in his path. As it was they collided and Cato's chin was badly knocked when it struck the other person's head.

'Oi! You stupid bloody . . . Lavinia!'

Rubbing her head, Lavinia stared at him, wide-eyed. 'Cato!'

'But . . . why . . .' he mumbled as surprise overcame loquacity. 'What are you doing here? How did you get here?'

he added, remembering the muddy tracks that had sucked down the baggage wagons.

'With the artillery train. As soon as they could move, Lady Flavia left her wagon to follow on with the rest and we hitched a ride with a catapult crew. What happened to your face?'

'Someone ran into me, quite a few times. But that's not important now.' Cato wanted to fold his arms about her, but there was a strange, distant expression in her eyes that discouraged him. 'Lavinia? What's the matter?'

'Nothing. Why?'

'You seem different.'

'Different!' She laughed nervously. 'Nonsense. I'm just busy. I've got an errand to run for my mistress.'

'When can I see you?' Cato risked taking her hand in his.

'I don't know. I'll find you. Where are your tents?'

'Over there.' Cato pointed. 'Just ask for the Sixth Century of the Fourth Cohort.' The sudden image of Lavinia wandering through the darkened tents surrounded by thousands of males made him worry for her safety. 'It'd be better if I waited for you here.'

'No! I'll come and find you, if I get time. But you must go now.' Lavinia leaned forward and kissed him quickly on the cheek before pressing her hand firmly against his chest. 'Go on!'

Confused, Cato backed off slowly. Lavinia smiled nervously and waved him away, as if joking, but there was an intensity in her eyes that made Cato feel cold and afraid. He nodded, turned and walked away, round the corner of a line of tents and out of her sight.

As soon as the tents blocked her view of him, Lavinia turned and hurried down the via Praetoria along the line of torches leading away from the legate's tents.

Had she waited a moment she might have seen Cato peep cautiously round the tent line. He watched her almost run in the opposite direction, and once he was sure that he could remain out of sight in the shadows on this side of the via Praetoria he followed her, padding softly from tent to tent, keeping her in view. She didn't go very far. Just to the first of the six big tents of the Second Legion's tribunes. The cold anxiety he had felt a moment earlier turned to a sickening, icy dread as he watched Lavinia boldly pull open the flap of Vitellius' tent and step inside.

Chapter Forty-Seven

With a grand flourish Claudius whipped back the silk sheet covering the table. Underneath, illuminated by the glow of dozens of hanging oil lamps, lay a contoured reproduction of the surrounding landscape, as detailed as the staff officers could make it in the time available, based on reports from the scouts. The legions' officers crowded round the table and examined the landscape intently. For those who had arrived after sunset this was the first opportunity to see what lay ahead of them the next day. The Emperor allowed his officers a brief moment to familiarise themselves with the model before he began the briefing.

'Gentlemen, tomorrow m-m-morning we begin the end of the conquest of this land. Once Caratacus is beaten and his army wiped out, there will be n-nothing between us and the capital of the Catuvellauni. With the f-fall of Camulodunum the other British tribes will bow to the inevitable. A year from now, I th-think we can safely say, this island will be as peaceful a p-p-province as any in the empire.'

Vespasian listened in silent contempt, and judging by the arch glances being subtly exchanged by other officers, they shared his doubts. How could there be a complete conquest in just one year? No one even knew the extent of this island; some explorers claimed that it was just the tip of a vast landmass. If so, and if tales of the savage tribes of the far north were true, it would take many more years before the province was pacified. But by then Claudius would have had his triumph in Rome and the mob would have long forgotten distant Britain, distracted by an endless orgy of gladiatorial contests, beast hunts and chariot races at the Circus Maximus. The last page of the official history of Claudius' conquest of Britain would have been written then copied onto scrolls to be placed in every major public library across the empire.

Meanwhile Plautius and his legions would still be occupied extinguishing all the minor strongholds that insisted on holding out against the invader. And while a Druid still lived, there would be constant, simmering resistance to Rome, which would regularly boil over into armed rebellion. Ever since their bloody persecution by Julius Caesar the Druids had regarded Rome, and all things Roman, with an unquenchable and fervent hatred.

'In two days' time,' Claudius continued, 'we will be feasting in C-Camulodunum. Think on that, and in years to come you w-w-will be able to tell your grandchildren of the d-d-decisive battle you fought and won at the side of Emperor C-Claudius!' Eyes gleaming and mouth grinning lopsidedly, he looked round at the faces of his staff officers. General Plautius quickly put his hands together and launched a round of applause that was rather more automatic than enthusiastic.

'Thank you. Thank you.' Claudius raised his hands and the clapping obediently died away. 'And now I'll let Narcissus talk you through the details of my p-plan of attack. Narcissus?'

'Thank you, Caesar.'

The Emperor stepped back from the table and his trusted freedman took his place, a long thin baton in his hand.

Claudius limped over to a side table and began picking at some of the elaborate pastries and tarts his team of chefs had managed to conjure up. He paid little attention to Narcissus' presentation, and so missed the sullen resentment of the senior army officers at being given their orders by a civilian bureaucrat, and a mere freedman at that. Narcissus was relishing the moment and looked thoughtfully at the model before he raised his baton to begin his address.

'The Emperor has decided that bold tactics are required to crack this nut.' He tapped the stumps of twigs which represented the British palisade on the ridge. 'We can't use the ground to the south because of the marsh and we can't get through the forest. The scouts report that thick briars grow right up to the edge of the tree line.'

'Did they manage any penetration of the forest?' asked Vespasian.

'I'm afraid not. The Britons sent out chariots to chase the scouts off before they could have a good look. But they report that, as far as they could see, the forest is impenetrable and there were no signs of any open trails.'

Vespasian was not content. 'Doesn't it strike you as suspicious that the Britons didn't want the scouts getting too near the forest?'

Narcissus smiled. 'My dear Vespasian, you shouldn't presume to judge others by your own failure to reconnoitre adequately.'

There was a sharp intake of breath around the tent and the other senior officers watched for Vespasian's reaction to this outrageous attack on his professionalism. The legate clamped his jaw shut to bite off the outburst that rose in his throat. The charge was grossly unfair; he had been acting on Plautius' direct order, but it would be most unseemly to say so now.

'Then it would be wise to reconnoitre adequately on this occasion,' Vespasian responded in an even voice.

'It's been taken care of.' Narcissus waved his hand airily. Behind him the Emperor left the tent with a plate piled high with delicacies. 'Now then, on to the details. The artillery will be deployed in range of the enemy defences under cover of night. The army will be drawn up behind the Praetorian Guards, with the elephants on our right wing. The bolt-throwers will lay down fire on the palisade until the Praetorians and the elephants start advancing up the slope. I should think the mere sight of the elephants will unnerve and divert the Britons for long enough to enable the Praetorians to scale the defences. They will take and hold the palisade. The Twentieth, Fourteenth and Ninth Legions will advance through the gap opened up by the Praetorians and fan out on the far side of the ridge. The Second will remain in reserve, after leaving four cohorts, along with the auxiliary troops, to guard the camp and baggage train. Once we've dealt with Caratacus it's a straight road to Camulodunum. That's all, gentlemen.' Narcissus let his baton slip through his fist until it thumped the wooden flooring.

Aulus Plautius quickly stepped up to the head of the map table. 'Thank you, a most succinct delivery.'

'I try not to say a word more than is completely and utterly necessary,' replied Narcissus.

'Quite. Now then, are there any questions?'

'If there were any questions,' Narcissus cut in, 'they would simply indicate a failure to listen properly. And I'm sure your men are as professional as they seem. There is one final item on the agenda. Word has reached me that there might be an attempt on the Emperor's life over the next few days. I have to deal with such rumours all the time, and I am sure this will prove to be another false alarm.' He gave Vespasian a slight nod and continued, 'But we can never be too sure. Accordingly, I'd be most grateful if you gentlemen could keep an eye and an ear out for anything remotely suspicious. General Plautius, you can dismiss them now.'

For an instant Vespasian was certain that his general was going to explode at the freedman's impudence, and he willed Plautius to do so. But at the last moment Plautius looked up, over Narcissus' shoulder, and saw Claudius watching them closely through a small gap in the tent flap as he munched on a pastry, oblivious to the flakes soiling his gorgeous imperial finery. The general curtly nodded to his officers and they quickly filed from the tent, anxious to avoid being drawn into a confrontation between Plautius and the chief secretary.

Vespasian waited by the map table, determined to have his say, and he deliberately ignored the warning look and beckoning wave from Sabinus who had paused briefly at the threshold. At last, only Vespasian, Plautius, the Emperor and his freedman remained.

'I take it you d-disapprove of my plan, Legate.'

'Caesar,' Vespasian began warily, 'the plan is excellent. You want to fight this war like a bolt of lightning, striking down your foe with one dazzling thrust that will overwhelm him before he can react. Who would not want to fight a war in this way? But . . .' He looked round to gauge the expressions on the other men's faces.

'Please continue,' Narcissus said coldly. 'Your silence is thunderous. But?'

'The problem lies with the enemy. We are assuming that they will simply sit on that ridge and defend it. What if they conceal troops in the wood? What if—'

'We've been through this, Vespasian,' Narcissus

responded, as if explaining something yet again to a particularly thick schoolboy. 'The scouts say that the woods are impassable.'

'But what if they're wrong?'

'What if they're wrong?' Narcissus mimicked. 'What if there are chariots hiding in ditches waiting to burst out on us the moment we approach? What if they have thousands of men hiding in marshes? What if they have secretly allied themselves to a tribe of Amazons to distract our men from thoughts of invasion and conquest?'

His mocking tone enraged Vespasian. How dare this fool show such contempt.

'The lie of the land has been thoroughly scouted,' Narcissus went on. 'We know where the enemy is positioned, we know how to play to our strengths and their weaknesses, and we have beaten Caratacus before and we'll do it again. In any case, we've issued all the orders so it's too late to change things now.'

Plautius caught Vespasian's eye and shook his head to forestall any more argument. The Emperor's word was law, for soldiers more than most, and there was no arguing with that. If Claudius wished to wage his lightning war, then no one could stop him – except the Britons.

Chapter Forty-Eight

The humidity of the last few days, and the proximity of the marsh and river combined to produce a particularly thick mist that lay most densely in the shallow vale between the two armies. Long before the sun came up and tinted the milky wreaths with orange, the legionaries had dressed and fed and were marching to take up their positions for the coming battle. From either side of the Praetorian cohorts came the mechanical clanking of the bolt-throwers as the artillerymen strained at the torsion levers and the ratchets dropped across cog teeth. Small braziers gleamed as incendiary missiles were made ready. Far to the right the elephants stuck closely together, thoroughly unnerved by the pallid wisps of mist that hemmed them in on all sides.

From a small grassy mound just outside the Roman camp, the Emperor and his staff waited for news of the battle preparations. Below them the mist blanketed most of the Roman army and only vague snatches of shouted orders, drumming hoofbeats and the clatter of equipment indicated the presence of thousands of men. A continuous stream of messengers went to and fro as Plautius struggled to co-ordinate his invisible army. Fortunately, he had foreseen the rising of the mist and during the night had ordered the engineers to lay out pegs to mark the start position for each unit. Even so, dawn came and went and the sun was well above the horizon before he was satisfied that the army was in position and ready to attack.

'Caesar, the eagles await your orders,' he announced finally.

'Well, let's g-get on with it, shall we?' Claudius replied, irritated by the delay; it had not been a part of his battle plan.

'Yes, Caesar.' Plautius nodded to his signals tribune to launch the attack. The massed trumpets of the headquarters staff blasted out across the vale, slightly muffled in the clammy air. Almost at once the British war horns began to bray out their defiant response, and swelling through the noise came cheers and jeering from the British warriors on the ridge. Down in the mist a sharp rhythmic clatter reached the ears of the Roman staff officers. The noise grew in volume and extended down the entire length of the Roman front.

'What is that racket?' snapped Claudius.

'Just our men announcing themselves, Caesar. They're hitting their shields with their javelins. It makes them feel good and scares the enemy.'

'They d-don't sound too scared to me.' Claudius nodded across the vale.

'Well then, it'll just have to be for the benefit of our men, Caesar.'

'It's a bloody nuisance!'

A loud series of cracks sounded from within the mist and a volley of fire-bolts whirred across the British defences in blazing arcs before crashing through the palisade. Sparks, fragments of wood, sods of turf and bits of men flew in all directions as the heavy bolts stuck home. There was a sudden end to the battle cries from the British, but someone on the other side knew the danger of sitting and taking such punishment in silence. One by one the war horns took up their battle cry once again and they were quickly joined by the shouts of the warriors behind the defences.

From their position just outside the ditch of the Roman camp the men of the Second Legion were in a good position to view the bombardment. The artillery kept up a steady fire and the air above the British defences was continually scored by flaming bolts and dark smoke trails. Already a series of small fires had broken out and thick smudges of smoke billowed up on the far ridge.

'Poor sods.' Macro shook his head. 'Wouldn't like to be over there right now.'

Cato looked sidelong at his centurion, surprised at this evidence of empathy for the enemy.

'You've never seen what an artillery bolt can do, have you, lad?'

'I've seen the consequences, sir.'

'Not the same thing. You have to be on the receiving end of those things to fully appreciate the effect.'

Cato looked at the flames and thick black smoke on the opposite slope, hoping the Britons had the good sense to turn and run. In recent weeks he had come to value most the battles that delivered the least number of dead and wounded at their conclusion. But today he no longer cared. After the previous night's sighting of Lavinia his heart was in the grip of a cold despair that made life seem quite pointless.

The Britons were a game lot and raised their serpent-tail banners above their defences. The lack of any breeze meant the bearers had to sweep their banners to and fro to fully reveal the tails and in the distance they looked like frenzied worms twisting on a hot plate.

'There go the Praetorians!' Macro pointed down the slope. Just emerging from where the mist began to thin marched an uneven line of men in white crested helmets. Then came their white tunics as they drew free of the mist. When the first wave was clear, they were halted and the officers dressed the line, then with perfect military precision the Praetorians moved up to the first line of defences: a series of ditches. Already the second line was emerging from the mist. The fire from the bolt-throwers slackened and finally stopped as word reached the artillery crews that the Praetorians were nearing the enemy.

As soon as the Britons were aware that the danger from the Roman artillery had passed, they swarmed back up to their palisade and began raining down arrows and slingshot on the Romans as they struggled up the steep face of the first ditch. Small gaps opened in the lines of the leading cohorts but the relentless discipline of the Roman army proved its worth as the line instantly dressed itself and the gaps were filled. But the banks of the ditches were already dotted with the white uniformed bodies of the fallen. The first line clambered out of the last ditch, re-formed under intense fire, and began mounting the final slope to the palisade. Suddenly, all along the palisade, smoke spilled up into the air, and moments later great blazing bundles were raised with the aid of long pitchforks and lobbed over. They bounced down the steep slope, showering sparks in all directions before slamming into the Roman lines, scattering the Praetorians in all directions.

'Ouch,' Cato muttered. 'That's a nasty trick.'

'But effective. For the moment. However, I wouldn't fancy being a Briton when those Praetorians get in amongst them.'

'Just as long as they spare enough to sell for slaves.'

Macro laughed and slapped him on the shoulder. 'Now you're thinking like a soldier!'

'No, sir. I'm just thinking like someone who needs money,' replied Cato briefly.

'Where've those bloody elephants gone?' Macro strained his eyes to try and detect any movement out on the far right of the Roman line. 'Your eyes are better than mine. You see anything?'

Cato looked, but nothing disturbed the white bank of mist hanging over the marsh, and he shook his head.

'Bloody daft, using elephants.' Macro spat on the ground. 'Wonder which prat came up with that idea.'

'It has the touch of Narcissus about it, sir.'

'True. Look! In go the guards!'

The Praetorians had reached the palisade and managed to break down a few sections. As Cato and Macro watched, the thin slivers of their javelins rained down on the defenders before they drew swords and forced their way into the breaches.

'Up, Praetorians, and at 'em!' Macro shouted, as if his words would carry across the vale. 'Get 'em!'

The centurion's excitement was shared by those on the grassy mound. Officers craned their necks to try and get a better view of the distant assault. The Emperor was bouncing up and down in his saddle in unrestrained glee as the Praetorian cohorts charged home. So much so that he had forgotten the next phase of his own battle plan.

'Caesar?' Plautius interrupted.

'Oh, what is it now?'

'Shall I give the order for the legions to move up?'

'What?' Claudius frowned before he recalled the necessary details. 'Of course! Why h-h-hasn't it been done already? Get on with it, man! Get on with it!'

The order to advance was sounded, but the mist obscured any evidence of its being carried out until, at length, the front ranks of the Ninth Legion appeared as spectral shapes gradually emerging into view on the far slope. Cohort after cohort negotiated the ditches with painful slowness, or so it seemed when viewed from the mound. Some of the officers were nervously exchanging quiet words as they surveyed the advance. Something was wrong. The rear ranks of the Praetorian cohorts were still in view on top of the palisade. They should have advanced further by now but seemed to have been stopped dead by something not visible from this side of the ridge. The foremost legionaries of the Ninth were already in among the rear ranks of the Praetorians, and still the waves of the succeeding cohorts emerged from the mist and advanced up the slope.

'Won't there be something of a t-tangle if this carries on?' asked the Emperor.

'I fear so, Caesar.'

'Why isn't somebody doing something about it?' Claudius looked round at his assembled staff officers. Blank-faced to a man. 'Well?'

'I'll send someone to find out the reason for the delay, Caesar.'

'Don't bother!' Claudius replied hotly. 'If you want something done p-p-properly you just have to do it yourself.' Grabbing his reins tightly, he dug his heels into his horse's flanks and plunged down the mound towards the mist.

'Caesar!' Narcissus called out desperately. 'Caesar! Stop!'

When Claudius rode on heedless, Narcissus swore and quickly turned to the other officers, who were watching events in amazement. 'Well? What are you waiting for? There goes the Emperor and where he goes his headquarters follows. Come on!'

As the Emperor disappeared into the fog, his staff officers streamed after him, desperately trying not to lose sight of the ruler of the Roman Empire as he raced into danger.

'What on earth is going on?' asked Vespasian. He was standing by his horse at the head of the six cohorts of his legion. With no warning the Emperor and his entire staff had charged from the mound, and what looked like the tail end of a horse race was melting into the mist. He turned to his senior tribune, eyebrows raised.

'When you've got to go, you've got to go,' suggested Vitellius.

'Most helpful of you, Tribune.'

'Do you think we should follow them?'

'No. Our orders were to stay here.'

'Fair enough, sir.' Vitellius shrugged. 'The view's better in any case.'

Vespasian stood and watched the far slope where the succeeding waves of attackers had become hopelessly mixed up before any officers had a chance to halt the advance and reorganise their men. 'This could turn into something of a disaster if we're not careful.'

'Hardly an edifying spectacle, is it, sir?' Vitellius chuckled.

'Let's just hope that's the worst thing that will happen today,' replied Vespasian. He glanced up at the clear sky from where the morning sun now shone brightly, and then down at the mist. 'Would you say it's lifting?'

'What was that, sir?'

'The mist. I think it's lifting.'

Vitellius stared at it for a moment. The white threads of mist were definitely thinner at the edges and already the dim outline of the forest away to the left was showing through.

'I believe you're right, sir.'

That the Emperor survived the mad dash right through the middle of his army Narcissus could only put down to some kind of divine intervention. In the dense white mist it was almost impossible to keep up with Claudius. Men scattered to the left and right at the sound of approaching hoofbeats and watched in astonishment as Claudius galloped by, closely pursued by General Plautius and his staff officers. As the Roman lines became more congested, Claudius was forced to slow down, and at last the others caught up with him and fought to clear a path through the packed ranks. As they climbed the slope out of the mist, the full scale of the disorganisation became clear. Across the entire front men were being crushed together. It was worst by the ditches, where those unfortunate enough to be caught in the bottom were wedged in tightly, and any who stumbled and fell were trampled to death on the ground. Only by using the brutal force of their mounts did Claudius and his staff at last gain the palisade and understand what had gone wrong.

Caratacus had foreseen everything. The ditches and the palisade were just a screen before the real defences laid out on the reverse slope. For hundreds of feet on either side ran a system of concealed pits with spikes at the bottom – the 'lilies' so beloved of Julius Caesar – and finally a deep trench and yet another turf rampart defended by a palisade. With no artillery fire to support them, the Praetorian units had been forced to advance into this deathtrap alone, with the Britons fighting them every step of the way.

All across the slope were the bodies of Praetorians impaled on lily spikes or crippled by concealed caltrops, whose vicious iron points went right through the soles of their boots and into their feet. There were only a few paths through the spikes and the Praetorians had been funnelled into these tight spaces where they were kept at bay by a handful of Britons while their flanks were exposed to merciless fire from small redoubts rising above the traps all around. The arrival of yet more troops had made the situation progressively worse as the Praetorians were forced even further into the trap.

Claudius gazed upon the disaster in horror; Plautius was in a cold rage. Without waiting for imperial approval he shouted out his orders.

'Get a messenger to each legate. They're to withdraw their men immediately. Make for their start markers and wait for further orders. Go!'

As the staff officers fought their way back down the slope, Claudius came out of his frozen state and responded to the orders his general had just given. 'Very good, Plautius – a tactical withdrawal. Very s-s-sensible. But first, let's make good use of this d-diversion. The second can advance r-round the ridge and catch them in the flank. Give the order r-r-right now!'

Plautius stared at his Emperor, dumbfounded by the sheer idiocy of the order. 'Caesar, the Second is the last body of formed-up legionaries we have left.'

'Exactly! Now give the order.'

When Plautius didn't move, the Emperor repeated the order to Narcissus. At once the chief secretary glanced round for someone to ride to Vespasian.

'Sabinus! Over here!'

As Narcissus gave the order, there was a growing roar from the enemy as word passed down their lines that the Roman Emperor himself was within striking distance. Sling-shot and arrows from the British lines began to thud down around Claudius and his staff, and the imperial bodyguard hurriedly placed themselves round their master, raising their shields to shelter him. The rest of his companions had to dismount and take shields from the dead as the volume of missiles increased. Looking out from under the rim of a

British shield, Narcissus caught sight of a ripple of crimson cloaks in the mass of Britons swarming before them, and the roar in the throats of the enemy reached a fanatic pitch as Caratacus' elite warriors swept towards the Roman Emperor.

'Now we're for it!' Narcissus muttered, before he turned back to Sabinus.

'Understand this. If your brother doesn't move his men up in time, the Emperor will be lost and the army will be slaughtered. Go!'

Sabinus stabbed his heels into his mount and the beast reared before surging back through the packed ranks of legionaries. Behind Sabinus the roar of the Britons converging on the Emperor's position drowned out the other sounds of battle.

Desperate and confused faces flashed before him as Sabinus urged his mount on, brutally clearing his way through the dense mass, heedless of the cries of those men knocked down and trampled by his mount.

At last, the crush of legionaries thinned and he spurred his horse into a gallop up the slope towards the Roman camp. Through the mist his eyes anxiously sought for the first sign of his brother's legion. Then the spectral shapes of the standards appeared directly ahead. Suddenly, the mist cleared and, with a shout, Sabinus steered his horse round beside his younger brother, and breathlessly passed on the Emperor's order.

'Are you serious?'

'Quite serious, brother. To the right of the ridge and sweep round into their flank.'

'But there's a marsh over there. Where the elephants went. Where the hell did they end up?'

'Doesn't matter,' Sabinus said breathlessly. 'Just carry out the order. We might yet win the battle.'

'Win the battle?' Vespasian looked up across the thinning mist to where the other legions were crowding back down the slope. 'We'll be lucky if we aren't massacred.'

'Just carry out the order, Legate!' Sabinus said harshly.

Vespasian glanced at his brother, and then looked again at the battlefield before he made the decision all his instincts and military judgement told him to make.

'No.'

'No?' Sabinus repeated, eyes wide. 'What d'you mean, no?'

'The Second is staying here. We're the reserve,' explained Vespasian. 'If Claudius throws us away in some hare-brained attack then there's nothing left to meet any surprise the Britons throw at us. Not while the other legions are in that mess.' He nodded across the vale. 'We stay here.'

'Brother, I beg you. Do as you are ordered!'

'No!'

'The Britons have already sprung their surprise on us,' Sabinus argued desperately. 'And now we – you – can surprise them.'

'No.'

'Vespasian.' Sabinus leaned forward and spoke with quiet intensity. 'Do it! If you stand here you'll be accused of cowardice. Think of our family name. Do you want the Flavians to be remembered as cowards for the rest of time? Do you?'

Vespasian returned his older brother's stare with equal intensity. 'This is not about posterity. This is about doing the right thing. By the book. While the army is disorganised, we must have a standing reserve. Only a fool would disagree.'

'Quiet, brother!' Sabinus glanced round nervously in case Vespasian's intemperate words had been overheard. Vitellius stood to one side and casually raised a hand in mock greeting.

'Vespasian—'

But the legate was no longer listening. He was staring at the forest, more clearly visible in the thinning mist. Unless his eyes were playing him false, there was movement down there. From under the boughs of the trees at the edge of the forest, briar thickets were slowly emerging in dozens of places. What dark magic was this? Could those devils the Druids conjure up the very forces of nature to aid them in their fight against Rome?

Then the briars were thrown to one side and the true genius of Caratacus' plan became clear. From deep within the forest charged a column of chariots. The thunder of hooves and rumble of wheels was audible even up by the Roman army's camp. The heavy British chariots burst out into the open and charged down upon the artillery positions on the left flank.

The legionaries manning the bolt-throwers had no time to react to the threat and were cut down where they stood, trampled and ridden over by the chariots, or speared by the warriors riding on the chariot beds. In the wake of the chariots swarmed thousands of lightly armed men carrying pikes. They streamed across the rear of the attacking force like grey ghosts in the thinning mist. They paid no attention to the few cohorts of the Second Legion visible above the mist as they rushed to close the trap on Claudius and the main body of his army. More Britons appeared all along the edge of the forest and threw themselves upon the legions' tangled flank. The ferocity of the attack compounded the effect of the surprise and the Britons carved a deep swathe through the disorganised Roman lines. Panic welled up and swept ahead of the British onslaught and some legionaries backed away, while others simply turned and ran to the right of the line.

'Dear gods,' said Sabinus. 'They're trying to drive us into the marsh.'

'And they'll do it,' said Vespasian grimly, 'unless we intervene.'

'Us?' Sabinus looked horrified. 'What can we do? We should guard the camp, so the survivors have somewhere to run.'

'Survivors? There won't be any survivors. They'll run all right, straight into the marsh and drown, or be stuck in the mire and cut to pieces.' Vespasian reached over and gripped his brother's arm. 'Sabinus, it's down to us. There's no one else. Do you understand me?'

Sabinus recovered his self-control and nodded.

'Good!' Vespasian released his arm. 'Now go into the camp and fetch the other four cohorts and any auxiliary troops you can find. Get them formed up as quickly as you can and attack straight down the hill. Make as much noise as possible. Now go!'

'What about you?'

'I'll take my chances with what I've got here.'

Sabinus wheeled his horse and spurred it up towards the main gate of the camp, bent low across the beast's neck as he kicked his heels in.

With a last glance after his brother, Vespasian wondered if they would ever meet again in this world. Then he pushed the grim thought from his mind, and steeled himself for what he must do if the army and his Emperor were to be saved. He turned to his tribunes and called them over. The young men listened intently as he delivered his instructions as briefly as he could and then galloped away to deliver the orders to the senior centurions of the six cohorts. Vespasian dismounted, handed the reins to a groom and asked for his shield to be brought to him. He undid the clasp on his scarlet cloak and let it slip to the ground.

'Make sure that is taken back to my tent. I'll need it tonight if it gets cold.'

'Yes, sir.' His personal slave nodded with a smile. 'I'll see you later then, master.'

Having checked the chin strap of his helmet and made sure that his shield grip was dry, Vespasian drew his sword and rapped it on the rim of his shield to steady his hand. He glanced over his cohorts to make sure that all was ready. The men were standing to, silently formed up and intently following the action down in the vale as they waited for the order.

'The Second will advance, on the oblique!' he shouted out, and the order was quickly relayed along the line. He counted three before the execution phase of the order and then filled his lungs. 'Advance!'

At a steady pace the six cohorts moved diagonally forward and started down the slope towards the shouts and screams of the desperate battle being fought in the vale. The mist was rapidly thinning and starting to reveal the full scale of the disaster facing Claudius and the other three legions. Caught out of formation and sent reeling by the surprise attack from the forest, the rear ranks had broken and were blindly fleeing across the battlefield towards the marsh. Scattered pockets of resistance showed where a centurion had managed to show sufficient resolve and presence of mind to gather men to face the British pikemen. Ranged behind their closely aligned shields, small groups of legionaries fought their way towards each other but they were getting the worst of it because of the reach of the enemy's pikes.

The standards of the Fourth Cohort bobbed up and down with the rhythmic pace of their bearers and Cato's eyes were automatically drawn to them as their gilded decorations caught the sun and glowed with a fiery burnish. The cohorts were marching in two lines of three centuries, with the Sixth Century positioned on the right of the rear rank. Cato had a clear view of the line of advance. The tall oaks of the forest loomed up ahead and to the left of the Second Legion, wide trails leading into their shadows clearly visible now that the briar screens had been discarded. Ahead and to the right bodies were strewn across the trampled grass, which was still wet with dew that drenched his boots. The cohort passed over the remains of the left flank artillery battery. Most of the weapons had been knocked over, and the bodies of their crews lay crumpled all around. Cato had to sidestep the corpse of a centurion, and glancing down he felt the bile rise in his throat at the sight of the bloody gristle and severed tendons in the side of the officer's neck where a sword blow had nearly taken his head off.

They kept on moving and left the carnage of the battery behind. As they advanced, Cato saw that at last some of the enemy were responding to the cohorts' approach. The nearest of the pikemen had turned to face the threat and were shouting warnings to their comrades. More and more of them turned to attack the Second Legion, screaming their war cries as they levelled their pikes.

'Halt!' Vespasian bellowed.

The cohorts drew up one pace on, hands tightening round their javelins in anticipation of the next order.

'Prepare javelins!'

The legionaries of the front line of centuries hefted the shafts of their javelins and stretched their throwing arms back. The British charge faltered. With no shields to protect them, the pikemen well knew how vulnerable they were to a volley of javelins.

'Release!'

The legionaries' arms flew forwards, releasing a ragged belt of dark lines that arced up in the air towards the Britons. As they reached the highest point of their trajectory the javelins seemed to hang for an instant, and the war cries of the Britons abruptly died in their throats as they braced themselves for the impact. The tips of the javelins dropped, and the volley plunged down into the British ranks, tearing into and through the unprotected bodies of the pikemen. The charge collapsed at once and the surviving Britons glanced fearfully towards the cohorts as Vespasian called the second line to readiness. But there was no need for another shower of javelins. Almost as one, the Britons backed away, not willing to brave another volley and join their stricken comrades lying dead and wounded amongst the jagged hedge of javelin shafts whose heads had buried themselves in bare flesh and soil.

'Advance!' Vespasian shouted, and the cohorts moved forwards once more, retrieving unspoiled javelins and finishing off enemy wounded as they passed through the destruction they had wrought. The left flank of the legion was close to the edge of the forest now and Vespasian called for a realignment of the advance. The legion stopped and steadily altered its facing until they were opposite the left flank of the British pikemen, cutting them off from the forest, in a neat reversal of positions. Now it was the Britons who would be forced towards the marsh – for as long as the six cohorts could maintain the momentum of their counter-attack.

Unless Sabinus threw in the weight of whatever units he could lay his hands on soon, the outcome of the battle was still very much in doubt. Vespasian spared a quick glance back up the slope towards the Roman camp, but there was no sign of any help from that quarter yet. He ordered his legion forward, and as they stepped out towards the heaving mêlée sprawling across the vale, Vespasian started striking the rim of his shield with his sword. The rhythm was picked up by the men around him and quickly spread to the other cohorts as the double line closed on the pikemen.

They were now passing over the bodies of their comrades from the other legions and a firm resolve to exact a full and bloody revenge filled their hearts as they raised their shields and prepared to engage the Britons. The triumphant war cries of the pikemen died away as the Second Legion swept in towards them, and beyond the Britons the hard-pressed knots of other legionaries rallied with a cry of hope.

Vespasian halted his men one last time to release the remaining javelins, and then the Second charged home with a savage cry of battle-crazed exultation on the lips of every man.

Surrounded on all sides by wild-eyed legionaries, Cato surrendered to the moment and released the tension and aggression that had been building up within him during the advance. He screamed out a meaningless cry as he was caught up in the charging press of men racing towards the waiting enemy. With a crash of spear and shield the Second Legion smashed into the British line and the momentum of the charge carried them through the broken mass of British spearmen who only moments before had been screaming triumphantly as they swarmed around the disorganised turmoil of the trapped legions.

Cato lowered his head and pushed his way forwards into the dense press of men hacking and stabbing at each other. To his immediate right he was conscious of Macro bellowing encouragement to the rest of his century and waving his short sword up in the air to rally his men around him. Cato found himself confronted by a snarling Briton who was holding his pike in both hands and swinging it round and down towards his stomach. Cato chopped at the spearhead, knocking it to the right, and then charged inside the Briton's grip. The man had but an instant to register his surprise before Cato's sword spitted him high in the chest. He fell back, spluttering great gouts of blood as Cato wrenched his blade free, knocked his opponent to the ground with his shield and turned to look for another enemy.

'Cato, to your left!' Macro shouted.

The optio ducked his head instinctively and the broad blade of a spear glanced off the top of his helmet. The blow momentarily blinded him as his vision exploded with white. It cleared instantly but his head was reeling and he was knocked flat as the pikeman slammed into his side, sending them both sprawling in the blood-soaked grass. Cato was aware of the Briton's fierce breathing, the stench of his body and a vivid blue tattoo on the man's shoulder, which writhed before his eyes for a moment. Then the man grunted, gasped and was rolled to one side as Macro pulled out his sword and stood over Cato.

'Get up, lad!'

The centurion covered their bodies with his shield and watched for any attack as Cato clambered to his feet, shaking his head to try and clear his dizziness.

'All right?'

'Yes, sir.'

'Good. Let's go.'

The impetus of the charge had run its course and now the men of the Sixth Century closed ranks and advanced behind a shield wall, cutting down any enemy that stood in the path of their steady advance. The British ranks were tightly packed now, so much so that they were no longer able to use their spears effectively, and they were gradually being cut to pieces. From further up the slope the legions that had so nearly been defeated now turned on their foe, and savagely meted out their revenge. The triumph in the cries of the British warriors died away and changed to fear and panic as they tried to escape the wicked blades of the legionaries' short swords. In the tight press of bodies the short sword was the most lethal of weapons and Britons fell in great numbers. Those who were wounded and slipped to the blood-stained grass were trampled underfoot, their bodies crushed by the men fighting over them, and then by more bodies so that some suffocated horribly.

Cato thrust out his shield, stepped up to it and stabbed with his sword in a steady rhythm as he advanced with the rest of the century. Some of the men were filled with blood lust and surged ahead of the line, hacking and slashing at the enemy, exposing themselves to danger on all sides. Many paid the price for this loss of self-control, and their freshly slaughtered bodies were clambered over by their comrades. Cato was aware of the danger underfoot and placed his feet carefully as he advanced, in cold dread of stumbling and being unable to rise again.

'They're breaking!' Macro shouted above the din of clashing weapons and the grunts and cries of the combatants. 'The enemy line's breaking!'

From the right, above the seething mass of bodies and weapons, Cato could see more Roman standards closing in from the direction of the Roman camp.

'It's the camp guard!' he cried out.

The destruction of the enemy spearmen was sealed once the remaining cohorts of the legion and a scratch force of auxiliary cohorts charged into their rear. Hemmed in on three sides by an impenetrable wall of Roman shields, they were killed where they stood. On the only open side they dropped their weapons and flooded towards the marsh in a desperate attempt to seek salvation in that direction. At first the Britons caught in the armoured vice of Roman legionaries tried to resist even as they were forced to give ground. Then they suddenly disintegrated as a fighting force and became a torrent of individuals running for their lives, pursued by a merciless enemy.

Shouting with glee, the men of the Sixth Century charged after them a short distance, but their heavy armour and weapons forced them to give up the chase. They leaned over their grounded shields, breathing heavily, many only now aware of the wounds they had sustained amid the frenzy of battle. Cato was tempted to slump to the ground and rest his aching limbs, but the need to set an example to the rest of the men kept him standing erect and ready to respond to fresh orders. Macro pushed his way towards him through the tired legionaries.

'Hot work, eh, Optio?'

'Yes, sir.'

'Did you see 'em run at the end?' Macro laughed. 'Bolted like a bunch of virgins at the Lupercal! Don't think we'll be seeing much more of Caratacus before we take Camulodunum.'

A piercing sound, unlike anything Cato had ever heard, carried across the battlefield and every head turned in the direction of the marsh. It came again, a shrill trumpeting scream of terror and pain.

'What the fuck's that?' Macro looked around, wide-eyed.

Over the heads of the other legionaries Cato could see the low knoll on which the right-hand battery of bolt-throwers had been positioned. Like their comrades on the left wing they had been quickly ridden down by the British chariots. The Britons were still there, and had turned a handful of the weapons round to face the marsh. And there in the marsh stood the elephants, stuck in muddy slime up to their loins, frantically being urged on by their drivers as the Britons used them for target practice. Even as Cato watched, a bolt arced in a low trajectory right into the side of one of the elephants.

It had already been struck in the rump and a bloody smear ran down its back legs from the bolt which protruded from its wrinkled skin. As the second bolt struck, the elephant whipped its trunk up into the air, bellowing and shrieking with agony. The force of the bolt carried it right through the thick hide and buried the head deep within the animal's vitals. With the next cry of agony came a thick crimson spray from the end of its trunk, which hung in the air like a red mist before dispersing. Thrashing wildly in the mud, the animal rolled onto its side, dragging the driver down with it. More bolts slammed into the other animals stranded in the marsh and one by one the British charioteers picked off the remaining elephants before the nearest Roman infantry could reach the knoll. The Britons bounded onto their waiting chariots and with a loud chorus of shouts and cracking of reins the chariots rumbled diagonally up the slope, past the Roman camp, and escaped round the edge of the forest.

'The bastards,' Cato heard a legionary mutter.

An appalled stillness hung over the vale, made more unbearable by the terrible cries of beasts in their death throes. Cato could see British spearmen skirting the edge of the marsh as they took full advantage of the pause to escape. Cato wanted to point them out and yell out an order to pursue the enemy, but the screams of the dying elephants mesmerised the Romans.

'I wish someone would silence those bloody animals,' Macro said quietly.

Cato shook his head in astonishment. All across the vale lay bleeding and butchered men, hundreds of Romans amongst them, and yet these hardened veterans standing around him were perversely fascinated by the fate of a handful of dumb animals. He banged a fist down on the rim of his shield in bitter frustration.

As the British spearmen fled, their comrades up on the ridge realised that the trap had failed. Uncertainty and fear rippled through their ranks and they began to give ground to the legions, slowly at first, and then more steadily, until they melted away in large numbers. Only Caratacus' elite band of warriors stood firm until the army had safely withdrawn.

From the crest of the hill the Emperor slapped his thigh with glee at the sight of the enemy in full retreat.

'Ha! Watch him f-f-fly with his tail between his legs!'

General Plautius coughed. 'May I pass the order for the pursuit to begin, Caesar?'

'P-pursuit?' Claudius's eyebrows rose. 'Certainly not! It would be n-nice if you fellows in the army would leave a f-few of those savages left alive for me to rule.'

'But Caesar!'

'But! But! But! Enough, G-g-general! I give the orders. As well I should. My very f-first effort at command and I win a resounding victory. Is that not proof enough of my military b-b-brilliance? Well?'

Plautius looked towards Narcissus imploringly, but the chief secretary shrugged with a slight shake of his head. The general pursed his lips, and nodded towards the retreating Britons. 'Yes, Caesar. That's proof enough.'

Chapter Forty-Nine

Two days later the Roman army arrived before the ramparts of Camulodunum. When news of Caratacus' defeat reached the town elders of the Trinovantes they wisely refused to admit the bedraggled remains of their overlord's army into their capital, watching with relief as the sullen column disappeared across the rich farmland to the north. Most of the Trinovante warriors who had served with Caratacus kept faith with him and sadly turned their back on their kinsfolk and marched away. A few hours later an advance party of Roman cavalry scouts approached warily, and nearly turned and fled when the gates were abruptly thrown open and a deputation rushed out to greet them. The Trinovantes were effusive in their welcome to the Romans and in their condemnation of those of their tribe who had joined Caratacus in his futile attempt to resist the might of Emperor Claudius.

The scouts carried the greetings back to the army marching several miles behind them, and late in the afternoon the exhausted Roman legions pitched camp just outside the Trinovantes' capital. The professional caution of General Plautius meant that the deep ditch and high rampart of a camp in the face of the enemy was constructed before the army was allowed to rest.

Early the next day the Emperor and his staff were

conducted on an informal tour of the tribal capital, a dour affair by imperial standards, mostly timber-framed buildings of wattle and daub with a handful of more impressive stone structures at its heart. The capital fronted a deep river, alongside which ran a sturdy quay and long storage sheds where Gaulish merchants plied their trade, carrying fine wines and pottery from the continent and filling their vessels for the return journey with furs, gold, silver, and exotic barbarian jewellery for the voracious consumers of the empire.

'An excellent place to found our first colony, Caesar,' Narcissus announced. 'Strong trade links with the civilised world, and ideally situated to exploit the inland markets.'

'Well, yes. Good,' muttered the Emperor, not really listening to his chief secretary. 'But I rather think a n-n-nice temple in honour of me should be an early p-p-priority.'

'A temple, Caesar?'

'Nothing too fussy, just sufficient to insp-sp-spire a little awe.'

'As you wish, Caesar.' Narcissus bowed and then smoothly moved the conversation on to more pertinent schemes for developing the colony. Listening to them, Vespasian could not help but wonder at how easily the decision to erect such a monument was made. A mere whim of the Emperor, and it would happen just like that. A vast colonnaded shrine dedicated to a man ruling from a great city far away would rise above the meagre hovels of this barbarian town just as surely as if Jupiter himself had ordained it. And yet this man, this Emperor, who aspired to be a god, was just as vulnerable to the thrust of an assassin's knife as any other mortal. The threat to Claudius was still very much on Vespasian's mind, as was the fear that Flavia might be involved in the plot.

'How is the planning for tomorrow's c-ceremony going?' Claudius was asking.

'Very well, Caesar,' Narcissus replied. 'A state procession into the capital at midday, the dedication of an altar to peace, and then a banquet in the centre of Camulodunum in the evening. I've had word from our new allies. Seems that they know of Caratacus' defeat and are anxious to pledge their allegiance to us as soon as they can. Should make a dramatic centre-piece to the banquet. You know the sort of thing: the savages led into the presence of the mighty Emperor, before whose imperial majesty they feel compelled to fall on bended knee and swear eternal obedience. It'll look terrific, and make for great reading in the Rome gazette. The plebs will love it.'

'Good. Then see to the appropriate arrangements, please.' Claudius stopped in mid-stride, and his staff officers had to pull up abruptly to avoid running into him. 'Did you hear that last sentence? I didn't stammer once! Gracious me!'

Vespasian suddenly felt very worn out by the Emperor's presence. The endless and effortless arrogance of members of the imperial family was born of the cringing obeisance presented by all those who surrounded them. Vespasian was proud of his family's genuine achievements. From his grandfather who had served as a centurion in Pompey's army, to his father who had earned sufficient fortune to be elevated into the equestrian class, and thence to his own generation where both he and Sabinus could look forward to glittering senatorial careers. None of it was a mere accident of birth. All of it was the result of a great deal of effort and proven ability. Looking from Claudius to Narcissus and back again, Vespasian experienced his first pang of desire to be as venerated as was his due. In a fairer world it would be him, and not the inept Claudius, who held the destiny of Rome in his hands.

More galling still was the greeting Claudius had made to him after the crushing defeat of Caratacus' army. As Vespasian galloped up to make sure that his Emperor had survived the battle unhurt, he was surprised to see Claudius' air of smug satisfaction.

'Ah! There you are, Legate. I must thank you for the part you and y-your men played in my trap.'

'Trap? What trap, Caesar?'

'Why, to lure the enemy into a p-position where his true strength would be r-re-revealed and led to its destruction. You had just the wit to fill the important r-role I had assigned to you.'

Vespasian's mouth had dropped open as he heard this astonishing version of the morning's events. Then he clamped his jaw firmly shut to stop himself making a remark that would threaten his career, not to mention his life. He had bowed his head graciously and mumbled his thanks and tried not to think about the hundreds of stiffening Roman corpses sprawled across the battlefield in silent tribute to the Emperor's tactical genius.

Vespasian wondered if it might be so terrible if Claudius fell under an assassin's knife after all.

The tour of the Trinovantes' capital came to an end and the Emperor and his staff returned to the Roman camp to discover that the representatives of twelve tribes had arrived and were waiting at headquarters for an audience with the Emperor.

'An audience with Caesar?' Narcissus sniffed. 'I think not. Not today at least. They can be presented to him tomorrow, at the banquet.'

'Is that wise, Caesar?' Plautius asked quietly. 'We'll need

them when we renew the campaign. It would be better for them to feel like welcome allies rather than despised supplicants.'

'Which is what they are,' Narcissus interposed.

Claudius turned his face towards the skies as if seeking divine advice, and gently stroked his chin. A moment later he nodded and turned back to his staff with a smile. 'The tribesmen can wait. It's been a long day and I'm t-tired. Tell them . . . tell them that Caesar welcomes them warmly, but that the ex-ex-exigencies of his office prevent him from greeting them in p-p-person. How's that?'

Narcissus clapped his hands together. 'A paragon of elegance and clarity, Caesar!'

'Yes, I thought so.' Claudius tipped his head back in order to look down his nose at Plautius. 'Well, General?'

'Caesar, I am a mere soldier, and lack the necessary refinement to judge the aesthetic merit of another's loquacity.'

Claudius and Narcissus regarded him silently, one with a look of benign incomprehension, the other with close scrutiny as he looked for any trace of irony in the general's features.

'Well yes, quite!' Claudius nodded. 'It's a good thing to be aware of one's d-d-deficiencies.'

'You speak truly, as ever, Caesar.' Plautius bowed his head and Claudius limped off towards his tent, with Narcissus scurrying along to one side. Then the general turned to his officers. 'Vespasian!'

'Yes, sir.'

'You'd better deal with our tribal guests.'

'Yes, sir.'

'See that they're made comfortable and are well looked after. But keep them under close guard. Nothing too obtrusive but just enough to let them know we're watching closely. Can't afford to have them wandering around if there's anything to this rumour about an attempt on the Emperor's life.'

'Yes, sir.' Vespasian saluted and left. His charges were at the headquarters tent. As he entered he was immediately aware of a marked division in the tribal representatives, between those who rose to greet him with a weary acceptance of the inevitable and those who remained squatting on the ground, glaring at him with bitter hostility. To one side, trying to be dignified without looking smug at having sided with the victors, sat Adminius. A huge man turned towards the legate and looked him over with the distastefully obvious air of a man examining an inferior. He approached Vespasian, arm raised, and greeted the legate formally. When he began to speak, Vespasian quickly indicated that Adminius should translate.

'Venutius begs to inform you that he and the others here had the privilege of viewing the battle as guests of Caratacus. He says he still finds it a little difficult to follow the logic of your tactics in the battle, and would be most grateful if you would talk them through with him.'

'Another time. I'm rather busy at the moment,' Vespasian responded coldly. 'And tell him that whatever the tactics, the outcome was inevitable. It always is when ill-disciplined natives attempt to best an army of professional soldiers. What matters is we won and that this island will eventually become a Roman province. Nothing else concerns me right now. Tell him I'll look forward to seeing him, and these others, when they bow before Caesar and pledge their loyalty to him at the banquet tomorrow night.'

As Adminius translated, Vespasian cast his eyes over the tribal representatives and was struck by the sneering expression on the face of the youngest of them. Hatred burned in the young man's eyes, and his gaze was unfaltering as Vespasian looked at him. For a moment the legate considered staring him out, but then decided it would be a waste of time and turned to leave. A small smile of satisfaction played on the young Briton's lips. Vespasian cocked a finger at Adminius and ducked through the tent flap.

'Who was the youngster?'

'Bellonius,' replied Adminius. 'Son of the ruler of a small northern tribe. His father's dying and sent his son to represent him. Not the wisest choice, I think.'

'Why?'

'You saw him. Not hiding much behind that expression.'

'Dangerous?'

Adminius considered the young Briton a moment before responding. 'No more so than any teenager who has been exposed to Caratacus' propaganda.'

'And Venutius?'

'Him?' Adminius laughed. 'He was once a great warrior. But he's getting on. Spends all his time talking about the old days. Bit of an old fool really.'

'You think so?' Vespasian raised an eyebrow as he recalled the shrewdness in the man's grey eyes when he had stood before him and assessed his character.

Vespasian could not help thinking there was more to Venutius than Adminius gave him credit for.

Chapter Fifty

The legions camped outside Camulodunum were in high spirits. Despite being caked in mud and exhausted by advancing so quickly after a pitched battle, there was a palpable sense of celebration in the air. A decisive victory had been won and Caratacus and the remnants of the British army were in full flight towards those tribes still loyal to the confederation resisting Rome. The tribal representatives who had been awaiting the outcome of the last battle had hurried to Camulodunum to swear allegiance to Rome. The danger of being opposed by almost every tribe on the island had passed now that the most powerful of the native tribes had been soundly beaten by the legions. Until next year's campaigning, the Roman army would be free to consolidate its gains unopposed. Caratacus' capital had opened its gates to the Emperor, and the following day's festivities would mark the end of this year's bloody campaigning. Of course, the conquest of the island was far from complete but in the prevailing mood of celebration few men spoke of it.

The Trinovantes had saved themselves from having their capital sacked, to the disappointment of some hardened veterans, but there were already ample spoils of war in the form of the thousands of Britons taken prisoner, who would be sold into slavery. Each legionary stood to gain a substantial sum of money as his share of the booty realised from the sale of prisoners. But there was even more to follow.

'Word has it that the Emperor is going to pay us a donative!' Macro grinned as he dropped down onto the grass outside his tent, eyes glinting at the prospect of a large handout of money from the imperial treasury.

'Why?' asked Cato.

'Because it's a good way of keeping us sweet. Why do you think? Besides, we deserve it. And he's managed to persuade the Trinovantes to hand over a supply of booze so we can celebrate in style after tomorrow's ceremonies. I know it's only that crap Celt beer they insist on brewing – like that stuff we had to drink in Gaul – but whatever it is, it still gets you pissed without too much effort. Then we're going to see some sights!' The centurion's eyes glazed over as he recalled previous drinking binges he had enjoyed with comrades in the past.

Cato could not help feeling a little nervous about the prospect. His body had a low tolerance for alcohol, and the slightest excess left his head reeling and made him curse the day that men first fermented their drink. He inevitably threw up and continued spewing until the pit of his stomach felt raw and the muscles were strained by the effort. Then sleep came uneasily and he would wake with a dry mouth and a foul taste on his tongue, head pounding. If what he had heard about the local brew was accurate, the after-effects would be even more unpleasant than usual. But short of volunteering for provost duties, there would be no way of avoiding the drinking session.

'Is it wise to be drinking with Caratacus nearby?' he asked.

'Don't worry about him. It'll be a long time before he can cause us any more trouble. Besides, one of the legions will be on duty at the time. Just pray it isn't ours.'

'Yes, sir,' Cato said quietly.

'Relax, lad! The worst is over. The enemy's on the run, we've a party lined up and the weather's improved.' Macro lay back in the grass, tucked his hands behind his head and closed his eyes. 'Life is good, so enjoy it.'

Cato would like to have shared the mood of the centurion and the other legionaries but he could not feel content. Not while he was tormented by the spectre of Vitellius seducing Lavinia. The Emperor's entourage had joined the army at midday, and was busy making camp in the corner of the fortifications allotted to it by General Plautius. Knowing that Lavinia was near quickened Cato's pulse, but at the same time he was filled with dread at the prospect of encountering her again. This time she would be sure to tell him what he most feared, that she no longer wanted to see him. The thought tormented him so much that at last Cato could bear it no longer, and the need to know overwhelmed the fear of finding out.

Leaving Macro dozing quietly in the sunshine, Cato made himself walk through the camp towards the elaborate tents of the Emperor's followers. Each step towards Lavinia was an effort, and on all sides the light-hearted mood of the legionaries increased the weight of misery bearing down on him. It did not take him long to find the tent of the legate's wife and her travelling house-hold, but it took a while to steel himself to approach the entrance. A burly slave he had never seen before stood guard and from inside came the muffled chatter of female voices. Cato strained his ears to catch the sound of Lavinia's voice.

'What's your business?' asked the slave, intervening between the entrance flap and the young optio.

'Personal. I wish to speak with a slave of Lady Flavia.'

'Does the mistress know you?' asked the slave contemptuously.

'Yes. I'm an old friend.'

The slave frowned, unsure whether to turn this filthy soldier away or risk interrupting his mistress in her unpacking.

'Tell her that it's Cato. Tell her I'd like to talk to Lavinia.'

The slave narrowed his eyes before reluctantly reaching his decision. 'Very well. Stay here.'

He entered the tent and left Cato standing alone. He turned away and gazed out over the camp while he waited for the slave to return. A rustling behind him caused Cato to turn back quickly. Instead of the slave he found Lady Flavia facing him, a strained smile on her face as she held her hand out in greeting.

'My lady.' Cato bowed his head.

'You are well?' asked Flavia.

'I'm quite well, my lady.' He raised his arms and did a quick turn, hoping to amuse her. 'As you can see.'

'Good . . .'

The silence was awkward, and when Flavia's usually cheerful mood failed to materialise, a cold sense of dread welled up inside Cato.

'My lady, might I speak to Lavinia?'

Flavia's expression took on a pained look. She shook her head.

'What's the matter? Is Lavinia all right?'

'Yes. She's all right.'

Cato's anxiety quickly abated. 'Then can I see her?'

'No. Not now. She's not here.'

'Where can I find her, my lady?'

'I don't know, Cato.'

'Then I'll wait for her to return. That is, if you don't mind.'

Flavia stood silently and made no reply. Instead she looked him in the eye and her expression became sorrowful. 'Cato, do you respect my opinion as you once used to?'

'Of course, my lady.'

'Then forget Lavinia. Forget her, Cato. She is not for you. No! Let me finish.' She raised her hand to quell his objections. 'Cato, you deserve better. Lavinia is no good for you. She's changed her mind about you these last few weeks. She has . . . higher ambitions.'

Cato recoiled from Flavia, and she was distressed by the cold anger that hardened his youthful face.

'Why didn't you tell me about Vitellius, my lady?' he asked in a strained voice. 'Why?'

'For your own good, Cato. You have to believe me. I have no desire to hurt you unnecessarily.'

'Where is Lavinia?'

'I can't tell you.'

Cato could guess where Lavinia might be easily enough. He stared at Flavia, jaw working as he struggled to control his churning emotions. Then he suddenly clenched his fists, turned, and strode away from the tent.

'Cato!' Flavia took a few paces towards him, and stopped, hand half lifted as if to restrain him. She stared sadly at the thin, almost frail body of the young man striding stiffly away, the hurt he was suffering evident in the tightly clenched fists at his sides. Since she had been responsible for allowing the youngsters' relationship to flourish in the first place, and had used it for her own political ends, Flavia felt the weight of guilt descend upon her. Despite her private justifications for her deeds, the human costs they entailed were hard to bear.

Flavia wondered if a simple brutal statement of Lavinia's present location might not have been a quicker and kinder way to help Cato get over his youthful adoration of Lavinia.

Chapter Fifty-One

The setting sun flooded into the tribune's tent through the entrance flap, burnishing one side of its contents with a rich orange glow and casting long dark shadows over the other side. Lavinia snuggled her head on the tribune's shoulder and ran her fingers through the dark curls of his chest, each hair highlighted by the glow of the dying sun. His sweaty scent filled her nostrils with the sharp tang of his masculinity, and she breathed in rhythm with the smooth rise and fall of his chest. Although his eyes were shut she knew he was awake from the light touch of a finger on the curved cleft between her buttocks as he gently traced the contours.

'Mmmm, that's nice,' she breathed softly in his ear. 'Don't stop there.'

'You are insatiable,' Vitellius muttered. 'Three times in one afternoon is more than any man can take.'

Running her hand down his chest and over his stomach, Lavinia cupped the soft malleable flesh of his penis in her slender fingers and slowly worked it.

'Are you really sure?'

Vitellius raised his other hand and extended his index finger, the gesture of a defeated gladiator appealing to the mob. 'I beg for mercy.'

'I accept surrender from no man.' Lavinia chuckled as she continued her attempt to elicit a response.

'Not even that youngster you were involved with?'

The tone of the remark was just the wrong side of frivolous, and Lavinia withdrew her hand and shifted round, raising herself on one elbow and looking down at his face.

'What's the matter? Jealous?' Lavinia waited for a response, but Vitellius silently gazed back up at her. 'Could you really be jealous of a young boy?'

'Not so young that he didn't know his way around, apparently.'

'But young enough to need to stop and ask for directions from time to time.'

'From an even younger woman?'

'Ah!' Lavinia smiled. 'I had the advantage of a head start. Thanks to you, my very own tribune.' She lowered her head and kissed him on the lips, then slowly grazed her lips across the stubble on his cheek and kissed his eye and forehead, before reclining back on her elbow. 'I'm so glad we're back together. I can't tell you how much I've missed being with you like this. I don't think I have ever felt so happy.'

'Not even with that boy?' Vitellius asked quietly. 'Are you quite sure?'

'Of course I am, silly! I've told you, it just happened after Plinius threw me out when he caught us together that time. You remember?'

'I'll never forget!' Vitellius smiled. 'That pompous fool had it coming to him.'

'Plinius was all right. He looked after me well. I've a lot to thank him for. In fact I felt very sorry for him afterwards, for a while at least. And then Cato fell for me.'

'What on earth did you see in him?'

Lavinia pouted as she thought about her attraction to the young optio. 'I suppose he looks handsome in an odd way. He's tall and skinny to be sure, but he has lovely eyes. Very expressive. And there was something quite sad about him too. Always seemed preoccupied with how others saw him, never at ease with himself. Maybe I felt sorry for him.'

'Hardly an adequate reason to bed him,' protested Vitellius.

'Oh you!' Lavinia punched his chest. 'Why shouldn't I sleep with him? I enjoyed it. And I couldn't see you very easily as long as I lived with Lady Flavia. What was I supposed to do?'

'Wait until I found a way to get you out of there.'

'Then I'd have waited for ever. I'm only here now because I managed to give my mistress the slip. If she knew where I was I'd be given a thrashing I wouldn't forget in a hurry.'

'You're sure she doesn't know you're here now?'

'Of course not. I'll just tell her I went for a walk and got lost coming back. She'll be suspicious but I doubt she'll guess the truth.'

'Even though she saw us together the other day?'

Lavinia prodded his chest with her finger. 'I told her that you had approached me and that I told you to leave me alone because I loved Cato.'

'And she believed you?' Vitellius sounded sceptical.

'Why shouldn't she? Now, can we talk about something else? This anxiety you men have over the physical loyalty of your women is very tiresome. It's not as if you live by the same standard.'

'All right then,' replied Vitellius, pulling her forward onto him and kissing her with a passionate intensity that surprised Lavinia. Closing her eyes she surrendered to the moment, breathing in the scent of him and becoming almost dizzy with the desire that came with such physical closeness. When she drew back from his face and opened her eyes, she felt the hardness of his penis along her thigh.

'I thought you said you weren't up to it?'

'You have a way of provoking a man's desire.' Vitellius smiled and ran his hand up the inside of her thighs. 'Let's see what we can do about it.'

Later, after sunset, a slave came into the tent and silently lit the lamps before disappearing. By the pale loom of the lamps Lavinia rose from the bed and yawned, stretching her slender arms above her head. The action caused her breasts to lift and Vitellius reached a hand round to cup the nearest, marvelling at its smooth softness. Lavinia allowed him to continue a moment before slapping his hand away.

'Enough of that, you! I have to get back to my tent.'

'When will I see you again?'

'Tomorrow, after Caesar's banquet. I'll meet you back here.'

'You'll definitely be at the banquet?' asked Vitellius.

'Yes, to wait on my mistress and the legate. But I can't wait to see the entertainments the Emperor has lined up. Should be quite a spectacle.' Lavinia picked up her tunic from the ground where it had been dropped in their earlier haste and pulled it on over her head. Vitellius watched her, head propped up on a silk bolster, his eyes dark and cold.

'Lavinia, I need you to do me a favour.'

Her head popped through the top of the tunic and she tugged the long tresses of her hair free of the neckline. 'What kind of a favour?'

'It's a surprise for the Emperor. I need you to take something into the banquet for me tomorrow night.'

'What is it?'

'It's over there on that table,' he said quietly, pointing across the tent to a low, black, marble-topped side table in the far corner. Lavinia went over and picked up an object that glinted as she raised it into the glow cast by the oil lamps. It was a dagger, sheathed in silver inlaid with gold in swirling Celtic patterns, within which were set blood-red rubies. The handle of the dagger was jet black and polished to a high shine, with a huge ruby set into the gold at the end of the pommel.

'It's beautiful!' Lavinia marvelled. 'I've never seen anything like this. Never. Where did you get it?'

'My father sent it to me. It's a gift for the Emperor. I was told to present it to him as soon as we'd taken Camulodunum. Bring it here.'

Lavinia returned to the bed, carrying the dagger with reverence. 'Such a lovely thing. The Emperor will adore it.'

'That's what my father hopes. And I think it is the kind of gift that is best presented with some sense of occasion. So I thought I might hand it to the Emperor at the height of tomorrow's celebrations, before all his guests, so that they can see Claudius' reaction to my father's symbol of loyalty and affection.'

'They'll die of jealousy.'

'My thoughts exactly,' said Vitellius. 'That's why I need you to do me a favour.'

'What kind of a favour?'

'I need you to carry this into the banquet for me. No one is admitted into the Emperor's presence carrying a blade of any kind. His guards will be searching all the formal guests, but you can get into the banquet through the kitchen. All you need to do is hide it like this.' He reached under her tunic and pressed the scabbard against the inside of her thigh. Lavinia gasped and then laughed. 'You'll have to strap it in place. No one will know it's there.'

Lavinia took hold of the scabbard again and regarded it with a worried expression.

'What's the matter?'

'What happens if I get searched and they find it on me?'

'Don't worry, Lavinia. I'll be close by. If anything like that happens before I get the dagger back from you, I'll intervene and explain everything.'

Lavinia looked intently into his face. 'What if you don't?'

Vitellius' expression changed to a mixture of hurt and anger. 'Why would I want to get you into any kind of trouble?'

'I don't know.'

'Exactly. I'm hardly likely to endanger the woman I love, am I?' He reached his arms round her and pulled her towards his chest, waiting until her body felt more relaxed before he continued. 'Once you're inside, waiting on Lady Flavia and Vespasian, I'll find you and retrieve the dagger, as quickly as I can.'

'Not too publicly I hope!'

'Of course not. It wouldn't be seemly for a member of my class to be seen to be groping a slave in public.'

'Thanks for the concern about my reputation,' Lavinia replied bitterly.

'Only joking, my sweet. We'll just have to find somewhere quiet for me to retrieve it.' He squeezed her affectionately. 'Will you do this for me? It'll mean a lot to my father, and it'll help my career along.'

'What's in it for me?'

'As soon as I get my share of the booty I swear I'll buy you from Flavia. Afterwards we can see about having you manumitted.'

'Nice thought. But why should Flavia want to sell me?'

'I don't think she'd be wise to refuse me,' Vitellius replied quietly. 'Besides, I can present you to the Emperor at the banquet and ask that he makes you my reward for saving the Second Legion from Togodumnus. Vespasian could hardly refuse that. It'd look appallingly ungrateful. Just watch for my signal, and come straight to me.'

'You've got it all worked out, haven't you?' Lavinia replied, frowning.

'Oh yes.'

'And then?' Lavinia asked, eyes shining with hope.

'And then?' Vitellius held her hand to his mouth and kissed the soft skin. 'Then we can cause something of a scandal by getting married.'

'Married . . .' Lavinia whispered. She flung her arms round his neck and pulled him to her as tightly as possible. 'I love you! I love you so much I'd do anything for you. Anything!'

'Easy, I can hardly breathe!' Vitellius chuckled. 'All I ask of you is this small favour, and that you will consent to be my wife as soon as we can make it possible.'

'Oh yes!' Lavinia planted a kiss on his cheek and quickly pulled away. 'Now I must go.' She picked up the dagger.

'Here, wrap it in this.' Vitellius reached over the side of his bed and flicked his neckerchief over to her. 'Best that you keep it with you, well-hidden, until the banquet. It's the kind of thing some people might kill for.'

'It will be safe with me. I promise.'

'I know it will, my sweet. Now you must go.'

After Lavinia had left the tent, Vitellius stretched out on the bed with a smug expression of satisfaction. It had not been so very difficult to arrange after all. When the slave girl was presented to the Emperor at the banquet, the expressions on the faces of Vespasian and his wife would be priceless.

It was a shame that Lavinia could not be allowed to live. She was a most accomplished lover and showed a sophistication in the more esoteric arts of love well beyond her teenage years. She might have looked good on his arm back in Rome, a trophy to dangle in front of his peers, and a tool for buying favours. But in using her to get the dagger into the banqueting hall, Vitellius realised she would know enough to place him in danger. If his plan succeeded, she would realise at once that she had been used. As yet, he still did not know the identity of the assassin Caratacus had found for the job – thanks to that fool Nisus. Caratacus might yet get a message through to him, but if he did not, Vitellius could only hope that the killer would make himself known so that he could be given the dagger. Failing that, the knife would have to be presented as a gift after all. But one thing was certain, assassination or no assassination, Lavinia could not be permitted to know what she knew and live to tell the tale.

She must die as soon as she had served his purpose. He would be sorry to lose her but, Vitellius comforted himself, there would be other women.

Chapter Fifty-Two

The assembly ground was growing quiet now that the tail end of the procession had marched out of the camp and down the track towards Camulodunum. Distant cheering and the sound of trumpets still carried across the endless ridges of section tents. Flower petals and trampled garlands lay strewn across the hard-packed turf, and lifted in flurries as the wind gusted through the camp. Above, scattered grey clouds scudded across the sky and threatened rain.

A number of people were still milling around the assembly ground in small groups, Romans and townspeople alike. The latter had come to witness the start of the celebrations as Claudius formally saluted the achievement of his legions while they marched past, cohort after cohort, equipment and uniforms bright and clean after many hours of bullshine. Now the legions had been dismissed. The Emperor and the standards were marching in procession through the rough streets of Camulodunum, under the protection of the Praetorian Guard units. As their new masters passed by, the Britons lining the route watched with the sullen resentment of a conquered people.

Cato approached the assembly ground along the via Praetoria, having left his armour and weapons in his tent. Shortly before the Sixth Century had formed up for the parade he had received a message from Lavinia.

She had asked him to meet her outside the headquarters tents after the procession had moved on into the town. The message had been short and terse, with no indication of what she wanted to say to him, nor any personal endearment.

He entered the assembly ground and made his way towards headquarters looking for her. He spotted her quickly, sitting alone on one of the wooden benches that had been erected on the turf bank raised between the tent and the assembly ground. She was not looking out for him, but seemed to be examining something cradled on her lap in the folds of her tunic. As Cato approached her from the side he saw the glint of red and gold before she was aware of him, and quickly bundled the object away in a scarlet neckerchief.

'Cato! There you are!' She spoke with a nervous edge to her voice. 'Come and sit down beside me.'

He slowly sat down, keeping a distance between them. She made no attempt to close the gap as she would have done at once not so very long ago. She remained silent for a moment, unwilling to meet his gaze. Eventually Cato could take it no more.

'Well, what did you want to say to me?'

Lavinia looked at him with a kindly expression that was perilously close to pity. 'I don't know quite how to say what I'm about to say, so please don't interrupt.'

Cato nodded, and swallowed nervously.

'I've been thinking a lot about us the last few days, about how far apart our worlds are. You're a soldier, and a good one according to my mistress. I'm just a house slave. Neither of us have particularly good prospects, and that means we'll never be able to spend much time together . . . You can see what I'm saying?'

'Oh yes! I'm dumped. Pretty way of putting it but the punchline's the same.'

'Cato! Don't take it like that.'

'How should I take it? Rationally? Put all my feelings aside and see how reasonable you're being?'

'Something like that,' Lavinia replied gently. 'It's better than getting worked up like this.'

'You think *this* is worked up?' Cato replied, face drained of blood as love, bitterness and rage surged through his heart. 'I might have guessed this is how it would end. I was warned about you. I should have listened, but you just used me.'

'I used you? I don't recall any complaints about the way I was treating you that night in Rutupiae. I fancied you, Cato. That's all. Everything else is just what you've read into the situation. Now we've both had our fun it's time to move on.'

'That's all? Are you quite certain? I mean, there's nothing else I should be told?'

'What are you talking about?' Lavinia looked at him warily.

'I don't really know,' Cato responded coldly. 'I just thought you might mention something about the new man in your life.'

'New man?'

'Sorry, I should have said the renewal of a relationship with the man in your life.'

'I don't know what you're talking about.'

'Really? I'd have thought your little sessions with Tribune Vitellius would have been more memorable than that. I'm sure he'd be most hurt to think that he could slip your mind so easily.' Cato clenched his fist, and to avoid the impulse to hit Lavinia he tucked it into his tunic, found Nisus' bandage and wound his hand tightly into its folds. He drew it out and stared at it dully. Lavinia glanced down nervously at the bandage, and recoiled slightly, shifting her position on the bench so that she created more space between them.

'Very well, Cato. Since you insist on being hurt I'll tell you everything.'

'That would be a nice change.'

She ignored his sarcasm and met his look of burning hatred with a cold expression. 'I knew Vitellius before I knew you. I wouldn't say we were lovers. I had feelings for him but I doubt he returned them, at first. But in time his love grew, and then that idiot Plinius discovered us and wrecked everything. Then I met you.'

'And thought, *here's someone I can use.*'

'Think what you like, Cato,' said Lavinia, and shrugged. 'At the time, whatever security I had in the world had been shattered. I was afraid and alone, and I just wanted some kind of support. When I saw that you had taken to me, I jumped at you.'

'If you want to be strictly accurate, the preposition isn't necessary.'

Lavinia glared at him, and shook her head slowly. 'That's so typical of you. Always the smart-arse comment. And you really think that's endearing?'

'Not supposed to be. Not now.'

'Not ever. I can't tell you how sickening I've found it playing the naïve young illiterate slave girl.'

'I wondered where the sudden expansion in word power had come from. It must have rubbed off from the tribune.'

'Cato! Will you stop being so horrible!'

They glared at each other for a moment, before Cato's gaze wavered and he looked down at the bandage he had been winding round his arm. He froze as he stared at it.

'I did like you,' Lavinia continued as gently as she could. 'I really did, in a way, but the feelings I had for Vitellius were much deeper, and when he . . . Cato?'

Cato was frantically shuffling the bandage round his arm and was not listening.

'Cato? What's the matter?'

'B . . . e . . . l . . .' he read out quietly as the marks on the bandage began to align. '. . . l . . . o . . . n . . . i . . . u . . . s. Bellonius.'

Bellonius. Cato frowned at the name before he recalled the tribal representatives who had been formally presented to Claudius at the start of the morning's ceremony. He jumped up, looking around, and hurried over to the footrail that ran along the line of benches. Lavinia watched him in amazement. Quickly unwinding the bandage from his hand, Cato began to wrap it carefully round the rail, adjusting the alignment as he went along, working his way back from the end of the message.

'Cato! What are you doing?'

'Saving the Emperor's life!' he replied excitedly as he continued towards the end of the bandage, reading as he went along. 'Here, give me a hand!'

Lavinia watched Cato with a mixture of frustration and bewilderment. Then, with a shake of her head, she crouched by the footrail and carefully rolled the rest of the bandage round the pole. Squatting down, Lavinia slowly read through the message, making careful adjustments to the bandage to align the words more precisely. She frowned as she tried to understand what had so excited Cato. As she glanced over the opening section, her eyes froze on a Roman name.

'Oh no.'

'What is it?'

'Nothing,' Lavinia replied, unable to conceal a tremor in her voice.

Cato pushed her back and leaned over the rail. Behind him Lavinia bent down. Before he found the phrase that had so alarmed her, he sensed a sudden motion and looked up – just in time to see Lavinia swing her arm in towards the side of his head. In her hand was a large round rock.

There was no time to duck, or raise an arm. The stone crashed against the side of his skull, the world exploded into a brilliant white before turning into the pitch black of unconsciousness.

'Come on, lad!'

Cato was dimly aware that someone was shaking him, very roughly. The darkness was slowly thinning into a milky blur, and his head felt thick, like a lump of wood. Slowly his reason returned to him. He groaned.

'That's it! Wake up, Cato!'

His eyes flickered open, took a moment to focus, and he saw the familiar coarse features of Centurion Macro looming over him. Macro gripped him under the arms and raised him into a sitting position.

'Ouch!' Cato raised a hand to the side of his head, and winced as his fingers touched a bump the size of a small egg.

'What the hell happened to you?'

'Not sure,' Cato mumbled, still muzzy-headed. Then the jumble of events resolved themselves very quickly. 'Lavinia! She's got the bandage!'

'Bandage? What are you on about?'

'That bandage I found on Nisus. She's taken it!'

'She hit you because she wanted a bandage?' Macro looked at his optio with a concerned expression. 'Must have been a harder blow to your head than I thought. Come on, lad, it's off to the hospital with you.'

'No!' Cato tried to rise to his feet but became dizzy and had to slump back to the ground. 'There's a message *on* the bandage. It's a scytale.'

'A sky what?'

'Scytale, sir. A Greek encryption system. You twist a roll of linen along a length of wood and write your message on it. Once it's unwound the marks look meaningless.'

'I see,' Macro nodded. 'Typical bloody Greeks. Too clever by half. So what was in this message of yours?'

'Details about a plot to kill the Emperor.'

'I see, and Lavinia knocked you out to steal this bandage of yours?'

'Yes, sir.'

'How inconvenient.'

Cato rounded on his centurion. 'Sir! I swear to you, by all that I am and all that I believe in, there was a message on the bandage. It must have come from Caratacus. It said the Emperor would be killed by Bellonius during the victory celebrations, and that someone would have to get a knife to him after he'd been searched by Claudius' bodyguard.'

'Who?'

'Whoever the message was sent to.'

'You don't know?'

'I didn't read it all the way through,' Cato said desperately. 'Lavinia didn't give me a chance.'

Macro frowned at him, as if trying to work out if this was some kind of elaborate practical joke.

'I beg you to believe me, sir. It's true. Have I ever lied to you? Have I, sir?'

'Well, yes, you have. That business about being able to swim.'

'Sir, that was different!'

'Look here, Cato,' Macro relented, 'I'll believe you. I'll accept that what you are saying is true. But if it turns out that it's not, then I'll break every bone in your body, understand?'

Cato nodded.

'Fair enough. Now then, where's this girl of yours likely to go if she's got that bandage?'

'To Vitellius. It has to be him. He has to be the one that's plotting with the Britons.'

'Up to the same old tricks again,' sighed Macro. 'That fellow could really use a sword between the shoulder blades on a dark night. We'd better see if we can find Lavinia. Let's go.'

They ran back to the area of the vast encampment allotted to the Second Legion, and made for the line of officers' tents. The senior tribune's tent stood at the end of the line, nearest to the legion's headquarters, and the two guards assigned to Vitellius stood at the fringe of the awning, hands on shield rims and spears grounded. As Cato and his centurion approached the guards, Macro smiled good-naturedly, and raised his hand in greeting.

'All right, lads?'

They nodded warily.

'Tribune at home?'

'Yes, sir.'

'Tell him he's got some guests.'

'Sorry, sir, can't do that. Strict orders. He's entertaining and not to be disturbed.'

'I see. Entertaining.' Macro winked at them. 'Wouldn't be entertaining some young dark-haired piece, by any chance?'

The guards exchanged a quick glance.

'Thought so.'

Cato felt sick. Lavinia was here, in his tent, being 'entertained'.

Suddenly he was striding towards the entrance, bent on doing murder.

'Lavinia! Get out here!'

One of the guards, trained to react instantly to any threat to those he guarded, dropped his spear and thrust it between Cato's legs. The optio caught his shin against it, tripped and tumbled over. Before he could react, the guard was standing over him, spear tip pointed dangerously close to his throat.

'Easy there!' Macro calmed the guard. 'Easy. The boy's no threat.'

The flap flicked open and Tribune Vitellius, in a silk gown, ducked outside, bellowing angrily, 'What's all the bloody commotion?' He caught sight of Cato sprawled on the ground and Macro standing to one side of the guard who was threatening to impale the youth.

'Well! If it isn't my Nemesis and his little acolyte! What can I do for you, gentlemen? Keep it brief. I have a rather ravishing young lady on the go.'

The calculated remark had its desired effect, and Cato grabbed the shaft of the spear above him and wrenched it from the hands of the guard. He thrust the butt back into the man's face and caught him a sharp crack on the forehead, stunning him. Before the other guard could react, Cato had sprung to his feet and hefted the spear, ready to thrust it into the tribune's guts. But he never made it. A quick kick to the back of one of his knees floored him again. But this time his body was covered and held down by another's.

'Stay down!' Macro hissed in his ear. 'You fucking hear me?'

Cato tried to struggle, and was quickly kneed in the

groin. He doubled up in agony and felt sure he was going to throw up. Macro quickly got back on his feet.

'Sorry about that, sir. Lad's been under a lot of strain lately.'

'That's all right, Centurion,' Cato heard Vitellius reply. 'Nasty cut he's got on his head. I'd lend you a bandage, only I've just burnt the last of mine . . .'

There was a moment's silence; even Cato stopped struggling. Then Macro pulled him to his feet and thrust him away from the tribune.

'Sorry to have disturbed you, sir. I'll see to it that the lad doesn't bother you again.'

'Think nothing of it,' Vitellius replied flatly.

'Let's be going,' Macro said sharply and pushed Cato away from the tent. 'That'll teach you to disrespect our officers!'

As they passed out of earshot, Macro leaned close to Cato and hissed, 'You were bloody lucky to get out of that alive. From now on you listen to me and obey me.'

'But the Emperor—'

'Shut up, you fool! Can't you see he was trying to make you hit him? You know what the penalty is for assaulting an officer. You want to be crucified? No? Just keep quiet then.'

Once they were out of sight of Vitellius, Macro grabbed the collar of Cato's tunic and pulled him close. 'Cato! Get a grip! We've got to do something. The banquet'll be starting soon, and we've got to find some way of stopping Vitellius.'

'Fuck Vitellius,' mumbled Cato.

'Later. Right now we've got to save the Emperor.'

Chapter Fifty-Three

'Not bad,' commented Vespasian, mouth full of the salty pastry. 'Not bad at all.'

'Careful, those crumbs are going everywhere.' Flavia brushed them off the folds of her husband's tunic. 'Honestly, you'd think a grown man would spend just a little more time thinking about the consequences of what he chooses to eat.'

'Don't blame me, blame him.' Vespasian waved the pastry over towards Narcissus who was standing to one side of the Emperor's table while his master picked at a plate of garlic mushrooms. 'He decided on the menu, and he's done a first-rate job. What is this anyway?'

Flavia picked up one of the pastries and sniffed it with the refined contempt of those raised to look down their noses on the efforts of others. 'It's venison – left to hang a little longer than necessary, I might add – and marinated in fish pickle sauce before being shredded, mixed with herbs and flour, and baked.'

Vespasian gazed at her in open admiration, and looked again at the remains of his pastry. 'How can you tell all that? Just from the scent?'

'Unlike you, I actually bothered to read the menu.'

Vespasian smiled graciously. 'What else is on the menu, since you're the expert?'

'I've no idea, I only read as far as the introductory course, but I imagine it is simply a replay of every banquet Claudius has ever had.'

'Creature of habit, our Emperor.'

'Narcissus' habits unfortunately. The menu has his stamp all over it, fussy, pretentious and likely to leave you with a sick feeling in your stomach.'

Vespasian laughed, and spontaneously reached over to kiss his wife on the cheek. She accepted the kiss with a surprised expression.

'Sorry. Didn't mean to shock you,' Vespasian said. 'It was just that, for a moment there, it felt like old times.'

'It needn't feel otherwise, husband. If you would not treat me so coldly.'

'Coldly,' Vespasian repeated and met her gaze. 'I don't feel cold towards you. I have never loved you more than now.' He leaned closer to her, and continued softly, 'But I feel I don't really know you. Not since I was told about your involvement with the Liberators.'

Flavia took his hand and grasped it firmly. 'I've told you all you need to know. I've told you I have no connection with those people. None at all.'

'Now maybe. But before?'

Flavia smiled sadly before she responded in a quiet, clear voice, 'I have no connection with them now. That's all I can tell you. To say any more would endanger you, and maybe Titus . . . and the other child.'

'Other child?' Vespasian frowned before the sestertius dropped. He stopped chewing the pastry, breathed in to reply, and promptly started choking on the pastry crumbs. His face went red as he coughed frantically to try and clear his throat. Heads began to turn, and at the table of honour Claudius looked up, watched the spectacle and looked down at his food in terror. Narcissus rushed over to reassure him and quickly nibbled at one of the mushrooms on Claudius' plate.

Flavia was thumping her husband on the back, trying to dislodge the blockage, until finally Vespasian started breathing again, eyes watering, and caught Flavia's hands to stop the beating.

'I'm all right. I'm all right.'

'I thought you were dying!' Flavia was on the verge of tears, then suddenly she laughed at them both, and the other diners relaxed again. 'What on earth got into you?'

'The baby,' Vespasian managed to say before having to cough. 'You're expecting another child?'

'Yes,' Flavia replied with a smile, before sending Lavinia to fetch some water for her husband.

Vespasian, still red-faced, leaned over and wrapped his arms round his wife, burying his face in her shoulder and neck. 'When did you conceive?'

'Back in Gaul, shortly before we arrived in Gesoriacum. Over four months ago. The baby's due early next year.'

'Vespasian!' Claudius called out above the hubbub of conversation, which abruptly died away, 'I say, V-V-Vespasian!'

Vespasian released his wife and quickly turned round. 'Caesar?'

'Are you all right?'

'Quite all right, Caesar.' He turned to smile at his wife. 'Marvellous, in fact.'

'Well, you don't l-l-look it. You seemed to be on the verge of croaking just a m-m-moment ago! Lucky escape for me, I was thinking – someone poisoned you by mistake.'

'No poison, Caesar. I've just learned I'm going to have another child.'

Flavia blushed and gazed down at her hands with becoming modesty. Caesar reached for his gold wine cup and raised it in their direction.

'A toast! May the next Flavian to be born live to serve his Emperor with as much distinction as his father, and uncle of course.' Claudius nodded towards Sabinus, who smiled weakly. The rest of the guests in the brightly lit great hall of the Catuvellauni chorused the toast and Vespasian bowed his head in thanks. But the Emperor's light-hearted mention of assassination brought back Vespasian's fears over what Adminius had told him, and he glanced round the hall, eyeing the British contingent suspiciously. Venutius, the elders of the Trinovantes, and a score of other natives sat in self-conscious discomfort not far from the Emperor's right hand.

'What's keeping that wretched girl Lavinia?' Flavia muttered as she glanced round the hall. 'She was only supposed to go and get you a glass of water . . .'

A pungent aroma of spices and the richer undercurrent of sauces and cooked meats filled Cato's nostrils as he and Macro entered the open kitchen area at the back of the great hall. Huge cauldrons simmered over cooking fires tended by sweating slaves, while the cooks laboured over long trestle tables, preparing the plethora of dishes required at an imperial banquet.

'What now?' Cato whispered.

'Just follow my lead.'

The centurion marched up to the timber-framed door leading into the side of the great hall. A burly palace slave in a purple tunic held up a hand at their approach.

'Out of my way!' Macro snapped.

'Stop!' the slave responded firmly. 'No entry without authorisation.'

'Authorisation?' Macro glared back. 'Who says I need authorisation, slave?'

'Only kitchen slaves come through here. Try the main entrance to the hall.'

'Says who?'

'My orders, sir. Straight from Narcissus himself.'

'Narcissus eh?' Macro stepped closer, and lowered his voice. 'We have to see the legate of the Second right now.'

'Not without authorisation, sir.'

'All right then, you want to see my authorisation?' Macro reached into his purse with his left hand, and the moment the slave's eyes followed the gesture the centurion piled in a skull-shattering uppercut with his right. The slave's jaw snapped back and he dropped like a sack of stones. Macro shook his hand as he gazed down at the crumpled form at his feet. 'How's that for authorisation, you dumb shit?'

The kitchen slaves were nervously watching the centurion.

'Back to work!' Macro shouted. 'Now! Before you get the same treatment as him.'

For a moment there was no reaction, and Macro took a few paces towards the nearest group of cooks, slowly drawing his sword. At once they returned to their work. Macro glowered round, daring any of the others to challenge him until all the cooks turned back to their duties.

'Come on, Cato,' Macro said quietly and ducked through the door into the great hall. Cato followed him into the shadows behind a stone buttress. A warm fug wrapped itself round them.

'Stay back,' Macro ordered. 'I need to check the lie of the land.'

Macro peered round the buttress. The huge space was lit by countless oil lamps and tallow candles fixed to vast timber

417

crosspieces hanging from pulleys up in the dim rafters high above. In their amber glow hundreds of guests were ranged along dining couches on three sides of the hall. Before them lay tables heaped with the best cuisine that the imperial cooks could provide. Loud conversation and laughter overwhelmed the Greek singers battling to be heard from a dais behind the top table, where the Emperor reclined alone. In the space between the tables a bear was chained to a bolt in the floor. It snarled and swiped at a pack of hairy hunting dogs that darted around and snapped whenever the bear presented an unguarded quarter. With a shrill yelp one of the slower dogs was caught by a paw, and flew through the air to crash into a table. Food, plates, cups and wine exploded into the air while a female guest shrieked in horror at the blood that splattered across her pale blue stola.

As the roars of support for the bear died down, Macro turned his gaze to the British contingent sitting to one side of the Emperor. Most of the Britons had succumbed to the Celtic weakness for drink and were being loud and gauche as they cheered on the beast fight. A few, however, were sitting quietly, picking at their food and gazing at the spectacle with barely concealed contempt. On the couch nearest the Emperor sat a young Briton, chewing on a small plaited loaf, staring fixedly at the floor in front of him, quite outside the prevailing mood of the banquet.

'There's our man – Bellonius, I'd say.' Macro waved Cato round and pointed. 'See him?'

'Yes, sir.'

'Think we should rush him?'

'No, sir. We've no proof any more. We have to try and speak to the legate, or Narcissus.'

'The freedman is standing in his master's shadow, but I can't see the legate yet.'

'Over there.' Cato nodded directly across the hall. Vespasian's head was turned away from them as he kissed his wife. Behind them stood Lavinia, laughing happily as she watched the tormented bear. A simmering mixture of jealous loathing and remembered affection bubbled up from the pit of Cato's stomach. Lavinia looked to one side and smiled. Following her gaze, Cato saw Vitellius sitting with a group of staff officers opposite the Britons. The tribune was looking over his shoulder and smiling back at Lavinia, causing Cato to clench his fists and press his lips together in a thin line.

'There's Vitellius, by the Emperor,' whispered Macro.

'Seen him.'

'What now?' Macro eased himself back behind the buttress and looked at his optio. 'Narcissus or Vespasian?'

'Vespasian,' Cato decided immediately. 'There's too many of those German bodyguards round Narcissus. We'd have no chance of getting a message through that lot. Let's wait for the next change in course and use the waiters as cover to get close to the legate.'

'Wait? Can't afford to. Won't take that lot outside long to recover their balls report on us.'

'Sir, what do you think will happen if we're discovered in here without any invitation or authority, and carrying weapons?'

'Point taken. We'll wait a little longer.'

As they crouched down behind the buttress, the savage growls and roaring from the beast fight reached a crescendo. The banquet guests cheered and howled like beasts themselves as the bear and dogs tore at each other in a terrifying frenzy. With a final shrill yelp that was abruptly drowned by the triumphant roar of the bear, the fight came to an end and the cheers of the audience subsided into loud conversation. Cato risked a glimpse round the roughly hewn stone buttress and saw the bear being led away in chains by a dozen burly Britons, blood dripping from its jaws and numerous wounds. Its mangled victims were dragged away on hooks.

There was a loud clapping from outside the hall and the doors burst open to admit dozens of imperial slaves who flowed round the sides of the hall.

'Let's go!' Cato hissed, tugging at Macro's arm. The two of them rose and causally joined the slaves making for the far side of the hall, mingling with them as they threaded through the mass of entertainers and party guests. Cato's heart pounded and he felt cold and afraid at the dreadful risk he was taking. If they were discovered, the chances were that they'd be cut down at once, before they had any chance to explain their presence. Cato could see Lavinia standing behind her master and mistress. Not far beyond, Vitellius had risen from his couch and beckoned to Lavinia. With a quick glance to make sure her mistress wasn't watching, she ran lightly over to the tribune. Cato's heart hardened at the sight and he had to force her from his mind.

With Macro at his side, Cato shuffled into position behind Vespasian. Just then Flavia glanced round, and frowned as she saw the two soldiers amongst the slaves. Then she smiled as she recognised Cato. She tugged her husband's sleeve.

On the far side of the great hall the head steward clapped his hands, and the slaves moved closer to the guests' laden tables.

'Sir,' Cato said quietly. 'Sir, it's me, Cato.'

Vespasian looked up and exactly reproduced his wife's reaction.

'What the hell is going on, Optio? And you, Macro? What are you doing here?'

'Sir, there's no time to explain,' Cato whispered urgently. He saw Vitellius take Lavinia by the hand and lead her towards the Emperor's table. 'That assassin Adminius warned us about is here.'

'Here?' Vespasian swung his feet to the floor and stood up. 'Who?'

'Bellonius.'

The legate's eyes snapped towards the group of Britons opposite, all of them drunk and shouting now, except Bellonius. He, too, was on his feet, one hand hidden in the folds of his tunic.

'How do you know it's him?' He swung round to face Cato. 'Quickly!'

At the Emperor's table, Claudius licked his lips as he ran his eyes over the shapely slave girl standing before him. Far from being nervous at the prospect of being presented to her Emperor, the girl was smiling, coyly.

'She's quite something,' said Claudius appreciatively.

'Indeed, Caesar,' Vitellius agreed. 'And very willing.'

'I'm sure.' Claudius smiled at Lavinia. 'And are you ready to s-surrender to your Emperor?'

Lavinia frowned and anxiously turned to Vitellius, but the tribune was staring straight ahead, utterly unmoved by the Emperor's advances.

'Well, young l-lady?'

Vitellius glanced quickly towards the tribal guests then turned back to his Emperor. 'Perhaps Caesar would like a closer look at the goods.'

Without warning he grabbed Lavinia's tunic by the shoulders and wrenched it down violently to expose her breasts. Lavinia screamed and struggled, but Vitellius held her tightly. All eyes turned on them.

There was a sudden movement to the Emperor's right as

Bellonius sprang forward, racing towards the Emperor, a dagger glinting low in his right hand. Cato was the first to react, jumping up onto the table in front of his legate and launching himself across the hall towards Bellonius.

'Stop him!' Cato screamed.

Bellonius darted a look sideways, teeth bared in a snarl, with the wide, blazing eyes of a fanatic, and continued running towards the Emperor. Cato threw himself headlong at the assassin, grabbing at his leg. He caught it, held tight, and managed to bring Bellonius tumbling down. Both pitched forward, but Cato held fast to his man, digging his fingers in for a moment before Bellonius kicked out with his spare foot and struck Cato square in the face. Instinctively Cato relaxed his grip and Bellonius tore free, scrambled up and threw himself towards the Emperor.

The German bodyguards, momentarily distracted by Vitellius' exposure of Lavinia, were running between their master and Bellonius. Claudius had raised his hands across his face and uttered a tremulous scream. The Briton ran on, dagger ready in an underhand grip, making straight for the Emperor. As he reached the first bodyguard, the German leaned back and smashed his shield into the side of the Briton's head. Bellonius crashed to the stone floor.

'Guards!' Narcissus shouted. 'Guards!'

It took only an instant for Vitellius to realise that the assassin had failed. Snatching a dagger from the belt of one of the bodyguards, he flung himself on the writhing Briton. The bodyguards were moving in but by the time they had reached the spot, it was all over. Vitellius rose to his knees, cheek and tunic front splattered with blood. Bellonius lay at his feet, dead, the handle of the bodyguard's blade protruding from under his chin. The blade had been driven up through his throat into his brain and his eyes bulged with surprise. A dribble of dark blood formed at the side of his open mouth and rolled down his cheek.

In the Briton's hand lay the jewelled hilt of the Celtic dagger Lavinia had smuggled into the hall. She glanced down at it and then looked up at Vitellius with a terrified expression, slowly backing away from him even as she clutched the ruined tunic to her chest.

The bodyguards swarmed forward, weapons drawn. From the other direction the dinner guests and serving slaves were surging forward to get a better look. Cato rose to his feet and found himself surrounded by a dense press of bodies. He looked round and saw that Claudius was safe. Narcissus had slipped his arm round the Emperor and was shouting out orders to have the hall cleared. Cato turned his head and looked about anxiously for any sign of Lavinia. Then he saw her, struggling in the grip of Vitellius who was trying to drag her to one side.

The Emperor's bodyguards were forcing the crowds away from Claudius at swordpoint. At the sight of the weapons, there were cries of panic and the crowd recoiled, carrying Cato with them, and he lost sight of the tribune and Lavinia. His arm was wrenched in someone's powerful grip and he was spun round, to face Macro.

'Let's get out of here!' Macro shouted. 'Before the Praetorian Guards arrive and some fool starts a massacre.'

'No! Not before I find Lavinia!'

'Lavinia? What the fuck for? Thought that bitch was working with Vitellius!'

'I'm not leaving her, sir.'

'Find her later. Now let's go.'

'No!' Cato tore himself free and thrust his way towards the place he had seen Lavinia struggling with Vitellius. With no thought for the people around him, Cato forced his way through. Behind him he heard Macro calling out his name, angrily shouting at him to get out of the hall. Then a woman directly in front of him shrieked and through the crowd he saw Vitellius, drenched in blood and holding a knife that dripped crimson. He met Cato's eyes and frowned. Then, glancing around at the terrified faces hemming him in, Vitellius smiled once at Cato and backed away towards the Emperor's bodyguards, where he let the blade drop and raised his hands. Claudius saw him, and instantly rushed over to embrace him, face beaming with gratitude.

Cato continued to push forward, fighting to catch sight of Lavinia. His foot snagged on something and he almost tripped. Looking down he saw that it had caught on a fold of tunic. The tunic was wrapped about the still form of a woman lying on the floor, in a spreading puddle of blood that matted the long tresses of dark hair. Cato felt a chill wave of horror sweep through his body.

'Lavinia?'

The tightly packed mob heaved and pressed in all around as Cato knelt down beside the body and lifted the hair away from the face with a trembling hand. Lavinia's lifeless eyes were open, pupils large and dark, her mouth slightly open to reveal white teeth. Below her chin, her throat had been cut so deeply that bone was just visible beneath the severed tendons and arteries.

'Oh no . . . No!'

'Cato!' Macro bellowed into his ear as he finally broke through to his optio. 'Come . . . Oh shit.'

For a brief moment neither man moved, then Macro snapped back into action and viciously hauled Cato to his feet.

'She's dead. Dead, you understand me?'

Cato nodded.

'We must go. Now!'

Cato allowed himself to be hauled through the panicking crowd by Macro who kicked and thrust people aside in his desperation to get them both out of the hall before the Praetorian Guards added to the mayhem.

'Quick!' Macro grabbed Cato's arm and pulled him towards the nearest side entrance. 'Through here!'

Hardly aware of what was going on, Cato felt himself being pushed out of the hall, and the last image to burn itself on his mind was the sight of the Emperor clasping Vitellius in his arms as his saviour.

Lavinia was dead and Vitellius was a hero.

Lavinia was dead, murdered by Vitellius.

Cato reached for his dagger. His fingers encountered the handle and closed round it tightly.

'No!' Macro growled harshly into his ear. 'No, Cato! It isn't worth it!'

Macro dragged him away from the shouting and screaming mob, and thrust him through the small side door.

Outside the building Macro pulled Cato into the shadows as the first Praetorians charged into the hall and began to round up the slaves. Screams and cries rose into the air.

Cato tipped his head back against the rough stone wall. Far above, undisturbed and unconcerned by the miserable details of human existence, lay the heavens in a placid scatter of glittering stars. But they looked so cold, colder even than the vice-like grip of despair that clenched his heart and crushed any will to live.

'Come on, lad.'

Cato opened his eyes, blinking away the tears. Above him, black against the stars, loomed Macro, hand out-stretched. For a moment Cato just wanted to stay there, to be discovered with his knife by the Praetorians and be swiftly put out of his misery.

'She's dead, Cato. You're still alive. That's the way it is! Now come!'

Cato allowed himself to be hauled to his feet. With a gentle shove Macro pushed him away from the hall and back towards the safety of the camp of the Second Legion.

Chapter Fifty-Four

Some days later the Emperor left the island to return to Rome. Narcissus had received word that, in Claudius' absence, some of the senators had begun to mutter about the Emperor's suitability for the job. Left much longer, such muttering might well become more vocal. The time was ripe for a return to the capital. Without any delay the fleet was summoned upriver to Camulodunum and the imperial baggage was hastily stowed below decks. A long line of warships was moored along the crude quayside and sweating slaves scurried to and fro across the gangplanks, driven on by the Emperor's stewards wielding their canes with their usual lack of restraint.

Not all of the imperial entourage was quitting Britain. Flavia, and some of the other officers' wives, had been given leave to spend the autumn and winter with their husbands before returning to Rome at the start of the next campaign season. Flavia was not looking forward to spending yet another freezing winter on the harsh northern fringe of the empire. Britain was no place to give birth to the child she was carrying. She had half hoped that Vespasian might decline her offer and send her back to Rome with Titus. But he had insisted that she stay with him, pointing out that she should not be travelling in her condition. Privately he wanted to keep her away from the dangerous political intrigues of

Rome, and beyond the influence of the Liberators.

The morning of the official departure dawned with a clear sky and a light breeze. In the cool air and pale light, the men of the Second Legion rose early from their dew-drenched tents to snatch a quick breakfast and prepare themselves for the day's ceremonies. The Second had been given the honour of escorting the Emperor from the camp, through Camulodunum, to the quay where he would board his flagship. Full ceremonial dress was to be worn and stiff red horsehair helmet crests had been issued to all the men. Every item of equipment had to be spotless and the centurions made a thorough inspection of the men in their centuries before marching them off to the parade ground where the legion was forming up.

The standards rippled in the breeze and the officers' scarlet cloaks stirred behind them as the legion stood at ease and quietly waited for the procession to begin. Plinius was once again senior tribune now that the Emperor had cut Vitellius' tribune service short so that he could return to Rome with him and be presented to the capital as the man who had saved the Emperor from the knife of an assassin. Further back in the ranks of the legion Cato stood a step to the side and one step behind his centurion. Several days after the banquet he was still numbed by the events of that night, haunted by the image of Lavinia lying dead in her own blood. Although she had abandoned him for Vitellius and paid the terrible price that came with too close an association with the tribune, Cato could not help feeling bound up in the cause of her death. Macro was somewhat less circumspect, and while not going quite so far as to say openly she had got what was coming to her, his lack of compassion for the slave girl was very evident. Accordingly, a frosty formality had grown between them – much to the regret of both men – and they stood in silence as the other men of the Sixth Century chatted happily.

The light-heartedness suddenly died away as the tall crest of a senior officer approached. A gap opened in the ranks and Vespasian made his way through his men towards Macro.

'Centurion! A quiet word with you and the optio, if you please.'

'Yes, sir.'

The legate led the way out of the dense mass of legionaries and stopped once he was sure they were out of earshot. He turned to face his subordinates.

'Any change of mind about the matter we discussed? This is your last chance.'

'No, sir.' Macro replied firmly.

'Centurion, the fact that you two were instrumental in saving the Emperor's life might well help your careers. If Cato here hadn't stopped that assassin, I doubt anyone could have responded in time to save Claudius. Even now, people are still trying to discover the identity of the man who first tackled that Briton. I can find a discreet way of making sure your efforts are rewarded, if you wish. Cato?'

'No thank you, sir.' Cato shook his head wearily. 'It's too late, sir. You saw how the Emperor embraced Vitellius the moment the assassination attempt was over. He's found his hero. It would be dangerous for us to claim any part in the Emperor's salvation. We'd be dead long before we could reap any benefits from the deed. You know that's true, sir.'

Vespasian stared at the optio, and then nodded slowly. 'You're right, of course. I just wanted to see justice done.'

Cato sniffed with contempt at the thought of there being any justice in this world, and his centurion stood stiff with apprehension at this affront to the commander of the legion.

'Very well.' Vespasian's tone was cold. 'You'd better get back to your men.'

With the first five cohorts leading the way, the Emperor and his staff proceeded through Camulodunum to the quayside. At his side rode Vitellius, graciously acknowledging the cheers of the legionaries lining the route each time the Emperor gestured towards his new favourite. Behind them rode Narcissus, cold eyes fixed on Vitellius as he considered his options in silence.

At the quay the cohorts spread out on either side and the red crests of the Second Legion stretched in a line that extended along the full length of the warehouses. The Emperor dismounted and boarded his flagship, and then stood on a platform at the rear of the vessel, bowing his head as Vespasian led his men in a chorus of cheers for the Emperor and the glory of Rome. As the gap between the gilded beam of the vessel and the rough-hewn stonework of the quay widened, the cries of the legionaries continued to echo across the river. General Plautius eased his horse over to the side of Vespasian.

'Seems our Emperor will have his triumph after all.'

'Yes, sir.'

'While we are, of course, sorry to see our Emperor return to Rome, I rather feel that this army might be pleased to be spared the further benefit of his tactical genius.'

Vespasian smiled. 'Yes, sir.'

They watched as the great banks of oars on the flagship extended from the hull, and then, as one, dipped down into the water. The flagship got under way and began to surge downriver towards the sea, closely followed by its escort of triremes.

'Well, that's the campaign over for this year at least,' announced Plautius. 'Don't know about you, but I could do with a long rest before we stick it to the Britons again.'

'I know exactly how you feel, sir.'

'You'd better make the most of it, Vespasian. The Second will need to be ready for a pretty gruelling time of it, once spring comes.'

Vespasian turned his head to glance sharply at the general.

'I thought that might interest you. Next year, while the other three legions push on into the heart of this benighted island, I've assigned the Second the hardest task of the lot. You'll work along the south coast and compel any tribes that have not already done so to surrender to Roman rule. We already have an ally we can trust in those regions. Cogidubnus. He'll provide you with a base of operations and you'll work with the Channel fleet to secure the lands to the west. No doubt you'll be delighted by the prospect of an independent command.'

Vespasian tried to stop himself from smiling, and nodded gravely.

'Good. I'm sure you will make a good job of it. Be mindful, Vespasian, that this is the kind of duty that launches men on great careers.'

Once the flagship had rounded the bend of the river, the Second Legion was dismissed. The cohorts tramped off the quay, back through Camulodunum towards the camp. Macro had seen the raw hatred in Cato's eyes as they had watched Vitellius bask in the glow of the Emperor on the deck of the flagship. For all his bluffness Macro had seen enough of the world to know that this was the kind of rage that chewed away at men's hearts and led them down the path of gradual self-destruction. Cato badly needed some kind of diversion, and Macro decided he was just the man to provide it.

'Fancy coming into the town for a drink tonight?'

'Sir?'

'I said we're going for a drink tonight.'

'We are?'

'Yes. We are.'

Cato nodded vaguely, and his centurion could see that he would have to offer rather more of an incentive. Well then, there was something he could try. Not that it pleased him to take the risk of introducing the optio to his latest piece of romantic interest.

'There's this girl I'd like you to meet. Came across her in the marketplace the other day. She'll be coming along with us tonight. She's good for a laugh, and I think you'll get on with her well enough.'

'That's kind of you, sir. But I wouldn't want to get in the way.'

'Nonsense! Come along and get a skinful. Trust me, you could do with it.'

For a moment Cato considered refusing. He did not yet feel he could enjoy life again – he was too emotionally scarred for that. Then he looked into the eyes of his centurion. He saw the genuine concern for his well-being expressed there, and found that he was moved to push aside his self-indulgent grief. Very well then. For Macro he would get horribly drunk tonight. Drunk enough to forget everything.

'Thank you, sir. I'd appreciate a drink.'

'Good lad!' Macro slapped him on the back.

'So tell me, sir, who's this woman of yours?'

'Comes from a tribe up the east coast. Staying with some distant relatives right now. Bit of a fiery type, but she's got the kind of looks that stop a man dead in his tracks.'

'What's her name?'

'Boudica.'

Historical Note

The most significant account of the Claudian Invasion that has passed down to us from the days of the Empire is a scant eight hundred words penned by Cassius Dio. Writing over a hundred years after the event Dio was reliant on other sources. How accurate or detailed these sources might have been is anyone's guess and it is infuriating that the section of Tacitus' Annals relating to the invasion is missing. However, the historian's loss is the novelist's gain. Being as true as I can to Dio's account, and taking on board as much of the archaeological evidence as possible, I have fashioned my tales of Cato, Macro and Vespasian. That said, it would be nice one day to read of the discovery of a few elephant bones in the depths of Essex . . .

Despite the paucity of Dio's account it is clear that the success of the invasion was anything but a foregone conclusion. The assault across the Mead Way (Medway) was unusual in that the battle lasted two days – testament to the ferocity with which the Britons resisted the advance of the eagles. The reasons for the later halt on the far side of the Tamesis (Thames) is a matter of dispute amongst historians. Some argue that the Britons were a spent force after their failure to defend the river crossings and that the halt had been pre-arranged to allow Claudius to lead the assault on Camulodunum in person. Others have argued that Plautius' troops genuinely needed reinforcing after being roughly handled by the natives. In view of the Emperor's precarious political situation I tend towards the former interpretation.

I have tried to keep the tribal politics of the Britons uncomplicated so as not to slow down the flow of the story. At the time of the Roman invasion of 43 AD the island was riven by shifting alliances, and most tribes regarded the sweeping gains of the Catuvellauni with growing apprehension. Having snapped up the Trinovantes and made the wealthy town of Camulodunum their capital, the Catuvellauni were making great inroads south of the Thames. When the Romans landed, the Catuvellauni had a hard time recruiting their erstwhile tribal foes to the forces resisting Rome. Having little to gain from the victory of either side, most tribes delayed making an alliance until it was clear who would triumph.

In the event Caratacus was beaten once again, and the capital of the natives has fallen to Rome. But the conquest of the island is far from over. Caratacus is still free, whipping up resistance to the invaders amongst the proud warrior tribes of Britain. Nowhere is this resistance more determined than in the tribes of the south-west, scornfully daring the Romans to do their worst from the fastnesses of their great hillforts.

For Cato and Macro there is only a short respite before Vespasian will once again lead them, and the men of the battered Second Legion, against the formidable fortresses of the Britons, and a deadly new enemy.

Under the Eagle

Simon Scarrow

It is 42 AD, and Quintus Licinius Cato has just arrived in Germany as a new recruit to the Second Legion, the toughest in the Roman army. If adjusting to the rigours of military life isn't difficult enough for the bookish young man, he also has to contend with the disgust of his colleagues when they discover that, because of his imperial connections, he is to be appointed a rank above them. As second-in-command to Macro, the fearless, battle-scarred centurion who leads them, Cato will have more to prove than most in the adventures that lie ahead.

In a bloody skirmish with the local German tribes, Cato gets his chance to show that he's more than a callow youth. But then the men discover that the army's next campaign will take them to a land of unparalleled barbarity – Britain. After the long march west, Cato and Macro undertake a special mission that will thrust them headlong into a conspiracy that threatens to topple the Emperor himself . . .

'A thoroughly enjoyable read. The characters are so lifelike they almost spring off the page. An engrossing storyline, full of teeth-clenching battles, political machinations, treachery, honour, love and death . . . More please!' Elizabeth Chadwick

0 7472 6629 8

headline

The Anubis Slayings

Paul Doherty

Hatusu, the remarkable young widow of Pharaoh Tuthmosis II, has forced Egyptian society to acknowledge her as Pharaoh, and her success in battle is spreading Egypt's glory well beyond its frontiers. In the Temple of Anubis, negotiations are taking place between Hatusu and the defeated King Tushratta of Mitanni for a peace treaty that will seal her greatest victory. But in one night, two hideous murders in the temple and the theft of the Glory of Anubis threaten the tenative truce. The respected judge Amerotke must find the truth or Egypt's fragile peace could be destroyed.

'Paul Doherty's *The Mask of Ra* is the best of its kind since the death of Ellis Peters. As ever, Doherty dazzles with his knowledge and intimate feel for Ancient Egypt' *Time Out*

'Doherty excels at his historical detail, bringing Ancient Egypt to life in his descriptions of daily life and characters drawn from every caste' *Publishers Weekly*

'Paul Doherty has a lively sense of history' *New Statesman*

0 7472 6309 4

headline

Now you can buy any of these other bestselling books by **Simon Scarrow** from your bookshop or *direct from his publisher*.

FREE P&P AND UK DELIVERY
(Overseas and Ireland £3.50 per book)

Under the Eagle	£6.99
When the Eagle Hunts	£6.99
The Eagle and the Wolves	£6.99
The Eagle's Prey	£6.99

TO ORDER SIMPLY CALL THIS NUMBER

01235 400 414

or visit our website: www.madaboutbooks.com

Prices and availability subject to change without notice.